SIMON THE FOX

The *DEVIOUS LIFE*
& *ODIOUS DEATH* of
# SIMON The FOX

Part One:
THE YOUNG MacSHIMI

By
MARTIN PETER KIELTY

Cover quote courtesy of Brent David Fraser
brentdavidfraser.wordpress.com

Cover crest image courtesy of Karen Henry
outlandishobservations.blogspot.com

To Claire, as usual

**SENNACHIE
PRESS**

www.sennachie-press.co.uk
www.simonthefox.com

ISBN 978-1-326-10555-6

CONTENTS

CAST OF LEADING CHARACTERS

In order of appearance (* denotes fictional characters)

*Bolla: An Aberdeen beggar

*Colin Campbell: Clansman of the Earl of Breadalbane

Simon Fraser of Beaufort, "the Fox":
Second son of the clan chief, MacShimi

Lord Mungo Murray: Son of the chief of Clan Murray, the Earl of Atholl

*Ben Ali Fraser: Clansman and warrior

Lord Tom Fraser of Beaufort, The MacShimi:
17th clan chief and Simon's father, later 10th Lord Lovat

Alexander Fraser: Lord Tom's eldest son and Simon's elder brother

*Andrew Fraser of Tanachiel: A laird of the clan

John "Ian Cam" Murray, Earl of Tullibardine:
Eldest son of the Earl of Atholl, later Secretary of State for Scotland

*Kirsty Fraser: Clanswoman, later wife of Bolla

Lady Amelia Fraser: Wife of Lord Hugh, sister of Ian Cam and Mungo

Lord Hugh Fraser of Lovat: 9th noble to hold the title

Captain Archibald "Baldy" Menzies: Soldier in Lord Murray's Regiment

*Captain Diederick Ackermann: Dutch privateer and pirate

*Lord George Murray: Young son of Ian Cam

Alasdair MacIain MacDonald of Glencoe: 12th chief of that clan

*Cathal Hendrie: MacIain's ghillie

Alasdair Dubh MacDonell of Glengarry: Warrior and later clan chief

Father Robert Munro: Outlawed Catholic priest

John Fraser of Beaufort: Younger brother of Simon and son of MacShimi

*Sergeant Jamie Fraser: Clansman serving in Lord Lovat's Company

William Fraser, 12th Lord Saltoun: Member of junior sept of Clan Fraser

*Ben Callum Fraser: Clansman and warrior, brother of Ben Ali

SINCLAIR

MACKAY

MACLEOD

MURRAY

MACDONALD

MACKENZIE

ROSS

Aberdeen

MACLEOD

MACKENZIE

Castle Doynie
Inverness
MACINTOSH

Moniack

CHISHOLM

Stratherrick

GRANT

GORDON

MACDONALD OF GLENGARRY

GRANT

FORBES

Invergarry Ca

CLAN FRASER

MACPHERSON

FARQUARSON

Achnacarry Ca

MACDONALD OF KEPPOCH

LINDSAY

CAMERON

Inverlochy Ca

Loch Ell

Maryburgh
(Ft William)

MACDONALD

Glen Coe

STEWART

Pass of Killiekrankie

MENZIES

MURRAY

Huntingtower

CAMPBELL

MACLEAN

Kilchurn Ca

CAMPBELL

MACNAB

Perth

MACLEAN

Glen Dochart

Auchenbreck Ca

MACGREGOR

The Bass Rock

CAMPBELL

Glasgow

Edinburgh

KINGDOM
Of
SCOTLAND

reland

England

LIST OF GAELIC AND LATIN PHRASES

In alphabetical order

Amaideach: foolish, stupid

A Mhòr-fhaiche: Great restorer of ruins (Fraser clan slogan)

Athair: father

Audentes fortuna iuvat: "Fortune favours the bold" (Virgil)

Bean nighe: the washer woman, faerie messenger of death

Blaigeard: blackguard, scoundrel

Cac: rubbish (literally "excrement")

Cailleach Bheur: goddess of winter

Chan eil mi a' tuigsinn: I do not understand

Ciamar a tha thu?: How are you?

Co'an fear ud?: Who are you?

Concordia res parvae crescunt: "Through harmony small things grow"

Creachadh: plundering

Crom Dubh: "Crooked Black," an ancient god

Domus et placens uxor: "A home and a pleasing wife" (Horace) (**Et filiola:** "and young daughter")

Dealbh: doll

De tha thu ag iarraidh?: What do you want?

Duine uasal: Highland gentleman or nobleman

Dulce et decorum est pro patria mori: "It is sweet and fitting to die for one's country" (Ovid)

Durate et vosmet rebus servate secundis: "Carry on and preserve yourselves for better times" (Virgil)

Fas est et ab hoste doceri: "Right it is to be taught even by the enemy" (Ovid)

Fear-an-tigh: steward (literally "man of the house")

Forsan et haec olim meminisse iuvabit: "It may be that in the future you will be helped by remembering the past" (Virgil)

Gorach: fool, idiot

Gràdh mo chrìdh: love of my heart

Hiems: winter

Là Fhèill Brìghde:
first day of spring, dedicated to St Bridget or the goddess Brigid

Ma 'se do thoil e: Please (literally "if it is your will")

Nam tua res agitur, paries cum proximus ardet:
"It is your concern when your neighbour's wall is on fire" (Horace)

Nunc est bibendum, nunc pede libero pulsanda tellus:
"Now is the time to drink, now is the time
to dance footloose upon the earth" (Horace)

Non semper erit aestas: "It will not always be summer"

Ochone: exclamation or surprise or regret

Oidhche mhath, mo tighearna: good night, my lords

Parturient montes, nascetur ridiculus mus: "The mountains will be
in labour, and a ridiculous mouse will be brought forth" (Horace)

Pibroch: a piece of bagpipe music, usually military

Sassenach: southerner, Saxon

Scunner: strong dislike, or that which inspires it

Sealgaire-mhor: great hunter

Se do bheatha: don't mention it, no problem

'S fhada bho nach fhaca mi thu: it is long since I have seen you

Siuthad: go

Slàinte mhor a h-uile là a chi 's nach fhaic:
Good health to you, every day I see you and every day I do not

'S math sin: it is good

Tapadh leat: thank you

Thusa a-nise: now you, your turn

PROLOGUE
Sunday, April 9, 1747

I DID NOT BELIEVE he would manage to retain his good humour to the last; yet he did. He had asked the presiding sheriff if I might be allowed to help him onto the platform where lay the execution block, "For," said he, "Despite being the most malevolent creature who ever drew breath, as you know, I'm not fit enough to climb three steps myself." That permission granted, I held his arm as he made his way, slowly and painfully, onto the last stage he would dominate. Old he may have been; but there was no lack of performance in his mind or mouth – that mouth, more than one had said, which would send him and many others to their graves.

The Londoners gathered upon the viewing platform had been anticipating the moment since his sentencing a month previously. Pamphlets had been printed and songs had been made about his life and career – and he had read and listened to many of them for his own entertainment while imprisoned in the Tower. At last the crowd gained the opportunity to meet the subject of their hatred; and I believe he made as much, or more, of it than they did, as he offered a regal wave in response to their jeers.

"So passes a dark cloud!" called a well-to-do gentleman.

"And it's a grand day for it!"

"You're dead, you Scotch dog!" shouted a woman.

"And you're ugly, you English bitch!"

"There's a dungeon waiting in Hell!" a man bellowed.

"See you there!"

We stopped, and he beheld the block. "*Ochone*, it's lower than I thought it would be," said he. "They don't make it easy to die!" He called the executioner over and took a purse from his pocket. "It's an ugly wee bag," he said apologetically, "But it has ten guineas in it, to ensure a clean cut. It's not your first day, is it? It's mine, you see. This audience deserves better than two amateurs. May I see the axe?" The executioner nervously looked over to the sheriff, who nodded assent. "Aye, it'll do. It's not a good old Lochaber axe, but it'll do."

He turned to me. "Time to earn your shilling," he said for the last time. "See that the paper is finished and published. And now, my lad, these final steps are mine." I stammered silent syllables; but he smiled, touched my shoulder, and said: "Cheer up – don't be afraid. I'm not! *Dulce et decorum est pro patria mori!*"

If I failed him, the people of London did not: they fell silent as his face drew stern and still as he looked round in the light rain; but the twinkle in his eye and the edges of his mouth betrayed what was to come. "I have never," he began, "seen such a crowd of ugly hounds —"

The throng erupted in fury, and without the line of guards they might have rendered the executioner redundant. The dragoons held them back despite their pushing, growling and throwing of missiles; then a terrifying groan rose up from beneath them. Rage turned to horror as the great viewing platform gave way under stamping feet, and it thundered to the ground, taking much of the audience with it and leaving them broken and twisted, with many clearly dead.

Silence fell again – a shocked silence as a scene of blood and bones played out amid slowly-rising cries of pain and calls for assistance. Then, over and above it all, he laughed. "The more mischief, the better sport! It seems even gravity hates the English!" As some soldiers and onlookers went to assist the fallen, he called: "*Ochone*, let's get on with it, shall we? I expect to be in Heaven by one o'clock."

He knelt down, and, without prompting, placed himself in his final position on earth. He closed his eyes for a moment as he held up a handkerchief in his right hand. Then he looked at me, winked, and started laughing again. "It's a grand end, isn't it, my lad? Grand, just! Don't let them take it out!"

Then he dropped the handkerchief, and the axe dropped with it, and so ended the dance of Simon the Fox.

It was a dance that had begun for me fifty-eight years previously, near to the day. A dance between Clan Murray and Clan Campbell, who both saw our own clan as an instrument of war against the other. A dance of dead enemies, and as many dead friends, in a battle between kings that, I fear, will rage on for ever. A dance in which I gained all that I could ever have imagined – and yet lost more still.

His last charge to me was that I should ensure his story is told in his own words. Yet instead, I will perform one final act of betrayal; although I suspect he knew I would, and that he laughs at me still from wherever his soul now resides.

I will perform that act nonetheless: I will not tell *his* story. I will tell *mine*. Then I will leave this dance of deceit, depravity and death.

In reading this account, think nothing of me. Yet be cautious of thinking much of that Fox; for I can only hint at the amount of lives he touched — and I can only guess at the amount of lives he destroyed.

CHAPTER ONE
THE CUR OF THE COLLEGE

I WAS WAITING for the pain to stop. I had been hungry many times already in my young life and I knew from experience that, after a while, it hurt no longer; and instead, the difficulty would be forcing such food as I could find into my shrunken stomach. That was a different, but no less painful, moment to come – I hoped.

It had not been a successful day's begging. Indeed it had been a while since a day had gone so poorly. There was no reason to it, for the skies had been kind and even the late evening remained pleasantly warm for an Aberdeen spring. Then again, perhaps there was a reason after all: it was the time of year when attendees of the university found it impossible to ignore their studies any longer, and instead took to ignoring the ale-houses. The absence of drunk nobles was almost certainly directly related to the absence of coins in my pocket, and bread in my belly.

Three or four of us often patrolled the bridge, but my fellow unfortunates had abandoned their posts in the hope of better pickings further into the town. I had not joined them; for I well remembered the night, two years previously, when a desperate character, tear-stained and drink-riddled, had offered me two shillings to push him into the River Don beneath, lest he remain alive when his father discovered he had squandered the opportunity of learning and instead built up a gambling debt so great that there could be no bridging it. In exchange for money equal to a fourteen-night's eating I had agreed; then, ensuring his body did not fall direct into the deep water below and therefore deny him his exit, I had scrambled down the bank and recovered many more shillings from his earthly remains.

Not that I expected a second such bounty – only, I thought, it seemed sensible to remain upon a course of action once decided upon. Then, from the deepening gloom I heard a sound which seemed to justify my commitment: tuneless, mirthful singing, the sure sign of a successful evening's entertainment in William Ghillies' tavern. Soon three men clad in the near-clerical attire of students, aged close to my own twenty or so years, appeared through the dusk, delivering an increasingly shrill and rough ballad about the adventures of a brothel keeper.

"*Oidhche mhath, mo tighearna,*" I said to the first.

He stopped mid-laugh. "Well, it's been a good evening for us, I'll say," he replied. "It doesn't seem like you can say the same. *De tha thu ag iarraidh?*"

"Just a coin or two, my lord, if you can spare it," I said, attempting to appear attentive and respectful – although my instinct was near-shouting at me to disengage, having detected a threatening tone in the other's voice, and beheld a flash of vindictive spirit in his thin, sharp face.

"Is that right? And tell me, my fine lad, what are you prepared to do for this coin or two?"

Bitter experience told me the chance to gain any money was gone; and the opportunity to retire without some form of assault was receding rapidly. My luck, it appeared, had not turned for the better.

"Pledge allegiance to the king!" said one of his companions.

That elicited a smirk. "Aye. Aye, tell us of your devotion to the king. King William, God bless him."

"And Queen Mary," added the second.

"And be brave about it," continued the first, "For I am of the Clan Campbell, true servants of the right and proper king and queen."

"God bless King William and Queen Mary," I said dutifully, and it was no real hardship, since the name of whomsoever sat on the throne made little difference to the days of my life.

"God bless them!" the second of my opposites shouted warmly.

"Aye. But you've got to mean it," the first said, leaning towards me.

"My lord Campbell, I assure you I do —" I began, but stopped, for

16

the glint of a small blade lit the shadow of his midriff. There was no further time for speaking; I could only pray the drink taken by three well-fed students would aid the chance of my escape as I burst past them and sped with all the force I could muster in the direction they had come from, towards the university town.

My prayers were not answered. They had been deep in their cups, but they were fit and agile, and the prospect of violent and deadly sport gave them an advantage set full against my terror. For they knew, as did I, that as fellows of the university they were under protection of the church and not subject to the laws of mere townsfolk. They could kill and face no sanction — and I feared they planned to follow such a course of action.

I threw myself along the paths I knew so well, not so much running as falling time and time again, my chest tumbling to my knees with every stride, my forward foot somehow keeping me just enough aright to avoid complete collapse. The Campbell bellowed at his companions to stop me, and the knowledge he had breath to do so while running terrified me all the more. I should not have let it happen — but somehow in my mortal alarm I led myself into a vennel which stopped dead after twenty yards. Even as I realised my error, my assailants entered the alley behind me and slowed their approach, the better to enjoy the coming moments. There was but one chance of a haven: an open door with bright lights behind, while all else was dark and shut. I had no option; I paced forward and burst into a small ale-room where two young men sat eating and drinking, their conversation halted by my clattering entry. Bereft of breath and hope, there was nothing left for me to do but fall on their mercy, and I gasped: "*Ma 'se do thoil e!*"

The Campbell arrived in the doorway as I dragged myself behind the two mens' table. I could tell from their dress and manner that they, also, were students — if it turned out they were all companions together, then my hunger would never concern me again. One of those seated, with a face notable enough to strike an impression even in my dread, looked first at me and then at the Campbell, and it seemed he immediately surmised the situation.

"*Oidhche mhath,*" he said to the three at the door, each now with a dirk drawn. "This fellow is with us."

17

"He is to die for treason," spat the Campbell grandly. "And you may very well go with him — unless you step back."

The seated one who had spoken looked at his companion with an expression which transmitted a simple message of confidence in what was to follow. "Treason indeed," he repeated, presenting a show of deep consideration. "What did he do?"

Eyes flashing, but taken aback nevertheless, the Campbell appeared to take a moment to consider whether to respond, before saying: "He mocked the name of the king and queen." Then, as if deciding that was not sufficient, he went on: "I have two witnesses of good standing."

"Well, good staggering, I'd say," laughed the one who clearly now controlled the proceedings. "Mocked the name of the king and queen," he said slowly, before adding: "William and Mary – that couple of *gorachs*."

It might have been expected that three men, recently so favourable to the notion of taking arms against one accused of pronouncing a royal salutation without proper regard, might be more inclined to violence against one who truly could be said to have committed treason of voice and spirit. Yet instead they remained motionless near the doorway as the taverner stood silently in the shadows, watching.

He who had offended the royal names before witnesses then turned from the Campbell and lifted a bowl of mutton from his table before holding it out to me, saying: "Will you accept this?"

It is remarkable how our animal instincts, conspiring to keep us alive, will topple over each other when more than one requires service. I was in fear for my life – but I was also sick from lack of sustenance. I made to grab the bowl, but he pulled it back. "Tell me you accept it from me," he said, with a voice of command.

I stared at the mutton and then at him. His was a face of little beauty, with a notable flat nose, but of striking personality, and there was such life in his eyes that one felt it was the clearest and wisest thing in the world to do as he said. Later, and often, I was to have cause to regret experiencing such feeling.

"It's not a trick," he said. "Well, not much of one. Just say you take it."

"I take it," said I, and he handed me the bowl.

"Grand," he replied. "Because that means you are in my protection." He stood up and spoke as if he was continuing conversation with me, although his words were directed at the Campbell. "And I am the Young MacShimi of the Clan Fraser!" He pivoted dramatically upon his heels and pointed to those at the door. "Who the devil are you?"

My attackers seemed to have lost much of their confidence, and bent slightly as they became aware of their recent exertions. In truth there was simply no question of anyone breaking this man's mastery of the situation. Slightly breathless, the leader said: "I am Colin Campbell of —"

"There's a surprise, a Campbell," my saviour broke in with a roll of his eyes. "Well, Colin Campbell of —" he exaggerated the notion of not having let the other finish — "Your luck has failed you. Because the Young MacShimi, which is me, is in town as a guest of Lady Margaret Campbell, daughter of the tenth Earl of Argyll himself. Your clan chief – my good friend Archie."

He picked up a jar of ale from the table and continued: "So you are going to stand —" and here he raised his voice to a furious rage — "stock still, while I do *this* —" he threw the jar's contents over his counterpart's face — "and *this* —" here he struck him across the right, then the left, side of his face — "and *this!*" He felt in the terrified Campbell's outer pockets until he recovered a purse of money, and took the time to open it, appear pleasantly surprised by its contents, and throw it onto the table.

"And now," he began to shout again, "You are going to be off… very, very fast!"

Without a moment's hesitation the three turned and bolted from the room. My rescuer stepped out into the darkness behind him, where the entire vennel heard him shout: "And when you get there, be off from there too! Then do it again! And just keep being off!"

By the time he re-entered the ale-room he was shaking with unbound laughter. "Magnificent mischief!" he laughed. "Grand, just! What do you say, Mungo?"

His companion shook his head, but replied warmly: "Simon, you'll get us killed one day – and a whole lot of others with us."

"Good chance," laughed the first, then turned his attention to me. "And what was that all about, my lad?" I began an attempt at an explanation but he stopped me with, "Wait – haven't I met you before?"

I realised he had. "Yes, my lord," I told him. "You have been kind to me with a farthing or two when I sit on the bridge."

"The man with no clan! I remember!" he said, and I recalled the lightly-teasing title he had given when, on asking me about my family history, I had been unable to recount anything. "Still, it's strange to me – you'll take a farthing, but you'll not take good mutton? What's wrong with you?"

I realised I was still holding the food. Surprised, I went to return it, but he was holding a spoon out to me. "Sit and eat it. You've taken it in good faith. But it's unusual," he continued as I sat, and, finally, addressed the terrible hunger that now felt all the worse for my frantic escape. "Normally it would be a boll of oatmeal."

"I'm sorry, my lord, I don't understand," I said between mouthfuls.

He pushed a jug of ale towards me too, entreating the man in the shadows: "More fighting juice, Wattie — although you'll be taking that *gorach* Campbell's money for it!" As further provisions were prepared, I was told: "The Clan Fraser has a noble tradition. If you take a boll of oatmeal from the MacShimi, the chief of our clan, you fall under his protection, and that means every one of us is God-sworn to defend your life with ours. Lord Mungo here is a Murray of Atholl, son of the Earl of Tullibardine, but I'd like to think it applies to him too, at least in spirit."

"But of course," said he who had been introduced, bowing to me, although he did not stand up. His appearance matched his companion's in expense of clothing, yet his features were much finer. I often felt, and I know others agreed, that there was never a more pleasing countenance to a man. I did not stand either – and in truth I did not realise that it was appropriate, such was the shock of the evening's events. The man who had undoubtedly saved my life was no older than me, and perhaps a year or two younger; but he spoke with a voice of age and knowledge, despite his light tone. In his company it simply did not seem strange for a fatherless beggar to be taking food and drink with the close relative of a clan chief and the son of an earl.

"If you take the oatmeal you become what we call a 'boll o'meal' Fraser. But you – you're a 'boll o'meat' Fraser. Well, actually, 'bowl o' meat!' That's not happened before. So it's a good night! What's your name?"

I told him – and it is a name I have not used since that night, and will not use here, for it bears no relevance to the person I have become since that moment.

"I will call you 'Boll O'Meat', if that'll do," he said. "No, that's *cac* – I'll call you 'Bolla'. Aye, I like that. 'Bolla'. Will that do, Bolla?" I nodded assent. There was little else I could do. "You should think longer about it. Names are important. For example, I am not yet the MacShimi, but I am the Young MacShimi. Simon Fraser, of Beaufort, of Fraser —" he stood and bowed gracefully to me — "And that means something."

"My lord, I do not know what to say," I exclaimed. "You have…"

"Called a Campbell an arse?" he said. "Along with those usurpers of King Jamie's throne? Just another day in my life. But mind, there's a true and legal bond between us. You're a Fraser now. I'll have a letter of note drawn up and sent to my father, the MacShimi, and it will be legal. Now, you have to obey the word of your chiefs, as long as it's fair word, do you understand?"

I nodded. Part of me wondered, and will wonder until I follow Simon Fraser to the grave, if there was any other direction my life could have taken. Then I think on the moments I have lived through: moments of joy, fear, blood, riches, love, hate and rage; and — comparing those to what could only have been a hundred nights or less begging on the Bridge of Don, until a student passed with a knife, and there was no rescuer — I conclude that no other direction might have seen me truly alive.

He poured some ale into my jug from his, saying: "My first word is: drink this and let's talk *cac* with Mungo Murray. That's not too bad an order to follow, eh, Bolla? *Nunc est bibendum, nunc pede libero pulsanda tellus!*" There were to be many worse orders.

THE ROAD TO GOD'S MERCY trodden by those who struggle to find regular food and drink does not often lead through tavern doors. While many of those who fell on hard times (a phrase too short and simple to describe a procession of moments of hardship piled upon hardship) took themselves too readily into their cups, people like myself – who had never fallen on such times but instead had only continually struggled onward through them – were more given to remaining outside those premises, in the hope of gaining alms from those who entered with the intention of finding refuge in drunkenness.

So it was that, after an unexpected flight followed by an unexpected supper, it was beyond my capacity to manage well an equally unexpected supply of ale. I have little recollection of those first hours with Simon Fraser and Mungo Murray, save for his insistence that our meeting was ordained from on High, and his repetition of the phrase "*Concordia res parvae crescunt*," which I later learned was the motto of Aberdeen and means "Through harmony small things grow."

After a time we left Wattie Keith's ale-room and Simon led us back over the roads I had recently traversed in fear of my life. We crossed the bridge upon which I spent most of my days, where I do recall my lord arguing strongly that despite many generals' insistence that it was easily defensible, there was a form of attack which could provide great success for any who employed it. Mungo laughed down his suggestion and called on him to prove it; to which Simon replied that, in the fullness of time, he might very well do.

Presently we found ourselves climbing the stairs of a tenement towards the Fraser chambers, and my lord bade us both enter. The conversation was loud and the night was dark — and that, I submit, is how we came to be taken by surprise from out of a corner on the stairway. Without warning a shadow lurched forward. I was forced backward down the steep steps, only keeping my balance by throwing both arms towards the wall. By the time I secured my footing and looked up, Mungo was pinned against another wall by a tall, heavy-set character, while Simon was moving to make protest, arms outstretched.

"This does not concern you, Mr Fraser," shouted the newcomer.

Mungo exclaimed nervously: "Mr McCaig!"

"And who else?" said the one now identified. "Set to beat you to within a heartbeat of the grave!"

"Dear Mr McCaig…" began Simon, only to be stopped again with a warning the matter was not his business. "That's fine with me. But can we move the performance to somewhere a little more private?" He pushed on his chamber door and stepped aside; and after a moment McCaig, still grasping Mungo firmly, marched them within.

"Everything is well, sir," Mungo pleaded as Simon lit some candles. "We've not been up to anything at all."

"That is exactly the problem, young sir," McCaig snapped back. "Yet again you have abandoned your studies — and I warned you what would happen. When your father learns of this…"

"There's nothing to learn, sir," Simon said easily, having recovered his composure. "We studied for some hours, then went out for a short break."

"We've been in our books since before lunchtime," offered Mungo.

"Aye," said Simon. "See how drunk we're not?"

McCaig let go of Mungo, who looked at me apologetically. "Mr McCaig, my tutor, engaged at my father's request," he shrugged. "His duty is to ensure my education."

The size of the man made it unlikely teaching was his first profession; but it was clear to understand that someone of Mungo's ilk, particularly in the company of someone of Simon's ilk, might require a dominie of a more violent persuasion than some others. McCaig held up a book.

"And this —" he flipped through it by candlelight — "This is what you were studying."

"I assure you my friend Mungo has been paying much attention," said Simon.

McCaig held it up for us all to see it was a volume of illustrations of an erotic nature. "How is this of help to learning the law, Mr Fraser?"

"I prefer to be addresses as 'the Young MacShimi.'"

"And maybe you do," replied the tutor, "But it is not your title — and you do not answer my question, sir!"

"You can expect nothing from such as him," Mungo said. "As you say, he uses a title that's not his to use…"

"What's this?" Simon exclaimed. "You challenge the very word of God, Mungo, and I will answer on His behalf with my sword!"

McCaig had clearly been the victim of such misdirection before. "Enough. Both of you," he said, adjusting his posture in a manner slight but yet effective in making it clear the discourse was over. "Lord Mungo, you will come home with me now. And Mr Fraser, I will write to your father."

"And I'm very sure," beamed Simon, "That Lord Tom will write back to you."

Mungo bid a brief good-night to us both before the shadow of McCaig, then the closing of the door, took him from our sight. "He's in for a bit of a beating," Simon half-sang. "Probably do him good, may the devil choke him. Now, Bolla — pour me a claret, from that bottle there, and let me show you your couch."

I did as I was bidden, with some little spillage as a result of my condition, and when I followed Simon into the small side room he had entered, I beheld him staring doubtfully upon a tent bed, over which he leaned to pull the blankets away. "What are you doing here?" he asked in surprise, as some of what I had presumed to be bedclothes resolved themselves into the form of a young woman, barely in any of her own clothes.

"You told me I could stay," she told him in a tone which suggested she had just awoken from a long, deep slumber.

"No I didn't!" he cried.

"Yes you did," she insisted. "A shilling a day until the end of term, you said!"

Simon dropped the blankets down upon her, raised his eyebrows and looked towards me, before taking the glass of wine from my stilled hand. "Sorry, Bolla," he said, looking back to the bed. "This is —" he gestured with his free arm, then dropped it — "a lassie."

"Here!" she objected. "It wasn't that last night!"

"It won't be that tonight either," he said firmly. "Get dressed and be off."

"You promised!" she cried angrily.

"I must have been drunk." He regarded her as she climbed from the bed and moved to gather her clothes from a corner of the room. "I absolutely must have been completely drunk." He felt in his pocket and removed a few coins. "Here, take this. For services rendered… whatever they were."

The girl grabbed the money quickly, as if she expected it to be removed from her reach. "What's he got that I haven't?" she demanded, gesturing her head towards me. "Oh, I see," she grinned nastily. "It's like that, is it?"

"You can give me a shilling back for your cheek!" Simon shouted, before laughing. "Just get out of here."

"See you next week?" she asked, giving me a considered glance as she passed me, while I attempted not to start back from her proximity.

"Maybe," he said after a pause.

She threw a single finger in the air at him then moved towards the door, closing it silently behind her with the air of one who had reason to have practiced the operation. "Women... eh, Bolla?" Simon said with a sigh. "And where was I? Aye, so — this is your bed."

It was a reflection of the impact made by that one's character that at no moment did I feel required, or indeed able, to remove myself from his company. A simple bar-brawl, no matter its import to me, could not be said to be reason enough to attach oneself to a noble Highland clan; and yet it was clear that a contract had been made and set. So it was no great surprise that I was to spend the rest of our time in Aberdeen laying upon that tent bed as my own. Stranger than my change of fortune itself was my simple acceptance of it — and I settle that upon the fact that Simon at no time offered the suggestion that I owed him anything, regardless of whether I did; and instead we both understood that contract between us, which he told me he wrote to his father, the MacShimi, that same night. Since I had no reading or writing it would be have been valueless to let me see it, save for the notion of knowing I was worth having been read and written about.

Yet in the months to come, alongside several adventures equalling and surpassing that of our first, Simon ensured through his own labours that I became versed in certain skills such as shaving, the management of clothing, and those other abilities required of what he called his "footman", the duties of which I undertook — although our understanding was never so simple and direct. He set me up with fine clothes of my own, once noting, "You're tall enough, and good-looking enough, to get away with this stuff better than me," followed with the addition of: "You handsome hero..."

Soon I was accustomed to a task which, at first, I dreaded: the running of errands to certain shops, the owners of which would have thought nothing of taking a broom to my back, had I dared to enter during my days on the bridge. I quickly became versed in the name and prices of bananas, pineapples, coffee, spices, and most particularly,

25

claret, which was a great favourite of Simon's.

Less than two months after my change of fortune a small event was unveiled in my lord's favourite vintners, which explained clearly to me how much the direction of my life had been altered: attending to procure a claret, I observed there was but one bottle remaining upon the shelf. I stretched out to recover it, only to find another hand within inches of my own, set on the same course. I glanced over — and there stood that Colin Campbell, so recently intent on my death. There was a moment between us; but I detected he was as doubtful as I over the outcome of our encounter; and so I bowed slightly to him and turned my hand over from the act of taking to the act of gesturing. He slowly took the bottle, and, still staring, bowed even more slightly than I had.

Then his demeanour changed, and I beheld something of the dark humour I had seen in his face the first time we had met. He offered a tight grin and said, so quietly that no one else could hear: "Do you think you've been saved? Do you think you've been bettered? That Fraser of yours has need of a footman — why? What happened to the last one?" With that he pushed past me, leaving a chill thought in my mind; for it was a fair question, and one I had not thought to ask myself.

On my return, Simon expressed himself disappointed to spend a night without claret, turning instead to whisky. I said nothing about my encounter with Campbell, telling him only that there was no wine to be had; and though I considered a number of ways to pose the question that other had raised, I could not find the strength even if I had found the words. Yet soon I managed to put the thought away from me, reflecting instead that, had I met the Campbell once more in any other manner than which I had, I could never have hoped for an outcome as positive as simply missing a bottle of wine.

Another task to which I quickly became accustomed was preparing for the visit of Simon's many ladies (as opposed to the passing "lassies," like she whom I had encountered upon my the night my fortunes changed). Each lady had her own preference of wine, food and flowers, which required my attention, and my lord had a collection of paintings, kept in a cupboard, one of which was to be hung above the fire according to the identity of that night's visitor. It was clearly a conceit which entertained him alone, for no matter how late into the night each of his visitors remained, I never saw one of them declare an interest in the painting he had related to her. Frequently as a lady retired from our chambers and Simon sat back with a drink, he would turn his head slightly sideways in a gesture of knowingness, and say: "You know how it is, my lad: a man for all seasons needs a woman for all night."

SPRING CHANGED QUICKLY to early summer, by which time the drinking, the fighting, the womanising, the arguing and the learning of letters were part of my everyday throng, such that I no longer considered a return to a life on the streets of Aberdeen. As I think back, I consider it may have been the happiest time of my life, and certainly my most carefree. Yet it lasted only weeks; and it was over when Simon first said to me: "Time to earn your shilling, Bolla."

In the days before he said it, he had been unusually attentive to his writings, dashing off masses of discourse to the exclusion of all else – including, even, drinking with Mungo. The writing itself was not my main concern, astonished though I was to see him racing through bottles of ink, while I struggled beside him to make sense of the most basic shapes upon his papers. I was more intrigued by his behaviour after he seemed to have satisfied himself with the contents of a page: he then took the document and painted it with a brush from a pot of light brown liquid, before laying it carefully on the mantle above the fire.

Eventually I asked him what he was doing – and that triggered his first use of the sentence I would come to dread. "Time to earn your shilling, Bolla – I was going to do it myself but, damn it, why should I when I have you? Do you remember me talking about the Lady Margaret Campbell?" he went on. I confirmed it; in truth he spoke of her often, despite his many other admirers. "Well, I made a bit of a mistake with her... I wrote her some letters I probably shouldn't have. So now, a certain distant relative of hers —" he nodded slowly and intently to me — "Well, he's told her father, the Earl of Argyll, that she's kept them all in her chamber. I've asked Mags to return them to me but I haven't heard from her. I don't think she's in Aberdeen.

"So the problem is, Bolla... Archie Campbell will be here soon. He's going to want to see some letters. And he can't in the name of God see the real letters. But — he can see these!" he waved at the fruit of his labours and read from a small number of them. "My dear Lady Margaret, it was a great honour to dine with you last Tuesday… Dear respected cousin, I was delighted to hear of your continued good health since last we met in the company of your noble father… Greetings, my Lady, and best warm wishes to you and all your exalted clan… Pish, pish, pish and more pish! But," he grinned, "A lot better for keeping on the right side of Archie Campbell."

"So you are going to replace one set of letters with the other?" I said. "*Ochone*, no, Bolla. You are!"

Naturally I had no taste for the enterprise; yet again, equally naturally I understood there was no question of dissuading Simon from his plan. I had, it must be admitted, some experience of gaining access to the homes of such as those who might provide for my requirements, without their assent. On many occasions, particularly on winter nights, I had found shelter in outhouses or lofts, then made off with whatever I could hold before the house rose the next morning. Entering the private chambers of a noble lady — and such a noble lady — was, of course, far from my expertise. The nearest I could offer was that, on one freezing yuletide, I had broken my way into the ice store under the grounds of a laird's big house, and it said much for the weather than I was warmer in an ice store than outside; and, on being marched into the mansion to be dealt with by the chief ghillie, I was welcomed and bade to share meat with him before being sent on my way with a few coins in my pocket and a fresh-cooked salmon. There would be no such timely generosity on breaking into the Earl of Argyll's townhouse.

Simon knew what I was thinking, or at least surmised my conclusion, for he said: "You are the bowl o'meat Fraser, the one and only. We have a bond, and I am the Young MacShimi."

It was fortunate I had kept my beggars' plaid, old and stolen as it was: its dull browns and greys were much more in keeping with my mission than the brighter red and green tartan in which Simon had dressed me. I took hope from my knowledge of making the most of such a disguise — until my lord told me the entire transaction would take place in mid-morning. "It's a *scunner*, to be sure," said he, "But you can get in from an outhouse round the back, and it's so easy I've done it myself a hundred times." His words brought me no comfort.

So it was that, on the appointed day, one of those few still and silent summer mornings where the heat seems to stifle sound itself, Simon sat beside me on a rear wall and we looked over the yard of Argyll's lodging in Aberdeen.

"You see that window, Bolla? Right above the lean-to roof? That's the one. You get in there and it's a wee chamber, and her room is right in front of you. The letters were in the bottom drawer of her wardrobe last time I saw them. In and out, and I'll see you in Wattie Keith's in, what —" he rested his hand warmly on my shoulder and shrugged — "Twenty minutes? Good luck, my lad." He thrust the bundle of forged papers into my grasp, patted my shoulder and wandered away as if strolling in the sunshine.

Fortunately there was no activity in the yard. I assumed the earl's household would be making final arrangements within for his imminent arrival — then realised that, if true, it made easy my approach, but nigh-on impossible my invasion. There was no other course than to push the letters into my plaid, drop down, and move swiftly and silently (a fashion known well to beggars) until I crushed myself into the corner between the yard's far wall and the lean-to. A convenient ale barrel assisted my climb onto the low roof, but here the challenge became more alarming: I was standing over the yard with the sun behind me, casting a shadow so large it seemed to shout of my presence; and if anyone should approach I would be seen immediately. My next pause was under the window, mercifully open. I planned to gather my senses before climbing in, but the noise of motion below threatened fast detection, and so I rolled through the window as quietly as I could.

I might as well have been blind for the effect the indoor light had upon my eyes. If I was already seen I was lost; but there remained silence, save for low sounds of people moving on the floor below. I did not dare wait too long so I stepped fitfully towards where Simon had told me Lady Margaret's chamber would be. I lifted the latch, ensured no one waited within, then swiftly opened, stepped past then closed the door, all in one motion.

My vision was still limited to vague shapes, but I could make out a bed, a washbowl, a foot-locker, a dresser – and a large wardrobe by the window. I crept over, opened it, and pulled open the topmost of three drawers. It was empty; and after a frantic moment in which my panic led me to be louder than it was safe to be, I found the other two equally empty. I looked round again and gently stepped to the dresser, finding its six drawers full of the accoutrements of a lady's dress, but no letters. I found the bedclothes bereft of papers, under or in pillows and mattresses; the washbowl stand contained nothing; and unless there was some secret compartment in the room, of which I could know nothing, it had to be the foot-locker.

At that moment I became aware of sounds I should have been attending to more shortly: the arrival of horses outside, orders being shouted, and the household being summoned. Argyll had patently arrived — and there was little time left for care. Bellows of rage came from a man in the rooms below, while two women seemed to argue back. I threw open the foot-locker to see a container near full of clothes, shoes, and ladylike possessions. Furniture rumbled and clattered beneath me as the pattern of shouting, I could tell, reached the point at which conversation was no longer worth pursuit. I became frantic, pulling dresses, boots, combs and books out and letting them fall wherever they may. There came the thunder of footsteps on the stairway, and if I had been hot in the sun under my plaid before, I was in rivers of sweat at that moment. Finally, like a burst of gold light matching the weather outside, I spotted what could only be a set of papers like my own. I grasped them, pulled the new ones out, and without even pausing to compare the bundles I exchanged their places.

Immediately then the door burst open; and I stared into a noble, and black-furious, face. "*Co'an fear ud?*" spluttered he, astonished. There followed several moments of doubt on his part, and calculation on mine; had I moved faster I might have pushed him aside and made off through the window of my entry. But there had passed enough time for him to recover, and therefore I had two paths remaining: surrender, or test my fortune with the front window.

It too, was open, due to the weather. As I dashed towards it I saw there was a straight drop beneath, but hardly higher than the back wall. Yet Argyll (for I assumed it was he) had come to his senses and was a footstep or two behind me — leading me to vault through the open

30

space then swing myself round so I was facing the building, all pivoted on one hand on the windowsill. It is not an act I could have completed had I planned it; but somehow I broke my fall into two movements with the pivoting action, and landed, somewhat heavily, into the open street. Argyll appeared above me but I was not simpleton enough to look back. As he raged at his servants to follow me I was already off, running as hard as I had on the night I encountered his clansman.

Beasts, when hunted, will turn themselves toward high ground. I do not know that men have the same instinct; however, I know that we often face a crisis, even within panic, between choosing to continue our flight or seeking cover. I knew the streets of Aberdeen well, but I knew not whether those following me shared my wisdom. And even though Wattie Keith's was just a moment away, I could not risk it. Instead I made full-pace for the Bridge of Don. As I crossed the college park, abloom with couples and friends enjoying the day, I took the chance to look behind and beheld two tall, thin men giving chase, without sharing the exhausted gait under which I now laboured. If my previous dash had been hampered by lack of nourishment, I fear this one was victim to the opposite problem. I made the bridge with Argyll's men a matter of feet behind me; and I prayed my judgement was correct, for I had not been paying attention to the rainfall of recent weeks. I paused, just once, in the vain hope I was no longer chased, and in that moment it became impossible for me to avoid their grasp for more than a few seconds. Then I threw myself over the wall.

Over many nights in our cups, Simon, Mungo and I had cause to discuss the nature of existence, and whether it could be said to be broadly similar for all men, and whether it ended with the last beat of one's heart. I was never confident enough in my views to express a strong opinion, but I do know that certain moments of one's life last much longer than the mere counting of hours might insist. So it was with my fall into the Don – in the lives of Argyll's men, watching from above, it could only have lasted moments, but for me it continued far longer. I had time to consider many things about my time on earth, before I experienced the not unpleasant shock of impact with the cool rushing water. I had time to consider many more things while the forces of nature kept me beneath the surface. By the time my head rose above

31

the waves and I gasped for air, I felt I should be many miles from the bridge. I was not; I was only a matter of twenty paces — but it was far enough to secure my escape from the enraged Argyllmen, who watched helplessly as the current took me beyond their grasp.

I had observed the river in spate many times, and I knew the current appeared to curve towards the north bank some forty paces beyond the bridge. I could paddle, but not swim; yet that was enough, with the help of the watercourse, to settle me upon land just a short run from our chambers. I looked back to see the Campbells starting to give chase again, but as I closed the chamber door I knew I was safe.

Simon had persuaded me of the urgency he felt in setting his hands on the letters I head recovered; so, briefly stopping to ensure they were not seriously damaged, which they were not, I changed into my footman's clothes. That alone would secure my identity, I was sure, even if an entire clan of Campbells waited outside.

There was no one there; but on my return I found there was still much consternation in the town, centred round Argyll's house. I was confident I had nothing to fear, such that I dared to pass the earl's building as I made for Wattie Keith's. The window through which I had escaped was now closed, and behind it I could see the figure of a lady, seemingly with her arms to her head in distress. I could imagine the reasons for her condition, but it was no concern of mine.

In contrast, the absence of Simon in Wattie's ale-room was a great concern. It was empty save for a handful of faces I knew well. I believe my thoughts played across my face because Wattie waved me over to the corner where he stored his wares and said: "Looking for the Fox? I know where he is."

He had been given the pet-name only the previous week, but all of us in attendance, in view of our knowledge of the man, had agreed it was ideal, and it had already stuck fast. "Well?" I asked Wattie; but he shook his head.

"I'm not to tell you," he replied, "Until you've taken a drink. He says you'll need it."

My lord was not wrong, and I gratefully accepted the jug of mild ale offered to me. It did not take long, after which the taverner quietly told me: "You'll find him at Jenny's." I thanked him and sped through the town to that other ale-room, only to find the same message: "I'll tell you where he is after you've taken a drink." I was no longer concerned. It was clearly another game of Simon's, and I suspected he had heard before my return that I had achieved at least partial success. Visits to four other establishments brought me the same message until, not entirely to my surprise, I was directed back to Wattie's – where I found Simon at table, with quite the most striking lady I had ever seen.

"Bolla!" he cried, pushing an ale jug towards me. "You made it! Spectacular sport!"

I sat down with the labours of the day beginning to tell on me. "A close thing, it was…" I said.

"Ach, *cac*!" he replied. "Nothing to a man of your talents. I'll bet they were never, what, closer than half a mile? *Audentes fortuna iuvat!*" he laughed long and loud. "This," he said, with his arm round his companion, "Is the Lady Margaret Campbell."

That noble smiled a beautiful smile to me. "The Young MacShimi tells me you have done him a great service," she said warmly.

"Aye, by drinking in every house in town before dinner-time," Simon said. "Naw, naw, that's not fair. You've done well, my lad." Then to Lady Margaret: "Balls of a bull, that one! That's what 'Bolla' means."

She laughed. "Simon, you introduce me to the most fascinating people!"

"That's what happens when you step out of the great castles and meet real folk," he replied. "Bolla, did you ever think you'd see the daughter of Scotland's foremost earl in Wattie's tavern?" I readily accepted I did not, and they both laughed again; before, turning serious, Simon said: "But, so — do you have something for me?"

I drew out the bundle of letters and offered them over. Simon took them, almost as if there was a fragment of the True Cross in his hand, gazed at them then looked up at me. "Good man," he said quietly, then, louder: "Good Fraser man!" Laughing, he took the papers over to the stove where Wattie kept a kettle warming, and began forcing them into the flames, where, after smoking for a few moments following their recent dampening, they burst alight one by one.

"What are those?" Lady Margaret asked me as we watched his actions.

Confused, since I had assumed she must know, I muttered, "Just papers, my lady."

He glanced over each page before casting it into the fire, his face betraying delight in some of the passages he read. One caused him to let out a great yell of pleasure, and he leaned over to let Lady Margaret see the words. Almost immediately she stared up at him, her eyes and mouth rounded in horror, followed by a burst of mischievous laughter – most unladylike. "You filthy hound!" she exclaimed.

Simon smiled wickedly then returned to his task until all the papers were gone. Despite my tiredness and the effect of several cups of ale, I began to realise all was not the way I might have expected it to be. He saw my mind at work, shook his head slightly with a conspiratorial glance, then said, "Come on, let's find a better drink."

The townhouse of my earlier adventure lay between Wattie's and Mungo's residence. While much of the clamour had died down in the street without, there remained a number of men and horses – and the lady I had earlier seen remained at the window. As we passed, she began knocking on the pane; and, at last opening the window, she shouted Simon's name across the road.

He simply looked surprised and waved politely back. That elicited a scream from the window, soon followed, as we moved on, by the appearance of Argyll himself in the street. "Simon Fraser!" That man shouted.

He turned. "It's yourself, good baillie!" Simon said. "How the devil are you?"

I was no scholar, but I was sure insulting an earl in such a manner could almost certainly be said to lead to a death warrant, legal or otherwise. Instead, the other replied angrily: "What devilry has been done in my house this day? In your name, I warrant, Fraser!"

Simon looked shocked. "I haven't a clue what your head is telling you," he said calmly, before looking to the sky. "Have you had too much sun? There's a lot of it about this weather."

The other turned back to his house, where the lady in the window was crying bitterly, still shrieking the name of my companion. "Jane! Shut up and close that window now, I warn you!" From behind her appeared four arms, pulling her away from the glass and closing it.

"Sounds like you're having a bad day," Simon offered. "My mate Bolla here, he's had one like it. So if you don't mind we're off for a drink. Oh – sorry, introductions." He became the embodiment of grace as he said: "Lady Margaret Campbell, may I present Baillie Wishart of Aberdeen, as fine a local man as ever you'll meet."

She smiled, and the man I had thought was her father found some resilience of position, calmed himself and bowed: "My lady…"

Simon nodded politely and gestured for us to take our leave; but just as we turned away he added: "I trust you found those letters? The ones someone told you were shameful? And I trust they weren't shameful in the least? Good. See you later, my dear baillie." He put his arms round Lady Margaret and I, steering us away from the shocked townsman.

"What do you make of all that, my lad?" he asked me so that our companion could not hear, nudging my elbow. It seemed that my expression was more than enough answer, for, grinning, he nudged me again and said: "You'll have gathered I wasn't completely honest with you. The letters had to be rescued – but they were nothing to do with Margaret here. Poor Jane… Ach well, experience teaches fools. And, indeed, Baillie Wishart!" I suspect my face continued to betray me, as he continued: "No harm done for a wee tale, Bolla – and the more mischief, the better sport! But let's find another tavern. Someone somewhere must have managed to get some damned claret."

CHAPTER TWO
THE BRIGAND OF THE BATTLE

"OF COURSE, I'D HAVE AS MANY OF THEM KILLED as I had to," Simon explained as we rode toward the castle. "But I'd much rather they were clever enough to just be off." His discourse on the politics of war had lasted the three days of our journey from Aberdeen to Inverness, but I confess much of it had been wasted on me – although doubtless it did not concern him greatly. Which is not to say I had not listened. In my previous desperate profession I had learned the value of that art: a conversation overheard on rabbit snares could lead me to fresh meat long before those who had laid the traps returned; silence in the shadows might reveal the whereabouts of a dropped coin, whose owner would soon give up the search; and the passing comment: "No one will find it there," could result in the recovery of unimagined riches.

In my last months as a beggar I had heard much talk of kings and queens; or, in fact, two kings and a queen. I knew the monarch of Scots — not of Scotland, my lord advised me — James, had been forced from his English throne and replaced by a Dutchman called William and his wife, James' daughter Mary. I knew also that many of the nobles in Scotland had taken issue with his removal, saying the northern kingdom should choose its master for itself. There had been a great gathering in Edinburgh, where Scotland had decided for William; but not without intrigue, for John Claverhouse, now Viscount Dundee, had vowed to go to war to protect James' claim to the crown.

Such intelligence was worth not a single corner of bread to me, and therefore I was given to discard it all. Had I been more aware I might have realised that, as a part of the conditions around me having changed, I was now sharing bread with some whose lives and futures were vested in the international argument. It was not until Lord Mungo Murray had come to take his leave of Simon that I realised how close the fight had come to me.

"I'm needed at home," he had explained in Simon's chambers one afternoon. "It looks like there's going to be a fight."

Simon had laughed. "I've heard. Your baillie has taken Blair Castle for King Jamie, and your brother's besieging it in the name of William. Your own home – magnificent mischief!"

"I'm glad to hear you think it so," Mungo said without his usual light-hearted spirit.

"And where's Atholl himself in all this?"

"Father... can be a right *gorach* at times. He's trying to stay out of it."

Simon laughed again. "I can see his point – Jamie's doing well in Ireland. If he brings over an army from there, he might be able to force and end to things . But if he doesn't, you could lose everything by being on the wrong side. Murray has been out of favour often enough in recent times. And no one knows if Dundee will catch Mackay, or if Mackay will catch Dundee, or if the two of them will just dance round Scotland till the Last Day. Spectacular sport!"

Mungo had shaken his head. "It's not funny. All these people running all over our country with guns and swords — someone's going to get done in sooner or later."

"Ach, come on!" Simon had demanded. "A fight on your own lands between Dundee and Mackay? I'd pay good money to see that."

"You'd likely be in it," Mungo replied. "Or do you think Fraser can stay out?"

"I sincerely hope not," my lord had said flippantly.

"I have to go. I'll see you again."

They had locked arms briefly. "Take care of yours," Simon had said. "But take care of you, and all." After Mungo left, there had scarce been another hour pass before I was told it was time, once again, to earn my shilling: "Go and get three horses. We're going to a fight!"

We had wound our way westward with my lord explaining the details of how the current conditions had come into being between Jacobites and Williamites – regardless of my limited ability to follow his monologue. My clearest memory of the journey is something which became a regular feature of our travels in the future: before setting out he had supplied himself with a large purse of farthings, and every beggar we passed became the beneficiary of one or two of those coins. He conducted a brief conversation with each and every one, often asking his opposite's name then recounting a short tale relating to it. On occasion he simply directed a line of his discourse to the pedestrian; and although it would have been near impossible for them to make sense of it, the spirit in which it was delivered left no doubt of his genial mood. By the time we reached the Fraser country outside Inverness – – and I had been told I was home, for it was now my country also — the dispensation of coins had increased threefold. Later, as we approached Moniack Castle, my lord's own home, it seemed that every man, woman, child and animal in the street had a word for him.

"Back from university already?" said one. "Were you thrown out?"

"No, I knew it all already," Simon replied.

"Your head's got even bigger," called another.

"That's impossible," said my lord.

"What did you bring me from Aberdeen?" asked another.

"A good beating," Simon called back. "Do you want it now?"

Moniack was a dog-leg building of three floors, its small entrance up a steep flight of stairs in a square tower which crowned its apex, its outhouses and land around it busy with people going about their daily business. As we dismounted, a truly massive man – near seven feet in height and not much less in girth, and with a thickly-bearded face like red rock – came down the stairs, his right hand across his belly, ready to pull his sword. "What is your business?" he shouted.

Simon turned to him, saying: "Murder!"

I beheld a transformation I will never forget: the human hill, clearly built for war and work, released a wide, explosive, heartfelt smile that spread beyond his mouth and made use of every single sinew in his face. The effect was to behold a giant newborn babe expressing pure joy for the first time. "Simon!" he bellowed – and I swear I heard it echo back from the mountains on the horizon around us.

My lord went to embrace him, but was picked up and swung around as if it was he who were the newborn. "Ali! How the devil are you? Put me down!" Placed at last on the ground again, he turned to me. "Bolla, it's my great pleasure to introduce Alistair Fraser, the living mountain – – Ben Ali to his friends. Ali, this is my good friend Bolla, and he's a better man than you."

It was my turn to be lifted into the air, at once terrifying and exhilarating. "Bolla, you're a good man if you can put up with that *gorach*," said Ali, and I thought it best to smile as best I could. As he dropped me and I recovered my balance, he continued to Simon: "Are you here for the fight?"

"We'll see."

"We'll *do*!"

"Time will tell." By this time Ali had directed someone to take care of the horses and we were climbing the stair single-file, as that is all its breadth would allow. "How's Himself?" The big man made a grumbling noise, to which Simon responded: "Ah, well…"

There was no time for me to savour my first experience of entering a castle. I caught a glimpse of a huge smoke-clad kitchen down stairs in front of me, and a great hall, full of noise and bustle, to my left; but we climbed immediately up the spiral stairs to the right, and on the floor above, Simon pushed a great curtain and we made our way into the lord's chamber. Within, a young man was marching back and forth between two spectators, angrily remonstrating with an old man on a seat by the fireplace; who waved for silence and stood up, with some little difficulty. "Simon!" he said. "It's good to see you."

"Father!" replied my lord, embracing his father. "Bolla, this is Lord Tom Fraser of Beaufort, the MacShimi himself – and this is my older brother, Alexander Fraser of Beaufort. Father, Alex – this is Bolla."

"Ah, the boll o'meat Fraser," smiled the chief gently. "You are welcome." Alexander gave me a terse nod, and I bowed carefully to both of them.

"So what about the fight, then?" Simon said. "When are we going to kick some arse – and where?"

"Trust you to act the fool!" cried one of the other two, a tall, slim character with dark eyes which seemed to be permanently enraged, and a notable sharp nose and downturned mouth which gave the impression he was enraged at whomsoever he looked at. "This is no game, Simon!"

"Ah, Andrew," my lord bowed towards him, a neutral expression upon his face which still managed to portray an amount of distaste. "It's sometimes good to hear your thoughts." He turned to me. "Andrew, Laird of Tanacheil," he told me, although my bow received no response. "And this," he added, gesturing to the last man in the room, who aged with Lord Tom and wore a beard to match Ben Ali's, "is the Reverend James Fraser, our sennachie." That man returned my bow with one which matched mine to an almost eerie extent. "Anyway, back to kicking arse!" my lord said.

"Whose arse? That's what I want to know," Alexander said with a glare towards his father. Simon turned to the chief with a questioning look.

"This is no easy matter, son," Lord Tom said after a pause. "Things are difficult to see clearly —"

"*Cac*!" Alexander cut in. "The clan stands with King Jamie, and there's nothing more to be said."

The MacShimi shook his head. "Alex…"

"What's the argument?" Simon asked. "Campbell is for William. Murray is for William. Fraser needs to be with Campbell and Murray, so Fraser needs to be for William too."

"Fraser is for Jamie, the rightful king, as well you know," Alexander said, waving toward the window. "Ask any of them out there. You won't get any other answer."

"That's the way of it," Ben Ali agreed, his bulk seeming to carry the weight of more than one voice. Tanacheil growled his assent.

Simon looked at them both and nodded thoughtfully; then, as his brother made to launch into another outburst, waved him down and turned to his father, now seated again. MacShimi paused for some moments before speaking. "This isn't all about kings and crowns. It's about the clan – Fraser has to win, whatever that involves. I've been in these fights before and I'll tell you: it's never simple. Say we join with Dundee, and we win. Now, that's grand — but we've made enemies of the Campbells and the Murrays, and everyone in the government, while King Jamie is… where? In Ireland? And what do we get for our win? A letter of thanks from him, and letters of fire and sword from

Edinburgh."

"We must stand for the king!" Alexander insisted. "He will send an army from Ireland."

"But he has not," MacShimi said. "He sent just five hundred men when Dundee asked for six thousand. And they got their supply ships caught by the English navy. I hear their General Cannon is a *gorach* and Dundee says he'd rather fight without swords than with him."

"We must fight for Jamie!" Alexander insisted. "He is rightful king and no act of man removes that right."

"True!" Tanacheil added.

"Ask the Campbell about that," Simon said. "His father and grand-father both lost their heads after following the wrong rightful king."

"Politics!" spat Tanacheil.

"Poison words!" Alexander said. "Jamie was appointed by God. Right is right and wrong is wrong."

"If only, son. If only," said Lord Tom, shaking his head. "The fact of the matter is we're completely surrounded by men of William. That's an end to it."

"You go out, then," Alexander shouted. "You go out and tell everyone we're fighting for William. Start with Ben Ali here!"

We all turned to the giant, who stared his chief in the eye for a many long moments, before stating in strong, quiet words made of stone older than the hills: "Fraser is for Jamie."

Alexander let out a nasty laugh. "There! You see?"

Into the difficult silence which followed, Simon spoke. "Father, better men than us have faced this kind of *cac* and come out smelling of flowers. I wonder if we should take a lesson from history."

"What do you mean?"

"Up till now it's all been talk. Dundee marches up and down, then Mackay marches up and down after him. There's going to be a fight for sure – and a Highland charge might wipe out a Saxon army. But what then? Campbell and Murray fight with their pens in courtrooms. The best general in the world may not win that fight."

"Pen and paper against the true word of God!" Alexander said. "And a Saxon army wiped out is all the chiefs of Scotland need to remind them of their duty." He and Tanacheil shared a glare of agreement.

"You're not wrong," Simon said, looking them both in the eye in turn. "But that makes it more complex, not less. It's not going to be decided in one move, you see? We can't tell how long it'll go on, or how it'll go down. So if Fraser is to be on the winning side, Fraser must be on *both* sides."

"*Cac!*" Tanacheil replied. "Political *cac!*"

"Your tongue will get you killed, wee brother," Alex warned. "That's the kind of talk that leads to treason. Jamie has the word of God—"

"Aye, but which God, Alex?" Simon said impatiently, clearly determined not to hear the same outbursts again. "The God who asks for Catholic worship or the God who sends Catholics to the gallows? The God of the presbyterian polity or the God of the episcopalian polity? If there are two religions in this country, and two types of one religion in this country, doesn't it make as much sense there should be two armies?"

His brother looked confused. "What is that to mean?"

"I'm saying if God is on so many sides, what's wrong with Fraser being on so many sides?"

"Your words are all *cac,*" Alexander protested. "They'll see you killed, and anyone who follows you!"

There followed another silence. Then Lord Tom asked: "Well, son? Do you have more than clever words?"

Simon nodded. "You know Mungo Murray and I are friends — well, he's with his brother, Ian Cam, besieging Blair Castle for William's army. I can take a wee band of the lads and join him. Alex, you take the rest of them to Dundee. As long as none of us are stupid enough to take each other's heads off, Fraser will be seen to be on the winning side."

Tanacheil and Alexander exchanged bewildered glances, before Simon's brother spluttered: "That's just... pish. No sense to it."

"Is there any sense to much of this?" Simon said quietly. Then he turned to Ben Ali. "Fraser is for Jamie, pal, I know. But Fraser needs to be for Fraser too — do you agree?" The big man thought for a moment then nodded slowly. "So what if I was putting a band together to stand with Murray, on William's side? Would you come with me?"

"Well, aye, I suppose. But I wouldn't like it."

"I know. But do you think, between you and me, we could get a band of fifty together?"

"Oh, aye; they'll do what I tell them or get a sore face. But —"

"But we'd have to be careful, and we'd have to watch who we were fighting, and we'd have to watch what we were saying."

"If someone tells me to pledge allegiance to King Billy, I'll —"

"Find a way round it," Simon nodded. "We don't need to shout 'For William and Mary,' we can shout 'For Fraser,' instead. For *Fraser*. Not for anyone in England."

"Aye, well…" Ali said with a shallow nod. "I don't like it, mind."

"Neither do I," Simon assured him, touching him on the shoulder. Then he turned to MacShimi. "What do you think?"

His father paused, then looked expectantly at the Reverend Fraser, who appeared to wait for some moments until it was impossible not to feel that whatever he said would be of great import. "We are all sons of Simon," he almost sang in a deep, melodic voice which carried the weight of generations of memories – as was fitting for the clan story-keeper. "He stood with Bruce, and won this country as his reward for following the rightful king, even when but six men believed he was the rightful king."

"You see?" Tanacheil cried with victory in his voice, gesturing towards the sennachie; but the other simply stared at him, until the joy appeared to drain from his face and outstretched arm.

"Simon had a cousin who stood against Bruce, yet not against Simon; and if those last six men abandoned Bruce, Simon was set to be welcomed to the other side. The fighting Frasers were forged out of knowing how to win." He tapped his aged brow. "For some of us," he said, "This is simply a place where our eyes sit. For others, it is a place where battles are fought in advance, and won the faster for it."

He fell silent and directed a glance towards Lord Tom, the understanding being clear: that all had been said and it was time for the chief to make a decision. That man sighed; and, after a meaningful stare at Alexander and Tanacheil, looked at Simon and nodded. "Best of a bad job, son. Best of a bad job," his father said.

"Political pish," Alexander muttered, and Tanacheil agreed.

"For God's sake, Alex," Simon said, finally losing his patience. "What we're trying to do here, in case it's beyond you, is to avoid sending the clan out to die for no reason. We're trying to make absolutely certain there's something in it for us, no matter who wins the war. A war run by bigger clans than us – aye, and don't deny it! So do you have any better ideas?" His brother looked at him, then at Tanacheil, then turned to stare out the window in silence. "Right. What's the latest word? How much time have we?"

"No more than a few days," his brother said, as if he had finally reconciled himself to the business in hand. "Stewart of Ballachin holds Blair, with Murray outside. He's told Mackay he'll back off if Dundee gets there first, so it's a race to Atholl."

"Aye, he can besiege his own home but he'll be damned if he's going to attack it," Simon laughed. "You see how senseless this all is? And where's the Earl of Atholl himself?"

MacShimi smiled. "He's left Ian Cam in charge. He's gone to take the waters in Bath."

Simon exploded with genuine mirth. "As befitting the Captain General of the Royal Company of Archers!" Even Alexander allowed himself a small smile. "Right, this is what we do, then: we'll all head for Blair together. You join Dundee, I join Ian Cam and support the siege. Then — we'll just need to see what happens."

"I'll tell you what happens," Tanacheil said darkly. "Frasers fight Frasers in front of Blair Castle."

"Frasers will never fight Frasers!" my lord cried, punching his fist into his other hand for emphasis. "No general is going to be stupid enough to line you up opposite your own clan — he'd be asking to have his own battalions broken. Forget that. We'll be seen to be part of both sides, meaning Fraser wins. And if you can think of another way to make that happen, Andrew, now's the time to say so." He looked round the room, daring anyone to gainsay him; but no one offered further comment. "So let's get on with it, my lads! Better or worse." Alexander made to speak, but Simon marched out.

CLAN FRASER DID NOT MAKE USE of the burning cross to summon its men to war, preferring a more ancient custom. Lord Tom appeared before those who lived in the castletown, carrying the dulled

45

sword of the chiefs who had gone before him and the ancient white wand of his office. All having observed his undeniable authority, he took a large oak staff and thrust it into a fire. He then drew his dirk, and, taking grip of a goat tied to a post, slit the animal's throat in one motion. Before it was dead he cut open its belly, then took the smoking staff and pushed it into the goat's entrails, throwing up a cloud of hissing steam. Then he handed it to a ghillie, who made off to the north; when he reached the nearest village they would accept the call to arms, and another ghillie would carry the staff onward. That done, it took until the following afternoon for near two hundred men to have assembled at the castle. Thomas declared himself satisfied with the response as he led Simon and Alexander down the stairs to stand among the clan. And, since the older brother was to lead them, their father told him to speak.

A small dray had been brought out for a platform and he jumped up upon it, to which the low talk between clansmen faded away. He looked round, seemingly unsure of how to begin, then called: "Clan Fraser!"

"Fraser!" the men replied as one.

"The king has need of us," Alexander began strongly. "And Clan Fraser has never ignored the call of the king." It was a good start — and I noticed no one was in any doubt to whom he referred. Yet his next words quickly appeared to sow a great seed of doubt among those who listened. "Needs must that we sometimes do things we would rather not do… and I want to assure you there will be no black thought from your clansmen if…"

"Where's the fight?" Someone called.

"Put me at the front!" shouted another.

"Give us a song!" came another voice, causing laughter, to which Alexander seemed to lose heart. At that moment Simon jumped up onto the dray, to scattered cheers of approval.

"I'll give you a song, you *gorachs*," he shouted strongly. "It's about looking after the friends of Fraser and sending the enemies of Fraser to hell!" To wider cheers he continued: "It's over forty years since this clan, and others, stood with Montrose against those who wanted to take our lives, and our wives and our weans. What was it like, Father?"

Alexander and Reverend Fraser gave Simon a strange look as all eyes turned to MacShimi. Although he was in his sixties, and climbing onto the dray would be a longer affair than it had been for his sons, the clan afforded him the reverence of silence.

"Some hard fights, indeed, hard fights," he said, his voice stronger than I had heard previously. "I was a young man, if you will believe me —" many laughed warmly, and he smiled. "Sometimes it was all I could do to keep awake and moving. But we fought well, and we won, and for years after everyone spoke of Clan Fraser and our bravery!"

Simon allowed the cheers to die down. "Aye, so this song you want," he continued, "It's about our bravery. But we need to go out and fight before Reverend Jamie makes the words. Can you get that into your thick heads?" More cheers. "But things have changes, lads. With Montrose we fought for the king and against Campbell. This time, we fight for the king – but we fight with Campbell too."

He paused to allow the muttering to spread across the castle yard, before sharply shouting: "Why? Why? Why fight with Campbell? Because Campbell is now our friend. For how long? God knows – or more likely, the devil knows. But I'll tell you this: it's not for Clan Fraser to break the rules of friendship, is it?" The listeners agreed. "So there you are, lads. Most of you are to go with Alex and fight with Dundee, in the name of King Jamie. But a wee dod of you is to come with me and Ben Ali, and look after our friend Campbell – and our friend from the next glen, Murray. And if that's not good enough for you, Ali will give you another song — what will that be about?"

Ben Ali did not need to stand on the dray to be seen. He turned round and bellowed: "Wee *gorachs* who don't want to fight… getting their heads broken!"

Laughter and cries of support rang out across the throng, and Simon finished: "So, lads, are we going to sing about Clan Fraser getting their heads broken, or are we going to sing about Clan Fraser looking after its friends… and fighting like heroes?"

"Heroes!" Ali shouted back, then led the clan in a chant of the word. Thomas gave a nod and a dozen servants appeared, each carrying bottles of whisky, which had soon been passed round the assembled clan to seal their union of purpose.

WE SET OFF ON OUR SOUTHWARD JOURNEY soon afterwards, there having been some discussion about choosing the best road to avoid detection from those sympathetic to William and those actively supporting James; the point being that, since the clan was to split, it was important for no one to know its full number. Eventually a route was chosen through Glen Mhor, turning east about Lochaber towards Atholl. Clan Fraser kept a good pace, as did most Highland troops, and it was expected we would see Blair Castle within four days.

"There have been letters passing back and forward," Alexander told us as we led on horseback, the men behind us on foot and Ben Ali walking beside us with no difficulty of pace or breath. "Mackay has been seeking to buy the support of the chiefs."

"How is he hoping to work that?" Simon asked.

"He thinks a lot of folk are supporting Campbell because they owe him money. He's hoping if he offers to cover the debts, they'll change sides."

"As he did," Simon mused. "Mackay fought for Jamie at Monmouth a few years back. Then changed his mind."

"Turncoatery!" Tanacheil said angrily. "You take us too close to these people, Simon!"

"Maybe," my lord replied. "But there have been letters from Dundee as well, eh?"

"Well, aye," his brother allowed. "To tell us Jamie is waiting for his moment, and we'll all get our reward when the time comes."

"What do you think of that, Ben Ali — a war of letters?"

"Break their hands," he replied, "And if they try to speak it instead, smash their teeth in." All in hearing distance laughed at the disgust in his voice.

The land changed such that Simon and Alexander moved slightly ahead while I proceeded alongside Ali. It was not often my choice to open a conversation, being aware of my own history and the great distance of experience between my own life and the lives of those by whom I was now surrounded; but the big man had such a magnetism or gravity about him I felt completely safe in his presence. So I said, "Simon gave a good speech there."

He laughed. "He always does. I swear his gub is a musical instrument, near enough. He could play it less often, mind, if he wanted to stay out of trouble."

"I do not think the Fox plans to stay out—"

"The Fox? Is that what you call him?" He exploded in mirth. "That's just grand! Wait till I tell the lads!"

"Will he one day be clan chief?" I asked.

"He'd make a good one. God knows we'd follow him to hell if he asked us. After Tom it's meant to be Alex, but…" I said nothing, waiting to see what would follow. "Tom was never meant to be MacShimi. We made him chief because Hugh, the Lord Lovat, was meant to be — but he's not even worth talking about. So we chose Tom. When Alex gets it, well, there's no guarantee he'll keep it."

"The clan would take it away from him?"

"Perhaps," Ali replied after a moment. "He's an honest man, to be sure. With King Jamie home and the kingdom at peace, he'd be a grand MacShimi."

"And without it?" I prompted.

He shrugged. "God will sort it out. God and fighting. You know, my father fought with MacShimi. My father, he was a really big man…"

Alexander made certain to send scouts ahead in several directions, aware that, as two armies made to meet, there could be any number of unexpected developments, and they could arise from any quarter. So it was that, as we came to the edge of the lands of Murray, we learned Dundee was a day behind us and on a similar route from the west, while Mackay was several days south of us, his departure from Edinburgh having been delayed for some reason. At this point Simon called for our company to split. Ben Ali had chosen five dozen men to travel on to Blair Castle, while the other part, some three times that number or more, were to wait with Alexander for the Dundee's arrival. There passed words of warmth and goodwill between the two parties – although Alexander could not keep his disapproval from his face.

"For Clan Fraser and King Jamie," Simon assured him with a smile. "And if you have to attack us, please don't take my head off."

"I hope you don't live to regret all this, wee brother," Alexander replied; but they locked arms before we moved off. Tanacheil, who went with the larger party, expressed his disapproval with a glare towards

Simon, who grinned cheerfully by way of response.

It had been decided that the main body of Frasers would keep the clan flag, while we would remain unidentified, at least from a distance; for that reason, as we drew close to of the home of Clan Murray, we observed that we were being shadowed from a hill above the road by a small unit of cavalry. Simon called for Ali and me to follow him and we went briskly up towards them; seeing what we did, six of their number came down to meet us. As we came within easy sight of them Simon called: "May I fall without rising – it's Mungo Murray!"

"Simon the Fox!" cried Mungo, galloping forward, to which Ali laughed and grinned at me. "And Bolla – good to see you!" As the Athollmen drew up to us, however, an expression of doubt came across their leader's face. "Why have you come?" he asked.

"What kind of a question is that, you *gorach*?" Simon replied. "Fraser has come to support Murray, of course!"

The other looked confused. "We were told Fraser is for Jamie."

"Aye," said Simon, "And I'm told Mungo Murray doesn't buy his drink, but I know better. How's Ian Cam?"

"He won't see you. He's not seeing anyone. Says he's had enough of all the talking and just wants to do his duty."

"I've been hearing a bit of that myself," Simon replied, giving Ali a glance. "You know Dundee is about a day behind us?"

"Aye. We were expecting his scouts. What brings you in from that direction?"

"We had to be careful," my lord said brightly. "Everyone seems to think we're for Jamie, so we couldn't go past Ruthven Castle or Mackay's garrison would have had us. That's why we're going without a flag. A pathetic state of affairs — war by letter? You can get that to hell."

"Well, I'll take you in," Mungo said, "But Ian won't talk to you."

"Fine," Simon replied. "Then you can command us. We'll line up with your lads and help besiege your own castle. Fraser is here to help!"

The other seemed satisfied, and led us the remaining way to the giant castle, a sprawling edifice with strong walls and high windows. Despite being far greater and grander than Moniack it bore the scars of battle, caused, Simon told me, by the Saxon Cromwell during the Wars of the Three Kingdoms. Its battlements appeared defensible enough to me;

upon them we could see armed clansmen, and before us, as near the walls as caution allowed, were arrayed ranks of red-clad government dragoons. "I don't believe it," Simon whispered to me. "You see how powerful this war of letters is? Murray's baillie holds their own castle for Dundee, and Murray must bring soldiers from England to stop it being used against him. All done by pen and ink. Spectacular sport!" It had not occurred to me that Ian Cam, being a captain in King William's army, would have brought Saxon troops into his own lands.

Mungo again protested that his brother would not see Simon, but when my lord insisted on making the effort, he unhappily described the true reason behind such withdrawal. "Ian gathered the clan about a week ago… about twelve hundred came in. But when he told them to fight with Mackay they all ran to the river, filled their bonnets with water and drank the health of King Jamie." At this my lord let out a great bellow of laughter, an act so out of place in this field of tense spirits that troops of both sides turned to watch. "I'm glad someone finds it funny," Mungo continued. "It could be the end of Murray if they go and join Dundee!"

Simon laughed again. "*Ochone*, Mungo, a wee bit of knowing your own clan would make you less of an arse! The men of Atholl won't just bolt up the road to Dundee — some of them will, but most of them will go home and wait. There's going to be a fight in their country. They'll wait till it's done then see what's what."

"The men of Atholl—"

"Aren't as stupid as their chiefs, I think! Ach, don't take it personally, Mungo. I'm just joking." Then he changed his manner. "But it's even more important to talk to Ian, then. He needs a wee bit of good news." After a moment his friend finally acquiesced with a slight nod, and I followed as the pair entered a large tent attended by two redcoat guards.

"I will see no representations!" barked the English voice of a tall man, stood behind a desk, resplendent in his own bright uniform.

"No representations, your lordship — merely the salutation of friends!" Simon replied.

Mungo cautiously introduced them. "My lord, I present Simon Fraser of Lovat, my associate from Aberdeen University. Simon, I present my brother, Captain John Murray, Earl of Tullibardine."

"I prefer 'the Young MacShimi'," Simon said cheerfully, sketching a bow.

"What's this, Mungo?" the earl demanded. The accent was alien; although I spoke good English, his was difficult to follow.

"Fraser marches to join us," Mungo replied flatly.

"Fraser? They're rebels!"

"Not at all, your lordship — we're friends from the next glen, you might say," said Simon. "With news that Dundee is but a day behind us, I bring sixty men to help ensure he cannot gain access to the castle. With the compliments of my lord Thomas Fraser, the MacShimi."

"A day?" the earl barked. "A day? Why wasn't I told?"

"You wouldn't see us," Mungo told him. "But we think it could be two days…"

Simon made a disapproving face and drew his breath in with a hiss. "I've never known my scouts to be wrong. They tell me a day, maybe a day and a quarter — but no more."

"Then we must be off!" said the earl. "Summon my officers! Order the striking of camp!" Mungo looked at his brother, then to his friend, and hurried out. "You're sure, Fraser?"

Simon bowed. "I'm sure. But I'm also sure we can hold the siege if—"

"Don't be a fool. With Dundee on one side of us and that knave Stewart in the castle… It cannot be done. Mackay has been told that. We will fall back."

"Then, sir, will you do Fraser the honour of allowing us to act as your rearguard? Since all and sundry tell me that I already fight for Dundee, perhaps he thinks so too, and that may allow you extra time to withdraw."

Tullibardine stared at Simon for a moment, then smiled thinly. "Oh, yes, Fraser. Your men may act rearguard. While *you* come with me, and we join up with General Mackay."

Simon bowed again. "Truly an honour, your lordship. I will go and make ready." We left the tent as a dozen officers ran in and Tullibardine began shouting once more. The Fox smiled. "That was easy!"

"What?" I asked.

He shook his head. "Wake up, Bolla — it's mission accomplished! Spectacular sport!"

"I do not understand."

"You will. Come on, let's get Ben Ali sorted out."

Within minutes the hundred or so government troops had brought up their baggage horses and were packing their belongings away, while a third of them kept watch over the castle. Simon told me not to fear any violence at this stage, "Because," said he, "Stewart gets to keep the castle and he'll be happy with that, and Ian Cam wants to get out of here without smashing his own windows. We're perfectly safe."

Ben Ali and the Frasers, at any rate, were delighted with developments, and for their duplicitous behaviour to have ended with such speed and ease. Simon told the big man: "Just sit here until Murray's gone, then tell Stewart who you are. If he wants to wait in the castle until Alex arrives, just sit outside. If he's happy with you — and why wouldn't he be? — there's a night on the drink for you. There's nothing to this warfare *cac*, is there?"

Within an hour Murray was ready to march, and sent Mungo to ensure Simon went with his company. "You come too, Bolla," my lord told me. "We're going to see a real fight." Just before we left, he dismounted and ran up to Ben Ali, who lifted him into the air as he had a few days previously. "Take care, you great lump," he said.

"If you get yourself killed, I'll kill you," the big man replied.

Then we trotted up to join Murray, who led his troops out towards the south at a quick march. From the castle a few muskets were fired into the air, and some questionable pieces of advice were shouted; but as Simon had predicted, the movements passed without any injury.

"Tell me more of what you know, Fraser," the earl ordered soon after we were clear.

"Certainly, your lordship. I can say James Stuart sent only five hundred men from Ireland, and they —"

"I know that, man! Do you think I haven't kept in touch with Mackay?"

"My apologies, sir. With respect, I do not know what you know or not. Are you aware, then, that Dundee dreads entering Atholl?"

"Really?" Murray seemed pleased. "How so?"

"Well, after that business at the castle with Stewart, it's been said in some quarters that Clan Murray wants to fight with Dundee. But after the whole nation has heard that you, sir, were prepared to fire your own castle if it came into rebel hands – well, everyone now knows Murray is for the king. Dundee has little option but to continue his advance. But now, he knows he's in enemy territory. In terms of spirit, sir, you have reduced his number by hundreds."

Simon clearly played a dangerous game; but it appeared he had reckoned the earl correctly, for he seemed to be satisfied as he absorbed the words he heard. "And what is his number, Fraser?"

"Scarce more than two thousand, sir, while we number over three. And may I say it's a privilege for Clan Fraser to have offered some small service."

"Your company is quite small," Tullibardine said. "Only sixty men!"

"Alas, the vicious rumour of us supporting James Stuart has been spread by letter," said Simon. "It has proved difficult for us to move beyond our own lands. I fear some of His Majesty's soldiers are put to poor use, while many more of us could be here where we're needed."

The earl barked a laugh. "You have the rights of that, Fraser! Do you know it took the Secretary of State three weeks to decide how to provision Mackay for just two? What kind of a way is that to put down a rebellion?"

Simon made an aggrieved noise. "Then, sir, it is beholden on us who have had to fight our way *to* the battlefield to fight all the harder *on* the battlefield. Devil take the pen-men!"

Tullibardine laughed again. I noticed that Mungo, who rode not far from me, seemed intent on keeping one hand locked tight across his face, while he tried to stare blankly into the distance ahead.

We came presently to a steep and foreboding pass, that of Killiecrankie; and it was clear to even an untrained eye such as mine that, if held by an enemy, it would surely lead to death. Any company marching through it would needs be stretched long, while soldiers stationed above could pour down fire with those below having no hope of cover. Indeed, they could save ammunition by simply tumbling rocks into the gorge; there could be no positive outcome for any trapped in the pass. Murray wisely spent several hours sending scouts to verify it was not held, and, being assured such was the case, gave orders to proceed with all haste. Yet the uneven land and its river on our west flank was so unforgiving that even our fastest movement seemed dangerously, painfully slow. I was not the only one who often turned my eyes upwards, dreading the sight of another's eyes looking back down at me.

At last we completed the traverse – although it took much longer than the distance suggested – and had not continued much further south when the appearance of more redcoats (and some blue) in the distance told us we had finally met with General Mackay's army. Both parties called a halt; and I beheld the vision of over three thousand men gathered in one glen, an image that had never before come to my eyes, and took some time to digest.

Murray ordered us to attend him as he made approach to his general; but if the earl had expected a warm welcome, he was soon surprised. "I hoped to find you at Blair Castle, my lord captain," said Mackay, speaking English in a broad north Highland voice I could easily follow, dressed in a rich uniform but presenting the face of a clansman.

"You have had my letters, sir?" he protested. "I held Blair as long as I could — and I have sure word Dundee was less than a day from me when I withdrew."

"That would seem to be an exaggeration," Mackay said coldly.

"Fraser assured me —"

"You take the word of a Fraser? That may explain it."

"If I may, sir," Simon said, "I am Simon Fraser, the Young MacShimi, and I was able to advise my lord captain that Dundee's rebels were close behind us as we approached his siege."

"You approached? I have it on authority —"

"Please, sir, I beg you not to repeat the accusation of rebellion which I have heard so many times in recent days," Simon cried. "In truth, if our position were better understood I would have been able to bring many more men to your cause through the barriers we met as a result of orders from Edinburgh."

"*Gorachs!*" spat Mackay. "The whole business would have been done two months ago if they'd done what I said. Very well, Fraser, explain yourself." Simon repeated his story; and, perhaps because the general was from the north, with understanding of clan relationships, he seemed to find happiness in the tale faster than had Murray. And yet I was sure my lord would be undone when he was asked: "Where is your rearguard now?" For the truth was that by now Dundee would have word they were waiting to welcome him at Blair.

"My last orders were to hold the pass for us," Simon said. "It's a treacherous piece of land, but we must march back through it. I have charged my man-at-arms Alistair Fraser to ensure the rebels cannot take position above us. They will die to keep that charge."

Mackay nodded. "Killiecrankie's a hard one," he agreed. "We need to get through it fast, and on to Blair Castle, to stop Dundee coming any further south. You are welcome here, Fraser," said the general; then, turning to Murray, said: "You too, Captain Murray. It's a sad day when a man had to take arms against his own house — but you were ready to do your duty, and have done all you could. That will be noted." Simon and Murray bowed while I stole another look at Mungo, but that one remained in control of his expression. "We will traverse the pass of Killiecrankie in the morning, and seek to take Dundee tomorrow."

LATE IN THE NIGHT, soon before the moon rose, I was shaken awake. "We must leave," Simon told me. "No, forget the horses — more trouble than they're worth where we're going." He presented me with a bag while I shook down my plaid, took some water and made to follow, not yet sufficiently awake to query his latest manoeuvre.

We had stopped, as planned, at the southern end of the pass, and as he led me north I realised he intended for us to walk the treacherous road alone at night. As we passed Mackay's sentries he gave them his compliments and advised them the Fraser rearguard had need of its leader, but he hoped to be waiting for the government army at the far end of the pass the next day. Believing, as did I, that it was madness to take the journey for any other reason than a matter of gravest urgency, the sentries were satisfied with his explanation. "Good luck – rather you than me," said one.

Yet I was wrong; it was not an unpleasant night, and with the river singing to our left, the moon casting blue-silver silk upon us, and the perfection of a careful but steady pace, there seemed something unworldly and incongruently peaceable about the journey. I remember it to this day as a magical interlude, and I suspect Simon felt the same way, for even though I wanted the knowledge of his plan, and I felt sure he wanted the sharing of it, neither of us spoke; until the river fell to the distance behind us, the moon began to set, and we found ourselves north of the pass and seated at the edge of a forest near an ancient standing stone.

"*Parturient montes, nascetur ridiculus mus,*" Simon said quietly – and, at last, the moment passed into memory. "Aren't you going to ask what we're doing?" he said to me.

"What are we doing?" I asked.

"You've got to mean it."

"I assure you, I mean it. What are we doing?"

"Well, since you mean it... Dundee and Mackay are both brilliant generals. So which side would you rather fight on?"

I believed, for once, I understood. "Neither?"

"What a man – right first time!" he touched me on the shoulder. "I knew a lot about Dundee from listening, but I didn't know anything about Mackay. Now I've met him, I reckon they're going to be evenly matched.

"Think about this: Dundee's a Saxon at the front of a Highland army, and Mackay's a Highlander with a Saxon army. But we're in Highland country. What do you make of that?" I felt I had achieved all I was going to do in my attempts at following my lord's thoughts, so I simply waited for him to continue. "What I make of it is, the man with the biggest character will win tomorrow.

"I've been weighing it up. Dundee's men have one tactic: the Highland charge. To get the best out of them you need to know them inside out. And he does. He marches with them, he talks to them, he tells them stories of their own folk and knows the names of their chiefs back into the mists of time. He knows they'll only fight if they love him, so he makes sure they do.

"Mackay understands all that, but he also knows it's meaningless to conscripted troops outside their own lands. The only thing they'll follow is strict leadership. So he gives them that. Dundee gets one moment of military might, but Mackay gets more men obeying more instructions more often. It's anyone's to win — providing the land doesn't favour one or the other. And the land round Blair doesn't."

"Won't Dundee try to attack while Mackay's in the pass?" I offered.

"*Ochone*, no," Simon replied scornfully. "That's no way for men like these to wage war. There are rules, you know – you can't just say and do what you like!"

I decided not to challenge that last; instead I told him: "I did not realise you were so interested in warfare."

"Aye," he said. "I might have read art at Aberdeen, but it was the art of war I read. It's the dance, you see. Getting people to do what you need them to do. Spectacular sport!"

I forbore to ask why one might need them to do anything.

The following day we spent several hours proceeding back and forth on the hillsides between the pass and the castle, watching for scouts from both armies; for Simon did not want to encounter any Jacobites for fear of having to line up with that army and miss a more advantageous viewpoint. At last our sightings of both forces became more regular, and we began to retreat to the east while Dundee came south and Mackay moved north.

When the meeting came it was a surprise to them both, although not to us; commencing his march after completing the journey through the pass, Mackay began to climb a hill, only to behold Dundee's advance guard coming down it. Almost at once it was clear both generals were decided for combat, for battle lines began to be drawn.

The Fox offered commentary as Mackay made a last desperate attempt to secure a promontory above the field where his troops waited; but, failing, began ordering his men so they could fire musket rounds in a three-deep formation. Meanwhile, Dundee, presumably delighted with having taken the hilltop, began to split his battalions in order to match the dimension of his enemy's wider line, and laid his men one deep. Soon afterwards Mackay re-arranged so there was a space in the centre of his formation, with his two troops of horse behind it; which showed, said my lord, that he was well aware of the power of a Highland charge, and aimed to wrap his men around it quickly enough to destroy it from its rear. "But if Dundee can persuade them to give it everything," he said thoughtfully, "It might be too little, too late."

Finally, after an hour or more of final movements, both armies seemed to stop dead in the bright summer's day. I noticed that, as my lord had predicted, the number of Athollmen lined up with the Jacobites was relatively low; probably two hundred from the twelve hundred who had gathered. "It's up to Dundee now," Simon observed. "But he won't charge with the sun in his eyes."

It appeared to be the case, for matters remained in a similar state until the warmth was going out of the day and the shadows lengthened from the west. Then my lord tapped my arm and pointed to movement from the hilltop. A group of no more than twenty men were creeping out from the front line, near bent-double, and making briskly down the slope. It seemed they were making for the small stone building which stood mid-way between the armies. "Sharp-shooters," he said. "Probably Lochiel's men. If they can set up in that house…"

Immediately afterwards there came near a hundred government men out from their right flank and rushed towards the building, stopping after a short run to make fire at the Highlanders; who, shortly, began firing back from crouched positions. "Saxon muskets against Scots rifles," Simon explained. "Rifles are better over long distance, but that's no good to them here. They need to get to that house."

The musketeers continued to shoot, reload and run forward, while the riflemen found themselves unable to continue their advance. Soon Mackay's greater fire-power was showing its ascendency – as plumes of smoke rose and the sound of gunfire passed into our hearing some moments after firing, I beheld two, three, then five Scots fall motionless in the field, with several others limping a painful retreat. Their bid had failed; but the rifles' greater accuracy began to show as they kept firing, and as several musketeers fell, their companions began also to retire. Neither side held the little house. "That's it started now," Simon said as the gunners returned to their respective ranks.

He was right: a few minutes later we beheld much more movement from the hilltop. At first I mistook it for a failure of sight, to be expected as the day began to dim rapidly; but what seemed like a slow, unsure slide soon revealed itself to be the Highland advance. There came a flurry of upward motion as clansmen lifted off their plaids and dropped the garments behind them, then bent forward behind their targes for protection as the men at the hillfoot prepared to react.

59

It seemed to happen in gruesome silence: Dundee's men began to pick up pace while I could see Mackay's generals shouting orders, although no sound reached my ears. At last there rang out a great round of musketry — it seemed a thousand men fired in one move; and straight away followed the giant explosion of four cannon shot in quick succession. The Highlandmen seemed untouched and continued to increase their pace. But then Mackay's right flank, closest to the enemy, opened fire into Dundee's left flank, and each cloud of smoke rose to reveal another cluster of three or four Highlanders thrown to the earth, dead, dying or mortally wounded. Their companions did not falter; the advance did not slow, even as a sickening line of disfigured men became the trail marker of Dundee's movement. Then the government front line launched a second series of musketballs, and the quickening Highlanders, in much closer range, suffered another twenty or thirty casualties. Finally, as if they had taken enough, they stopped — but only for the final stage of preparation. As one they shot what guns they had, pistols for some, muskets for others; then, discarding their spent firearms and targes, they took up their double-edged broadswords or Lochaber axes. Then there came the noise of military legend, the sound most certain to dismay those standing against it: the furious Highland charge, begun with each man shouting for his clan then continuing with the roar of a devil as he fixed his eyes on the two men before him he was about to kill. Screaming for hell they broke into a run, raging like a winter river in spate, ignoring the muskets and cannon, seeing only the soldiers who would, in moments, be victims. Mackay's frontline struggled with their bayonets – the old threaded type took painfully long seconds to affix – but the effort of watching one's gun and also the approaching enemy was too great. The Highlanders arrived, swords and axes swinging — and where previously there had been plumes of smoke there rose sickening plumes of blood as hands, arms and even heads were thrown into the air. And still the Highlanders screamed.

"*Ochone* – they're going to break!" Simon breathed. Sure enough, many government men were already fleeing from their positions, including the separate force placed on the hilltop. Muskets and cannon kept firing, but far less regularly; and the neat lines of soldiery recently arrayed across the hill had become no more than a mass of animal movement, akin to cattle being herded through a glen.

"Dundee's going right for Mackay — look!" I beheld a figure which could only be the viscount, mounted and slightly ahead of his horsemen, making directly for his counterpart's position. Moments later the Scots had ridden straight through it and broken it in one move. Without stopping Dundee led them on to the cannon position, sending the gunners running and removing that powerful asset from the government armoury.

The remains of Mackay's horse, led by the general himself, had somehow regrouped and were preparing a counter-attack. He led his men round his own right flank, the apparent aim being to finish off the job his musketeers had started on the Jacobites' left; but consumed with doubt and panic, many of his horsemen wheeled into his own flank, smashing what was left of its formation. Seeing this, a battalion of Highlanders turned to wipe them out, but they were not needed: the sight of them sent cavalry and infantry into instant retreat. "Mackay still lives!" Simon pointed to him, leaning back and waving his arm as he galloped out of the melee. He only went far enough away to ensure he was not followed; but that was enough time for the battle to have effectively ended. Of his army there was almost nothing, only the wounded lying dead or sitting defeated; small groups of his dragoons were making their escapes in any direction; others were being pursued down the river by still–raging Highlanders; but the majority of Dundee's men were on the riverbank, tearing their enemy's baggage to shreds in a looting frenzy.

"Fire upon me," Simon said. "That was… something else." In all it had lasted barely the time it takes to walk a mile. Uncounted hundreds, many more lowlanders than Highlanders, lay unmoving across the darkening hillside. Mid-way upon a hill terrace, Mackay could be seen with those of his army he had gathered: possibly one in ten, who he was forcing into something assembling a marching order. "I think he's going to come this way," said Simon. "Let's be off." Yet we sat watching for some moments longer, reflecting on what we had seen and what we yet saw: the silence had returned, and the night was very soon to join it, as if the heavens were placing a mortcloth over the dead. But soon we awoke from our reflection and made to find safety.

"I did not see how our men fared," I said.

"I think the left were good. The right really got its head broken, did you see? Lochiel's men – Camerons and Macdonells and God knows who else. But I think our boys are safe."

"I thought to have seen Ben Ali."

"There were a couple of big lads on our side, so I couldn't be sure," Simon replied. "Did you see that MacGregor, the tall one with the great longsword? Giant of a man. If they were on the right Ali will do well. It would take more than a musket from a distance to stop him.

"That was textbook," he went on. "It takes a special general to know how to work untrained Highlanders. They don't think – they kill. You need to know how to wind them up and turn them in the right direction. Mackay would have known that. He must have known he didn't stand a chance."

"Then why fight?" I asked.

"He was counting on greater numbers. And he needed the victory to secure the government's proper support. Now the word's going out of a great victory for King Jamie – and, mark me, that's going to change things."

Suddenly he stopped, turned to me, grabbed me by both arms and let out an excited scream – this despite our cautious withdrawal in a world surrounded by murderous, furious armed men. I could make out a face of almost mad delight through the gloom. "What a fight, Bolla! Magnificent mischief! I wouldn't want to be one of Mackay's men tonight. Poor *gorachs* will be strung up by every Athollman they meet, once word gets out. They'll be lucky if fifty of them get home."

Once we were a mile or two clear of the battlefield I began to wonder if we were safe. "It's best not to think so," my lord told me. "If I were Mackay I wouldn't be going back down the pass – that would be almost certain death. I might even head north-east in the hope of getting clear quickly. And that's assuming they're sure of where they're going. No, we'd best be careful."

It seemed he was proved right not much deeper into the night. Through the trees we made out a small point of light, which we soon saw was a night-fire, with the matt shapes of men moving around it. We attempted to pass as far as we could away from it; but soon found that, with a steep ascent to the west and a confluence of two steep rocky rivers to the east, we had no recourse but to travel past it, painfully close. Simon whispered to remain quiet, although I needed no warning. Slowly and cautiously we moved forward, expecting at any minute to be challenged by a guard. Eventually we were so close we could hear muttered voices — and they were speaking English. Simon cocked his pistol, and bade me do the same.

I feared my heart itself would give me away, so loudly did I think it beat; as, painfully slowly, we clambered through steep and dogged undergrowth as far from the flames as we could be. Then a large branch gave way beneath my feet. It was so old and worn it made almost no sound, but instead half of it rolled downward, taking a stack of twigs and stones with it, and the whole lumbered into the clearing where the Englishmen waited. "Over here!" One of them shouted, the accent unmistakably from the very far south. A great shadow appeared between the fire and us, clearly a large man, and clearly carrying a gun. We froze, stock-still, desperately hoping the darkness would shroud us. But it seemed the shadow came directly towards us. It looked down and kicked at the broken branch, then its head moved back up to where we, merely seven feet from him, waited to be seen.

Suddenly there was a hiss, a flash and a bang. Simon's pistol lit us up as it fired, and the shadow collapsed from the near point-blank attack. "Move!" said my lord, and we scrambled along the undergrowth. "Shoot if you hear them!" he told me, and, a few moment later, partly for fear and partly in the hope of putting off any followers, I discharged my own gun in the direction of the fire.

After it became clear we were more likely to injure ourselves through scrambling onward than through assault from behind, we slowed and searched for stronger, smoother ground beyond the trees. No one had followed us. Simon led us for a mile more or so, before we found an old roofless cottage and decided to settle for the night.

"That was a grand day, Bolla," Simon grinned, offering me a drink of whisky as we wrapped ourselves for the night. "Tomorrow we'll get some horses and we'll be home in a day or two. Dundee was brilliant – he'll get more men now, from here and from Ireland, and if he pulls a few more shows like that one, the crown is Jamie's again."

"Aye," I breathed; for, despite the drama of the day, it still made no difference to me who was king.

WORD MOVED FASTER than did we. By the time we entered Fraser country and met friends to ask the news, they were able to tell us that, even in the moment of victory, Dundee had been shot dead from his horse. He had taken a bullet in the gap between the shoulderplate and breastplate of his armour, just as he had secured Mackay's cannon and turned to chase the general himself. He had ridden for just a few moments longer, and by the time he hit the ground he was already dead. Simon had laughed – a bitter laugh, in truth, but a laugh nonetheless. "The better the sport," he had said. "Who can replace Dundee?" Indeed it seemed a question difficult to deal with, for we soon heard Lochiel had marched away from the Jacobite army after the Irish general, Cannon, had claimed the leadership. Simon had shaken his head. "That man is a *gorach*. Lochiel's no soldier, but he's brave and he's loved. With Highland troops that's four-fifths the tale. But — there is still a victory, and that'll bring out the clans."

We were unsurprised to discover Alexander, Tanacheil and their men had reached Moniack before us. Simon's brother and father did not wait to receive the Fox in the castle, but came out as soon as word of his arrival reached them.

"I'm glad to see you safe, son," said MacShimi, warmly.

"So am I, Father," Simon replied. "Alex – how did it go?"

"We lost eight," Alexander said, "But we took down two hundred and fifty for King Jamie."

"Well done!" his brother replied. "How was it?"

"You would have known if you'd been there."

"Alex —" began Lord Tom.

"You were on the right when the advance started just before sunset," Simon broke in. "You stood through four rounds of musket from the line, then scatter fire, before launching one round yourself and charging. The right was the first battalion to break and you cut them up before outflanking the next battalion, who broke as well. By that time everyone was engaged and you chased them into the river before filling your pockets from Mackay's bags." He finished with a look which could have meant almost anything, but was doubtless an insult.

"I did no such thing," Alexander snapped back. "We fought for the king and there was no —"

"Yes there was," Simon said. "Maybe you took no part, but tell me none of the lads did and I'll call you a liar." Alexander stared angrily, but said nothing. "Congratulations on your victory, brother," my lord finished, as that man strode off. Tanacheil made to say something, but crumbled in the face of Simon's demanding glare.

"How did it go with you?" Lord Tom asked. "I heard the siege did not go well for Murray. Blair Castle is held by Jamie's men now."

His son grinned. "I did what could be done. Fraser was seen to be with Murray when we met Mackay, and Mackay seemed to like Murray. I don't know what that does for us, but it's something. I suppose it depends on whether Murray got out."

His father laughed. "He was one of the first out — maybe even before the fight," he said. "But you were right. It was important to do what you did. For the clan."

Simon nodded.

"Where's Ben Ali?" I asked, for it seemed a question begging to be voiced.

"He's not back," MacShimi replied. "I would not think he'll be long."

He was not. Barely an hour later we were summoned from the castle hall, where plans were being made for a victory feast. Simon, Alexander, Thomas and I came down the stairs to see Ben Ali, laid on a litter of young trees; and he was quite dead. Most of the folk employed in or near the castle had stopped work and made a procession behind the two dozen or so Frasers who had returned from battle with their fallen fellow. All was silent asides from the low sounds of chickens and goats around us. The four who carried Ali laid him on the ground and stepped back reverently. Lord Tom strode forward and stared at the body. Simon pushed past and knelt down. "What happened?"

One of the clansmen spoke, cautiously. "We got cut off after the fight. There were Saxons everywhere and we had to find a long road round. But we got a few of them for ransom. It was Ali's idea – he said we should bring something home for the lads. We must have been followed, but. They came in the night to rescue their own. Ali got shot trying to stop them."

Simon stared at his dead friend. "Where did it happen?" I asked, at which the Fox looked at me sharply.

"Not even two mile from the fight," the clansman said. "We had a fire. Ali said it would be fine." By way of completing their explanation, two others brought up three government soldiers; whereupon one look at their red jackets and white trews told the tragic truth: they were simple dragoons, the lowest of the low, and the paper on which a ransom note was written would be of more value.

Simon turned and went up the stairs into the castle. I followed, while MacShimi took charge of arrangements for Ben Ali and the hostages. Up in the great hall, my lord stood silently at the window, until Alexander entered.

"What did you have Ali doing?" he demanded.

Simon shook his head. "Nothing."

"One of your political games, no doubt. Playing games with good folks' lives —"

"Are you listening?" Simon turned and his eyes flashed. "He was with you before the fight! This was none of my doing."

"And Ben Ali took hostages by himself? That's not his way." Simon shook his head again, but his brother pressed: "That *wasn't* his way —"

"Say one more word, Alex," Simon snarled furiously through clenched teeth, staring him straight in the eye. "Please. Just say one more word."

After a moment his brother turned and stamped out. "My lord —" I began quietly, but he stopped me.

"No, Bolla, not now. Keep quiet, my lad." I decided it best to follow Alexander out. In the castle courtyard Reverend Jamie was comforting a crying woman while three small children wept at the side of Ali's litter.

WHAT WAS TO HAVE BEEN A CELEBRATION feast became Ben Ali's wake. As Highland tradition demands, it was a celebration of the big man's life rather than his death; but amid the emotion and energy of recent events it seemed more difficult to focus on thoughts of a

66

bright or positive nature. In addition, the coldness between Simon and Alexander had reached levels clearly never previously known, and nothing could force them to speak to one another, even with the best attempts of their father.

More Frasers attended the funeral service than had responded to the call to arms, but there were no recriminations, and the Reverend James united us all with a soft lament delivered in his melodic and heartfelt manner. Tom, Alexander, Tanacheil and Simon were first to pass the big man's open coffin and touch his forehead in the traditional farewell; they were first to take their turn carrying him on his final journey; and then first to throw a handful of soil into his last resting place. They were also first to toast the departed when the feasting began.

I had not spent enough time in Moniack to come to know its inhabitants, save Simon; and while I felt no unwelcoming spirit from anyone there, I was reminded of how, until a few months ago, I would have been unable to partake in such an event. That memory, along with the thoughts of the battle I had witnessed, and my concerns over the tragedy concerning Ben Ali, left me feeling somewhat distant. So it was that, as the hours passed, food and drink was taken, and songs of affectionate sadness transformed into tears of equally affectionate laughter, I took myself to the height of the castle tower and looked down from the roof walk. It was a clear night with a near-full moon, and I could perceive the mountains which towered over Loch Ness to the south-east, and those that rose less sharply, but higher, to the west. Directly below, where torches lit the ground, I watched Frasers talking, singing and dancing, and I also observed Simon conversing in a friendly fashion with a piper.

"I don't know you, do I?" came a voice from behind me. I turned to behold what I could tell was a female figure, probably of an age similar to my own; but in the darkness I could make out no more.

"I am with Simon," I said.

"The Fox!" she laughed. "Did you know they're calling him that now?"

"I had heard so," I replied.

"I'm Kirsty Fraser, the daughter of Colum the blacksmith."

"They call me Bolla."

"Oh, you're him! Tell me, are you his footman? No one seems to know."

"I do not, either," I admitted honestly. "I would not say I was his servant, but I am not sure I would say we were friends."

She laughed again. "He likes to keep things… interesting, that one. So, are you going to be staying in the castle? I'm in the kitchen – I might see you, sometimes."

At that moment I realised I was engaged in the longest conversation I had ever conducted with a woman who might be said to be close to my own position in life. I might have reflected I was not performing poorly; but instead I felt a panic rise within me – such that the concept of jumping from the roof entered the back of my mind. "I am needed downstairs," I mumbled, inching carefully past her to keep a respectful distance, although she made no effort to assist in that.

"Well, I'll see you later," she called after me.

In the hall I was relieved to find Simon near the doorway, attending upon a young serving girl, while a hundred people and more created the noise of a thousand around him. "Bolla! Having a grand time?" he asked, removing his arm from around her shoulder and throwing it around mine. "*Ochone* – it's a grand send-off. Let's have a drink. Let's have a drink with Alex, eh?" Surprised, I followed him to a table near the fire, where Alexander sat with Tanacheil and others. Simon raised a bottle of whisky from another table and slammed it down opposite his brother. "Alex, will you drink with me? To the memory of Ben Ali?"

If he was surprised, Alexander hid it well; or perhaps he was already in his cups. "Aye, for Ben Ali," he said, looking up. "And, despite it all, brothers and clan. For we, Simon, we are brothers and clan."

"Brothers and clan!" Simon agreed, taking a mouthful directly from the bottle then offering it to Alexander, who did the same. "Fraser!" he shouted, and everyone in hearing distance shouted the same in return.

We sat down, with Simon pouring more whisky, and discussion moved the way it does at such events, (as I came to learn), stopping every now and again to echo the sentiments of a toast, sometimes to the clan but more often to Ali himself. The piper started playing once again, having enjoyed a few drinks of his own, and the room danced, clapped or struck tables to the rhythm he dictated. "Give us another!"

called Simon as a *pibroch* ended in cheers and tears. "Give us another!" The musician laid down his pipes and took up a stock-and-horn instead, and was joined by a singer, who began encouraging the clan to clap along with a high-paced tune. Yet instead of clapping, my lord looked surprised and concerned. "Never mind it, Alex," he said loudly to his brother.

"Never mind what?"

"Ach, just, never mind it. Ben Ali!" Those around the table repeated the toast, but something had changed in the spirit of the hall. At once I realised it was that many were beginning to listen carefully to the song. By the refrain it seemed to be called *The Tale of MacThomas*; and the suggestive nature of it was not lost on the Frasers, who were glancing cautiously towards Alexander and Simon.

MacThomas thinks to steal an ox
But runs off with a dog
He seeks to marry a lady fair
But lies instead with a hog

MacThomas sups with a fearsome king
He hopes he long will rule
Alas he has not brains to see
He's supping with the fool

MacThomas plays with dirk and sword
He thinks himself so clever
He's answered by a hangman's rope
That ends his dance for ever

MacShimi himself made to end the song — but with a roar of fury Alexander rose too, casting whisky bottles and cups aside. Simon attempted to push his brother down, saying: "Never mind it!" but he would not be stopped. Drawing the dirk that might easily have been the one referred to in the song, he threw himself across the floor to where the piper and singer stood. The latter, aware of what was unfolding, stepped behind his partner; but the piper, entirely collected upon his stock-and-horn, knew nothing of the furious attack until he lay sprawling against the fireplace with Alexander's dirk in his chest. A horrified silence fell as Simon arrived behind to see the piper staring up, shocked, at the man who had wounded him. He opened his mouth as if to speak, but instead could only render a sickening noise as blood dripped from between his teeth. In seconds he had died.

"Andrew! Bolla! Get him upstairs!" Simon ordered, to which Tanacheil and I took Alexander by the shoulders and did as we were bid. I heard my lord calling for men to attend the piper while others were asked to clear the hall, as, the full drama having become apparent, children began crying and dogs joined in with barking.

In Lord Tom's room upstairs Alexander was near deadly calm with rage. "That *gorach*!" he said. "What was he playing that for? How dare he insult a Fraser under his own roof, and him a guest…"

"Sit down," Tanacheil urged, but he was not obeyed. Presently Simon and Lord Tom came up, and my lord simply stared at his sibling, seemingly unsure of what to say.

"A shroud upon you, Alex!" he finally exclaimed. "You killed him."

"No, just a wee —" his brother seemed to wake from his stupor. "What did you say?"

"The piper's dead, man. And everyone saw."

"May I fall and not rise…" Tanacheil muttered.

Finally Alexander sat down. "I didn't mean to… I lost my head a bit, just —" he began. "They're all Frasers. We can pay his family, can't we?"

Simon shook his head. "He's a Campbell, Alex. They weren't all Frasers downstairs – there were guests from outside."

"There are senior Campbells here on my invite," groaned Tom.

"But… that song was… It was about me!"

"It wasn't," Simon said. "But it sounded like it, the *gorachs*," Simon said. "Still, you can't be killed for it." Alexander placed his head in his hands and fell silent. My lord continued: "I need to think. Let me think…" Then after a few moments he said: "I have it. Alex, the government will take any reason they can find to turn over Jamie's man. They know we were with Dundee at Killiecrankie. But they know we were also with Mackay at Killiecrankie. So… if we send those hostages to Edinburgh with a note from you, saying you saved them from certain death in enemy lands, you'll look good."

"Do you think so?" All signs of drunkenness had long since left Alexander's behaviour, his redness of face replaced by a grey pallor, and a look of fear in his eyes.

"Aye, I do. But you'll need to take yourself off for a while, I think, to make sure. A few months, until it dies down, just. And in the meantime we'll see about paying the Campbells. If they're honourable folk it should be well."

Alex nodded. "Where should I go?"

Simon shrugged. "A good way. Out of Scotland, certainly. Not Ireland because it's all for war there…"

"Dunvegan?" Tom asked. "The Macleods are our family."

"And for Jamie, and closer to Campbell." Simon said. "Too risky for everyone. What about… Wales?"

"Wales?"

"Aye — no one will look for you there, man. Just keep down and quiet for a month or two, then come home. We'll send ahead and sort something out for you. Won't we, Dad?"

"Of course we will. You'll be back by summer's end. What do you say, son?"

Alex nodded uncertainly. "If you think so," he said.

"Aye, I do. It's grand," Simon said with confidence. "Thank God for Ben Ali bringing in those hostages. We'll sort it in the morning — get some sleep, Alex. Try to calm down."

By the time Alexander arose, still bewildered and upset, my lord had put everything into action. He explained a message had been sent to a family in south Wales with whom he had made connection in Aberdeen; another had been sent with the body of the piper to his Campbell home; the hostage dragoons were bound and tied behind our horses; and all was waiting upon his brother's departure. "Bolla and I will take you to Loch Eil," Simon grinned encouragingly. "Make sure you're fit for it all. By the time we get there a boat will be waiting."

The clansfolk kept their distance as Alexander locked arms with Lord Tom and Tanacheil, then mounted his horse beside Simon as I prepared to ride behind, ahead of the three miserable soldiers. As we rode out of the castle yard a remarkably handsome woman with blazing red hair waved to me from the stairs. I waved back doubtfully — I could only assume it was Kirsty, she I had met on the roof.

There was little conversation until we had passed out of the castletown, then Simon stopped and cut the dragoons' bindings. "You're deep, deep in Highland country, my lads," he told them in English. "If you run off, the first of my clan to set eyes on you will know you for what you are, and you'll be dead. To be honest," he laughed, "I had to pay my own men not to hang you from a tree last night. They all blame you for the death of our big friend. The only way to stay alive is to stay with me – I'll get you to the fort at Inverlochy. Do you understand?" They cautiously nodded their assent.

As the day went on and we travelled south-west down Glen Mhor, Alexander had time to think about the previous night's happenings, and began to speak of it more. "I can't believe I did it," he finally said.

"You were provoked, man," Simon told him. "Ali's funeral, drink, then a stupid song. It's just one of those things."

"Aye, but — killing someone…"

"No one's perfect. Maybe you've been trying to be for too long."

"What do you mean?"

"Well, look, I know you've been worried about the stuff I've been getting up to, with the Murrays and the Campbells and all that. You don't like it one wee bit."

"I just think we should keep it simple…"

"I know. But others don't think the same. For those who do, your approach is perfect. For those who don't, mine is needed. We didn't invent the dance, but we're called to join in."

"Maybe… And if it's all for the clan…"

"For Fraser, now and for ever." I had not previously heard the pair converse so agreeably; and I began to wonder if, even from this dark episode, there could come some light.

At dusk Simon stopped us at a fork in the road near the end of Glen Mhor. He told the soldiers: "You're on your own from here, but Inverlochy fort is just a wee bit down the road. Don't speak to anyone until you're there. And remember: tell them Alexander Fraser of Lovat protected you." He shook hands with them one by one and wished them luck, giving each of them a few coins, to which they muttered thanks and moved off into the night, while we took the western road.

Some time later, when the moon was high, we gathered close upon the banks of Loch Eil. "We need to be quiet," Simon told Alexander. "There are patrols about, looking for stragglers from Killiecrankie. We don't want to answer any questions. I'll take you down to the boat — Bolla, keep a sharp eye out. Any movement, make sure the horses stay hidden and give me a whistle. You can whistle, can't you?" I blew a noise to prove I could. "Good lad. No end to your talents, just." He touched me on the shoulder.

"Safe journey, Alexander," I offered. He took my hand and nodded.

"Look after my brother – he's not a bad type at all. But he'll need good friends," he said. He turned away and they stepped into the shadows, until they became too difficult to pick out from trees, brush and the moonlit movement of the water beyond.

Soon Simon returned; but he seemed suddenly tired. "And there it is: an end to all this *cac*," he smiled. "It's been a long few days, Bolla. Let's go home — then maybe back to Aberdeen for some easy times. And easy lassies. What do you say, my lad?" We set as brisk a trot as the horses could manage in the dark, and as we could manage in our exhaustion. On climbing a hill heading north, I looked back over the loch to see if there was any sign of Alexander in his boat, but there was not; it seemed he was wisely keeping close to the shore, out of sight of dragoons who, by now, would have heard from our three hostages and even now might be scouring this country looking for us.

CHAPTER THREE
THE COZENER IN THE COMPANY

THE LONG SHADOWS cast over the field of Killiecrankie were not as long as those which the battle cast over Scotland. The kingdom remained in arms for nearly a year following that day, and although Clan Fraser continued its involvement with the Jacobite cause, Simon and I saw no further military engagement. That was not to say my lord became inactive — in fact, despite his suggestion of spending time at leisure, it seemed he remained almost always on horseback; and when he was not, he was instead mounted at a writing-desk.

A month after Dundee's victory and death, his successor Cannon presided over the Battle of Dunkeld, which resulted in what was generally held to be an ignominious loss, both in terms of result and reputation, for the Jacobites. Listening afterwards to accounts of the action, which danced up and down the streets surrounding the cathedral, Simon was overjoyed to be told of the destruction of a house belonging to the Marquis of Atholl, and then disappointed to hear about the death of the government's general. "Will Clelland gone, so soon after Dundee?" he cried. "That's a *scunner* — he beat Bonnie Dundee fair and square at Bothwell Brig. With a couple more years on him he'd have been a great leader." Indeed, it seemed the man dug deep for a last act of heroism, as, knowing himself to have been shot dead, he crept out of sight so his army would not know it and lose heart. "Street fighting," Simon reflected sadly, "Is no place for generals. Besides, where would you watch it from?"

As the days of the year shortened, the prospect of more large-scale action receded, and the weapon of choice became the pen – despite my lord's claim to despise the measure. When not writing letters he circled his way around the country of Clan Fraser, meeting first with one and then another of its lairds; and, I noted, spending considerable time with the daughters of several.

We were seldom at Moniack, meaning I had little opportunity to discover more about Kirsty, the red-haired girl; although I thought of her often. Then, as the cruel Highland winter moved in and it behove us to choose a location to shelter for a longer time, Simon directed us to his estate of Stratherrick, on the banks of Loch Mhor. He explained at some length as to how the lands came to Fraser: a bewildering series of strands drawn together into a deep, diverse weave; but I confess I was not able to retain the image of my adopted clan's history in anything akin to the rich detail Simon clearly beheld in his mind.

Presently the snow began to loosen its grip, and I sensed an increase in the tension of debate in my lord's correspondence in the expressions of his face. There had been ale, wine and whisky aplenty for months, but the turn of the season brought a change in spirit, and soon we were once again riding across the hills and glens, where Simon stopped at house after house and engaged in deep conversation behind closed doors with his allies. As ever, he made much use of his stock of farthings — and in one instance handed over near a full bag to the angry father of one girl heavy with child. Despite such occasional inconveniences (as he called them) and the ongoing conversations, he continued to find time to speak to almost every man, woman or child he passed; and they also to him.

I concluded later that many supporters of King James wanted to recommence military action at an early date, but that others, including Simon, intended to hold off, to see whether they would receive more than mere promises of reinforcements. When it seemed that the king's word would be no more followed by deed than it had before Killiecrankie, and but a small force came across from Ireland under one Major-General Buchan, the majority of the Jacobite party vowed to wait until their land-tending chores were complete before committing to arms. Buchan, however, was not for waiting; and so it was that, ignoring the advice of his Scots counterparts, he marched his twelve hundred men too far east, losing near a third in the process to desertion, and was surprised and destroyed at the Haughs of Cromdale. Simon had little to say of the affair worth repeating.

When James himself was defeated by William in Ireland that summer, and then fled to France, Simon expressed much more in words. "There you have it, Bolla," he said, pointing at a sketch of a map where he had attempted to interpret the reports gathered from the Battle of the Boyne. "The arrogance of a king who insists God put him on the throne and no one can take him off it, against a general who'll damn your divine right and hack the legs off the chair! It's not even that, although that's enough," he went on. "Jamie needed France and the Pope together, but the Pope was with Billy because it was the only way to move against France. Then — then you have Jamie's old matchlock guns against Billy's brand-new flintlocks.

"It's this simple: Jamie Stuart took the throne off himself." Then, after a moment, he threw his head back to the rafters and laughed long. "Magnificent mischief!"

IF ANY DARED TO HOPE for an end to the royal intrigue, they did not seem to be among those who were most involved. Fraser remained loyal to their Jamie, vocally at times, and certainly in their cups — but when the Marquess of Atholl and the Earl of Breadalbane both declared, once and for all, for William, my clansmen remembered in sobriety that both powerful families leaned heavily, and leaned close; and so it was that Hugh, Lord Lovat, called a gathering at the clan seat of Castle Dounie.

"Pick a window, Bolla, and it'll be yours one day," Simon grinned at me as we approached what was a far grander building than the castle of Moniack, just southwards of the wide basin of the Beauly Firth. It stood three storeys high, with, again, its guarded entrance one floor above the ground, and it had a bustling castletown around it, seeming home to as many folk who had gathered at Moniack ahead of our expedition to Killiecrankie. My lord hailed his father merrily, on sighting him at the foot of the stairway. I had not seen the MacShimi in many months and his appearance surprised me, so dull was his pallor and so tired seemed his eyes. "How's it going, Dad?"

"It is not so bad," replied the other. "Aye, not so bad."

"No word?"

Lord Tom shook his head. "Nothing. Nothing at all."

"Ach, I'm sorry. Maybe he's just too busy? We don't know what's going on, Father – it's stupid to assume the worst."

The chief offered a thin grin. "Aye, I suppose."

Simon turned to me as he dismounted. "Alex," he said quietly.

The interior of Castle Dounie seemed similar in plan to Moniack, but on a greater scale. The spiral stairs led past the kitchen entrance to the main hall above, and there I beheld near a dozen lairds of Fraser assembled, Tanacheil among them, all chattering with the pleasant energy of those with much in common but who spend too little time in common. It was impossible to ignore the most handsome woman who appeared to be at the centre of such energy: tall and blonde, with rich clothing and voluptuous shape, she seemed to brighten the room merely with her presence. "Tom!" she cried on seeing our entry. "Save me from these bores!"

She hurried up to embrace that man, who seemed to recover some of his former posture. "How are you, Amelia, lass? Still causing bother for your poor man?"

"If he was poor I'd be gone," she laughed. "And — my apologies, sir, is it… Simon?"

My lord's face froze like ice for a moment, before he cried: "You know very well it is — come here, you!" She threw herself into his arms as they both laughed. "This is my good friend Bolla," he said after some delay. "And this is the Lady Amelia Lovat."

"The boll o'meat Fraser," she said, giving me a stunning smile. "You're welcome to Castle Dounie. Even if you brought the Fox!"

Simon shook his head. "I wish people would stop calling me that."

"No you don't," she giggled. "Come and say hello to Hugh." She led us to the high table, before which stood a man I recognised as John Murray, the Earl of Tullibardine, along with another. Both turned as we approached, but their reactions were very different. "The Lord Hugh Fraser of Lovat," Lady Amelia said grandly, her hand out towards a young, thin man who looked ill at ease, and ill of health. "And my brother Ian."

"MacShimi," Hugh said stiffly, the suggestion of a sheen of sweat upon a brow hardly hidden by thin, greying hair, despite his age. His watered eyes failed to hold a glance for long and his mouth seemed unable to stop moving.

Lord Tom offered a shallow bow but Simon grinned brightly and asked: "How's yourself, my lord?"

"Concerned, Simon, concerned," replied the other, and clearly it was no exaggeration. "As is our good-brother here."

"Haven't seen you since Killiecrankie, Fraser," Tullibardine said in the voice I found difficult to follow, as he brushed down his traditional dress, since he was apparently here as a Highland gentleman rather than a government soldier. "I mean, the night *before* Killiecrankie."

Simon bowed. "I'm grateful you remember at all, my lord. It was indeed difficult to operate my rearguard action in that hell-hole, but I'll warrant it saved many a good Saxon's life. As he ran away."

Lady Amelia's laugh made it impossible for any further tension to develop; but Lord Hugh moved away to find repose in attending to his guests. After some time it was decided that all were present who were needed, and a dozen and a half men sat round the high table, with Hugh and Thomas perched closely together at the head. Simon motioned me to stand behind him, mid-way down the table, in the position of a servant. "Watch and learn, Bolla," he whispered with a twisted grin. I noticed Lady Amelia leaving the hall, and her closing of the door seemed to change the spirit within to one of serious business.

"God bless all here," began the Lord Hugh, his voice not fully matched to the challenge of sounding as grand as his attire. "I welcome John Murray of Atholl, Earl of Tullibardine, as our guest – and he has news."

That man, seated to the chief's right with Tom between the two, cleared his throat. "Indeed, your lordship. I have come to tell you that after his recent victory at the Boyne, King William has favoured the Clan Murray with his full support in any future dispute over the crown of Scotland. And that Campbell of Breadalbane has been named also as the king's beloved ally." During Murray's opening words Simon had created low chuckles by making gestures to suggest he could not understand the words; yet the mirth abated as he continued: "It is beholden upon Clan Fraser to assist its friends in maintaining the king's peace, and to that end I propose to raise a company of Frasers to serve in Lord Murray's Regiment of the King's Army."

The response to that was instant and aggressive. Lairds ordered Tullibardine not to overstep himself by telling another clan what to do; men cursed him for a Saxon; and others muttered to each other with shaking heads making plain their position. "Enough!" MacShimi cried, mustering all the power he could into the word. "Murray is a guest in the house of Fraser!" That brought the clamour to an immediate halt.

Lord Hugh spoke, albeit with less authority: "It is an offer extended in the spirit of continuing friendship between clans – and we thank my good brother for bringing it to us in person."

Into the suspicious silence Tullibardine said: "It is simple. King William will have peace in all his lands, and that includes our country, and yours. There was a time when you and I were not at odds —"

"Never!" someone called, leading to laughter, even a small smile from the earl.

"Well, there have been times when our respect has led to... understanding," he continued. "When we looked after our own and tended our lands."

"And lifted Macdonald beef," said the same wag from the far end of the table.

"Quite," Tullibardine nodded. "But the current matter affects all clans, and all futures. It warrants an ending, so we may all get back to that which concerns us most."

"More Macdonald beef!" the wag added, to laughter.

This time the earl ignored the joke. "You may know I have raised the matter of a Lord Lovat's Company in the past. Now I must give a solemn warning that, should my father's regiment be asked to assemble for the king, and should it lack any of the Clan Fraser within its ranks, and should the king ask me why — I will have to answer. It is down to Fraser whether that conversation arises."

There came another uncertain silence, but it seemed the earl had finished, and, bowing to MacShimi, who thanked him for his words, he left the hall. "You have all heard," said the chief. "Now speak."

A chatter of voices began but over the top of all one shouted: "Fraser is for King Jamie!" and the others changed to sounds of agreement.

Lord Tom raised his hand. "There is something Murray did not mention," he said. "Hugh will be captain of the company, of course —" no one offered an opinion on that point, although it was clear what was thought — "But he wants you, Simon, to raise it."

All eyes turned to the Fox, who seemed to be caught off guard for a moment — and I could count on one hand the amount of times I beheld such an expression on his face. He stared at the Lord Hugh, then very briefly at his father, but neither betrayed any emotion. Then he laughed. "Spectacular sport!" He looked round, taking note of the expressions of those around him, then said: "It is well, Father. If the clan approve, I'll do it!"

Cries of rage filled the room until Simon turned angrily to Tanacheil, who was seated down the table and opposite from him, seemingly silent among the fury. "Call me traitor, Andrew?" he demanded loudly, bringing other conversations to a halt. "It wasn't so at Glengarry, was it? When you went on your arse while the Macdonalds chased us, and I went back for you — and your sheep!"

There was some laughter at this, while Tanacheil looked somewhat shamed. "Aye well, Simon, that was a clean case of fighting and running," he said after a pause. "Maybe times change."

"They do," my lord agreed. "And we need to change with them. Just like Killiecrankie."

"Where were you at Killiecrankie fight, you Fox?" called another laird, causing yet another explosion of voices.

Simon stood up and made two fists far apart from each other. "Heres changed times, my lads," he shouted. He raised one fist and said: "Murray," then the other and said: "Campbell." Then he slammed them together and let them bounce an inch or two away again, before adding: "Fraser."

"Not without a fight!"

"A fight against the Earl of Tullibardine and the Earl of Breadalbane, two bigger clans, both of them with allies in England, and with King Billy's ear? And how much help has King Jamie sent in recent fights?"

81

That caused more furious explosions. Lord Hugh called for silence but the room was beyond sense, and it took for Tom to slam the hilt of his dirk on the table and shout: "Castle Dounie!" before silence fell once again.

Simon nodded to his father. "Fraser is for Jamie," he said. "But Fraser must also be for Fraser. Think about this — how do you raise a standing troop, ready to fight for Jamie at any moment, when his enemies are all around you?" He looked each man in the eye, slowly, ensuring he had their full attention. "So I'll muster a Lord Lovat's Company for Lord Murray's Regiment," he said. "But I'll tell you this: the minute Jamie sends enough men to make a stand against Billy, that company will strip off their red coats faster than Ian Cam bolted from Killiecrankie. And they'll be shouting 'Jamie Stuart' the next moment!"

If my lord had been expecting a chorus of support he was disappointed; instead, the lairds looked at one another, then to the top of the table. Tanacheil muttered something clearly negative under his breath and glared at anyone who caught his glance.

Finally Lord Tom spoke. "We're the fighting Frasers," he said to sounds of agreement. "It's not been for us to take part in wars of words, or letters, or lies. But this is a time of change, and there's no denying those letters and lies are working well for Murray and Campbell. It's not our dance — but we still must bide in the hall.

"So, Simon, if you'll take on this duty for Fraser, and you can make it work, you have the thanks of us all." Simon nodded. "But not one of us —" his father raised a warning finger and looked round the table — "is to speak of this outside the gathering. We will all find it hard to explain this policy if asked, so silence is best."

"Very well put, Thomas," the Lord Lovat nodded, in an attempt to act the noble, the which was clearly tolerated by all on the understanding that all knew it was tolerated. "I approve." One by one the lairds supported the decision, if doubtfully, and Tanacheil was the last to gruffly growl an "Aye." If Simon had achieved a victory, no one was sure of it. Yet he glanced round at me and clenched his fist, a look of satisfaction on his face.

THERE WAS MORE TO DISCUSS and so the lairds of Fraser were to remain in Castle Dounie that night; and it seemed that the day's talking had caused much thirst, for the hall was entirely drunk before the sun set. I observed Simon in discussion with Tullibardine before the earl's departure, but I could not read their expressions in any meaningful way — which itself said enough.

"You're never a laird already?" a voice asked from behind as a cup of ale appeared in front of me. Turning, I saw it was Kirsty, the red-haired girl from the roof of Moniack.

"Not at all," I assured her, accepting the drink but finding it difficult to look her in the eye, while also careful not to gaze at any other part of her either. "I am here with Simon."

"The Fox!" she laughed, then laughed further at my shock. "Lady Amelia told me the name. I'm in her household now." She looked over to where the lady was talking brightly to three lairds, all clearly besotted with her attention. "Do you think she's beautiful?"

"Yes," I said simply and quickly.

"What about me?" Since I did not reply with enough speed or alacrity she took me by the shoulders. "Well, you've not had a good look, have you? Go on."

I had never felt so bewildered and unsure; yet I settled my eyes on her forehead, instantly surprised that I could have any kind of reaction to which I had previously regarded as an indifferent part of the body. It was impossible then not to move to her own eyes: bright blue, round and lively; and below, a dimpled smile that was both friendly and challenging. "You are very beautiful," I finally let out.

"So are you," she said. "Much more than Simon."

"What's that?" said my lord, approaching from my line of sight, although I had not seen him. "Much more what than me?"

"Much more *everything* than you," she said, turning to him and laughing.

"Bolla, you've met Kirsty Fraser then?"

"Aye," she said, "And he can meet me any time he likes." Again she laughed, before letting her fingers drop down my arm and walking slowly away.

"Well done, my lad!" Simon said, touching my shoulder. "Best lassie in the castle, and no mistake. Well, except Amelia herself… *Ochone*, go after her, man — are you mad?" He pushed me towards the door through which Kirsty had disappeared; but, frozen in doubt, I could not follow. He shook his head. "Aye, you're mad," he muttered.

"Simon! What are your intentions with my handmaid?" Lady Amelia demanded, having made her way across the hall to us.

We both turned to her and my lord bowed. "Nothing for myself," he replied, "But I think Bolla has his own intentions."

"I'd say so," the lady smiled, draping herself against Simon, who wrapped his arm around her waist. "You should take her while you can, you know. Everyone wants her, but she wants you — for now!"

"You know that feeling, eh, my lady?" Simon said, and they both laughed. "But tell me, is my lord the earl away?"

"Aye, well, you know Ian Cam," she replied. "If there's a good party, it's only good because he's gone." I realised she was drunk even before she affected mock despair. "Oh, God – my brother is such an arse!"

Simon was careful not to agree. "Lord Hugh dealt with him well today, though," he said.

"*Cac!*" she replied scathingly. "You and Tom dealt with him. And all the better for it, I tell you. Hugh has already let him run round our country, trying to raise that company, free as you like without any Fraser keeping an eye on where he goes or what he says."

"I heard," Simon said. "He spent five days on the road and wound up with not a single recruit."

"After certain letters went out, I understand," Lady Amelia said with a cunning glance. "But — did you know about Breadalbane's plans for peace?"

"No," said my lord, suddenly serious. "Not a word."

She rolled her eyes. "He's been sent money by King Billy to buy off the chiefs," she explained. "He's going to pay them to agree to peace."

"That won't work…" Simon began.

"It's not like you to be so stupid," she interrupted. "Of course it'll work — if he makes sure no one knows everyone else is getting paid too. And he'll find a way. They don't call him Slippery John for nothing."

"Aye, that's true. But it won't work for long."

"It doesn't have to. If they sign a bond of peace for a year, maybe two, that's enough to keep the wind out of Jamie's sails. By that time he'll have a nice serving-girl or two in France to keep his mind off things. And those Stuarts were always terrible drinkers. A man who likes his drink isn't going to rush out of France, is he?"

Simon looked thoughtful. "Are you certain?"

"Stupid boy! Who do you think my Hugh asks for advice when your father isn't here?" She gestured towards herself. "The Lady Lovat."

"Of course – I'm sorry," he said.

"He's such a lovely man, my husband," she said to me, making an act of appearing to prevent Simon from hearing. "But he's no man of words or letters. Either my brother or Campbell of Breadalbane will have Fraser country if something isn't done. And there's only one man here who can do it." She kissed Simon on the cheek and moved away, a little unsteadily, leaving my lord deep in thought.

The gathering was still lively with song and laughter, but I, too, had a head filled with distractions, so I took myself without; and presently, possibly because of the similarity in form with Moniack, I found myself on roof, looking over another moonlit night. I should not have been surprised, yet I was, to hear the same voice once more: "It took you long enough to find me."

I could make out very little in the night, with my eyes unadjusted to the gloom, so there was no warning when I felt thrust upon by a silhouette from my side — and before I had any understanding of events I was locked deep in the first kiss I can own to have been passionate. I had been kissed before; there were a wide variety of social understandings amongst those of us who fought to survive in the vennels of Aberdeen, but those cold, dank fumblings in drink or sickness riddled hovels had no comparison with the activity I now found myself engaged upon. Yet, suddenly, it was over. "Come on," Kirsty told me, and led me by the hand back into the castle, down the stairway, out into the yard and into the road beyond. I remembered the night climbing the Pass of Killiecrankie, and indeed there felt some similarity to that sensation of moving unsensed in another world. This, of course, was different, and new in an altogether mystical manner; and I will admit to a small moment's fear in being convinced I was being abducted by a faerie. I could not have said how far we walked, although later I established it was less than a mile, until we came upon an open field beyond a churchyard. At its centre was a standing stone, of the type carved by the ancients. The moon was high and I could follow the lines as Kirsty pointed out an eagle-headed man. "I love this place," she whispered. "They say if you press the eagle-man's eye and make a wish when the moon's full, it'll come true."

"The moon is not quite full," I said slowly.

"Try anyway," she replied, crouching down by the carving so they were both lit in the silver light; and, comparing the two visions, I realised I had no further interest in the stone.

HAD I BEEN MORE ADVANCED IN YEARS, or had I spent more time in the company of Simon Fraser, I would have reacted with no astonishment when, the next morning, he told me: "Time to earn your shilling, Bolla." At least he had paid me the honour of waiting until late in the day to call for me (as indeed had Lady Amelia to Kirsty) and, instead of the bawdy comments I expected, he had simply touched me on the shoulder and said: "Good man," before adding: "Take that look from your smug face." We were in his chamber and he was bent over a bundle of letters, as was so often the case. "We need to move fast," he explained. "And in two different directions, so you need to go one way while I go the other."

He paused before explaining: "Breadalbane must be intercepted before he kicks off his grand plan, but he won't wait much longer now that Ian Cam got what he wanted from us. Two things need to happen – and that takes two letters." I was hardly aware he was taking me into more confidence than he had previously done, in as much as he was not simply giving me instructions. "This one —" he held up a document — "must be delivered by a complete stranger. Then this one —" he held up another — "must arrive by your hand the next day." He realised I was not paying full attention and ordered me to repeat what he had told me, and it took a second attempt for me to do so correctly. "*Ochone*, Bolla," he sighed. "Take her with you." That woke me from my mind's slumber. "I'll clear it with Amelia. We all set off as soon as we can."

"Where do you go?" I asked, attempting to act as if I was interested;

although he was not convinced.

"Inverness," he replied. "I need to get this Alex thing sorted out. You can see what it's doing to Father. It has to end." I was doubtful as to what he could achieve – it had been over a year and a half since we bade his brother farewell on the banks of Loch Eil. Yet there could be no doubting the effect on the MacShimi of the lack of later knowledge; and I was reminded of Simon's attention to the detail of his clan and history. "Remember," he said, staring into my face and pointing at me, "The first letter gets delivered by a stranger. Pick the poorest bairn you can find and give him a shilling to do it. Make his day, and he won't know who you are. It's important, Bolla — of all the things you might get wrong in this life, don't get this wrong." Impressed at his determination, I confirmed that I understood, and he touched me on the shoulder once more. "Good man, Bolla. The best."

I barely dared to hope; but when Simon called for my horse in the castle yard the stable boy brought two, and Kirsty appeared with him. She gave me a bright smile before turning to my lord. "Thank you," she said, and made to kiss his cheek, but he directed her into a fuller embrace, from which she disengaged as quickly as she could. He laughed and waved us off. Mindful of his urgings I aimed to set as fast a pace as our mounts and weather would allow – even if Kirsty set the pace of our night-time travels when we stopped at the houses of a Fraser, a Cameron and a Stewart on our southward journey to Kilchurn on the side of Loch Awe. Nevertheless, the journey felt more like a happy excursion than a mission on which the future of our clan (if Simon were to be believed) relied. All too soon we overlooked the prospect of Breadalbane's castle, much taller and grander again than was Dounie — and, in a way I could not explain, much more dark and threatening.

Riding along the lochside nearby I beheld a young wretch who fitted the description I had been given; I do not think even I, in my worst moments, ever looked as poor and unwanted on earth as that lad of about a dozen years. I waved him over, holding up a shilling, marvelling at how my life had turned to one of opposites in the very way I now looked at the other side of that coin than once I would have done. "Deliver this to the castle guard," I told him, handing him the first letter,

"And when you see me here again I will give you another shilling."

He ran off, while I watched to ensure he went in the correct direction. "You could have been nicer about that," Kirsty told me. "Simon would have asked his name, his history, and given him two shillings in the first place, then two more."

I decided not to explain that I understood all that to be pointless; that when I had been a beggar I was suspicious of those who asked questions, and never believed there was a second coin in anything. "I am not Simon," I said simply.

"No," she smiled, taking my hand. "You're not."

That done, we found a Campbell household who took us for the night in return for a guest's politeness and a small consideration. The most challenging aspect of the trip, I reflected, was already completed. The following day I went alone to the castle, and begged entry in the name of the Lord Lovat. As I was led to the main house within the walls I beheld the business of Breadalbane's garrison, who thronged the courtyard. A gallows had recently been constructed, and by the surrounding assembly of soldiers it seemed about to be put to use. A secretary bade me wait in a downstairs antechamber while my lord Breadalbane, above, read the letter I had brought.

I had no idea how long I might have to sit; but it was mere moments, before I heard a thundering cry, followed by the secretary's return, and a frantic order to attend the earl at once. Upstairs, that noble – a large, well-appointed man who wore a remarkable periwig upon his head, elaborate to the point of ridicule – was standing behind his desk, his chair thrown to the floor behind him, staring intently at the letter I had so recently carried.

"My lord," I began, "I send greetings from Hugh, Lord Lovat, and his brothers Thomas and Simon —"

"That Fox!" cried the earl. "Don't tell me anyone else wrote this!"

"I have not read it, my lord."

"Have you not? Have you not?" he stared at me ferociously, then let out a laugh. "Well, it's worthy of him, anyway, I'll say that." I heard a commotion from the grounds without, and assumed the gallows was in operation. "Damned perfect timing, mind you. I wouldn't have credited it…"

"My lord?" I asked.

"Tell me what you know of the chiefs and their plans towards the king's peace," he demanded.

I thought for a moment, attempting to establish which king he meant, and what he might know of the Frasers' recent discussions. "Only that my Lord Lovat is to raise a company in the Lord Murray's Regiment," I replied carefully.

"Aye, aye; about time too," the Campbell replied. "But what of next year? Or the next?"

"My lord?" I repeated flatly.

"Never mind it," said he. "Lovat needs a fast answer, and that's what I'll supply. You will wait outside."

I bowed and departed, informing the secretary he could find me in the courtyard. On my arrival there I must have been seen to jump back as if I had been shot — nothing could have prepared me for the shock of the sight I beheld. The soldiers, having hung and killed their victim on the gallows, were in the process of cutting him down; and it was the poor boy I had charged to deliver Simon's letter the previous day.

My mind sped in a thousand directions, so fast I could not catch a thought. Yet I was certain of one thing: Simon's letter was the reason that lad had lost his life, and therefore I was also the reason. I watched without movement as two men cut the rope and another two caught the body, then they placed it in a sack and carried it off. I stood there for many more minutes, gathering myself, for I knew I would soon have to speak as if not in shock. In due course the secretary returned with a letter of reply from Breadalbane. Dry in the mouth I feigned carelessness as I asked: "That boy they hanged – what did he do?"

"Eh?" the secretary replied, surprised I should ask. "Damned Stuart spy, apparently. You didn't know him, did you?"

"No," I said truthfully. "But I once knew someone like him."

If my sudden change of fortunes with respect to Kirsty had affected me more than the change which brought me to Simon's table, I had not realised it until I found myself weeping in her arms for the young man I had inadvertently sent to his grave. Feelings of sorrow, remorse or pity were expensive in my world, and certainly not to be wasted upon others. After I mustered my powers of speech and told her what I had witnessed, she silently stood with me beside the horses; and after I said nothing for some time, she quietly offered: "You have to watch him, Bolla. Simon is a *blaigeard*. A complete *blaigeard*."

"He is my friend," I replied.

"No, *gràdh mo chrìdh* – you're his friend, but he's not yours."

I shook my head, and she fell silent again. I began to speak seemingly unconnected thoughts, fighting to catch the fragments of ideas in my head; and, presently, I realised I was telling her about all my experiences at Simon's hands. I do not know how long I took over it, but when I had finished she simply wrapped her arms around me, until, eventually, I became aware of how remarkable we must have looked, standing in the castletown, our horses round about us, embracing for long minutes in apparent silence. "Come on," I said at last. "We must go back."

"WHAT MORE CAN I SAY, MY LADS? A fine red coat, a fine new flintlock, sixpence a day — and you'll be with me!" Simon held out his arms from the dray he used as a platform to the assembled audience, who laughed and applauded. He took a moment to look some of them in the eye and winked or nodded in recognition; the village in which he stood was not far from Moniack and so it was easy to imagine how many knew my lord well, and how many had been beneficiaries of his bag of farthings.

"I won't lie to you, there's work to be done," he went on. "But we're Frasers. We've never run from a fight and we're not going to start now. We'll be part of a big army to help look after our own in these difficult times. And I swear to you: we will not fight a single one of King Jamie's men. Ever. You can trust me, can't you? Have I ever led you wrong — except all those times?"

He bowed to even more laughter and applause, and near twenty of those listening moved towards the sergeant of militia who was taking names beside him. "Bolla!" he said, spying me as he jumped down from the dray. "Is all well? How's Kirsty?"

"All well," I said. "Your letters were delivered, and here is a reply from the Earl of Breadalbane."

If he detected a change in my demeanour he did not show it, and instead fell upon the document like a hungry wolf; moments later he was grinning and touching my shoulder once again. "Well done, Bolla. Good man. Good man!"

I nodded. "It appears you have done well yourself," I observed.

"Just short of three hundred recruits," he said proudly. "This was my last stop — you can ride home with me tonight."

"I heard your speech," said I.

"Aye, it's fair enough. And as far as I can go in public, just," he nodded. "Are you joining up?" His question took me by surprise. "I mean, there are limits to the boll o'meat agreement," he continued rapidly, apparently somewhat flustered. "But there are things to do, man, and I can't do them alone. Damn it — I don't want to do them alone."

"I had not thought about it," I said slowly. "But I will."

"I'll keep you a uniform," he grinned.

"Yet you will not serve in Lord Lovat's Company?" I asked. "Tullibardine wants you near him, I think."

He nodded. "Aye, but I'll soon sort that out. How much good do you think Lord Hugh will do as a captain? I don't see him coming out of the alehouse to watch muster without being dragged."

"I will consider it," I said after a pause.

"Good man. Now — what did you make of Slippery John's wig?"

"I have never seen the like," I said honestly.

After some days' thought the spectre of the poor lad's death had receded somewhat, and I had reflected that I was fortunate indeed to have reached a position in life such that a similar tragedy was no longer likely to befall me; also, that similar events transpired across the world every day; that Simon had saved me from a such an undeserved demise; and that if such was the case then perhaps the books were balanced. Kirsty said nothing against my argument, although she could easily have done so. She was much more vocal on my decision to join the army – it was our first real fight, and it ended only after an hour when I said: "He needs me."

"Aye, he does," she agreed, a sadness upon her face.

My lord was delighted when I told him of my choice, touching my shoulder and apparently genuine in his gratitude, before telling me that, should I have doubted it, my mission to Kilchurn had wrought a great success. "There was a big talk," he explained. "Breadalbane got all the chiefs together in Achallader and persuaded them there was no point trying to kick off this year." He read from a paper: "To testify our aversion of shedding Christian blood, and that we design to be good Scotsmen, we agree to a forbearance of all acts of hostility until the first day of October next. The chiefs give bonds, wherefore it is most necessary, just and reasonable that no acts of hostility should be committed on King James' generals or officers, or anyone they command, or upon the chiefs, or their kinsmen, friends, tenants or followers, etcetera…

"You see? A truce! Think how many died at Killiecrankie and Dunkeld and Cromdale — and think no more will die this year or next. Well done, Bolla! Well done, myself!"

"I thought Breadalbane was already committed to that cause, without any letters," I said doubtfully.

"Aye, he was, but his way wasn't going to work," Simon said excitedly. "He was going to try buying the chiefs off. Sooner or later someone would have asked how much someone else was getting, and the whole thing would have fallen in. I suggested a way to do it without being so short-sighted."

"What was the first letter about?" I asked.

He looked at me carefully. "Part one of a two-part plan. He needed to know his secret was out, then he needed to know there was an alternative."

"Was his secret out?"

"Of course it was, Bolla. What are you asking me?"

I could take the point no further. Instead I asked: "What about Lady Amelia's argument that two years is all William needs to make sure Jamie never comes back?"

"Aha! The big question!" he cried happily. "Don't you worry about that, man. I've got a plan. It's so good that even knowing about it in advance can't stop it working. But I need two years to get it moving. The time that's meant to work for Billy is going to work for Jamie — and Fraser. I'm brilliant!"

"So… is there any need to form a company?" I asked.

"Maybe not now," he told me, "And on the other hand, maybe.

92

Either way, we're going to have some fun. And what's more, everyone will be getting paid…"

I DO NOT THINK SIMON OFTEN FAILED to receive whatever he desired; but it seemed the Earl of Tullibardine, if not determined to see such failure, was at least minded to make my lord's route to success as difficult as possible. I attended when he presented himself at Blair Castle – now held once again by the earl and his father – to become commissioned into the Lord Murray's Regiment. He was resplendent in a richly-appointed uniform as a secretary guided him into an office, wherein waited two other similarly-clad officers.

"Fraser, you know my brother Mungo, of course," — the old friends shook hands, realising this was not the moment for their more usual form of greeting — "And this is Captain Colin Campbell of Glenorchy. I believe you know his father, Breadalbane?"

Simon grinned and held out his hand. "He knows me too," the other said sullenly. I realised that I did also — it was none other than he who had attempted to kill me in Aberdeen, leading to my meeting with my lord. The colour drained from me with the memory, despite so much having changed since then. Yet Simon seemed unaffected.

"Captain Campbell!" he said. "Ah, yes — a trifling error of youth, I think, brought us together in an ale-room one night? I trust you hold no grudge? I certainly don't."

After a moment Campbell stretched out his hand. "Of course not, Fraser. A long time ago. And now we are on the same side."

"Indeed," said Simon.

"I'm glad of that," Tullibardine said. "Because Breadalbane has specifically requested that Captain Campbell serves with Lord Lovat's Company, acting in command for Lord Hugh, who must attend to other matters. A request I am pleased to grant in the interests of all parties."

There was a twisted look in that man's face. Simon caught it and asked quickly: "There are to be two captains?"

"No, no, Fraser — that's ridiculous," the earl replied. "Captain Campbell commands. You will be his lieutenant, and I am pleased to offer my own brother as second lieutenant. A well-led company, to be sure!" he laughed.

A moment later Simon did too; but it was steeled. "Of course, sir," said my lord.

After the papers were signed and arrangements put in place, Simon marched out into the castle yard quickly, with Mungo and I struggling to keep up. "What was that about?" he demanded.

"Ian Cam is —"

"A *gorach* arse!" roared Simon. "Everyone knew Hugh was never going to command. The deal was that I'd raise the company, and become captain the minute Hugh ran out!"

"The deal?" Mungo asked, confused, before appearing to understand. "Oh, for God's sake, Simon."

My lord threw his hands in the air. "And what's worse – a Campbell in charge of Clan Fraser! They'll shoot him before they shoot anyone else – and I'll cheer them on!"

"Listen!" his friend bellowed back as the pair stopped and faced each other. "Look, man, I don't know about any deal, but you know how it is with Ian. You've been seen on one side then the other. He's got to make sure you're on *his* side. This is how he finds out."

"What?" It was unlike Simon to understand anything so slowly.

"Just follow orders for a month or two. Pass the test, buy Campbell out of his commission, then you're captain. That's what Ian told me, and I'm guessing he knew I'd tell you."

"Did he?" Simon replied through a scowl. "Well, it's probably *cac*, then!"

"If you think so, you can buy yourself out your own commission. Which you didn't have to go through signing."

"Of course I can't, Mungo. I can't leave Bolla here, and all the lads who signed up, along with a Campbell – and whatever it is you are." Mungo went to react furiously then realised it was a joke. "Seriously, I can't do that. But, if you think a month or two... Well, after that we'll see." He smacked himself in the forehead. "What an arse!" Then he laughed. "That brother of yours isn't stupid!" Tullibardine and his new captain appeared in the courtyard, some distance away, and Simon gave them a companionable wave of his arm, followed by a salute. "Good luck to you... you pair of *gorachs*," he muttered through a frozen grin.

94

So it was that, when three hundred men of the Clan Fraser stood to attention in red coats and arms, we stood before a Murray general, a Campbell captain and three lieutenants Fraser – Simon and two others of that ilk, James and Charles, from the south of our country. (No one mentioned Lord Hugh's absence at any time, it being clearly understood that it was for the best.) I stood alongside them as sergeant, the position Simon had secured for me, causing me to reflect that such a situation made as much sense to the lifelong Frasers beneath me as did the order of command above.

Having received several weeks' training – a dull procedure involving instruction on wearing uniforms, caring for weapons, how to walk and how to salute – we passed muster in Inverness, following which half of us were sent home, to be called upon when necessary, while the rest remained in cantonment outside the town, preparing for our first mission. Breadalbane's successful negotiations with the Jacobite leaders had led to some immediate thawing of relations between King James' men and King William's, with the result that many prisoners were being released. Such it was for sixty-seven MacDonalds of Glen Coe, held since the Battle of Dunkeld the previous year. Despite the thawing, Breadalbane did not trust such men, who had long been in feud with his own, to traverse his lands without exacting vengeance; and therefore they were to be escorted, by one hundred and ten of Lord Lovat's Company, from the outskirts of Edinburgh home to Glen Coe.

Captain Campbell appeared the model officer as he rode at the head of our party, with Simon at his side and I heading half of our troops in front and alongside our charges, while Mungo led the other half who followed. Nothing so complimentary could be said about the MacDonalds, who had suffered the depravity of a pauper's prison since the previous summer. All were pale in complexion and drawn in expression, while many coughed and sweated with a sickness come from lack of air, exercise and food. Yet their Highland pride was undiminished – especially for one man, who had clearly led them in exile.

During the first two days of our march, through Stirling and Crieff, Simon gave his usual performance: going amongst the MacDonalds, making use of his bag of farthings and exchanging words of friendship and encouragement with them all. Shortly it was returned by many, and

I have no doubt the hearing of speech and stories in the style of their own country represented a wakening from the nightmare of entrapment in a *Sassenach* city. Yet that one man would hear nothing of my lord's words, nor partake of his offerings; and those around him made it apparent that, should Simon continue with his efforts, he might lose the goodwill he had already engendered. Matters came to a head once we had set camp for the night outside Crieff: as he persevered with his attempts to start conversation, one of the MacDonald leader's companions spoke up. "I tell you the last time: leave it well alone, Fraser," he said darkly. "Alex here has given us everything to keep us alive, and we will give our lives up to gain him peace from your chatter."

As a number of our charges muttered their approval Simon replied: "Alex, is it? My own brother is named Alex and I've never known a better man — until today!" That created all the space my lord needed, and he continued: "So you'll be Alexander MacDonald of Caolasnacon, third son of the laird of Caolasnacon. And you paid the last of your money to give all your men a yule feast in prison."

"That he did," confirmed one of the companions, as that man looked cautiously at Simon.

"Then why so angry, friend? *Ochone*, you're going home to a grand welcome. Have any of you started making a song about him?" There came a few murmurs in response, from which it could be gathered that, if anyone had thought of such an act, it had proved beyond them. "It's not for everyone, that game," Simon continued. "What about calling it *Alex Who Laughed at Prison*? It could go something like this —" here he hummed a tuneful pibroch melody while slapping his tartan trews with his hands — "Although, I'm not the man to make it. All my songs are about lassies you wouldn't want your mother to meet." That raised a laugh. "But if you'd allow me, MacDonald of Caolasnacon, I'd be honoured to pay for a better man to make one?"

There was another murmur from the prisoners; but it was of approval, as MacDonald finally met Simon's glance, and his mouth turned upward for, it might be guessed, the first time in a twelvemonth. "As long as I can sing it to my mother," he said; and the two laughed together, to the great satisfaction of those around them.

From that moment the spirit of our endeavour was transformed from one of military coolness to one of, almost, the hunting parties following harvest season. Or at least, it did for a short time – until the afternoon we marched along Glen Dochart; and Captain Campbell, feeling the confidence of one within his own country, took issue with Simon. "Lieutenant Fraser," he began with a barb in his voice, astride his horse while my lord and MacDonald walked past, "It is unfitting for an officer in the king's army to consort with rebel prisoners."

The march halted at once as Simon replied: "They're not prisoners any more... sir."

"They are prisoners until we get them off Campbell lands into their own corner of hell," said the captain. "These hounds know full well what they did to my cousin Glenlyon's country. They near ruined him with a vicious attack."

"That wasn't us. It was Glengarry," MacDonald protested. "We were in Edinburgh at the time – and you know it."

"It was rebel MacDonalds returning from Dunkeld, where they fought against King William — and you fought with them," Campbell replied. "And that makes you every bit as bad as every other MacDonald scum. Or Glengarry." He turned to my lord. "I want this worthless cattle watched doubly carefully until they're off my good land, Fraser!"

"MacNab land," said MacDonald. "Stolen by Campbell lies."

"Enough!" the captain snarled, and, jumping from his mount, struck his opposite with his horsewhip. Surprised, that one reeled back; but not for long, before he threw himself full upon the body of his assailant. Campbell lost the whip immediately but went for his dirk even as MacDonald forced him to the ground. They rolled in the dust, struggling to catch command of the blade, as soldiers and charges alike gathered round to watch the fight. Campbell's grip loosened but he managed to cast the weapon beyond MacDonald's reach; and that man immediately disengaged to scramble after it. But warning shouts were raised as the captain went for his pistol — and in seconds both men were armed, crouched, and facing each other across eight feet of space, one with the dirk, the other with the gun. A shot rang through the sudden silence: but it was not fired by Campbell. Instead Mungo Murray, his hand raised into the air and still clouded in powder smoke, stood in the battleground.

"It would be a shame to be shot dead when you're so close to home," he told MacDonald quietly, then, turning, said: "Captain Campbell, sir, these men are guaranteed safe conduct in the king's name."

"These *prisoners*!" Campbell spat breathlessly, still glaring at MacDonald.

"As you say, sir," Mungo replied.

Simon, who had remained silent during the episode, appeared brightly beside Mungo. "Sir, it's getting late – maybe we should camp here for the night?"

Campbell looked round the glen, seeing an open, flat area beside its loch, while mountains allowed ease of movement only east, from where we had come, and west, where we were to proceed. He nodded. "Double guard!" he added before striding off. MacDonald made to return to his own men, stopping briefly as Mungo pointed at the dirk and opened his hand. He surrendered the weapon and exchanged a hard glance with Simon before moving past. "All's well," said my lord. "Let's make camp."

It was a cold, clear night at the base of Glen Dochart. The lights of two farmsteads twinkled in the distance while the loch silently glistened against the flat summer half-night. MacDonalds sat round their fires while Frasers alternated between doing the same and acting sentry round the field. I attended Simon as he shared a drink with Campbell, Mungo and the Fraser lieutenants. "Damned fine claret, this, Fraser," said the captain, who appeared to desire distance from the afternoon's bad feeling.

"Best I could find, sir," my lord replied. "It's from Aberdeen. I think you used to use the same vintner as I did. And Mungo." Campbell spluttered slightly and his eyes darted round the company, even landing on me for a moment; but Simon and Mungo had assembled their best careless expressions and the moment passed. "That's Lochdochart Castle over there, isn't it?" Simon asked, pointed at a small island on which the jagged remains of a large building could be seen. Campbell acknowledged with a grunt. "Built by Duncan of the Cowl, if I'm not mistaken," the Fox added.

"No, you're not," the captain replied, impressed. "A great man and a relative of mine. They called him Duncan of the Castles as well, because he put up so many. He founded the Breadalbane ambition – to walk from one side of Scotland to the other without leaving our own country."

"A massive undertaking, sir. But how will you achieve it with Argyll so strong in the west?"

"Argyll? An idiot, man!" Campbell stood up and marched stiffly back and forth. "I tell you, Fraser, it's not long before that one gets what's coming to him. He's a fool!"

"How so, sir?" Simon asked innocently.

"You would think, would you not –" it was clear from the first words that this was a speech often rehearsed – "That a man whose father lost his head, and whose father's father lost his head, would learn what had to be learned in the affairs of state? But no! He does not! Still, Breadalbane watches and waits. My father dances carefully and well, and he knows when to cut in. There will soon be a time when everyone knows who leads Clan Campbell… and it will not be Argyll!"

"As long as the lochs don't freeze," Simon said into the pause.

"What?" Campbell demanded.

"Sorry, sir. I said, 'as long as the lochs don't freeze.'"

"I know what you said, man! Explain yourself!"

"The castle, sir. I'm sure you know this was once MacNab land before —"

"They lost it to my family through poor management!"

"Indeed, sir. And Black Duncan built the castle on the loch. Then, one night, about forty-five years ago, the loch froze over and some MacNabs – some say it was two, others say it was three – came over the water and burned it down."

"Nonsense!" Campbell raged. "It was a brutal assault by hundreds of invaders!"

"If you say so, captain. But I'm thinking, any clan who falls for something as obvious as that, just, they're stupid enough to —"

"You forget yourself, sir!" the captain threw his glass into the fire. "You are on Campbell land under Campbell command, and you will show respect! Bloody Frasers – you're as bad as these cursed MacDonalds. Cattle, all of you! So, you want a walk over the loch like your precious MacNabs, do you? A pity it's the wrong time of year.

Assemble fifty of your men at once, Lieutenant Fraser!"

Simon stared for just a moment while his fellow officers stared at him. Then, with a stiff, shallow, bow, he went off to follow the order. In a matter of minutes fifty men were standing to armed attention in two ranks of twenty-five, while those of us around the fire were treated to a dazzling series of insults regarding our history and heritage. Then Campbell stalked over to the men and shouted: "Fraser! Your men will march across the loch fifty times. Do it!"

Simon looked at the furious captain's face, then steeled his own. "Right turn!" he bellowed. "Quick, march!" The captain called for more wine as our clansmen doubtfully moved towards a stretch of the loch about thirty paces wide. The first of them were soon splashing into the freezing water, where it could be seen they disappeared to their waists. It became clear they were struggling through thick mud, for their progress was painfully slow.

"Keep those muskets dry, or you'll answer for it!" Campbell bellowed. The men were forced to continue their struggle while holding their weapons high above them. Simon glared at him; then, before the last men had entered the water he ran over and joined their labours. That raised an unpleasant mirth in the captain, who commented on Fraser *duine uasals* being no better than Fraser cattle; but no one else found enjoyment in the exertions of those fifty-one men for an hour or more, and by the time they returned, places close to fires and cups of whisky were waiting for them.

IT WAS TESTAMENT to Clan Fraser's loyalty to Simon that not a single man of the company disappeared that night in search of respite. It would have been scant surprise had I been woken to the news that some of our own had absconded – instead, to be shaken into life at the coldest point of the night and told ten MacDonalds had vanished was a great surprise; for they were now just two days from their own lands, and freedom.

Part of Captain Campbell's orders included counting our charges every two hours, and since he had instructed a doubling of attention they could not have been gone for longer than half that time. Therefore they could not have got far; and it could be safely assumed they had travelled west towards Glen Coe. As the officers roused themselves, James Fraser ordered me to gather twenty men to give chase, which I duly did; and as we presented ourselves outside Campbell's tent that man appeared, his uniform not quite properly presented, and demanded to know where Simon was. After a moment's delay Mungo admitted no one was certain. "Treachery!" screamed Campbell — but as he did Mungo pointed towards the west, where a torch was being waved from the middle-distance. "Follow me at once!" barked the commander, and we set out in pursuit.

A few minutes later we found ourselves beside the widest part of the watercourse, parallel with the castle on its small island; and found that the torch was being waved by Simon himself. "I gave chase, sir, but I think they split up at the head of the loch," he gasped, out of breath. "They must be headed for Glen Coe."

"Of course they are!" snapped the captain. "Do you think —" Just then there came a flash in the sky which turned all our heads towards the loch; and there we beheld a great flame reaching skywards from the remains of the old castle itself, its source hidden by the walls standing between the fire and us. Then above the sound of frantic soldiers in action we heard that of a low, loud bell ringing slowly across the water. "What in God's name...?" cried Campbell.

"The devil choke me!" Simon said. "The bell of Saint Fillan!"

The captain turned on him. "What?"

"An old, old story, sir, since before this country was your own," my lord replied, holding the torch at mid-height so that its light flickered across one side of his face, throwing the other into deep shadow. "It's said that when the laird of Glen Dochart was about to die, the wee folk would come out and ring Saint Fillan's bell, which was kept here in ancient times. He had a cell just up the glen —"

"Utter *cac*!" Campbell bellowed. "Are you mad? It's clearly those MacDonald scum! Boats! Get me boats!"

I ordered six men to run to the nearest farmstead and bring back what boats they could. Meanwhile, we could make out dark figures moving within the castle, as they cast moving shadows against the walls and trees behind them.

"They say there's a faerie island on the loch," Simon continued. "It moves wherever the wee folk want it to go. Once, long ago, a wife of MacNab got lost on her way home. She was bringing her newborn son to the glen for the first time. It was a moonless night so she lay down near the loch to sleep. When she woke up she saw the island floating away with her son on it, and the faeries waving and laughing at her. She tried to jump across the water, but she fell in. They say she found the saint's prayer bell in the loch before she drowned. The wee lad was never seen again, but she comes back to the glen and helps the faeries ring the bell when another son of MacNab is under threat." the Fox paused for effect. "Of course, now, sir," he went on, "it would ring for Breadalbane instead of MacNab."

The captain said nothing. The flames of Simon's torch danced in the low breeze while the shadows on the island followed with an eerie matching pattern, and the bell tolled every ten or fifteen seconds. It seemed my heart stopped when I had counted time and expected to hear it again, only starting up when the chime rose across the glen. The spell was broken with the return of my men with two small boats, each with capacity for four. "Right, lads, let's get to the bottom of this!" cried Simon, but Campbell held up his hand.

"Not a chance, Lieutenant Fraser," he said with a twisted grin. "I'll deal with this MacDonald mischief myself. You!" he shouted at me. "With me, and detail six to follow." I glanced at my lord but he gave me no signal, so I followed the captain into the boat with two Fraser privates, while four others boarded the second vessel. "I'll bring back your precious bell – and melt it down for bullets!" Campbell shouted to the shore as we rowed across. The journey took almost no time, so small was the loch, as the bell became louder; and we disembarked at a low point on the east of the tiny island.

The rocky platform seemed to have been abandoned since the castle's destruction, for a healthy crop of trees, reaching as high as the ruins, had grown over the broken stone and rotting woodwork. We climbed with difficulty up the steep approach to the remnants of the walls, and Campbell directed us round the outside to the eastern face, as the path before us danced in firelight. The sound of the bell by now ensured no one – wee folk or otherwise – would likely overhear our movements. Finally I crouched under what was left of a stone wall, beside Campbell, and we peered over the top.

The scene we beheld would give even the hardiest head pause for thought. The large fire had been set at the centre of the square building and it towered above those around it: nine small figures wrapped in cloaks, each no more than chest height to a normal man, but each holding a torch of nearly double his size. They wove from side to side, never facing away from the fire, as their torches followed. I checked on my men, aligned beside the captain and I, and saw each of them drawing crosses upon themselves against evil spirits. Campbell drew his pistol and ordered us in a whisper to charge our arms, the which we did; then he pointed to a gap in the stonework where we could make entry, and motioned for us to surround the figures within before presenting weapons.

At that moment the bell was struck three times instead of its regular once; and we all looked to see a new figure, of greater than average height, stood upon a platform beyond the fire, backed against the tall remains of the castle fireplace. A giant shadow was cast behind him as he raised his arms to reveal a great rectangular object in one hand, and a stick in the other — then struck the former with the latter to reveal their identity as bell and beater. Next he began singing, a strange, foreign song with melody I could not follow and words I could not understand; and with each phrases the fire roared up in response.

Even Campbell with his cold attitude could tell this last was causing the Fraser troops' confidence to wane. "A trick of gunpowder!" he hissed loudly. "There are ten MacDonalds missing, and ten men standing round a fire! It's a pretty dance, but it ends now — move in!" He stood up and stepped forward; but as I made to follow I found I was unable to move, as if great arms were around my chest, preventing my escape. Then, instead of standing up and running forth, I felt myself pulled backward and dragged down upon my side, and a great darkness came across my vision. I could make out the lower portion of Campbell running forward, and I heard him bellow a challenge; but I saw no other movement, and then the darkness drew across the rest of my sight, and I fell unconscious.

"BOLLA! BOLLA! May I fall and not rise – are you with me?" I opened my eyes, but the bright daylight hurt; yet I was glad to discover I could again move as I covered my head with my forearm. "Bolla! Answer me, my lad! Come on!"

"I think so…" I muttered uncertainly.

Simon stopped shaking me and collapsed against the castle wall. "Thank God. I thought you were away, just!"

"What happened?" I asked after a moment. He opened a small flask of whisky and offered it to me. The drink spurred me towards full wakefulness and I glance around, my eyes still painful, to see the soldiers from the boats all in a similar condition.

"I don't have a clue, honestly. Come and see." He helped me to my feet and we entered the castle ruin, which looked greatly different from how I had seen it just moments before (as it seemed to me). The fire was replaced by a smoking pile of embers, and there was no sign of the figures who had danced and swayed with the flames. Yet the greatest difference was upon the platform where the bell-ringer had stood. It was a great stone slab, from some important part of the old building; but it had been decorated as if it were a kind of altar, with flowers and yew wands laid upon it.

And, laid out upon the top, arms and legs stretched wide, was the body of Captain Campbell, a dirk through his heart and a great slash across his neck, his head thrown back, eyes and mouth open in a furious and desperate scream. "*Chan eil mi a' tuigsinn…*" I whispered. "What can it mean?"

Simon shook his head. "Damned if I know," he said. "Let's just get this mission finished and go home." He gave orders for the body to be wrapped up and taken to the shore, while he and I sailed over ahead, where Mungo was waiting for us.

"Tell your tale, Fox!" he said sharply. "What has gone on?"

"I know nothing, Mungo," my lord protested. "If it was my affair I'd tell all. Stabbing a man isn't my style – you know that. And stabbing my own captain would be setting my own firing squad."

"Your marks are all over this page," Mungo insisted. "And you had plans for Colin."

"Everyone had plans for Colin, except you," Simon corrected. "He made enemies of the MacDonalds and the Frasers. He even went at his own kind – you heard. *Ochone*, one more glass of wine and he'd probably be calling out Murray as well."

"Ask MacDonald if he was involved. On oath."

"I have. He swears none of his men went off last night. And why would they? We'll have them home tomorrow, easier than it would be for them to make their own way through Breadalbane."

"All I know is, one moment the prisoner count is ten down, the next it's twenty down, then it's ten, then suddenly no one is missing," Mungo replied, shaking his head. "And the guards are all Frasers."

"Say what you mean," Simon challenged.

Mungo met his stare. "Things… *happen…* to people you don't like, Simon. You had a problem with Campbell, and he's gone. You have a problem with my brother. And maybe even with me. If I find —"

"Be off with that *cac*," Simon cut in. "How long have we known each other? How much trouble have we survived? Are you really saying everything that goes wrong in this kingdom is down to me? You might as well blame Bolla here — he was on the island. I wasn't."

I looked up, startled; but Mungo only glanced at me then gave Simon a withering look. "You know what I mean," he said. "And it doesn't matter what I think anyway. We've got to report to Ian."

"And Breadalbane," Simon said. "But first, we've got to get Alex and his lads home. So let's do that."

It was true that none in our company could say they were in any way disaffected by Captain Campbell's death; although its method was a different matter. As we set off towards Glen Coe the MacDonalds were delighted when Simon, now leading, offered Campbell's mount to Caolasnacon, and he rode with the officers. In fact, very little remained of the previous military order. Most of our discussion, of course, was about the events of the previous night, and the mysteries of missing men who had never left, faerie fires and deaths on altars. MacDonald could not offer any reason why the count of prisoners (now no longer referred to as such) had changed; but offered: "I can tell you none of my people ran off, and none have been replaced by changelings. But I'll be honest with you — if the wee folk had given me the chance to kill that Campbell, I'd have done a deal with them in a heartbeat."

"We should make that part of the song, then," Simon said. "MacDonald, who laughed at prison and treated with faeries. Sing it to your mother!" That raised laughter, but my lord continued: "Seriously, Alex, think about my point. We can tell people the devil took Campbell away while we were all asleep, or we can say someone struck a blow for MacDonald pride on the way home to start — well, whatever you're going to start when you get home."

That other gave Simon a curious look. "As I say, I'd have killed him if I could have."

"Well, let's say you *did* kill him, then. My Frasers aren't going to call you a liar, and I'm going to write the report. I'll say we marched all the way to Glen Coe in good order, but Captain Campbell had behaved grievously the whole time, and I'll bear witness to diverse allegations of impropriety levelled against you. He maligned your whole clan and people — he did as well — and you called him out to a duel. He chose dirks for weapons; I was your second, Mungo was his, and it was a tragic ending for a *gorach* who should have known better."

MacDonald nodded. "It's more or less true," he said.

"And no dishonour in any of it — except to Campbell."

That seemed an end to the matter, despite some expressions of doubt from Mungo; and after a stop at the ruined castle of Achallader – where Breadalbane had persuaded the chiefs to sign bonds of agreement – we marched onto the moor of Rannoch, beyond the end of that earl's country, and near the entrance to MacDonald's. He had begun singing to himself as the day grew, and as we approached the time to part he was bellowing out songs of his fathers and grandfathers. "You can't beat it, Simon," he cried happily. "That feeling you have as the hills begin to line up, the way you remember them from the day you were born, and you know you're home!"

"I know it well," my lord laughed, and Mungo agreed cheerfully.

We stopped for the last time, and friendships made down the ranks were sealed with vows to meet again one day, hopefully under the reign of a returned King Jamie. Just then one of our scouts galloped in (as best one could on the moorland) and spoke urgently to Simon, whose expression turned serious.

"Alex," he said, his arm round that one's shoulder, "There are

Campbells around. They've been following us since Glen Orchy – I should have realised they'd expect Captain Campbell to report in his own country. We'll need to put on a wee bit of a performance to get you away."

"What do you mean?" the other asked.

"We'll need to stage Campbell's death, right here. It needs to look good – but only from a distance. All they need to see is your lads heading off, and us trying to shoot you. Just a wee gunpowder trick, if you get my meaning."

MacDonald agreed; and so, our farewells concluded, Simon gave clear instructions to Frasers and MacDonalds alike: "The lads heading home are going off that way," he pointed, "And we'll line up over here. We'll fire two rounds of blank shot then give chase, but we won't follow MacDonalds into their own country, where they'd easily kill us all."

"Blank shot!" Caolasnacon called loudly.

"Aye," Simon agreed. "We're in more danger of setting fire to ourselves than we are of knocking you down!" He gave his orders, arranging some dragoons in three ranks, the MacDonalds aligned haphazardly beyond, then assembled a confusing melee of officers and bystanders between the two. "Looks perfect from a distance," he said, nodding. "Now, Alex MacDonald, be gone — and may I never see you again unless you're bearing whisky!" He bowed and turned away. "Clear the ranks!" Simon told those of us at the centre, and we ran to either side. "Now lads," he shouted from his command position. "These are King Jamie's men, just like us, and we're going to show them some honour after the year they've had. No bullets – load powder! Aim high! Fire!" The noise of muskets exploding bounced across the moor, and from a distance it would have looked exactly as if the king's men were firing on a band of fleeing clansmen. "Reload! Aim! Fire!" Simon ordered again, and a second cloud went up.

But as it rose, I saw one man before us had fallen. At first I believed he had done no more than stumble; but then I made out the stiff, inhuman movements I had seen at Killiecrankie: the unmistakable sign of one who lies shot and dying.

"Hold fire!" my lord cried. "Hold ranks!" I repeated the order, watching my men to ensure they stayed where they were, while craning to watch as Simon and Mungo ran to the fallen man and lifted him up. Even as the last MacDonald disappeared into the heather at the edge of Glen Coe it was obvious their companion was never going to behold his home again. They carried him back between them, his head drooped and limbs lifeless; and I saw, as they came closer, it was Alex himself.

"At ease!" I shouted and rushed forward to help; yet all I could do was make it easier for them to carry the body by lifting his feet. We laid him down at the very place we had bid him farewell, and under his breath Simon simply said: "*Cac.*"

"Someone fired a real shot," Mungo snarled angrily. My lord touched his arm.

"It's my fault," he said quietly. "I gave the order to load, not load powder."

"No!" Mungo replied. "Everyone heard what you said. Someone's going to be hung —"

"Leave it," Simon insisted, shaking his head. "No one else should be dying today."

It was a quiet moment as MacDonald's body was wrapped and tied to a litter, and joined Campbell's in the middle of our company. There was nothing to do but begin the march home, the which we did. Some miles before Glen Dochart Simon took time to write a letter, which he pushed into Lieutenant James Fraser's hand. "Take the bodies to Breadalbane at Kilchurn Castle," he said, "And give him this."

Mungo and I stood with my lord as he watched the sad funeral band move south-east towards Loch Awe. "What have you done?" Murray asked.

"The best I could, Mungo," he replied quietly. "The best I could to prevent any more deaths. I sent Breadalbane the body of his son along with the body of his son's murderer. MacDonald will be remembered as a hero and Campbell will have had his revenge."

"And Fraser is friends of all." Mungo said darkly, moving away as Simon stared after him.

"I hope our Alex has fared better than Alex MacDonald," I said by way of something to fill the void of conversation.

Simon turned back to watch the bodies being carried to their final destination. "No. At least, I don't think so," he told me. "He's been declared dead."

That caused me to start. "How?" I asked after a moment.

"You could see what the worrying was doing to Father. I went to Inverness and had the lawyers deal with it. If you haven't heard from someone in a year you can make it official." I said nothing, my mind in turmoil; but at last he turned back towards the company, and, passing me, he touched my shoulder. "This way, if Alex comes back, it'll be spectacular sport."

I stood for some moments longer, unable to trust myself to move or say anything.

CHAPTER FOUR
THE RAPSCALLION ON THE ROCK

IF THE MEN of the Lord Lovat's Company were of strong opinion over the events of our march, they had made no display of it by the time they were ordered to return home. Such was their silence on any great matter that I, for the first time I could remember, felt a distance between them and myself; for the reactions in my own mind were like screams across an empty glen, and I often found myself glancing round my companions to see whether my most recent silent outburst had somehow been detected by others. But then, these were proud members of Clan Fraser, on the business of the one they hoped would one day be their chief; and as long as he did no wrong by them they would be unlikely to raise any objection.

The question of whether he had indeed committed the acts of which I suspected him hung heavy with me, but still I said nothing, and that itself seemed to increase my distance from those with whom I travelled. Yet, by the time Simon, Mungo and I arrived in Edinburgh, I was once again questioning my previous position, and beginning to recall how much my lord had done for me since our first meeting.

It was a warm evening with a light breeze that sent the heavy odour of the city far away from us as we passed through its West Port; and Simon was entertaining us with an account of a recent affair which, he said, illustrated why King William could not be trusted. "If you asked me for an example of a good man," he told us, "I'd point you in the direction of one called Leisler.

"He was a magistrate in New York in the Americas, and he met a family looking for help, so poor they were sharing clothes between them. They had to move as a group, all together, within the one set of clothes. That's incredibly poor, wouldn't you say?

"The governor of New York says, 'These folk are too destitute to be any use to us, so let's sell them into slavery.' His officials agree. But Leisler says: 'You do that and I swear you'll have five thousand men knocking your heads off by the end of the day.' And the whole town, all the working folk, all stand behind him and say: 'We're on his side.' So the poor family, instead of being sold as slaves, are given help — and they end up the best clothmakers in New York. Spectacular sport!"

He stopped mid-flow, and, clasping Mungo and I by our shoulders, said: "It's weeks since I've been drunk. Crawling about on my hands and knees, banging into walls and throwing up every time I do, drunk. What's the best ale-house in this town, Mungo?"

That one directed us to a conveniently nearby inn, which, my lord observed, lay not far from a leasing of Lord Lovat where we could bed down later. "Once I've finished howking my guts up," he added, proclaiming: "*Nunc est bibendum, nunc pede libero pulsanda tellus!*"

There commenced a fast and eager consumption of ale, followed by an order of two bottles of claret; and I confess to desiring the use of a couch long before my colleagues appeared to need the same. In fact, Simon appeared to become more energetic with each drink, and was soon embarked upon a barrage of bawdy stories, which, for his volume, began to generate a notable negative reaction from those around us.

"Have a care," Mungo said warningly, nodding to a group of men in uniform similar to his own, and who had already glanced in our direction more than twice. "Keep your voice down."

"Aye, aye," my lord said, waving his hand dismissively. "Now, wasn't I telling you *gorachs* a story? Aye, Leisler in New York… After saving those folk from slavery, and giving the place its first decent trade since it was founded, Leisler goes on to become an official himself. Most of the others don't like him, remember, for standing up to them.

"Now, most of them are Jacobites, and want to keep New York for Jamie, even after King Billy beat him at the Boyne. But Leisler takes over the fort and says he'll hold it against the governor until Billy sends a new one.

"He's no soldier. He's just trying to do what he thinks is right. But he holds the fort – which he called Fort William, by the way, just like the one we're about to have here – he holds it against all comers, and he even extends the town's lands. For six months at least he's in charge, with no word from home. Eventually a new governor turns up and Liesler surrenders the fort — and next thing he's in jail for treason, then hung for it.

"Hung for treason after defending the interests of the rightful King William!" the Fox's voice at this point was aggressively loud, but he seemed to revel in the attention he was receiving from the room, as he took a large drink from his cup then spat: "The devil choke a king who'll kill you for supporting him!"

"Calm down, Simon!" Mungo hissed. "You're not among friends!"

"I care not," my lord replied, grinning round at the onlookers. "Simon Fraser, the Young MacShimi, at your service," he said loudly, raising his cup to them. "And here's to the king," he continued, taking a drink, before quietly adding, "Just don't ask me which one."

"Seriously, man – end your madness," said Mungo tersely.

"Get me another drink and I'll think about it." Mungo stood up and moved towards the housekeeper while Simon looked sadly into his empty cup. "Do you know what I'm saying, Bolla?" he went on. "They call it a 'glorious revolution' – but you tell me what's changing. Same *cac*, different arse on the throne."

"But if King Jamie comes back —"

"*When* King Jamie comes back," he corrected me with a leer, "He'll know who brought him back, and how they want things done."

"What about his belief in the divine right of kings?" I did not know much detail of the matter, but the phrase had been used in the midst of many arguments regarding monarchy.

Simon laughed. "It needs pointed out to His Majesty that every single thing that's gone wrong for him and his father was down to spouting that *cac*. I don't care what he believes, or what he doesn't. But there are ways of saying things and having them heard." I decided against referring to his recent outbursts, which, I was sure, would have been better off unheard. "It's all part of the plan, Bolla. The big plan where everybody wins. Well, everybody who matters, just. Where's the wine?"

113

Mungo had returned, after some discussion with the army officers. "We'll get it somewhere else," he said quietly. "We should leave."

"Why, is it shut?"

"For God's sake, Simon," Mungo glared. "You just told them who you were, and the whole town's been ringing with the story of how you killed Captain Campbell then blamed a MacDonald for it."

My lord shook his head dismissively. "You were there, you *gorach* – you know that's *cac*."

Mungo pointed dramatically behind him. "They don't! And some of them served with Campbell."

Simon stared at his friend intently for a moment, although it was difficult to tell whether he was looking upon or through him. Then he rose, and, slamming his empty cup on the table, while still staring at Mungo, he announced: "If anyone wants to discuss recent events concerning one Captain Colin Campbell of Lord Murray's Regiment, I'll be pleased to explain it — over a cup of their own wine."

Silence fell across the half-full room. I was aware of quiet, cautious movement around me, but I was too intoxicated with drink to analyse the situation fully, and I dared not look away from Simon, who, standing still, was turning his head slowly in every direction. Then one of the officers came over and stood opposite my lord. "You've had a good drink, Lieutenant Fraser," he said calmly but firmly. "Why don't you take some air?"

"Aye, you know who I am," Simon replied, "But who in the devil's name are you?"

"Captain Menzies of Lord Murray's Company," he replied crisply with a slight bow, although it was clearly unnecessary. "And I ask you to withdraw from this place." He was a gentle-looking character, slight of build and less tall than any of us, and already losing his hair despite being little older than were we; but there was a strength in his eyes and they did not shy from Simon's full glare.

"Order me," Simon said.

"All right. Lieutenant Fraser, get out."

At once Simon threw himself at Menzies. Cups and chairs were flung across the room as he tried to grab the captain in a choke-hold; but the other broke the grip by lifting his arms and pushing outwards. Even as my lord recovered and prepared to throw a fist, the captain landed one, then two blows into his torso. Simon staggered back, at which I went to dive forward — but I felt an arm round my shoulder and the unmistakeable cold pressure of a blade on my neck. A look to my left showed Mungo was similarly held; then a look back to Simon told me he had managed to pull a dirk from his waist. But Menzies had gone one better: a pistol was pointed at my lord. "Stop still, Fraser!" he cried; and after a moment, Simon dropped his blade, breathing heavily. Yet Mungo and I were still held at knifepoint.

"Let them be," the captain told our captors, and we were pushed towards my lord where the three of us stood, surrounded. I took a moment to glance at he who had held me, and I saw in him the same crisp, firm look that Menzies still retained.

"You serve with Fraser?" he asked Mungo, who nodded, and made to identify himself – the which might have simply resolved all that had occurred.

Yet Simon bellowed: "I prefer the Young MacShimi!" in an attempt to recover some of his poise; and Mungo's attempt at negotiation was forgotten.

"Fraser, the charge is assault on a senior officer. You have lodgings nearby? Very well, we will accompany you there and you will spend the night under guard. We will report to Colonel Murray, your brother —" he nodded acknowledgement at Mungo — "In the morning. March."

The walk was not long, but it was long enough for the evening air to reinforce my belief that I, if not we, should have stopped drinking some hours previously. I do not recall the expressions of our captors, or ourselves, as my lord regaled Captain Menzies with the proud history of his own clan: "A noble race," said he, "Brave men who have managed to keep their country to themselves despite the efforts of Campbells, Murrays and others – but not Frasers." I do not recall Menzies' reaction as my lord stopped twice or thrice on the road to deliver farthings into the hands of beggars, telling them, laughingly, to beware, for he was in the company of fearless warriors. I also do not recall the expression of Lord Lovat's housekeeper on opening the door of our chief's lodgings to a beaming Simon, who announced: "Good evening, Mrs McGourty – I've brought friends!" In truth, I recall very little until the following morning, when I was shaken awake by one of the captain's men who had stood guard over us all night. (I do, I admit, seem to remember Simon knocking me awake in the dark and attempting to persuade me to escape through one of the building's few windows, only to run into a chamber pot in his drunkenness, and his half-hearted plan dissolving into laughter as our guards threw him back on his couch; but I cannot certainly say it took place.)

It was an agonisingly bright morning, and an early rain had added a sheen to the town's stone surfaces which made my vision all the more painful. I can only believe Menzies marched us into the Earl of Tullibardine's chambers within the government buildings, for I do not remember the direction or any detail of the premises. I was still partially drunk, as was confirmed to me when I bowed on Tullbardine's entry via his private door, and my head felt as if it continued forward even though I had leaned back.

"What in God's name is this supposed to mean, Fraser?" barked the earl, with no preamble, in the voice I found so difficult to follow. "Attacking a senior officer? Explain yourself!"

"Your lordship —" Simon began in his usual bright style, then, with a frown, deliberately lowered his voice — "I throw myself on the mercy of yourself and Captain Menzies. It was simply a misunderstanding, but I have no excuse for my behaviour. Except, possibly, the exhaustion of a long mission so recently completed."

"We'll talk about that in a moment," Tullibardine said grimly. "You realise I can have you shot for this?"

Simon bowed his head. "I do not misapprehend the seriousness of the situation, your lordship. I can only repeat my apology to you and the good captain, who was only acting in my own interests."

"And you, Mungo — what is this game you play?"

His brother shrugged, but before he responded Simon said: "Lieutenant Murray also tried to have me take a different course of action. He is blameless in this – as is Sergeant Fraser, here."

"But what was it all about?" Tullibardine insisted.

"Sir, if I may?" Menzies interceded, to a nod. "There was some discussion of treason against the king, and Lieutenant Fraser became distressed at the thought of it. The rest, as he says, was nothing but a misunderstanding. For my part I desire no further action against him, and I appeal to your lordship to let the matter go."

The earl grunted. "This is the kind of officer you would do well to emulate, Fraser," he said; and although I dared not look round, I detected a certain air of satisfaction from Menzies' direction. "On his word – and only on his word – I will take no further action."

"I thank your lordship," Simon bowed, "And you, sir." the captain nodded, the air of him moving noticeably towards smugness.

Tullibardine sat down and turned over a few papers on his desk, as if to emphasise he regarded the matter closed. "Now you will report on events concerning the death of Captain Campbell."

"Sir," Simon began, "Again, I can only offer my regret at those events. The captain bade us camp at Glen Dochart, and, from what I have been able to tell, a small number of MacDonalds escaped from under guard and contrived to kill Captain Campbell – a contrivance, which, unfortunately, was successful."

"I know that, damn you!" Tullibardine said. "What's this I hear about witchcraft – and one MacDonald dead too, under your guard?"

"I fear your lordship has listened to poor rumours. Some of the escaped prisoners set up a defensive position in the ruins of Lochdochart Castle. The captain took a boat and just a handful of men to investigate, against my recommendation. I believe he misunderstood the seriousness of the situation in his desire to resolve it. Instead of calling for the prisoners to surrender he marched into their stronghold alone, where he was, regrettably, killed."

"I have had a different report, Fraser. It tells of… it tells of faerie islands and fire from nowhere."

Simon laughed. "Your lordship must know how dancing flames in a lonely dark night can set off the imagination. I can only tell your lordship what I saw with my own eyes – which was a brave but, I believe, a foolhardy attempt to recover escaped prisoners when they were in too strong a position."

"But why would they escape, Fraser, that's what I want to know?" Tullibardine went on. "What, two, or three days from home? They were being freed, by God!"

"All I can say is that certain men amongst the MacDonalds felt that

Captain Campbell was not affording them the respect they deserved."

"And what of men being marching fifty times across a loch?"

"The captain was pleased to give orders he believed to be appropriate," Simon said flatly. "And I was pleased to obey them."

"Tell me about Alexander MacDonald."

"Another tragic misunderstanding, I fear," my lord replied sadly. "After I took command we led the prisoners to the edge of their country, as ordered. Just as they were turned free I was told a party of troops were advancing from a distance. The MacDonalds suspected they were about to be tricked into being recaptured, and ran for freedom before I had given the word. Some of my men, acting in the spirit of Captain Campbell's orders, opened fire. MacDonald was killed."

"Why would anyone betray them in those circumstances?" the earl asked.

"I cannot answer your lordship. All I can suggest is that a year in captivity had rendered those men most suspicious in nature. They could see the hills of their home, and would not be turned back for anything."

"And what of the approaching troops you mentioned? Who were they?"

"Apparently another sad error," Simon said. "Your lordship may know the lands to the east of Glen Coe are barren and strange. Perhaps trees, or deer on the horizon, agitated the imagination of a poor cold scout. In short, sir, I cannot name any of my company for reprimand."

Tullibardine stared at the Fox for a long moment, then turned another paper. "I will require a written report, of course," he said, to which Simon bowed. "But, Fraser..." he went on, exasperated rather than angry. "Your orders were simple!"

"Captain Campbell's orders were indeed simple, sir. Alas, these are not simple times."

"Indeed." He shuffled some other papers, this time not turning any, and I received the impression he was not entirely convinced about his next course of action. Eventually he continued: "I have another mission for your company. A small number of them, at any rate. You are aware of this business on the Bass Rock?"

Simon nodded. "An irritation, sir."

"An embarrassment, sir!" Tullibardine shouted. "All across Scotland rebels are being brought into the king's peace – but just two dozen miles from his capital there remains an outpost held against him. It must be stamped out, Fraser. And your company must do the stamping!"

"Your lordship, perhaps the Royal Scots Navy —"

"The navy?" the earl bellowed with a laugh, and appeared set upon another tirade before thinking better of it. "No. We... you must deal with it, Fraser."

"I await your orders, your lordship."

"You will gather a squad – fifteen should do it – and proceed to Canty Bay, there to confer with one Sea Captain Ackermann, who is already engaged in guarding the Bass. Find a way onto that accursed rock and break the forces upon it."

"Yes, your lordship," Simon said with a suggestion of sarcasm, which Tullibardine ignored.

"Getting on will the the hard part. Once you've done that you'll find barely twelve in the fort. Break them, Fraser, and bring them back — and that will secure your captaincy."

Simon looked surprised. "I do not have it already... your lordship?"

Tullibardine slammed his fist on the table. "God damn it, man, how can I promote you in these circumstances? I'm all too aware it was my idea to have you join the army. But... things *happen* around you, Fraser. Things that could reflect badly on you, me, and your entire clan. You could have got my brother killed!" Simon went to reply but the earl held up his hand. "If I'm to believe you, it's all just bad fortune. But if that's so, it is down to you to change it. I advise you strongly: find a clean, soldier's way to follow these orders. It will lead to your captaincy." A shadow of a grin came across his face as he added: "In the meantime, Menzies will command your company."

"Sir? My lord?" that man said, surprised.

"Your orders, Captain Menzies, Lieutenant Fraser, Lieutenant Murray," the earl rapped, presenting papers. "I wish you good fortune." With those words he made it clear the interview had ended, and we all saluted as he left the chamber. After a moment, we filed through the other door and made our way into the bright sunshine.

"Thank you, sir," Simon sighed, nodding at Menzies while covering his eyes.

"It was nothing," said the other. "Although, it could have gone better for myself."

"I'm sorry about that. I did expect to be made captain of my own company – it was understood before I signed up."

"I have to agree with the colonel," Menzies said. "You're not making it easy for him to back you."

"Or for anyone else," Mungo added.

Simon sighed again. "I want the hair of the dog that bit me. And what a big dog it was. Bolla, time to earn your shilling." I was shaken out of my half-daze, but I need not have worried. "Send an express messenger to Lieutenant Charlie and have him bring himself and fourteen men to Canty Bay as soon as he can. The captain will write the orders – if you don't mind, sir?" Menzies scribbled onto a tablet while I waited, and handed a torn off sheet to me. "Meet us back in the ale-house when you're done," Simon told me, then added: "And tell Charlie to make sure he brings Neil Fraser of Bona." With that he turned to his superior officer. "What do you say we continue where we left off – over the table instead of under it?"

Menzies allowed a gentle laugh. "Well, to start with anyway."

By the time I had completed my brief task the three officers were sailing away from sobriety at a rapid rate; fuelled, I suspected, by the amount of drink remaining in Simon and Mungo's veins, along with the captain's clearly lesser abilities with his cups. All unpleasantness appeared forgotten as Mungo poured me a drink, gesturing that I should not interrupt my lord's speech.

"A very fine race indeed," he was saying, in continuation of his salute to the Clan Menzies.

"I know," said the captain, in a tone which indicated it was not the first time he had uttered the words.

"To hold their lands while others known for their swordsmanship – and their penmanship – tried their best to take them. Brave, and noble!"

"I know."

"Not the most numerous clan in Scotland. But then, God himself would have trouble finding the makings of many more of that quality."

"I know."

"How do you come to soldiering, then, sir?"

"I know —" Menzies took a moment to realise he had been asked a question. "Ah, well… same as everybody else, I expect: no inheritance and no money to speak of." Simon nodded understandingly. "To have risen to the rank of captain already… Besides, I always wanted to serve. To see some action."

"Aye, action — spectacular sport!" Simon slurred. "Your cousin, Major Duncan, wasn't it, who broke the government line at Killiecrankie? Now there's action!"

The captain frowned. "Duncan Menzies found himself on the wrong side of battle. We had good men fighting with Mackay."

"I did too, I did too," Simon said encouragingly, touching the captain on the shoulder. "Action, though. Here's to action in the king's name!" We smashed our cups together before he added, in the way he had done the night before: "Just don't ask me which king."

"Watch your words, lieutenant," Menzies said in a cold tone. "I know Clan Fraser finds itself recently changed of mind, but treason reamins treason."

Simon paused, shocked, but then laughed again. "Well, then, another toast – to action and the Lord Lovat's Company!" Cups clacked again and the moment seemed passed. Yet I watched carefully, and I was convinced a misunderstanding had arisen between the two. I glanced to see whether Mungo had gathered any of it; but he was intent on the task of drinking; and, soon, so was I.

IT SEEMED TO ME that the road from Edinburgh to Canty Bay, which could easily have been travelled in one long day, became no more than an endless row of inns and ale-houses of various quality – even the worst of which we deemed as acceptable surrounding for our happy company. My lord (who frequently extended that company with the addition of local womenfolk) countered Captain Menzies' urges for speed by explaining, hands wide open and apart, that we could achieve nothing until Lieutenant Fraser arrived from Inverness, a charge which our commanding officer found more easy to accept every time it was pressed. It was a warm, still summer which leaned towards the unpleasant in the way of high temperature; but each slow, delayed step towards the coast brought us closer to a cool sea breeze. It was a delight to arrive at our destination to behold a pleasant and inviting inn, where we were to be billeted, overlooking a small beach. To the east Berwick Law rose up above the flat lands, while to the west stood the silent ruin of the once-great Tantallon Castle; yet the scene was dominated by neither of these. Instead our eyes were drawn to the Bass Rock itself, a white monster of stone which seemed to have been lain there entirely by powers other than nature. It stood in the near-still waters of the the firth of Forth, its steep sheer sides soaring high into the air, topped by a clearly treacherously steep slope; while, around it, a cloud of countless thousands of birds spun and wove endlessly.

"That's a big boat," Mungo said after time, referring to the three-mast vessel settled in the sunset scene within the bay.

"That's a crock of *cac*," replied Simon. "Don't you remember the ships at Aberdeen? It's a flyboat, and it's an old one at that. But it looks like that's what we've been given."

"Well, let's get out there," Menzies said after a doubtful pause.

We made our way down to the beach, where Simon pointed to a small skiff on which a man busied himself with work, while all the other vessels appeared abandoned. "Hello!" the Fox cried. "Will you take us out to that flyboat?" he asked.

"Who's asking?" came the reply.

"I'm the Young MacShimi," said my lord with an elaborate bow. "Who's asking me?"

"Vinner, son of Vinner," the sailor called back.

"Vinner? I've not heard that name, my friend — where's it from?"

As ever, his personal deportment won him that which he intended to receive, and minutes later we were being taken out of the harbour aboard the single-masted boat while Vinner discussed the history of his father's name with Simon. "So you're off to see Dandy Dapperman?" he asked my lord between measured breaths.

Simon laughed from his seat and let his arm slip over the side. "Dandy Dapperman? *Ochone*, it's a day for new names. Don't you mean Ackermann? I think he's Dutch."

"Aye, his real name's Ackermann," Vinner replied with a roll of his eyes. "But they call him Dapperman. You'll work it out for yourself."

In time he pressed his oars against the bow of the flyboat and called up to its deck – which was not entirely as poor in appearance as Simon had suggested. There was a great lion carved upon her prow and another on the side of her stern that I could see, so that I assumed there to be a third on the other side. Six closed gunports attested to at least a reasonable amount of firepower, and I could make out small cannon fore and aft on the vessel's deck; presumably, again, there was the same configuration on her far side.

At that moment a dishevelled-looking sailor peered down at us and called out: "*Wat wil je?*"

Simon made to shout back but instead Menzies stood up and announced: "Throw down a ladder in the name of the King!"

The sailor turned away and held a brief conversation with someone behind them, then a rope ladder was lowered, and he shouted something in broken language which had the effect of: "Permission to come aboard." I had never climbed a rope ladder before, and soon had occasion to wish I should never face the challenge again. Of course I was the last of us to begin the ascent, by which time all but Mungo had arrived on the deck above, and none of them had to deal with the sensation of abandonment as the skiff disappeared from beneath me, leaving me nothing but deep, cold water to receive me if I fell. By the time a sailor grabbed my arm and pulled me over the last rung – during which I shortly became convinced I was indeed destined for the depths beneath – I expected I would have missed all introductions. Yet instead, I beheld my colleagues standing with bemused interest at the sight of a sailor engaged in a swordfight with one of the most overdressed gentlemen I had ever observed.

The exchange was clearly not in anger; nor was it a simple matching of blades. Instead the sailor was embarked upon a precise attempt to disarm the gentleman using a heavy cutlass against an ornate rapier. The most remarkable feature of the performance was not the ferocity and expertise of the swordsman; but that, despite the energy being expended, the gentleman kept up a commentary throughout. "No... no... yes!" He proceeded. "Pointless! You know I have more strength in my right. Now, strike! No, not like that, like... this! Yes! But from higher up... no... not even worth a word... strike... *alas!*"

I had not had time to notice at first, but those crewmen surrounding the display appeared to be far less engaged upon it than were we. It seemed strange once I had realised it – for there was no doubting the calibre of martial art on display. Then it was over: with a smooth solid movement the gentleman powered forward and the cutlass flew into the air, to land too far away to offer any hope of retrieval. The sailor, shocked to have been torn from his labours so quickly, stood, breathless, facing the gentleman, who stepped forward, rapier extended, then flashed it to the air before his face and bowed sharply. "You are good, Vonders, but you must listen more. Dismissed."

The sailor and his companions returned to their usual labours without any further acknowledgement of the gentleman's achievement – which, again, seemed notable. As he smoothly dropped his sword into its scabbard and approached us, however, I became more conscious of his elaborate apparel; an enormously-plumed black round hat over a tightly-curled periwig, and a carefully-powdered face with an elaborate twisting light moustache and chin-beard. Beneath he wore a dark purple cloak and deep red jacket and trews which billowed at his extremities, white bejewelled shirt and gloves, a white belt with a large gold buckle and knee-high leather boots dripping with gold ornaments. The effect was overwhelming as he bowed to us. "Sirs! I bid you welcome aboard the *Lion*!" he said in a heavily-accented voice, although it was much easier to follow than was Tullibardine's. "I have the pleasure of presenting myself Captain Diederick Ackermann – as you may have gathered." He stopped, presenting a gap-toothed grin as part of his delicate facial adornment, striking a pose as if he were prepared to remain statue-like while we admired him; and I was not the only one of us to be rendered unsure of how to proceed.

"In the name…" I heard Mungo mutter.

Finally Menzies spoke. "Captain Dapper — Ackermann, I am sent by Colonel the Lord John Murray," he said, presenting papers which the other opened with a flourish and read with head held so high above them that I was certain he could not make out the words.

"Captain Menzies," he said with a nod as if he were impressed, but pronouncing the name in the English style.

"Actually, it's 'Ming-iss'," he corrected.

124

"Of course it is," Ackermann said quickly. "I wasn't sure if you knew that. In the Highlands I would have said 'Ming-iss' right away, but I assumed since we were in the lowlands, on English business, you were probably a 'Men-zies'."

Our captain made to respond but decided to say nothing; which allowed Simon to join the fray. "Allow me to present myself Simon Fraser, the Young MacShimi, to be chief of the Clan Fraser," he said brightly.

"Ah, yes," replied Ackermann. "Lieutenant Fraser. And Lieutenant Murray – the Lord Mungo Murray? Lords and chiefs as lieutenants," he muttered to that man's response. "But, we all start as babes in arms. Good luck to you, gentlemen!" He bowed once more and Simon followed with enthusiasm.

"Captain, we are instructed to engage your assistance in a matter of military importance," Menzies said, appearing to have recovered.

"The Bass Rock," Ackermann nodded. "I'm sure I could deal with it myself, but of course I'm not part of your navy. Such as it is. But I have sailed on your *Janet*. A fair vessel – considering."

"Better than a flyboat," Mungo said under his breath.

Yet Ackermann caught his words. "No it's not," he said, then corrected his manner. "The *Lion* is not a flyboat, Lord Mungo. That's an English term. She's a fluyt, from the Dutch word for flute, named after the gracious shape of the hull. She's sleeker, more manoeuvrable and lighter than anything you can build. She can be managed with just twelve crew, and she can carry a greater cargo than anything else on the seas. That's why the Dutch lead the world in merchanting. And the *Janet*, may I add, is a French frigate," he went on, adopting a tone even more haughty than his last. "Not built by you Scots, but captured, although refitted by you. I have as many guns on the *Lion*, a fluyt, as you have on your proudest warship!"

"Which is why we're lucky you're here," Simon cut in. "I'm sure your assistance will be invaluable in our little endeavour."

"An act of war is no little endeavour," Ackermann scolded. "If a life is in peril, the matter must be taken seriously."

"Then I have already learned a lesson from you, sir!" Simon grinned. "Tell me, what have you gathered about the rebels who hold the Bass?

Since you're sure you could deal with it yourself?"

The Dutchman wavered. "I haven't gathered anything," he said before recovering. "That is to say, it ill befits a guest in your land to go meddling without permission. Especially in matters of kingship. But, to me, your King William will always be the Marquis of Veere."

"Campvere?" Simon inquired.

"That's what you call it," Ackermann shrugged. "A great trading bond we have, the Scots and Dutch. It's kept you going as a country and made us rich all the world over —"

"Except the Indies," Simon interrupted, "Where fluyts are easy pickings. And the Americas, for the same reason."

My lord's warm grin made it impossible for Ackermann to acknowledge the wound. Instead he smiled back and snorted through his nose. "I love the Scots humour! But, Captain Menzies—" he used the Saxon pronunciation again — "have you brought a plan of attack? The Bass Rock is no easy piece of land to reclaim, as you can see." As if he had planned the move in advance, he bowed and stepped aside with hands gesturing towards the sea behind him, where the mountain grew out of the water, set in late evening shade and beautifully decorated by the colours of an oncoming dry dusk.

"Have you a telescope, Captain Dapperman?" Simon asked. He carefully tripped over his pronunciation so no one could be sure whether or not he had actually said "Dapperman" – a trick I suspect he had been practicing in silence for some moments ahead of its performance.

"No," Ackermann replied. "But I do have a Lippershey glass."

"I'm sorry?" my lord asked, ready to laugh at the absurdity of the conversation.

"The telescope, as you call it, is an adaptation of a Dutch invention – the viewing glass was invented by my countryman, Lippershey."

"So he does have a telescope," Mungo said to no one in particular.

"Yes," Simon replied, making his response seem as if it had been directed to Ackermann. "May I borrow it, sir?" With another flourish and an unrepressed sigh from Mungo, the Dutchman drew a battered old metal tube from a pocket and held it out for Simon, who took it, pulled it to its full length and placed it to his eye. "It's not a crock of *cac*, it's a fluyt," he muttered, before exclaiming: "The birds!"

"Solan geese," Ackermann said. "Tens of thousands of them live on the Bass. You see it looks white? That's their droppings. You'll smell them before you hear them, I warrant."

"How is the fort supplied?" Mungo asked.

The sea captain shrugged. "They have two small boats, taken out of the water by derrick and stored on land. They drop one in the water and sail north or south, depending on where the navy scouts are – if there are any."

"You haven't intercepted?" Simon inquired.

"I would have done, and made fast work of it. But my... agreement with your government is to keep my distance, and only patrol if there are larger vessels nearby."

"Agreement?" Menzies repeated.

Ackermann shrugged again. "I have been pleased to make an arrangement —"

"Trading rights," Simon cut in.

"— with Edinburgh. If you ask me, it would be easy work for two or three navy vessels to capture the boats from the rock, were they only manned by Dutchmen and not commanded by the Royal Scots Navy." he expressed mock concern with his eyebrows. "Your Admiralty is not the best of your naval service."

"We know it," Simon said, looking through, then at, the tube he bore. "I think we're too far away. We'll need to get closer to the Bass."

"Tomorrow night is best," Ackermann replied. "No moon. I was just correcting the navy tables this afternoon."

"Ideal," Simon said, turning to Mungo and me. "I need to go and buy a telescope." Even Menzies came close to forgetting himself.

IF THE CREW OF THE *LION* had become practiced in remaining quiet for fear of becoming involved in conversation with their captain, then his influence served us well as the Dutch proved the efficacy of their vessel. Our small company of Frasers having arrived the next afternoon, when Simon had returned with his new telescope, the *Lion* waited until the sun set then pulled out of the shelter of Canty Bay in near silence, matched by the almost dead-calm waters beneath her. It could not be said to be fully dark (it never can be so in Scotland in summer, unless the clouds hang heavy) yet it was certainly so shaded that she would not be instantly detectable. As she moved closer – the crew pulling and pushing on wooden wheels and blocks to control ropes which operated the sails – the size of the island became increasingly apparent. On three sides it rose steeply from the water to a height many times that of our vessel; while on the side facing the south it climbed less steeply, although still extreme enough to offer a challenge to traversing it. I beheld the lights of what I thought was a small house, but on closer approach I could make out the extent of a reasonably-sized castle with three main buildings. There came a flash of light and the sound of an explosion – Ackermann assured us it was simply a warning cannonshot, and he doubted whether there was any ball in flight – and shortly we sailed round and away from the south face, the better to keep away from any real threat. As we came closer it was apparent that keeping silence was not an issue, for the countless large white birds which lived upon the rock created an endless cacophony of high-pitched cries, which served to give the impression that an unimaginably large group of people were conducting an animated conversation, all speaking at once.

"Fraser of Bona!" Simon called, as our company stared at the giant rock, beholding the near impossibility of landing upon it. A thin, lithe character with strong lines upon his face and a gait which spoke of great strength stepped forward in effortless silence, his move more like a dance than a walk.

"Aye, Simon," he said with a soft voice, the pair of them peering upwards.

"It's impossible, isn't it, Neil?"

"Well…" the other said after a pause. "Let's keep looking."

"What are you thinking, Fraser?" Menzies asked.

"Neil is something of a climber," my lord explained. "He's happier on a cliff face than on the ground. I've seen him hanging off precipices with just one finger. Isn't that so, Neil?"

The clansman grinned. "Ach, it's a wee trick, just."

"So," the Fox continued, "I'm thinking that there's only one obvious way onto the Bass, and that's directly in front of the castle. We'd be shot down in seconds. We need a way to land one or two people out of sight and arrange things in the castle, so that, by the time we're landing, it's impossible to stop us."

Menzies was unsure, but his expression revealed he could offer no solution to a problem Simon had clearly defined. "And?" he asked shortly.

"And," my lord replied, "it's impossible, I fear. Is it so, Neil?"

"Let's keep looking," that one said again, and we continued staring at the wall of rock as the *Lion* sailed round. Eventually Ackermann observed that to continue onward to the south side would result in our being caught within easy distance of the castle guns, and ordered his crew to change course.

"Aye, impossible," Simon sighed.

"Actually, it's not," Bona said suddenly.

"Is that right? How will you do it?"

Neil pointed towards a recess in the west face of the Bass, where an inlet the size of several boats lay. "I'll use that rope."

"Rope?" Simon cried, pulling out his telescope.

"Have you ever eaten solan goose?" Neil asked. "It's a great delicacy, in high demand on the tables of the well-to-do. It stands to reason some folk would have found a way to take a few."

My lord, who almost certainly could not make out the detail he required, turned to his clansman. "Sharp-eyed *gorach*," he grinned. "So what do you need?"

The other shrugged. "Just get me to the bottom of the cliff. The rest depends on what you've got planned."

"What have you planned, Fraser?" Menzies asked.

"Test my thinking, sir," the Fox offered. "Neil and one or two others get on by night, find out what they can about the castle and its garrison, then climb down again. We pick them up, make up a course of action from what they tell us, then put them back on. They go down and get the gates open — and we're waiting for them on the other side."

"That's not even near half a plan," the captain replied scornfully. "You can't be sure they'll come back. Or that that they'll have anything useful to tell us if they do."

129

"I await your suggestions, sir," Simon said with a blank look.

Menzies took off his hat and ran his fingers through what remained of his hair, staring up at the huge body of stone which bore down upon all our thoughts. "What if it doesn't work?" he said at last. "What if we arrive to find the castle ready to be defended?"

"There'll always a risk, sir," my lord said. "That's what happens... with action."

After a long pause, during which Simon made a point of not moving so much as a finger, Menzies nodded. "When, then?"

"There's no moon tonight, or tomorrow," Ackermann said.

""I can go right now," Neil said. 'If you can get me into that bay."

"Easily," the Dutchman grinned with a flourish. "Captain Menzies?"

"Alright," the commander nodded. "Do it. But don't get it wrong. And don't make it any more difficult than it needs be."

Bona asked for a spare rope, in case the one he had seen was not to be relied upon. Supplying it, Ackermann explained he was sorry to offer a left-handed rope when he would recommend a right-handed one for an endeavour such as his. Simon then demonstrated a little too much satisfaction when Neil asked for a wide-brimmed hat to fend off bird droppings from above; my lord's response was to snatch the Dutchman's elaborate headgear and give it to the clansman, who took his dirk and tore off the peak on its front. The strange-looking item in place, Bona declared himself ready – and when he suggested that two of us went with him, I realised Simon would send me, and was not proved wrong.

Neil, one Private Dougal Fraser and I were lowered onto the water in a cutter, in which six of the *Lion*'s crew rowed us swiftly into the recess the climber had chosen. Within, the sense of disorientation was overwhelming as the calls of solan geese far above combined with the echoes of water lapping against the walls of stone. It felt as if we were contained within a solid chamber of rock, as the edges of the fault climbed out of the water so steeply that we could lean against them from the boat. Indeed, that is how we steadied ourselves as we clambered from the vessel onto a lonely outcrop of stone above the waterline.

Neil bade us wait until the cutter had departed, then spent some moments pulling on the rope to ensure it was safe. "It's going to be slippy with bird *cac*," he told Dougal and I. "Take it slow, and put your feet exactly where I put mine. It won't be difficult but it'll take a wee while." He began to climb and Dougal followed, then I came last, my eyes keen upon making out where footsteps fell in the dark, while the bird calls echoed strangely around us and the dark waves whispered below.

Of a sudden, Dougal fell — I could not make out how, and I do not know how I managed to prevent following him as his full weight struck me from above and he plummeted past to the rock below. "Get down!" Neil cried from above. "Get back down!" I froze, terrified, as he used the rope to swing himself off the cliff and drop at a great rate, the movement he caused leading my own footing to falter; but I think he realised his reaction was putting me in danger, for he stopped just above me and told me to make my way downward as carefully as I could. "We're coming down, Dougal!" he called. "Are you alright?"

"I've broken my leg!" came the response.

Neil swore every step of the descent, which, at least, was nowhere near as long as it could have been. There was only just enough room for him to lean over the sprawled dragoon while I stood aside, clinging to the cliff for security. "You're not joking," Bona said as he examined Dougal's leg, to some cursing from the victim. "You're going to have to stay here. We'll have to come back and get you later."

"What about the tide?" Dougal asked — a wise question.

Neil glanced round. "Look at the water marks," he said. "You're above high tide, and it's not far off now."

Neil felt in his pocket and offered him a flask of whisky. "I've got my own."

"Have mine too — it's going to be a cold one tonight."

Dougal readily agreed, and, with some issue, we managed to wrap him in his plaid and sit him as comfortably as possible. Bona again vowed we would return, but just as he began climbing again he added: "It might be tomorrow." The wounded man could do nothing but nod acceptance; and soon he was some distance beneath us as I followed the climber's steps as accurately as I might. All the time I was aware that, should either of us lose our footing, it would almost certainly be fatal for he who lay at the bottom of the cliff. Every time I felt my grip

131

slide on the rope, or my foot slip against the cliff, I became sure I was set to rejoin Dougal much sooner than he expected. It seemed like an eternity, but in truth I do not think it was very long before Neil dragged me, gasping in agony, onto the surface of the Bass Rock. I immediately beheld we were nowhere near the top, for the island loomed steeply above us to the north, and almost equally steeply to the south, where we could see a few points of light from the castle.

"Are you well?" Bona said loudly, to be heard above the protesting birds all around us, some of which flapped their wings in fury, although few left the holes in the ground they used for nests, and none came close. "What a God-forsaken stench!"

"Yes," I replied equally loudly to both of his points. "What next?"

"There's that building," he said, pointing to a roofless structure not far away. "Probably best to stay there for a while. We'll take a look at the castle when it's lighter." First, however, he located a large, solid outcrop of rock to which the rope was secured, and tied the new one around it, hiding the rest of its length among the stones.

We made our way along an old path until we arrived at the building, a small, ancient ruin which offered little shelter from the sky but at least some from the constant cries of solan geese. I raised a fire from wood which, I think, had once been part of the roof, while Neil disappeared for some minutes before returning with two newly-killed birds, which he had soon prepared for cooking. It was not without a pleasing taste, although Neil told me the eggs and chicks were regarded as a delicacy rather than the older creatures we feasted upon; sadly, it was too late in the year to sample such delights. As we sat back in our plaids, sharing my flask of whisky, I began to believe the evening would prove to be an almost enjoyable one. Yet it was not to be, for the weather rapidly turned on us – and as cloud cast the night into complete darkness and the wind and rain exploded around us, I heard a new sound: seemingly the very noise of Hell itself, thundering up through the Bass. "What causes that?" I said, in no little fear.

"It's likely a betrayed water beastie," Neil replied. "Calling the name of the one who was false."

"What do you mean?"

"The poor creatures are everywhere," the other said, the strong lines of his face highlighted by the flames before us. "There was once a wee princess crying by the edge of a loch. A water beastie came up and asked her what was wrong. She said, 'I've to marry a man I don't love.' The beastie said, 'Climb on my back and I'll take you to Ireland, where there's a man who needs your love.' So she did, and she found the man, and she fell in love. She thanked the water beastie, who told her its name and said, 'On the very moment you get married, say my name three times and I'll be set free from this form into my real form – for I too am a princess, only bewitched by a jealous stepmother.' The princess promised she'd do just that.

"But on the day she got married, she was so happy she forgot all about the water beastie. She didn't say its name one time, never mind three, and it's still out there, calling out for the princess to help it, crying her name when the wind blows and the seas rage."

I said nothing for a time, watching Bona's face as he fell silent. Eventually I asked, "What was the princess' name?"

"You listen," Neil said, and I set my mind upon the terrifying noise from beneath us.

Finally I ventured, "Mona?"

"Maybe," Neil said. "It depends where you listen. The sea is full of beasties with broken hearts, with broken promises from princesses." He shook his head. "Most women think they could be a princess – but they end up as jealous stepmothers."

Sensing a downward mood, I changed the subject. "What do you think of Simon?" I asked.

"As little as possible," he replied, a quizzical grin giving him the look of a gargoyle from some ancient church. I offered no comment and he continued: "I'm meant to be the laird of Bona. Maybe thirty, forty people, I'm supposed to look after. I'm not interested – my brother is laird in my place. But Simon… he wants to be MacShimi. I don't follow his mind." He stared into the fire. "It probably takes someone who wants it to be good at it. God knows Hugh's no use. He'd rather be drinking with his family in London."

"So would Simon, I think," I said softly.

"Ah, but he doesn't, does he?" Neil replied, waving a finger to demonstrate he'd come upon an important issue. "He used to – he used to spend months in London, drunk with Hugh, while Lord Tom got on with running the clan. But he doesn't any more. He didn't want to join the army, I hear. Hugh and Tom told him the clan would be in trouble if he didn't, so he did."

"There is some truth in that," I offered cautiously.

"I wouldn't know. All I know is I get paid. I get to climb and explore. So I can't complain about Simon."

"How did you come to find an interest in climbing?"

Bona's face tightened for a moment. "Where I grew up," he said, "there's a castle on a wee island. They call it the Castle of Spirits – and they're right to. If you think this place is scary you should hear the sound of the trees around the castle when it's dark like tonight. It's said every one is the spirit of a murdered man, waiting to take revenge on whoever killed him. And if they can't find him, they'll take revenge on whoever they can reach.

"I got stuck there one night when I was young," he continued, staring into the flames for a long moment. "They let me live. But I realised the spirits – the trees – got their power from being so close to the loch. After that I went climbing, so I'd be as far away as possible from that power. I've been climbing ever since. It's a different world up there, away from battles for land, battles for thrones and water beasties. This here is just a wee hint. Here – come on!"

Despite the weather he urged me out of my relaxed position and led me, step by careful step, higher up the slope of the rock than I felt was safe. "Isn't this amazing?" he asked calmly, although his voice was raised above the storm. I had to admit to a sensation of being separated from the world I knew: a feeling of apartness, that the concerns of those below us were not mine. It quickly passed as a powerful gust of wind near threw me from my feet, and Neil led me quickly back to our shelter. From there we listened to the thundering rage around us for a time longer; and, again, I was forced to allow that I had experienced nothing like it before (although I preferred not to comment upon whether I would want to again); then it occurred to me that Neil spoke of sea monsters in the same breath as clansmen – and it seemed odd. "Do you believe in the beasties, then?" I asked.

"I've seen them," he told me shortly, with a tone which suggested there could be no argument.

"You will tell me next you have seen the one in Loch Ness."

Without directly facing me he rolled his eyes to present a fixed stare. "Aye," he said firmly.

"Really?"

"Aye," he repeated with more cheer in his tone. "But I don't think anyone will see her again. The last person she spoke to was St Columba – and he tried to curse her. Ordered her to hide her face from menfolk for the rest of forever."

"It seems to have worked, more or less."

"That it didn't," Neil grinned. "She just decided she couldn't be doing with our *cac*."

"I HEAR THERE'S TWENTY-ONE BARRELS of that new drink, port, in the castle," Simon said. "Funny that – there's twenty-one of us, isn't there?" The men on the lower deck of the *Lion* snarled an almost animal laugh; they were ready for a fight. Too much time in cantonment at Inverness had left them like dogs kept unfed to turn them mad.

"Lieutenant Fraser," called Menzies, "Your attention, please. It is vital we get this right."

"Sorry, sir," the Fox replied, saluting smartly to the captain, who stood above us upon the stair leading from the *Lion*'s afterdeck; while, from above, we could hear Dutchmen shouting as they prepared to set sail once more.

"Sergeant Fraser, you will correct me if I miss my mark?" the captain asked.

"Yes, sir," said I, giving Bona, who stood beside me, a short glance – for in truth I was concerned that I might mistake the details of what we had seen on the Bass myself, since we had had no sleep during our hours upon the rock, even after the storm abated, nor since we had been collected. We had briefly scouted the interior of the castle from above at first light, before returning to where Bona had secured his new rope, then climbed down the cliff to rescue the injured Dougal (who was in better condition than we, I felt, since he had slept) and returned to the ship by cutter. Despite Canty Bay's distance from the island I felt

135

certain I could still hear the noise of Hell and the relentless screech of countless birds.

"The castle is not well defended," Menzies told his assembled troops. "There may be as many as twenty enemies or as few as eight. We will land in plain sight of the ramparts, so caution is of the essence. There is a curtain wall with a small gate, which will be opened for us —" here he nodded towards Bona and I — "allowing us access to a courtyard where two boats are stored out of the water. A small unit will drop them off the rock, so that our enemies are without the means to resupply themselves. Meanwhile, another unit will enter the castle by its main gate, which will already be open —" again he nodded at us — "and fire the stores. At that point, if it is easily possible to overwhelm the enemy, we will do so. If it is judged not so easy, we will retire and leave them to surrender in due course."

"No we'll not – we'll fight!" growled an unidentified clansman.

"I'm looking forward to it," Ackermann said quietly from his place beside Simon. "Although I doubt they'll be a challenge to me."

"Our orders are to secure the castle's surrender!" Menzies barked. "There will be no fighting if it is deemed too risky."

"But there's eight of them and nearly two dozen of us," the Dutchman said. "It makes sense to —"

"It makes sense to follow orders in the simplest way possible! Minimal risk means minimal chance of failing."

"Minimal chance of action," Simon said sullenly.

"I will decide!" Menzies cried. "And you will all remember it!" There came no reply, and after glaring round the deck, but failing to meet any eyes, he climbed the stair and disappeared. Ackermann, Mungo and Lieutenant Charlie followed him, but as I made to ascend I sensed Simon turning away behind me. "One wee thing, lads…" I heard him begin, but I caught no more.

With dusk fallen and the brief voyage to the far side of the rock completed once more, two cutters descended from the *Lion*: the one carrying Bona and me, to make our third excursion upon the hidden cliff, and the other containing the rest of our party, who would be waiting in position for our arrival. The climb was easier for the use of the new rope, unscarred by seasons of storms and bird droppings; and

Bona, who led again, made use once more of Ackermann's hat, the sea captain having refused its return upon seeing its condition. Once upon the clifftop we followed the steep downward path discovered the previous night, until, very soon, we were close to the main rampart of the castle. It crossed the full width of the accessible part of the lower island, with one gate leading to the courtyard where lay the boats, and on to the outer defensive wall, with a second gate, leading down to the water. Above all, towering around us in fact and in thought, were three large keeps – from which one man's voice could end our endeavour.

The first gate required only the lifting of a well-greased bar to open it, the which we did carefully and silently – although the noise of solan geese meant such caution was not necessary. That done, we pulled it shut behind us. As we crept towards the small outer gate, pressed tight against the outer wall where it met the main rampart, we knew we could not be seen from above, and it was difficult to think otherwise than that the worst of the night was over.

Opening the second gate presented no more problems than had the first; and on doing so we beheld the shadows of our main force, crawling, bent double against the outer wall, towards us. Once all were within the first courtyard, Menzies gestured towards the two boats and the derrick used to lower them. "We can take both from out of their hands," he said, just loudly enough for all to hear. "The store rooms are dead ahead through there —" he pointed towards the second gate — "and we can easily fire them. Fraser, detail ten men to lower the boats, and take the others to set the fires."

Ackermann looked unhappy. "Since we are here and undiscovered, why don't we just walk in, fight and end the siege?" he said.

"Because we find the simplest way to follow our orders," Menzies replied impatiently. "That's the rule of good soldiering – captain."

I looked at Simon, and I believe Mungo did too, but he offered nothing to the discussion. Instead he said: "Bolla, Neil, with me." Bona grinned encouragingly at me as we moved towards the inner gate, leaving Menzies with the task of dropping the boats into the sea, from where they could not be recovered by those on the rock. Slowly I pushed the gate open, every bird's screech matched by an urgent thought of how we could be undone in the next moment; and yet the courtyard was as we had left it: dark, empty and silent, with the three keeps looming over us, and one light in the main tower the only sign of occupation.

I waited as Simon gestured for one small group of men to move toward the furthest-away keep, then signalled for me to take four others to the building before us; while he, Bona and three more made for the only one we knew to be inhabited. Carefully I crept toward my target, once again finding the door open; but as my eyes adjusted to the gloom I beheld there was nothing in the store, save a bundle of empty sacks, which were not worth the burning. I waved for my men to turn back for the wall; and we were mid-way through that cautious navigation — when, from my left, I heard Simon shout: "Fire!" and his men launched a volley of musket shot.

I swear they shot into the air rather than at any real target, for there was none to be seen. Just moments later came a reaction from the tower above in the form of shouting, a door opening and a number of bodies appearing on the rampart, complete with weapons. Our position was such that our enemies were mere paces away from us, and far above, meaning they could draw fire upon us easily – especially if they were given more time to prepare. "To arms!" I cried to those with me – but by the time they understood me I heard a gunshot from terrifyingly close range and found myself blinded by the flash of fire.

"To the gate!" I shouted and began stumbling towards where I believed it lay – yet the agonised moans I heard from around me told that not all my companions were able to follow me. Several more shots rang out from above, and some balls bounced off stone near me, forcing me to change my direction and lose my footing. As I crawled blindly towards the outer gate, I became aware of Simon's men returning fire, and it seemed to draw attention away from me.

There came a pause in shooting, but not in shouting, while the combatants reloaded their weapons. I felt an arm thrown round my shoulder and I was lifted to my feet as Simon's voice said, "Run with me, Bolla!" He led me to where I knew the gate stood, even though I could not see it, and I confess my running was more an exercise in raising my feet and pushing against him in the hope of remaining upright. He led me onwards towards the outer gate, and I heard more of our party come alongside us; then, just as my sight began to return, I found myself forced down steep, damp steps cut out of the rock, all but falling into the water as I went, and then I was thrown into our cutter and told to remain still, while the Fox gave the same instructions to others, who collapsed beside me, breathing harshly.

A volley of shot burst towards us, but landed nowhere near, and I realised they had not been aimed directly at us – instead our enemies were shooting for three figures, who had only just emerged from the outer gate and were being pursued by men from the castle garrison.

"Cast off!" cried Menzies, seated near me. "Go!"

"No! Don't move!" Simon shouted furiously.

Our companions began their painfully delicate climb in darkness, an act more likely to send them into the water than the boat – and it was clear they could not complete the task in time. Just as the last started to descent, two of the enemies caught him up, and I saw him turn to face what was about to befall him. The chasing shadows had raised swords, and in a fraction of a moment so did our man, and I realised it could only be Ackermann. "Cast off!" the sea captain shouted as he turned to take on his opposition, which now numbered three.

"No!" Simon shouted again. "Get down here!"

I could not credit what I next heard: Ackermann began fending off three swordsmen on a treacherous ledge – while commenting on their bladework. "Pointless! What was that to achieve? No…No… not even close! Yours is a single-edge sword — it doesn't do that! Yes, but if I sweep like this… See? No, you missed — *alas*!" Suddenly one of them fell, crying out in pain, and another followed. Two more men behind, but their fallen companions appeared to be blocking any hope they had of catching Ackermann. Even so, the Dutchman reached forward with his blade and dealt a piercing blow to another enemy, who joined his associates on the stone.

"Dapperman! Move!" Simon shouted, to which I made out the Dutchman sketching a bow towards his foes in the darkness, then leaping from the rock into the boat.

"Now, Beeks, will you please cast off?" he said, hardly breathing heavily at all.

The sailor had not waited for the request; we were already moving

139

off. "Fast as you can, boys," said Simon. His urgency was soon justified: an explosion of cannon came from the battlements, and we were nothing close to far enough away. Yet we were not struck. "Leather guns," Simon said. "Can't hit a crock of *cac*. Or us."

At that one of our men spluttered a short laugh, and I realised it was Mungo. Simon soon joined in; but Menzies silenced them with one command: "Count off." In detailing who was present, we soon knew who was not. We had lost six men: three privates in the outer courtyard, Lieutenant Charlie beyond the outer wall, and two more privates in the inner courtyard — and one, to my anguish, was Neil Fraser of Bona.

I had been closer to losing my life in my begging days, and I may have been closer than I had known in previous adventures with Simon. Yet the harsh, monstrous horror of gunfire at close range on that animal island felt more stark than anything I had previously encountered. A beast of Hell had breathed fire upon me and I had escaped with no more than a singe, while three men within my arms' reach – and he who had so lately offered me an unseen aspect of the world around me – had been burnt to ashes. As our cutter was wound back on board and made secure, the weather began to change as it had the previous night; and in almost no time at all, the ever-present cries of the solan geese was joined by the accursed noise from within the Bass Rock itself.

Ackermann ordered the *Lion* back to port, called for brandy to be served, and summoned his two officers to a gathering on the afterdeck, where I could hear him regaling them with an account of his recent bravery. There was no need for him to add fiction to his endeavour, but almost as soon as he began to speak he was introducing creative elements to his narrative. (I am convinced he claimed an eagle swooped upon him during his sword fight.) Having ensured our remaining men were free of dangerous injury, I joined our officers on the foredeck, where Captain Menzies was listening to Simon's account of what had taken place on the rock – and was clearly finding a challenge in the control of his sentiments.

"I trust Neil Fraser with my life," my lord was saying in agitation. "If he says he saw —"

"Neil Fraser of Bona trusted *you* with *his* life," Menzies interrupted. "And he lost it."

Simon fell silent for a moment, then continued in a more measured tone. "Neil pointed to the castle and said: 'They're moving.' I was right beside him when he did it. Private Neil is — *was* — one of the best huntsmen in the clan. His eyes were sharper at night than they were in day. And if Private Neil tells me he can see movement, I'll believe him even when I can't. Sir."

"You gave an order to fire?"

"Yes, sir."

"At *what*, Lieutenant Fraser?"

Simon shook his head. "At whatever Neil told me to fire at."

Menzies shook his head in turn. "You're telling me you broke our cover because someone told you they saw something that no one else saw. It's clear to me the reason no one else saw anything was there was nothing to see. This was to be an easy mission —"

"We lost them one of their boats, sir. I'd say that's a partial success."

"*I* lost them one of their boats! And it doesn't matter – there's only about eight of them, maybe fewer now. One boat is all they need! And the cost, man… the cost! Six dead! Is that how a Fraser chief looks after his clansmen?"

Simon said nothing for a moment. "I know my men," he said quietly. "Every man, woman and bairn called Fraser is my responsibility. They trust me, and I trust them. Neil Fraser told me he saw something. I believed him. I still do, sir."

The captain moved in close to Simon and met his gaze. "Some might talk of murder," he said quietly.

My lord looked back at him. "Some might talk of action," he replied evenly.

They both held their ground in a silent battle. Menzies, it seemed to me, was struggling with so many accusations in his head that he was at a loss to select just one to deliver. Finally he muttered "Dismissed," and strode away, leaving my lord seeming forlorn for a moment. He turned to face Mungo and me, looking us both in the eye in turn; but neither of us said anything, although we returned his gaze. It seemed to me he wanted to explain something, but only if another would ask it of him; and regardless of how Mungo considered the situation, I could not formulate an appropriate question.

"Come on, let's get a bloody drink," he said at last, and we followed him to the afterdeck, where Ackermann was still fighting off men and beasts on the island, to the dull middle-distance glares of his officers.

"One of the fools didn't even know his sword had only one sharp edge," he was saying. "Isn't that how it was, Fraser?"

"What? Aye. You stabbed a few *gorachs*, Dapperman. Well done." Both Dutch officers failed to stifle a short laugh, and Ackermann, finally lost for something to say, looked in several directions before offering a dry cough and moving quietly away. "Thank God for silence," Simon said, gesturing for a bottle of brandy. "Ding doon Tantallon... mak' a brig to the Bass!" He laughed shortly. Yet I could still hear the distant furious noise of the rock as we sailed back towards Canty Bay, and the rain began to assail us with strength.

BEFORE THE SUN was fully risen it was apparent our mission had been more successful than we first imagined; for the first sight to appear in the lightening sky was a great plume of smoke growing out of the island. It could only be the castle stores burning. The development lent a small amount of cheer to our proceedings later that day, when we went ashore for a council-of-war at the inn. Several bottles of wine were consumed during the conversation, but I observed Menzies retaining a distant attitude towards Simon, even though he was not fully dismissive of his company. My lord, for his part, appeared to accept the captain's position, turning instead to Ackermann for entertainment. "The Scottish Staple," said the Dutchman, "is a prime example of how a great nation like ours can help a... friend like Scotland. For many years now you have enjoyed the advantage of low taxes on the export of wool, coal, whisky and flax. We pay you a fair price and sell on to a far greater number of customer than you could ever hope to attract on your own."

"It sounds like paradise," Simon said encouragingly.

"Well, there's no such thing as paradise," the sea captain replied without a change of tone, "But it's certainly a wonderful place. The Ackermann family are among the foremost merchants in Veere. We have even intermarried with the Scots. It's difficult not to – more than half the townspeople are from here. And why wouldn't they be? With their own laws, taxation and even their own church, and the prospect of merchant riches... it's any man's dream to be in Veere."

"Indeed," Simon said. "What made you leave?"

"Oh, you have to leave to enjoy it the more when you go back," Ackermann replied. "And my father wants me to learn the business from the ground up. That's why I'm a sailor just now – but I'll be a gentleman merchant in a few years. Have you seen the tiled roofs of Fife?" he went on. "If you see a tiled roof, and there are lots of them in Fife, it's a sign of someone who's made his money thanks to Veere. We use our tiles as ballast, you see, then sell them to Scots merchants when we fill our ships with their stock. It's perfect roofing against Scottish rain."

Even Simon was finding it difficult to feign interest in the constant monologue; and that was one of the reasons he jumped to his feet, delighted, when one of the *Lion*'s crew entered the inn. "Aha — here's news!" my lord shouted.

"What is it, Beeks?" said Ackermann in English, but the sailor replied in Dutch, meaning we were not acquainted with developments until he had left. Afterwards the sea captain told Menzies: "It would seem the rebels want to parlay. They want to send a boat to the *Lion*."

"They want to send *the* boat," Simon emphasised.

"Murray, you and I will go," said Menzies, abandoning his silent disposition. "Captain Ackermann, I require you to remain on land with Lieutenant Fraser, to watch proceedings from a safe distance. If anything happens to us, you are to send to Edinburgh for new orders. Is that clear?" He directed that last at Simon, who confirmed his understanding. The Dutchman made a show of being more interested in the wine than in military developments, suggesting he was satisfied with a lack of participation.

Yet soon after Menzies followed the sailor to the harbour and onward to the ship, the three of us who remained were stood outside the inn. I took care of the wine while Simon and Ackermann peered towards the *Lion* with their telescopes. "I see their boat," said the Dutchman. "A skiff with a single mast. But I can't make out how many are aboard."

"Three," Simon replied. "Under a white flag of parley."

"It might be the flag of France," Ackermann said. "It's white too." He did not observe the pointed stare Simon gave him as he briefly removed his eye from his spyglass. "The Auld Alliance, you see, Fraser. But it might have some *fleur de lys* if it's French."

"It doesn't."

"Don't be ridiculous – how can you tell from this distance?"

Simon looked over at me and made an act of striking the other with his telescope. "Perhaps my telescope is cleaner than your, what was it, Dapperman stick?"

"Lippershey glass," said Ackermann without any sign of being aware he was the subject of derision. "And it's unlikely – good glasses improve with age."

"Yeah, the more you use them the brighter they get," my lord said with a roll of his eyes.

"Exactly," replied Ackermann. They continued to watch as the boat from the Bass approached the ship, and even lacking a telescope I beheld Menzies and Mungo boarding under the white flag before it began its return journey. "I didn't see them getting into the boat," the Dutchman muttered.

"They did. They're sitting at the back, side by side. Captain Menzies is waving to the *Lion*."

"Oh, yes. Sorry – I was admiring my ship instead of looking at them. Do you know it's named after a lion my family once gifted to King James the Fifth?"

"You gave James the Fifth a lion called '*Lion*'?"

"I didn't say it was me. It was my family."

"I need a drink," Simon said, closing his telescope and taking the bottle from my grasp. Ackermann made to follow but my lord observed casually: "It's amazing, Dapperman, it really is."

"What is?"

"Well, the fact that you have so few crew on your ship, and yet they can obviously run it perfectly without your input. I'll wager they could keep on trading for years without you."

Ackermann gave a dry cough. "Actually I was about to return to them," he said. "They're a good crew, you're right – but you don't really think they could do without me?"

Simon laughed. "Of course not! See you later," and turned away briskly, leaving the Dutchman no option but to bow with a flourish and retire. "Let's have a nice quiet dinner," my lord said as he directed us back to the inn. Our meal, and the drinks which followed, were indeed quiet; I had no desire to support Simon's efforts at making light conversation, and he was not disposed to forcing the issue. Our minds were set upon the matter of the recent deaths among our number, mine more so on the young laird I felt I had begun to know well after our night on the island. I do not believe the Fox's thoughts matched mine when it came to the matter of conclusions. He looked at me with that questioning gaze, but still I could not form a communication which would not raise too light a response, or too heavy. Eventually he introduced himself to some of the locals in the drinking room, and by the time I heard him climbing the stairs towards his chamber, with female company, I was asleep – or at least I wished him to think so.

The following afternoon found us taking wine, once again, upon the beach, with Ackermann's company proving as trying as ever. Our light discussion about the advantages of Veere (which Simon continued to call Campvere) was broken by the puffing noise of a far-away explosion. Without hesitation our eyes turned to the Bass, where we beheld three clouds of smoke rising from the castle area; and as we watched, the puffing associated with the lower two reached our ears. My companions at once opened their telescopes, but after a moment or two of frantic twisting and turning of the column, Ackermann gave up on his and asked Simon what was happening. "It's another fluyt," my lord reported. "It's too close to the Bass – it's trying to get away. They're firing down on it. Just leather guns, but at that distance they'll do enough damage to a ship that size."

"They must return fire!" Ackermann cried.

"I think they can only place one gun – but they're using it," Simon said as more clouds appeared. "They must have lured the Dutchman in. How did they do that? And why leather guns? They must have something better... they're in a damned castle!" In the coming moments, as more puffing noises reached us, Simon reported the ship had surrendered and moved in towards the dock. He could only make out small movements but they suggested that, after some discussion, the fluyt's crew were engaged upon carrying cargo onto the dock, under the armed watch of those who held the Bass. While Ackermann lamented the embarrassment to his countrymen, and asked no one in particular whether he was the only captain left with the sense to navigate through contested waters, Simon informed us that the Dutchman was leaving the island, and another boat was making towards us. It did not come all the way to Canty Bay, but stopped midway and engaged in a shouted discussion with a passing fishing boat, which then turned and passed a message to the *Lion* – by which time we were aboard. The message was simple, as translated by Ackermann from one of his sailors: "We have reprovisioned ourselves by capturing the fluyt. As a result we no longer wish to parlay, and Menzies and Mungo are our hostages."

"The bastards!" Simon said, yet there was some tone of approval in his voice. "Hah! Bass-tards! See what I did?"

"Indeed," Ackermann replied, missing it. "You must send to Edinburgh for orders."

"No time," my lord said. "We don't know what those people are capable of. My captain and my friend need me — I'm not waiting to be told to help them."

"Then, what do we do?" asked the sea captain.

"We need to act, tonight."

"So soon? Perhaps we should wait until their guard is down, like it was the other night."

"There isn't time!"

"Surely there's time to make the right plan?"

"No need. I know what to do — just give me half an hour." It did not take my lord so long before he sprang into action and began directing Ackermann through a list of instructions, in too low a voice for me to follow, although I saw the sea captain appeared to approve. Finally the pair nodded, Simon touched the other's shoulder and grinned, and came over to me while the other began issuing orders to his crew. "Time to earn your shilling, Bolla," he told me, and I was not surprised to hear those words. "Tonight it's just thee and me... but that's all it'll take."

Soon after midnight, when the still sky was adjudged as dark as it

146

was to become, the *Lion* stole away from Canty Bay to a point north-east of the Bass, far beyond the castle's line of sight, there to meet with two patrol boats of the Royal Scots Navy, a gathering Ackermann had arranged at Simon's bidding. The vessels were not together long; my lord and I jumped aboard one boat and made for the recessed cliff to the west, while the other headed to the east side and the *Lion* held position, ready to steer directly towards the enemy stronghold. All was arranged carefully upon a series of signals, designed such that our forces would see them all, and know what their colleagues were doing, while the castle would see none until it was too late.

We managed, through slow, carefully progression, to climb the rope left by Neil Fraser; and I was glad to hear my lord expressing amazement that I had now managed to traverse the cliff four times, this last the most challenging, since I had additional bulk upon my back in the form of a large torch. Soon enough we were crouched above the castle yard, within its furthest defences. "This bit's a right *scunner*, Bolla," Simon said in a voice that could have been lower. "But it has to be done. You know what you need to do?"

I nodded. "Go back up to the ruin," I repeated, "Then light the torch and wave it while coming slowly back down the hill."

"Really slow – one pace every five heartbeats. No faster. Got it?"

I nodded. "Then what?" I asked.

He paused. "Keep watch on my movements and follow me wherever I go." He gave me a strange look through the deep gloom, then touched my arm and grinned. "All will be well," he said. "God be with you." And he rushed off into the night.

Using the torch as a climbing aid, I scrambled directly up the slope rather than follow the less direct path I had taken previously. Such navigation was no thoughtless task, surrounded as I was by howling solan geese in their nesting holes. After looking back once I resolved not to do so again, for the extremity of the ascent offered the impression of a near-vertical drop. Behind the old building (I did not enter, my memories of my night there with Bona too distracting for the moment) I took out my tinder and fired the torch, waiting until it was fully ablaze before turning it out towards the waters beyond the castle. A few moments later I saw a light flash briefly from somewhere on the firth, soon extinguished because its message had been sent. Our action had begun.

Almost immediately I saw more flashes, followed by the rumble of explosions, and then more lights appeared on the water. Soon there came sharp, heavy noises from the hillside below me; and, as expected, the castle broke into life with doors opening and voices shouting. I began my slow descent, waving the torch as I went. The *Lion*, having launched a barrage of ranging shots, started to fire the eight cannon it had placed towards the Bass. The patrol boats, now lit up, began to approach from their positions. The scene as beheld by the enemy would be one of all-out assault – and sure enough, their own cannon began to reply. Proceeding down the hill I saw a light flash from the shadows of the castle: Simon's signal to me. That was where I was bound, then. Yet the noise of ship's cannonballs striking the rock was becoming louder and louder, and presently I could detect clouds of stone and soil being thrown into the air ahead of me. With each strike they seemed to land closer – and all the time there came more explosions from the *Lion* and more missiles took to the air.

Fear began to overtake me. I realised, suddenly and with unbridled horror, that *I* was the target — that Ackermann was firing upon the torch I carried, and that my approach to the castle gave him opportunity to draw perfect range for accurate striking. Yet still I did not break the orders my lord had given me. As balls landed, bounced and threw up soil around me, I kept slowly moving towards the castle, drawn towards new terrifying sounds which added to the increasing noise of the Bass itself. As if in a dream I simply moved at one pace every five heartbeats, although that count naturally grew in pace with my panic, as I held my death above me and the missiles landed ever closer.

Of a sudden I heard nothing — all the noise simply stopped. It could not be that the action had ended, for I could see cannon firing from the castle and from the *Lion*, and smaller shots being launched from the three boats. I realised I was standing in a storm of debris thrown up from the land around me; so how could there be silence? Then I realised I had dropped the torch; and that, when I went to retrieve it, I could not manage to raise my left arm from my side. My vision began to falter; distraught, I drew my right hand across my forehead, and felt the unmistakeable damp, clinging sensation of blood. At last it became clear to me that I had been shot, although I felt no pain. Bewildered, I resolved to continue moving downhill as I had been told, and turned to recover the torch with my right hand; but the act of turning was the undoing of me, and it seemed the light tumbled up and away from me, before I realised I was falling down the hill into the barrage of cannonballs.

I RECALL SPENDING many years enveloped in a dark world full of the noise of the living Bass – birds, wind, crashing waves, and the water beastie's horrifying cries – and that, every time I attempted to rise out of it, I was struck with a debilitating pain in my head which rapidly took over my whole body. In later attempts I experienced a white-hot agony as I tried to open my eyes; and if I tried to speak, I am sure hands took my shoulders and pushed me backwards. Often I fancied myself crouching in the shadows of the bridge at Aberdeen, or among the castle ruins at Loch Dochart. In the best of those years I was bathed in moonlight at Killiecrankie, and in the worst I lay at the foot of the gallows at Kilchurn.

Gradually I began to perceive that perhaps only hours, rather than years, had passed, and soon I was able to make out a large white room containing a number of beds, in which I made out the presence of Menzies, Mungo, and Simon – who always appeared close to me when I tried to rise.

"St Baldred once lived in that wee church up the hill," he told me on one occasion. "He was one of those early priests – half monk, half warrior, and he was scared of no one. If you didn't want to hear the word of Christ he held you down until you listened. Magnificent mischief, Bolla! By the time he died he'd created three houses of God, and each one of them wanted the honour of burying him. So they brought his body back to the wee church on the Bass and left it overnight, and prayed to God for an answer. Next day, when they went back, they found three bodies of Baldred waiting for them, and they all went off happy with one each."

Another time he said: "You have to believe that wasn't the plan,

Bolla. You were never to be hit by cannonball. Well, you weren't hit – if you had been you'd be gone from me for ever. You must have been hit by rocks thrown up by a shot. I told you before never to pull this *cac* on me. Drink some more water."

On another occasion: "The Vikings were here nearly six hundred years ago. They had a big fight with the tribe who lived here, but there was never a winner. It's said the fight went on so long each side had bairns, and the bairns eventually intermarried, and over time everyone forgot what the fight was about and they all just settled down. But the solan geese – they've been on the Bass since before Vikings or Scots. Since before time began."

When the noise from the rock seemed the loudest it had ever been: "There's a great cave all the way through the Bass – that's what causes the screaming sound, the wind and waves echoing through it. When the day is calm you can walk through it. Just you wait, Bolla; we'll be doing that soon enough. Walking through the middle of the Bass Rock."

One time, during the night: "I needed cannonball on the island, you see. If the Saxons ever send an actual warship the castle won't stand a chance. They had cannon and powder but no balls, which was why they could only use leather guns. I needed to get them the balls. But I didn't know Dutch balls were a different size – how was I to know that? I don't know what to do next, Bolla. But it was the only thing I could think of. I should have known it had been tried before…"

Again: "Every Stuart king has tried to buy the Bass off the Lauder family. Ever since Robert the Second was imprisoned here the crown has wanted to own it. But Lauder would never sell. He finally lent it to Jamie the Sixth but it was meant to be given back. Jamie was an expert in witchcraft. They say the Bass has the soul of a devil trapped inside… but it's just the noise from the cave. Probably."

As my periods of awareness become more frequent and lasted longer, my physical condition began to concern me. I had not been able to ascertain whether I was permanently injured, and memories of my left arm failing haunted me. But as I came closer to full consciousness Simon would not let me rise; until at last I could move my head fully, and discovered, thankfully, that my arm was still part of me, but that it was strapped tightly in bandages red with the stain of blood. My head, too, was bandaged, but as the pain above my eyes faded I felt sure I had sustained no serious injury there.

Each time I woke I noticed Captain Menzies spoke little; and I began to perceive that the coldness which had arisen between he and Simon had been nourished by recent events. Mungo seemed himself, although a little sullen, which was to be expected of a prisoner on an island of unearthly noise.

My first attempts at getting out of bed were dramatic failures. On the third effort I managed to stand, but only for a moment before I crashed forward to the floor. It was then I discovered another set of bandages on my left leg, and almost immediately I realised it was the most serious of my wounds, at which point I lost consciousness again. When I next woke, Simon and I were in a different, smaller room, with just two beds. "I pushed you too hard," my lord said, smiling. "We won't try walking again till you're ready."

"How long have I been... ill?"

"This is the sixth day."

"Keep pushing," I urged him. "I need to get up."

It took another series of collapses, but eventually I was able to walk slowly round the prison cell. After a few more cautious, painful days Simon asked me if I felt ready to try going outside, and I agreed immediately. The moment he knocked on the cell door it was opened for us, to my surprise. The guard without bore a face of concern rather than enmity, as I would have expected. "Is he faring well?" that one asked with a slight accent.

"Getting better every day," my lord replied with a grin. "We're going to take a wee wander round the yard."

"Good luck, Bolla – go easy," the guard said to me, and I nodded my thanks with doubt.

"I'll explain later," Simon whispered. "This way." I stumbled along a corridor with his help until I saw a door with daylight seeping around its edges. He gave another knock and this barricade, too, was opened by a stranger with a concerned expression.

"Today's the day?" he asked.

"We're trying," Simon replied.

"Good upon you, lad," the other said, patting me on the shoulder as

I passed him. Simon grinned at me.

There were many places to rest round the small courtyard, which was a blessing, since I had need of them all. A walk which should have taken mere moments was a staggered struggle lasting many times as long. Yet when I sat again near the door, the task completed, I heard applause coming from the battlement above, and raised my eyes to see two more men showing support for my efforts. "Come down and meet Bolla!" cried Simon. As they approached he introduced them. "This is Lieutenant Middleton, who commands the Bass, and this is Crawford of Ardmillan. They both helped save you – Crawford in particular, who dug out all the stones from your wounds."

"Well, I hope it was all of them. Any sharp pains, you let me know," the last man said.

"Thank you," I stammered. "Thank you both. I —"

"Have done enough for one day!" my lord cut in. "Back to bed, and I'll tell you a wee story." Once the long, strenuous journey back to our room — I could no longer call it a cell — was complete, he endeavoured to explain. "It's like I tried to tell you, Bolla. I needed to make sure the Bass had armaments and provisions so they can hold it for as long as possible."

"For King Jamie?" I said, beginning to understand.

"Of course, for King Jamie! We want an end to the fighting, but at the same time we don't want it going all the government's way, or they'll have nothing else to do but march all over the Highlands. Including our country!"

"How many of our men know about — *this?*"

"All the Frasers. You know what I've said since the start: we wait to fight for Jamie. And we take our turn when we can, like in this wee adventure."

"Mungo? Captain Menzies?"

"Mungo likes good sport," Simon shrugged. "I don't know what side, if any, he's on. Menzies..." he trailed off. "I thought I understood him. I think I was wrong."

"He is a dutiful soldier," I said.

"He's a *gorach*," my lord nodded. "A jumped-up lapdog who's only happy when he knows he's got masters to obey. It's a problem. That's another reason we moved rooms. He had something to say about everything I was trying to achieve. You can't say a word without him shouting about duty, honour and him being in command."

"Another reason?" I asked.

"What?"

"You said that was another reason for moving. What was the first?"

He grinned and touched my shoulder. "To make sure you got better, Bolla."

"What happens next?" I asked after a pause.

"We wait. Dandy Dapperman is on the high seas… and he has work to do. I just hope I've got him right. I can't believe I missed the mark with Menzies."

WAITING TOOK A FURTHER six days, by which time I was nearly able to hobble round the castle alone – although not quite. Crawford dressed my wounds, which were beginning to look less angry, and as he did he told me about his dramatic escape from the tolbooth at Leith, where he had been sentenced to death or King's service for an unidentified offence; and had decided to exercise his own judgement in the matter.

Manning the castle was a business which took up most of the garrison's time, such that I was uncertain how many, or in truth, how few they were. I met gunners named Swann and La Fosse, and Crawford's Irish manservant whose name I could not pronounce and whose words I could little understand, although his ability for making good solan goose stew was welcome. We lived through a period of warm, calm weather, which made it easier to sleep at night, although the birds never let up their constant calling; and I came to know Middleton to a certain extent as he played the role of my companion during my slow marches along the castle rampart, repeating the exercise more and more frequently as the days passed.

"I've been here since the fight at Cromdale," he told me. "There were a few of us, all captured by Tom Livingston up there. If only he'd been on our side – a top quality soldier, he is. One of the few as good as Dundee was. He treated us fairly as well, and there's not many on the government side you can say that for." It seemed that the taking of the Bass from its masters had been an easy and almost comical task. "Fletcher, the governor, was no leader," Middleton said. "He took most of his men over to Canty Bay on an errand, and there were just a dozen left to keep us. A coal tender came in and they all went down to unload it. All we had to do was close the gate behind them and fire off a few shots. They all got on the tender and sailed over to Fletcher, to tell him he wasn't governor any more! We hadn't found the telescope by that time. I'd have loved to have watched that little conversation!"

One Captain Fraser (the lieutenant was unable to inform me whether that man was a member of our clan) had commanded at first, and arranged a series of daring raids to provision the castle. Yet things had come undone when they forced a wheat ship to halt upon pain of being sunk. "We went out and took the ship, but a great storm blew up. We lost control of her and wound up having to land at Montrose. We abandoned her, of course, and split up to try and make our way back here. I got back. Captain Fraser and a few others were captured. I don't know what happened to them. Hung, I expect."

"Surely there have been attempts to take the rock by force?" I asked.

Middleton laughed. "Aye – pointless ones," said he. "They had two Saxon frigates firing nearly a hundred guns on us for two days. They both had to retire, near to sinking, and this place took almost no damage at all. Problem is, that was the end of our cannon shot. Which they don't know — and neither do you!" He grinned and tapped his nose.

"Surely they will succeed at some point," I said, although I did not mean to direct the comment to Middleton.

"Maybe," he shrugged. "The last time Jamie held it was just before Cromdale. His man only surrendered because they offered him a year's pay, a pension and a ship to France." He laughed again. "No, as long as there are people on our side on the mainland we should struggle on. They've made it a death sentence to help us, but that hasn't stopped anyone."

"I think Simon hopes to help," I observed.

"A good man," Middleton nodded. "Jamie has need of such able thinkers and risk-takers. He's the only person who realised our problem was lack of shot. His solution didn't work, but that's not the point. Now

154

he's working on something else, of course."

"Of course," I said quietly. "I wonder if it will succeed."

"It sounds good to me — but it depends whether we can trust that Captain Dapperman as much as we can trust the Fox." I offered no response.

It seemed that everyone including the imprisoned Menzies and Mungo (the latter kept below, said Simon, in order to maintain their understanding that we two also remained in our cell) had an air of waiting over them. I am unsure how many of us were aware that it was the return of Ackermann upon which we waited. The *Lion* had gone, and the only government presence were the two navy patrol boats, not well armed and unable to approach – although certainly capable of preventing the one boat on the Bass from leaving. When at last a large ship was sighted in the firth, making for our island, Simon gritted his teeth and declared: "This is it, Bolla. Make or break."

It took me some minutes to climb onto the rampart, by which time my lord was peering at the oncoming vessel through his telescope. "I think it's the right one," he was saying. "No lions, so it's not the *Lion*. Looks more like a warship to me." He offered me the telescope and I leaned against the wall to operate it.

"French frigate, I'd say," Middleton offered, looking through his. "Flying Dutch colours."

"Well," Simon replied doubtfully, "let's make it look real — it might *be* real." At Middleton's orders the Jacobites loaded two cannon. It was not until the frigate opened fire from its deck guns they launched a return. But quickly Simon shouted: "They're aiming to miss!" and with Middleton repeating the information, the next salvos were deliberately shot to avoid the vessel. "It's got to be Dapperman," my lord muttered. "If it's not… we're undone."

Looking over the approaching ship I spied an easily-recognised figure standing in clear view. "It is him," I said, handing Simon the glass. "On the prow."

My lord laughed as he beheld the sea captain clinging to the foremast, waving his sword in a gesture of greeting. "He's got himself an even more ridiculous hat!" the Fox laughed. "Return fire — but miss!" I could not follow the reasoning behind the false fire, but I assumed it would become clear. When the vessel drew into the bay – so recently the scene of death – Middleton ensured every fit man was armed and sent them down to meet it. Simon returned the telescope to me and told me to wait where I stood. "Things might get tight again, and I'm not risking you twice," he told me. I forbore to mention it would have been far from the second time he had risked me.

At such a short distance use of the glass felt strange, because I could see faces closely enough to expect to hear the words they spoke. The developments of the next moments made events clear to me, however: the ship had been granted to Ackermann in the government's name, and its intended crew had included fifty redcoats plus officers and sailors of the Royal Scots Navy. The plan had been for those men to swarm up the hill and re-take the castle – but since leaving port all of those had been locked out of sight with their arms stowed beyond their reach, and found themselves prisoners, while Ackermann and the crew of the *Lion* took control. How the Dutchman had managed it was, I felt sure, likely to be a long story. The task of those captured men now was to unload the ship of its rich cargo, thus provisioning the Bass for a long siege. I beheld Ackermann waving towards me, and returned his gesture, then watched as he and Simon wandered up towards me as if they were merely enjoying an afternoon stroll, while betrayed soldiers and naval officers did their bidding alongside them. "I'm glad to see you on your feet," the Dutchman told me. "I understand it was a close thing."

"*Ochone*, it wasn't that bad," Simon said hurriedly. "What do you think of our plan, Bolla? This rock is King Jamie's for years to come."

"How could you be certain it was going to work?" I asked, astonished as I began to understand the scale of their deception.

"The challenge was making sure the men in the castle would believe me, and the men on the ship would believe him," Simon told me. "But the hardest part was believing he could do what he said he'd do."

Ackermann bowed. "How could I refuse such a great adventure? And the opportunity to command a great ship?"

"Where's her captain?" Simon asked.

"Before you, sir!"

"No, no — I mean her real captain."

"Ah, yes," Ackermann sketched a flowing gesture. "Captain Bird – that's him there, with the rich uniform. Carrying a bag of grain." They both waved to the unfortunate officer, a well-presented figure displaying a recently-inflicted sword wound on the side of his head; obviously unused to labours he felt were beneath him, he struggled with his burden; but found spirit to glare up at us. "Another bird swoops upon the Bass," said the Dutchman, laughing at his own humour, although we did not. He then drew a roll of paper from his tunic and presented it to my lord. "I took the liberty of writing an account of my actions," he said grandly. "I know how much you enjoy your letters – as do I." Simon immediately opened it and began to read, an expression of delight on his face. "You'll see I favour the classic German hand," he continued. "So much more balanced than the humanist nonsense that passes for writing these days. I would have chosen a darker ink, had I the opportunity…"

After a time the cargo was unloaded – and to Simon's satisfaction it included a good supply of the correct size of cannonballs. We prepared to take our leave on Ackermann's new vessel, with my lord assuring Crawford that the island would be reported as better armed, garrisoned and supplied than it truly was. Due to my condition I was hoisted onto the deck in a bosun's chair, a seat suspended by ropes which felt little more secure than the terrifying ladder I had used previously. Once the redcoats had been returned below deck, able only to report they had heard cannon fire and believed the ship to have been overcome, three of Middleton's men marched Menzies and Mungo aboard, each with disconcerted expressions. As we made off, Simon told them what he wished them to know. "They bested us – it's as simple as that," said my lord. "You heard the cannon. They defeated Ackermann's rescue mission and stole supplies. I persuaded them to us go. We were lucky they didn't want to keep us for longer."

"How many men bested us?" Menzies demanded. "Don't think I've forgotten how you talked them into letting you out of your cell. A hateful display of treason!"

"Captain, can't you see? I had to be in amongst them to work out their strengths. You couldn't bring yourself to say what had to be said. What good would it do to have another one of us locked up, when I could be spying on them?"

Menzies shook his head. "I don't believe you."

"Look at the result," Simon persisted. "We're free. No more dead!"

"But the Bass is better held now than it was, and the King has taken another defeat. These were not our orders, Fraser – they are the damned opposite!"

My lord shrugged. "I have saved your life, sir; I have tried every trick I know to get those men off the rock, and I have got every one of us – including Bolla – away alive. I do not understand what more you can expect of me."

"I expect nothing," the captain replied. "You will answer to Colonel Murray."

"In due course," nodded Simon. "But first I must stay aboard to persuade Captain Ackermann to return this vessel to the King. He plans to keep her."

"*Keep* her?" thundered Menzies, glaring round to the afterdeck where the Dutchman was forcing his officers to listen to another story.

"Careful, sir – there's Dutch all around us," Simon whispered. "He believes the *Lion* crew can handle her, and plans to put her own crew on land with us — with you." Menzies, shocked, could find no words. "Lieutenant Murray, you see all is how I say it is?"

Mungo nodded. "I will report exactly as I have seen and heard, Lieutenant Fraser."

Menzies removed his hat and ran his fingers through his hair, which seemed notably thinner than when last I had seen it. "Fraser, I find myself confounded by you," he said. "I cannot believe all is as you say, and yet I cannot prove otherwise. But I believe that if I remain in service with you, I will be killed. And I would rather die knowing the cause than doubting it." He glared directly at me. "Others could think the same. You've proved yourself to be foolhardy and untrustworthy. So I'm going to resign my captaincy in this God-forsaken Lovat's Company – and I wouldn't be surprised if that's what you wanted all along. It's yours for the purchase. I do not wish to encounter you again." With that he strode to the prow and stared across the water.

"As you wish, sir," Simon said quietly — but there was a gleam in his eye.

We marched the redcoats off the ship without arms, leaving them under the command of Menzies and Mungo for the march to Edinburgh. The last command I heard from the captain was to quick-march out of Canty Bay, the sooner to be safely beyond Fraser's treacherous guns. Then, some time after they had disappeared from sight, the *Lion* crew drew arms on the frigate's sailors, who had been trapped in another hold, and forced them ashore. Ackermann did Captain Bird the honour of escorting him from his own vessel with great grandeur and flourish – which served to make the victim even more furious. Then, slowly, and with admitted lack of grace, the vessel moved away from the harbour, her destination Inverness – and Kirsty.

"I knew you'd keep her," Simon said to Ackermann. "But won't it hurt your family business?"

"It's time to expand," the sea captain replied. "A fluyt is a wonderful, Dutch invention, but it has limitations, especially in the Indies and the Americas. Give me a good French frigate any day. This —" he flourished around himself — "is the *Janet*. I told you I'd served on her before. A nice ship; I always liked her."

"What about the *Lion*?"

"Sink her."

"What about her being named after a family gift to King Jamie?"

"Didn't I tell you? The lion was named *Janet*."

"You're a damned bloody *gorach*, Dandy Dapperman," Simon laughed, and the other bowed deeply.

At that moment I felt an impact at the back of my head as if one of the cannonballs on the Bass had struck me again. I knew I been shot as I fell. I wondered if the Dutchman's bow had been a signal, and then, as I recoiled from striking the deck, I wondered if Simon had been shot too.

CHAPTER FIVE
THE TRAITOR IN THE TOWER

THE NOISE HAD finally stopped. What seemed like an eternity of waves and howls had been washed away by an endless, deep silence from which I did not want to wake, although I knew I must. I sadly opened my eyes, aware that closing them again would not return me to that peaceable underworld; but in an instant that other place was fading into forgetfulness, because I was upon my couch in Moniack Castle – and Kirsty was seated beside me.

Like a new-born child I stared in silence up at her, attending more at first to the line of her hair above her forehead, before slowly drawing my glance down to her eyes. She was not returning my glance; instead she was intent upon something behind my head, and it gave me another moment to savour the delight of being awake, as that trance-like trap of an underworld receded into the past.

She looked down at me, realised I was awake, and smiled. "Good morning, *gràdh mo chrìdh*," she said, and hearing her voice in my new-found quiet world was as a song in my heart.

Then I began to remember what had gone before. "I was shot!" I rasped, finding it strangely difficult to speak. "Simon! Was he —"

"Shh!" she said gently, drawing her fingers over my mouth. "You're going to be well soon. Simon's well too. There was no shooting."

"Then…" I began.

"They say you had hurt your head but didn't know it. You just fell down on the boat."

"Ship. *Janet*. Dandy Da…" I found I could not speak the Dutchman's name, given or otherwise.

"All's well, *gràdh mo chrìdh*. You must slow down. You're doing better than you were earlier — you've been making me laugh with the nonsense coming from your mouth." She laughed at that, and the joy of the sound sent me back to a more restful condition. She leaned in and kissed my cheek. "But I've been worried."

"Simon?" I asked quietly.

"He's been asking for you," Kirsty said. "He'll be here soon."

Suddenly my entire recollection of the Bass Rock thundered across my thoughts, and I let out a cry of shock and sat up straight. Kirsty took both my arms, telling me all was well; but even as I lay back I knew I must say all that was in my mind. She listened as I recounted the darkness, the cannonballs, my sickness, the fight and my collapse – and the terrifying animal noise of that place.

She simply listened, holding me as I spoke. I swear I felt better for the passing of some ill humour, and I made no objection when she bade me lay back down and sleep. I must have fallen into rest almost immediately, for it seemed like the next moment that she was gone, replaced by the figure of my lord seated by me, reading a letter.

"Devil choke me, Bolla!" he cried, then, remembering himself, lowered his voice. "You know how to worry a man, I'll tell you. One minute you're standing beside me, the next you're on the deck. How are you feeling?"

I nodded slowly. "Better… I think. What happened to Dandy Da…"

"Dapperman? Of all the things that man is, he's not forgettable, surely? *Ochone*, he's well away – dropped us off Inverness then made a run for it. If he gets by the English he'll be fine. That couldn't have gone better, as it goes; Dapperman with a frigate is a very useful wee addition to my plan."

"Kirsty said… I was not shot?"

"You weren't," Simon said. "But you might as well have been, the way you went down. I had Paddy Abercromby, one of those physicians, look at you. He said something about a concussion of the brain. Auld Maggie the wife said it's a bad spirit you caught on the Bass. The funny thing is —" he held up two jars of powder — "They both prescribed foxglove! Maggie told me to boil the brain of a man who died in violence and feed you that too. But no one's been fighting recently – I think it's this lovely weather."

I smiled, enjoying the experience of Simon amid one of his performances, aware that some part of me had doubted I would live to experience such a thing again. I was not surprised at what came next.

"Anyway, time to earn your shilling… as soon as you feel able, that is," he said. "It's actually going to be good for you – Doctor Paddy says you have to keep your mind active. How's your sight, Bolla?"

"It seems good," I replied.

"Grand!" Simon said. "But you never kept at the reading and writing, did you?"

I decided not to discuss the point that, every time I had turned my thoughts to developing those skills, my lord appeared to find something other for me to do. "Not so much as I would have liked."

"Well, maybe we can do something about that," he said brightly. "Anyway, you're to sleep. *Durate et vosmet rebus servate secundis*. And don't let Kirsty keep you awake!" He offered me a leering glance, touched my shoulder and left.

I settled down to gain some more rest, the which I felt was much needed, even thought I had been conscious for only a few minutes; but as I laid back and began to settle I became aware of raised voices in the chamber beyond. From the tones I could tell it was Simon and Kirsty; and from the volume I could tell it was no minor disagreement.

With a struggle I managed to push my bedclothes away and raise myself up, then slowly, with the aid of every furnishing in the room, I made to the door. It was a heavy latch, beyond my limited abilities, but I was now close enough to hear what was being said beyond.

"I don't have to explain myself to you," Simon was saying in a rage. "Remember who you are!"

"I'm not scared of you," Kirsty replied. "And if you really are the Young MacShimi then you *do* have to explain yourself to anyone in this clan. He trusted you!"

"And I brought him home in a frigate! And I paid Abercromby a fortune to come out from Edinburgh and see to him. What else do you want me to do?"

"You know that's not what I mean. That's just you clearing up your guilty conscience. You set him up as a target!"

"You don't know the whole story. It wasn't like that."

"Bolla," Kirsty said slowly through teeth tight with rage. "On a hillside. With a torch. For a ship to fire on. What was it like, Simon the Fox?"

"He's not stupid!" Simon shouted. "He knew to get out of the way!"

"Oh, aye – he knew alright. But he did what you told him, and you told him to stand there while he was shot at. That's the price he pays for being your friend! And if that's how you treat friends…"

"Don't you lecture me. I'm doing things that have to be done."

"At any price?" Kirsty shouted. "Well, he might pay it, but I won't. You leave my man alone – or you'll answer for it."

"That had best not be a threat," Simon warned.

"That's up to you," Kirsty replied. "We both know some of the things you've done in your time. But I'm telling you not to do any more of them to him. He doesn't deserve it. He's a better man than you – and we both know it."

The outer door slammed and there was silence, followed by the low sound of sobbing. The thought of Kirsty alone and upset gave me the strength to lift the latch — not quite to openness, but enough so that she heard my attempt to enter, and opened the door for me.

"You shouldn't have heard that, *gràdh mo chrìdh*," she said, finding her own strength as she realised I could not return to my couch without her assistance. "But I don't want him hurting you any more. You're too important."

I shook my head. "What Simon wants…" I began.

"We won't talk about it now. Later. But just remember this, Bolla Fraser – you're mine. Not his."

From that moment Kirsty's nursing of my ills took on a more determined character; she vowed that I would recover fully from my injuries and suffer none of the permanent side-effects, such as loss of balance or vision, that the physician Abercromby had warned I might. Each day she set targets for me to achieve, such as walking fifty paces, then eighty, then a hundred, then two hundred; and only allowed me to fail when it became clear I simply did not have the power to succeed. Her approach towards me was attentive, caring but firm – and she encouraged me with the promise that she would lie beside me the very first moment she believed I was well enough to survive the moment.

It did not arrive for several weeks; and in the meantime, when I found myself confined to my couch or a seat in the late summer sun, Simon provided me with mental exercises instead. He took to arriving with the draft of a letter and having me copy it as best I could onto another piece of paper. When I had completed each laborious task – confusing to me because I did not understand the patterns I followed; they could have been Gaelic, English, French or even nonsense – he compared my work to the original and awarded me a mark out of five for the result.

"It's just a bit of fun, Bolla," he told me. "I came up with it when Abercromby said you had to keep your mind active. There's another couple of lads across the country doing the same – and they all say it's good for them." Indeed, after my first struggling experiences I began to enjoy the challenge of matching the shapes as best I could, even attempting to add my own vague concepts of neatness and balance to the pages.

My labours came to a temporary halt soon after Kirsty gave me the reward I had been most anticipating. Judging me near to full fitness, she told me we were going on a short journey on horseback for a few days, the better to enjoy what remained of the summer.

Staying upon a horse was a new challenge for me – another usually thoughtless procedure I was forced to re-learn. Our progress was therefore slow; but that drew no complaint from me as we made our way past the glens and bens of Fraser country, into Cameron country at the foot of Glen Mhor. We spent a night in the grand ruin of Inverlochy Castle, its curtain walls still more dominating than even Castle Dounie's frontage; and there we played a game of acting king and queen of our own domain – entirely childish, but for the way it ended.

We observed the new town of Maryburgh, growing up around the new fort named after King William at the head of Loch Linnhe; and there we were questioned shortly by two government soldiers. Their stern expressions softened as Kirsty explained I, too, was a soldier, wounded during the attempt to recover the Bass. It seemed Simon's version of events had become taken as the truth, for these men were convinced a small number of the King's troops had been overcome by a large and well-armed number of Jacobite rebels; and they gave me a bottle of whisky to help me on my way to recovery. I wondered, as I often did, whether they understood the lines of division in Scotland as clearly as their orders stated they should.

It was not until we approached Loch Eil that I began to suspect Kirsty had a secondary motive in devising our trip. When I stated, carefully, that I knew where we were going, she did not keep her intentions from me any longer. "I want you to show me where you last saw Alex," she admitted.

"Why?" I asked, although I had no need.

"I just want to see," she replied. "To see if, maybe..." she did not finish, but in truth there was no more to say.

I was not minded to refuse her; and indeed I had inquiring thoughts of my own, although I had no idea whether any answers might be forthcoming. The landscape seemed different, but I had only seen it by night before, and some of my memories appeared to have been dislodged during my illness. Nevertheless I was able to say with some confidence, when we reached a certain point on the banks of the loch, that we had arrived. "What happened next?" Kirsty asked. I sketched out my recollection of standing near the road with the horses while Simon and Alexander went further into the trees. By imagining my lord had been away for around ten minutes, we assumed they could have walked no further than four minutes from where we stood. We tied up our horses and set off along the lochside.

We did not find what we were looking for immediately. In fact, we found it by moving in the opposite direction from that which I had last seen Alexander following. Once out of my sight the brothers had changed direction, and so the scene we finally beheld was closer to where I had been waiting that night. Out from a rocky clearing under a tree there lay the rotting remains of a sunken boat, forced beneath the water in winter by the short mooring rope which connected it to the bank. Under the tree, scattered over several feet, we beheld small, bleached scraps of cloth; and intertwined within them a collection of white bones. "No..." I whispered, sitting down on the bank.

"It must be," Kirsty said equally quietly. "There's no chance of it being anything — anyone — else."

I remained seated, my heart racing, while she stepped among the remains. "You would never find a body," she said, shaken, but less than I. "Animals and the weather would have taken most of it away. But…" she leaned down and picked something up, then brought it over and sat beside me. She held what could be seen to be the bones of a hand, complete with part of a shirt cuff around where a wrist would once have been.

"It might not be… Alex," I said.

"Don't tell yourself stories, *gràdh mo chrìdh*," she said, quietly but sternly. "If you can think of any other explanation, I'll tell you why it's wrong."

We remained there in silence for a time. Part of me struggled to assemble a series of events which could satisfy every challenge to the evidence of my eyes. Yet the evidence of my heart, and the surety of my love beside me, bade my desperate efforts to depart. Finally I asked: "So what now?"

"I don't know," Kirsty replied. "We need to find a way to tell Himself."

"We cannot. He has never been the same since… this."

She nodded slowly. "We must tell someone; but how could we say it? I think the best thing is to talk to Lady Amelia. She'll know what to do." She brought out a small pouch and dropped the bones and cuff within. "Bolla, you need to be very sure of what kind of a man Simon is." I offered no reply — I knew she was correct, but as long as there was any shade of doubt I knew I would cling to it, as I was doing at that moment. She took my hand and kissed it. "Remember: you are his friend, but he is not yours." I put my arm around her; and we remained by the body and boat until I felt able to move away.

THE LADY AMELIA FRASER stared at the pathetic pile of remains Kirsty had poured from the pouch onto the table. Her expression must have been akin to those we had worn at Loch Eil. Yet ours were now faces of expectation; for, having become committed to the belief of

167

what had to be done, we wished to see a conclusion to the episode.

"You can't be sure," Lady Amelia said.

"Not fully, my lady," I admitted.

"Oh, come on, Amelia," Kirsty insisted, displaying a familiarity I dared not share. "You know what it means. And don't tell me you haven't thought about it yourself."

The lady sighed. "I wish you hadn't brought me this problem," she said. "It's the last thing we need."

"Something has to be done," Kirsty said firmly.

"Aye, lass – but what?" Lady Amelia replied. "Things aren't as simple as they used to be."

"Murder is murder," my love insisted stubbornly.

"Death is death," the other replied. "The death of our clan – our whole clan – is on the cards. And Simon, mark my words, is the only one who can prevent it."

"Forget what you feel about him —"

"That has nothing to do with it!" the lady flashed. "I don't expect you to understand, but listen. My brother wants to crush Fraser out of existence. He wants this to be Murray country. If he continues climbing the English ladder the way he has, the influence we currently have won't be enough to stop him."

"But Simon is building more enemies for us!" Kirsty protested. "He's not —"

"He's doing much, much more than you think he is."

"Amelia, is this the price of Fraser's name? Brother killing brother and waking up the next day to do it again if he feels like it?"

"That's what I mean," the lady said with a sigh, her fury passing like a blown candle. "That's why I wish I didn't know about this." She sat down at the table and peered at the long-dead hand, gently touching the shirt cuff while ensuring she did not make contact with the bones. "Alex Fraser was a good man. Strong. Loyal. But not a MacShimi. Ian Cam would have danced him into hell."

"And that makes this all well?" Kirsty said.

"Enough!" Lady Amelia snapped; and I had to concur that my love had said far too much in far too assertive a tone. "I'll consider what has to be done, then I'll do it. But don't expect anything soon – there are far more people involved in this than you may think." She gestured towards the bones. "Leave these with me. And you talk to no one about it. Not even Simon, do you understand?" She appeared to direct this last towards me, and I nodded in silence.

The interview appeared to be over; we left the lady's chamber and went out into the courtyard of Castle Dounie. "That could have gone better," I observed.

"It could have gone worse," Kirsty replied. "I knew she loved Simon. I didn't know how much."

"You mean —?"

"Oh, Bolla!" she sighed. "You miss so much, don't you? Yes, I mean that. And not just once or twice either. But I didn't think it was that serious. I hope we haven't made a mistake." I could not help wondering whether the trip to Loch Eil itself had been the mistake; but there was nothing to be gained from starting such an argument, and indeed, much to gain from not starting any argument at all.

THE SUMMER GAVE way to an equally pleasant autumn, in turn giving rise to much joy across the country, for recent harvests had been difficult; and that year's was expected to be one of the best in memory. Those conditions assisted in softening the sharpness of my Loch Eil memories; and the next time I met Simon, who had been absent for some weeks, I was able (I know not how) to set aside my concerns and instead delight in seeing him in spirits as high as my own. "It's spectacular sport, Bolla. Grand, just!" he laughed as he appeared outside Moniack Castle, where I rested in the sun. "It's like King Billy himself has approved the plan!"

"What do you mean?" I asked, pouring him a glass of wine – and wondering for a moment if the guilt I chose to ignore bore any relations to similar feelings of his own; and if so, to what degree.

He drew out a letter from the packet he had been carrying since my confinement in bed, which had started out in normal dimensions but now bulged with papers within; and, adopting a parody of an English accent, he read: "William and Mary, by the grace of God, King and Queen of Great Britain, France and Ireland, blah, blah blah... Whereas we did allow John, Earl of Breadalbane, to meet with the Highlanders, blah blah blah, in order to reducing of them to our obedience, blah blah blah, we understand their willingness to render themselves in subjection to our authority and laws.

"We being satisfied that nothing can conduce more to the peace of the Highlands, blah blah blah, in order whereunto, we are resolved graciously to pardon, indemnify and restore all that have been in arms against us, blah blah blah, who shall take the oath of allegiance before the first day of January next. Restoring all and every one of those persons who have been in arms against us to their lives, estates, dignities, fame and blood as if they had never been guilty. God Save King William and Queen Mary!

"Magnificent mischief, isn't it?" he grinned. "I couldn't have arranged it better myself."

"I do not understand," I admitted.

"A permanent peace accord, Bolla. Well, they say so anyway. Gives us all the time we need to get things moving behind the scenes."

"But... does it not give King William time to organise forces against the Jacobites?"

"*Ochone*, man, that doesn't matter! I keep telling you. Even if you know the plan you can't stop it working. It's that good."

"But I do not know the plan," I pointed out.

"It'll become clear to you," Simon said, "and it'll become clear just how much you've done to make it happen, and maybe even how many lives you've saved.

"But for us," he changed in tone, touching me on the shoulder, "it means another couple of journeys. One to sort things out with Ian Cam, and another to meet the best man in the Highlands. And I know it's not me, Bolla – we all know it's not me..." His expression was slightly different, but I could not level an estimation as to whether he referred to his argument with Kirsty, Loch Eil, or something other. "We're going to Huntingtower," he told me. "A nice relaxing couple of weeks with the Murrays. And you can bring that fine lassie of yours. In fact, I insist!"

It was a leisurely four-day journey to Murray's castle just north of Perth; under other circumstances it could have been covered in a little over two days, I believe, but Simon and Kirsty took efforts to ensure my comfort, and that I did not over-reach myself. With the exception of regular head pains and agonising moments with my left leg, I felt all but cured. I even began to feel that my sense of guilt around Simon was something I could live with as easily as the remaining symptoms of my injuries – especially as there came no disagreements in conversation between my companions. As ever, Simon's bag of farthings and knowledge of clan names were constantly brought into use, and it seemed a nonsense that we were travelling into an environment which could be plagued with dangers.

As we approached the unusual double-keep construction of Huntingtower we were accosted from the branch of a tree above the road by a young voice calling: "Stop in the name of the King!" Surprised, we halted and looked up, to behold a boy of eight or nine summers standing in the tree, brandishing a sword carved from a twig towards us. "Name yourselves!" he demanded.

Simon grinned. "I am the Young MacShimi, my lord. Come to rest with the Lord John Murray, Earl of Tullibardine. Might I know the name of he who has bested us?"

"I am the Lord George Murray," said the boy grandly. "I will provide safe passage to the castle – but first, name the others with you."

"This is Sergeant Bolla Fraser, who serves with me and the Earl; and this is Lady Kirsty Fraser."

He stared at us both with large round eyes under an unkempt brush of brown hair, and the thin character wore a most serious expression. "She is very beautiful," he said. "I will come down." he scrambled out of the tree with a most comical movement, but despite the urge to laugh we all managed to maintain our expressions.

"Will you ride with me, Lord George?" Simon asked.

"Or with me?" Kirsty added. The boy looked at them both then rushed towards Kirsty's horse and threw himself, rather than climbed, onto the saddle before her. "I must repay you for your protection, my lord," she said. "Will you accept a kiss?" He nodded and presented his cheek, but Kirsty turned his head and planted her lips on his; and despite myself I could not help feeling a little envy.

"No harm will come to you, my lady," said George. "You have my

171

word. And since these men are your friends they will be safe too."

"My hero!" she smiled and wrapped her arms round him, and as Simon grinned happily we made towards the castle.

I know not whether George truly did act the lookout, or whether there were other eyes watching, but as we entered the courtyard we beheld the Earl of Tullibardine, a woman who could only be his wife, and Mungo waiting upon us. George shouted: "Ma!" jumped off Kirsty's horse and ran up to her, while the menfolk waited for us to dismount.

Simon gave a smart salute. "Your lordship! Lieutenant Murray! May I present Sergeant Bolla Fraser, whom you know, and the Lady Kirsty Fraser?"

"Oh, I'm not really a lady," she said shyly.

"I think she's a princess!" George stated loudly, his arms round his mother's waist. She too was a handsome woman, tall and dark, and immediately shared a laugh with my love. The young man had bonded us all in friendship instantly. Indeed, it was clear to see that all the Murrays were uncommonly fond of him – and why.

"Shush, Geordie," Tullibardine said softly. "Captain Fraser, Sergeant Bolla, Miss Fraser, you are welcome. You've met my son Geordie, and here is my wife, the Lady Katherine."

We all started at his words. "Captain…?" Simon asked cautiously.

"Captain," Tullibardine confirmed. "Menzies has been granted a post elsewhere in the regiment. I Assume you are able to purchase his commission?"

Mungo winked behind his elder brother as Simon nodded. "Of course, sir. And… thank you!"

"We have much to discuss, though, Fraser. We must reach an understanding, the better to secure our future in this changing world. But — not tonight. Tonight we will take dinner on the lawn. I don't believe the warmth will go out of the day until midnight!"

So began another pleasant interlude of that summer; and if the Murrays had any discomfort with treating a common soldier and his woman as honoured guests (the opposite of which I could not believe, since they favoured the English manner of running their household), they did not display even a hint of it. Serious discussion could not wait long, of course; and so it was the next afternoon, seated in the shade of a tree near the castle, Mungo and I silently observed as Tullibardine and Simon conducted a conversation which could lead in any direction, with many of them threatening dire consequences.

"It is not a question of what you or I want," said the earl mildly in his strange accent. "We are not in charge of the game, but we must take part, even when the rules change."

"I understand, sir," Simon replied, equally mildly. "*Nam tua res agitur, paries cum proximus ardet*. But I fear we are not of the same view when it comes to following or bending rules."

Murray sighed. "My clan is as ancient as yours," he said, "but over the years we have perhaps stretched ourselves further. We have lands in England – I was born there, and I've spent most of my life there – but that doesn't mean Murray country in Scotland matters any less. Fraser could take the same view."

"That's not for me to say," Simon replied. "I'm given more orders to follow than I think you are."

"Everyone knows who wields the power of Fraser. It may not be you entirely, but you have a great say – and as time goes by I believe it will become greater. You are surely to be the next MacShimi?"

"It's probable," Simon accepted. "Unless Lord Hugh has a son – who lives."

"But you are now Lord Tom's eldest son." I did not dare change my expression, but in freezing my countenance I fear I revealed everything I wanted to hide, had anyone been watching.

"That's true," my lord agreed after a pause.

"Well, let me put it like this. Fraser's future is with Murray. Murray's future is with England. Therefore all of our futures are with England. The old ways are passing into history. I did not cause that and nor did you. But Scotland's a damn small place, man, and to stand still is to sink in the mire. As you say – well, as Horace says: *Nam tua res agitur, paries cum proximus ardet.*"

"It's your own concern when your neighbour's wall is on fire. I understand your point, sir."

Tullibardine laughed. "Yes, I'm sure you understand, but do you see? There can be no other way than the one foisted upon us. King James is gone. He will never return. William's pardon will wipe out most of the remaining resistance. All that is now set. And there's more. You know of the failed harvests in the last couple of years. This year is plentiful, thank God. But were the cold to return, how many would die if Scotland is an enemy of England?"

"I see that very clearly," Simon said.

"There is talk, you must know, of a united kingdom, of one government ruling all."

"It's nearly like that already anyway."

"I'll let that pass," the earl said with a smile. "But the point is this: Fraser must decide whether to be part of the future – or part of the past. You understand the old loyalties, and you understand the new realities. There is much need for men like you."

"I won't disagree with that!" Simon said to laughter from us all.

"I can give you orders you as a soldier, but I cannot give you orders as a chief, or as a future chief at least. Instead I must have your understanding – and that must include no more intrigue. No more letters, and certainly no more events such as… whatever went on in Glen Dochart and on the Bass."

Simon sighed. "You see, my lord, there we have a problem. I don't make these things happen. They were going to happen anyway. In both those places I did my best to see the right result. I would do it again – I have to. And even though you may not think so, I was following your orders all the time. Neither Captain Campbell or Captain Ackermann were present on my account. I cannot be held responsible for their actions."

It was Tullibardine's turn to sigh. "That damned pirate – running off with a warship in these times! One would think the Admiralty's failure to deal with it, among everything else they fail to deal with, would have forced some change upon them. Meanwhile all the best Scots sea captains join the English navy and take over the world! But… you are correct, Fraser. I cannot disprove what you say about how events unfold – and I should add that I'm not sure there's any disproving to be done.

"But this is my case: between you and I there must be no more doubt. I cannot be left wondering what happened. It would reflect poorly on me, and that would reflect on you, and your clan."

"I think my lord is some way above such suspicion," Simon said. "But I assure you it's not my intention to create any doubt. I hope I can prove that, now I'm captain of the Lord Lovat's Company. Which was, if you remember, the position you asked me to take."

Murray nodded. "I accept I underestimated you in that respect – and I can see how having a Campbell or a Menzies in command of a clan company leaves the door open for doubt. So let us hope your promotion marks an end to that. But I don't just mean in the records, man, I mean in spirit too."

He leaned towards Simon and changed his tone. "There is one more thing. When I say Fraser's future is with Murray, I should like it to be understood that Fraser's future is *not* with Campbell, and specifically, Breadalbane."

"I'm not sure what you mean," Simon replied quickly.

"I think you are. There are more reckonings to come after the matter of James Stuart. Think about it," he added by way of closing the conversation as young Lord George ran up, ahead of Kirsty and Lady Katherine. "Geordie, my lad – what have you been up to?"

"I was telling Kirsty about the kidnapped king!" the boy said excitedly.

"The kidnapped king?" the earl repeated.

"Don't pretend you've forgotten, Da! The king that got kidnapped and hidden in the castle!"

"That sounds like fun," Simon said, to a light-hearted warning glance from both Murray men. "What happened, Geordie?"

"The king was out hunting and they told him to visit the castle," the lad recounted breathlessly. "Then they took him prisoner and tried to kill him, but he wouldn't die. Then they told him to do what he was told but he said, 'No, I'm the king!' And in the end his friends came and got him and the baddies all went to jail!" He was flushed with delight. "I want to play kings and kidnap, Da! Can we do it tomorrow?"

Tullibardine looked apologetically at his wife. "I'm sorry, lad, not tomorrow. I have work to do." Then he looked at Simon. "You've seen the work we have on, building the two towers into one. These things are never as simple as they should be – I'll be tied up all day."

"We'll play with you, if you want," Simon told Geordie. "But who would be the king?"

The young man frowned. "Me, of course. And Kirsty will be my princess."

"Then Mungo and Bolla must be the friends who come to save you."

I nodded and Mungo said: "I'm your best friend, am I not, Geordie?"

The Fox mused. "That means… I will have to be the baddy!"

"You'll make a very good baddy," George said decisively.

"Geordie!" laughed Lady Katherine, failing to sound authoritative.

"Your majesty!" said Simon, bowing to the young man.

The following day, while Tullibardine busied himself with stonemasons, carpenters and papers, my lord spent some time exploring Huntingtower with Mungo, intent, he said, on making the re-enactment as authentic as he could. Later, with all set, Mungo and I rode on horseback through woods near the castle, behind Kirsty and Lord George on their own mounts.

"That's a fine lass you've got there, Bolla," Mungo told me conspiratorially. "I'll wager she's a bit of fun."

"She's a fine lass," I agreed cautiously.

"Aye, I thought so," he leered. "Do you think Simon's danced with her?" It was not a thought I wished to consider so I simply shrugged. "He'd love to, though. She'd keep a man busy…"

I chose to hear his talk as complimentary, but I was glad when the sound of a galloping horse signalled the game had begun. "Where are you, king?" shouted Simon, appearing from a bend in the path. "I have a message for you!"

"You will speak to your king properly, knave!" Lord George bellowed, standing up in his stirrups and drawing his wooden sword. Simon drew his also and the pair lunged at each other as their mounts circled.

"Save me! Save me!" Kirsty cried. Mungo moved ahead and I followed.

Simon managed to knock George's sword to the ground and shouted: "Surrender, king, or I will take this princess!"

"Don't you touch that princess!" Mungo replied, drawing his own sword. I followed the motion, feeling somewhat unneeded.

"Throw down your swords!" Simon told us, and we did so. King,

176

you will come with me to Castle Ruthven —"

"Huntingtower!" Lord George interrupted.

"It was called Castle Ruthven then," Simon told him, a hand over his mouth for dramatic effect. "So, to Castle Ruthven!"

"Very well, to Castle Ruthven," agreed the young lord.

"Count to a hundred then give chase," my lord whispered as he pretended to lead George and Kirsty away. She gave me a look of playful fear, her mouth wide open – but as she passed me her eyes settled on Mungo, which I did not like.

"She's really yours?" he asked me after they had disappeared into the distance.

I did not like the question. "No one belongs to anybody," I replied.

He patted my shoulder while looking along the path after her. "Come on, let's go," he said.

By the time we trotted back to the castle, Kirsty was waiting on the parapet of the east tower; on seeing our appearance she began crying for help, and we climbed the smaller building's stairs until we arrived in a room on the top floor.

"We have come for the king!" Mungo shouted, thumping the door.

"He's mine now!" called Simon from within. "You'll never take him alive, you hounds!"

"Your majesty! Are you in there?" Mungo shouted back.

"Kill this knave at once, my subjects – your king orders it!" came the reply.

Simon lifted the latch from inside, allowing us to gain entrance; and there followed a wooden sword fight with Simon fending off attacks from the three of us while Kirsty looked on. Mungo, of course, was no stripling in the art of the blade, and with their naturally competitive nature some of the blows became more aggressive than perhaps they should have been. At the same time George carried himself well too. It was no surprise that I was the first to fall, feigning death as Simon threw a stab at me – but without intention (I must believe) he struck me near the wound on my leg; and when I collapsed it was no play-act. Yet no one noticed, since I had fallen at the moment expected, and the game went on until, with Mungo pretending to be wounded, George disarmed Simon then made an act of beheading him after he had pleaded for mercy. "So end all enemies of the king!" the young lord shouted triumphantly. "Bolla! You are really hurt!"

In truth I was. Somehow a wound I had thought nearly healed had reopened, and it was almost as painful as when I first felt it. Blood had soaked through my trews and my head began to swim. I recall all four of my companions rushing towards me and George shouting: "Your king commands you to get up!" before I fell into darkness yet again.

I AWOKE WITH A SENSATION of events repeating themselves. As I had become familiar with the bewilderment which came with collapsing, I was able to spare myself worry and instead I waited until my eyes and ears began offering information I could understand. I was in my chamber in the west tower, and no one else was with me. I realised there was a small bell beside my couch so I rang it, in answer to which a maid entered.

"How do you feel, sir?" she asked.

"I think I am better," I replied, slightly shaken at the formality of her tone: something I would not have expected in Fraser country.

"I'll fetch Captain Fraser," she said and left the room. That man appeared shortly afterwards.

"This is becoming a boring habit, Bolla," he said, crouching beside where I lay and giving me a look of concern. "There aren't many worse things you can be, after boring."

"I am sorry," I muttered.

"Ian Cam has a physician on the way. That leg of yours wasn't quite ready to rescue a king, it seems. Is it sore?"

"It is not too bad."

"We must take more care of you, man. *I* must." Something about his emphasis on the last raised a concern.

"Where is Kirsty?"

He paused. "Little Lord Geordie is out on another adventure," he said. "And it's on your behalf. He's visiting St Conval's Well. The story goes that the waters can heal any wound, as long as whoever carries it doesn't make a sound. The wee lad's too excitable," he added with a laugh. "He keeps getting distracted. He's on his thirtieth attempt, just!"

"And Kirsty is with him?"

"Yes. She and Mungo…" I lay back, and while I said nothing a dark look must have passed over my face. "Bolla…" Simon began. "Mungo — *ochone*, you know Mungo. He's…" My lord stopped speaking as I shook my head.

At that moment the chamber door opened and Lord George, a look of severe concentration on his face, entered with a small bucket sat upon his outstretched hands. Staring directly at the container he walked almost as if in a procession, and his effort was such as to make me forget my concerns – until I saw Kirsty and Mungo appearing together behind him. "My lord," I began, but George silenced me with a glare. He tenderly placed the bucket on the floor then motioned for me to draw back the covers, revealing my bandaged wound. Then he cupped his hands and lifted some water up towards my leg. In truth most of it spilled on the floor, his clothing and my couch; but enough dripped onto the bandages to satisfy the young lord.

"There you go, Bolla – you'll be fine now!" he said with delight. "Do you know I had to do that in silence for it to work?"

I nodded. "Was it difficult?"

"It was one of the most difficult things I've done in my entire life," he said seriously. We all laughed, but I stole a moment to establish whether Kirsty and Mungo shared glances, and the evidence of my eyes distressed me.

In the days which followed my thoughts brought me more pain than my leg. Tullibardine's physician dressed the wound and left some ointment, saying I must rest easy for as long as my body told me so, or else I would end up visiting a surgeon to have the limb removed. The earl himself visited me on occasion, as did Lady Katherine; although I was aware his conversation was more pointed than hers, determined as he was to establish more details of the events at Loch Dochart and on the Bass. With the strain of loyalties preying on my mind I was happy to offer him the impression that Simon had done nothing but the which he believed to be for the best; an impression I shared to a great degree, having had time to consider matters. Tullibardine observed, more than once, that he was more convinced by the fact of my wounds that Simon was true than by any of my lord's words.

179

George was a regular companion, sharing stories which excited him about the adventures of his predecessors, and speaking at great length about how it would be when he were an earl leading a regiment. He asked me about my own experiences of soldiering and I felt comfortable enough to share more with him than I had with anyone – except Kirsty. She did sit with me on occasion; but each time the feeling in the room seemed to worsen. At first I tried to kiss her hand, but she preferred to simply let me hold it. I spoke to her the way in which I was accustomed, but she no longer called me by the names she had used, and so I let mine rest too. I could not bring myself to say that which I needed to say; yet on one occasion I came close, saying her name then falling silent, but saying all with my eyes. She looked back at me with sadness and said quietly: "I'm glad you're feeling better, Bolla." That name had never felt so like poison.

I had to draw the conclusion that she felt it better to play the mistress of a lord than the woman of a wounded soldier. I remembered those in Aberdeen who huddled together in relationships without love in order to survive the challenges of life, and I wondered if her choice was borne from a similar perspective.

It was Simon who kept my spirits alive, telling me about the history of Huntingtower, about how, when the work was finished, there would still be a bridge between the towers, half-way up, but there would be rooms around it; and about how King James the Sixth (the victim of the raid of Ruthven, which we had re-enacted) was twice the subject of intrigue at the hands of those who held the castle before Murray. When he and George both sat with me, great laughter was had – one time so strong that my leg bled briefly once more. Yet sometimes I would remember that if the three of us were here, two of us were elsewhere.

I do know know whether it was one of Simon's more understanding machinations; but when he suggested another re-enactment for George's entertainment, it appeared also to represent an opportunity for me to at least attempt a renews intimacy with Kirsty. "Do you know the story of Lady Greensleeves?" he asked the young lord, and when the reply was negative, he lamented: "What kind of times are we living in when you live in a haunted castle and you haven't even been told?"

"Haunted?" George repeated, eyes wide. "By a ghost?"

"Absolutely," Simon confirmed. "A long time ago Lady Greensleeves lived here, and she was in love with a servant. Same as now, the family lived in the west tower and the servants lived in the east. Well, the lady was in her lover's chamber when she heard her mother coming up the stairs to catch her. She tried to jump from one tower the other – and fell to her death." My lord allowed a silence to pass, while George, captivated, waited for him to continue. "They say when the moon is full you'll see Lady Greensleeves wandering in the castle, looking for her lost love."

"When will the moon next be full?" the boy demanded.

"Let me see," Simon replied. "What date is it? The sixth? Well I never – it's tomorrow night!"

"I want to see Lady Greensleeves!" George said excitedly.

"Well, we must see what we can do," my lord replied. "But it might mean staying up late. You're probably too young."

"I can stay up all night! I've done it before!"

"Good man, Geordie! I'll ask your father if it's all right."

"Ask Ma," he said cautiously.

Having secured permission to perform the feat, Simon gathered Kirsty and Mungo in my chamber and explained his idea. "I'll take him out on the east tower where there's not so much mason's mess for him to fall over. But the doors onto the parapets face each other so I need a reason to take him round the far side. So, Mungo, I need you in the trees waving a light as if it's a spirit moving towards us."

"Must I?" that man said, clearly uninterested.

"Come on – it's for your wee nephew!" Simon encouraged.

"Aye, come on, Mungo," Kirsty said. "It'll be fun!" At that he appeared to become more positive. I expected nothing less.

Simon continued: "Kirsty, you need to get yourself done up all in white, with your face and hair white too. Can you arrange something?"

"Katherine will help," she said. "Something wavy and ghostly?"

"That's it," my lord grinned. "Wavy and ghostly. Bolla, you need to look after the lights to shine on Kirsty on the west tower. It's a narrow wee parapet so you'll have to take care. When Geordie and I are round the other side watching Mungo's lights, you two get on the parapet. Bolla, you wave the lights, and, Kirsty, you act — well, like a ghost looking for something. After a couple of moments walk away round the back of the parapet, and as you go out of the light it should look like you're fading away. All clear?"

"I'll do the lights for you," Mungo told Kirsty.

"Use your brain, man, not your —" Simon said. "Think! Bolla here can't go running about in the trees with his leg, can he? Besides, I want to know if it looks good from above. If it does, you never know, we might use it again." He grinned, but he cannot have missed the looks which passed between Kirsty and Mungo, and between me and no one.

The following night arrived with the conditions my lord had stipulated, and he declared it perfect for an appearance of Lady Greensleeves. Lord George spoke about almost nothing else all day, sitting on Kirsty's lap and explaining in great detail how the spirit might be as beautiful as she, but would be no more so, and declaring that, if she appeared, he would ask her how long she had lingered and where she went during the hours of day. Tullibardine and Lady Katherine were both amused by Simon's scheme, and it appeared to bring the parties even closer than the previous days of discussion had done.

Soon after dusk – George's parents had urged us to send him to his couch as early as possible – I waited on the stair leading to the west tower's parapet, looking at the two lamps I was to control and attempting not to recall the night I had performed a similar duty on the Bass Rock. The appearance of Kirsty below gave me cause to start: dressed in a white undergarment with cloths sewn on to billow round her arms and legs, and with pasted-white face and powdered-white hair, she seemed otherworldly enough without the assistance of lights. Laughing at my reaction, she asked "How do I look?"

"Astounding," I said. "Truly, astounding."

"Not bad for a wee bit of cutting and sewing," she replied, reaching the landing on which I waited. "Do you like it?"

"Very much," I said. Her face was close to mine as she looked into my eyes and smiled, the way she had done in the past. For a moment, I knew, she allowed her emotions to shine through, and they were still within her; but then she seemed to catch herself in the midst of an admission, and as she turned away I beheld the distance return to her expression.

182

"It's nearly time," she said, "Let's not let Geordie down." I did not reply; instead I gently opened the door to the parapet, pulling it closed again as I realised Simon and the young lord were in the process of stepping onto the platform on the tower opposite. I allowed a few moments to pass then tried again, and, seeing Simon disappearing round the corner, proceeded onto the high ledge.

My lamps were lit but I had put cloaks over them to keep them hidden. I placed them near one corner of the walkway and crouched, with some difficulty, into a corner where I could reach them both but remain unseen. I signalled to Kirsty that I was prepared, and she stepped into her position between the lamps. Just then I caught sight of a point of light which seemed to be floating through the trees beyond the castle. It flickered, then vanished, then after a moment reappeared a little further away; and the feat was repeated several times. Had I not known it was Mungo's work I might have believed I was seeing some form of apparition; I pointed it out to Kirsty and we both watched, a little transfixed, until it faded and did not reappear.

Soon afterwards we heard Geordie's voice from the other tower, and a moment later we made out the shades of he and Simon approaching us. I reached over and lifted the cloaks – but not fully away; instead I waved them back and forth so, I hoped, Kirsty's ghost would appear to flicker. The effect was impressive even from my viewpoint. She was dancing without moving her feet, making all motion with her waist and arms, while turning her head from side to side and letting her hair fly around her. Despite my concentration on managing the lamps, the sensual suggestion of her movements did not evade me, and the knowledge of what I no longer possessed saddened me.

"It's her!" I heard the young lord shout.

"So it is!" Simon replied loudly, although there was little need since the pair were but a few footsteps away from us, only separated by the space between the towers.

"Lady Greensleeves!" Geordie said in awe. "It is you! How long have you been a ghost?" His lack of fear was amusing. "Answer me!" he continued, then, when there came no reply (for clear reasons) he shouted: "It's not your castle any more – it's mine! So answer me!"

I sensed we had achieved all we could, and Kirsty seemed to think the same, for she began to step back from the lamps and turn to move along the parapet.

"Wait, Lady Greensleeves!" George shouted. "You couldn't jump! I'll teach you how to jump!" I heard running footsteps and Simon shouting a warning. Alarmed, I abandoned the lamps and made to stand up. Looking towards the far tower, I saw the shape of George, who had stepped back along the parapet, running towards me, with Simon appearing to make a grabbing motion in the air around him. "Wait for me!" the boy called — and leapt into space.

He vanished in the darkness almost instantly. Simon shouted his name into the air below us. Kirsty let out a startled gasp. I heard the sound of an impact not far below, almost certainly on the top of the wall the masons were currently building. Then, after a few moments of silence, there came a much worse and more final noise from the ground. Kirsty nearly toppled us both in her haste to reach the parapet edge, but I stabled us. There was nothing to see in the darkness, until the lamp Mungo had been carrying on his way back to the castle appeared, lit up a scene of disaster, and gave just a hint to the anguish behind the agonised scream the boy's uncle sent out into the still, silent night.

"HE WON'T SEE YOU," Mungo told Simon.

"He has to," my lord all but pleaded. "He has to be told…"

"He doesn't want to know. You should go — now."

Head bowed, face pale and shoulders slumped, Simon looked broken in a way I had never seen any man, let alone this fox of a character. Tullibardine wanted no explanation or apology, as Mungo had underlined; Lady Katherine, too, was unable to bring herself to speak, even to Kirsty. "Mungo… please."

His friend struggled with his expression for a moment, then achieved a level look, before saying: "Simon, you need to be off. He's done with you. And… and I'm done with you too. Just be off."

"Don't say that!" my lord cried.

But Mungo shook his head. "Ian's right about you. Things just… *happen* around you. You're a bad omen, or something. God knows you don't cause it all – but I know you cause enough. I've had it with you,

Simon. I want to do some good with my life. Not… whatever it is you do." A painful silence fell. The friends stared at each other, one having said all, the other knowing he could say nothing. We were already aware the interview would end with our departure — although the finality of it had certainly not occurred to me — and so our horses were ready. My lord and I turned away, knowing we would not be welcome as Mungo and Kirsty shared what they had to.

"I've been involved in some things in my life, Bolla." Simon told me quietly. "Never anything like this."

"It wasn't you," I repeated as the chorus it had become for me since the tragedy of the previous night. "No one could have guessed he was going to… do *that*."

"I should have. I knew him. I know everyone, Bolla – it's how I can do…" There was nothing I could add, so I did not make any attempt. Instead I mounted my horse with less difficulty than I had previously endured, and waited as Simon slowly mount his. A short time later Kirsty joined us, and we set off, alone and unaccompanied. Kirsty sobbed as we passed under the tree where George had met us, and I do not think it was a simple feat for any of us to retain composure.

We made as fast work of it as we could. The days were still bright and the nights warm, but without Simon's usual attempts at providing cheer – the beggars we encountered were even passed without the expected dispensation of farthings – together with my pain over my turmoil with Kirsty, the journey was an altogether dark experience.

We had not made more than half way to home when Simon diverted us onto an unexpected road, leading us westerly instead of the northerly route which led to Fraser country. I had not the spirit to question him, finding solace only in an enduring silence during which I barely saw the land around me; Kirsty, of course, was built of different stock. "Where are we going?" she asked.

"Work to do," Simon replied, almost brightly, making an attempt to break the despair which surrounded us. "We're off to see the best man in the Highlands. And we could all do with that, I think." Kirsty slowed her horse. I glanced at her, unable to look directly into her eyes, but she did not so much as gaze in my direction. Instead she directed a look of anger and hatred at Simon's back – for he had not slowed or turned –

and, without any further words, she turned and made for the road home.

To one who passed nearby, observing us, my condition might have looked exactly as it felt: mounted on my horse I turned one way then the other, unable to concentrate my feelings as my lord moved steadily along one road while my love set off on a different one. I do not know how long I remained in doubt – perhaps moments, perhaps until this day – but, finally resolved as best I could be, I turned and sped to follow Simon. When I caught him up he did not refer to the decision I had made; instead he grinned at me and said: "Well, it's not all bad, Bolla, is it? At least you know who your friends are." He patted his packet of papers. "And I have new information."

I said nothing. In truth I found it impossible to believe that he was able to put behind him so quickly such a tragedy as the death of Lord George; and to ignore the obvious distress my recent decision had caused me. "It seems Murray is moving faster than I thought," he went on. "I... found some letters at Huntingtower that made very interesting reading. Someone we're about to meet will agree with me."

"You stole letters from Tullibardine?" I asked, astonished despite myself.

He grinned. "I didn't say that, did I? But you didn't think I was just looking round the castle so that we picked the right room for a trick of the light — did you?"

I fell into a silence as deep as that which had previously held me; but the reason for it seemed far darker to me.

CHAPTER SIX
THE MUMMER OF THE MASSACRE

I PRIMED MY PISTOL as a light breeze rose from the west, whispering in my ears to add to the turmoil in my mind, then placed it within my jacket. I had already decided that, despite my soldier's comfort in using the weapon, today was not the day I would first kill another man.

"They're coming," Simon told me, examining his own two pistols before hiding them in the pack of his horse, then extracting two wine goblets and a flask from another pocket. "Remember, Bolla – if they're Campbells they can't be allowed to get away. This is about thousands; maybe tens of thousands." I did not know whether he meant lives or coins. It mattered not to me. After the ideas which had torn through my thoughts, waking and sleeping, in recent days, I felt myself to be loosing the chains holding me to him.

"But if they are Campbells, they are friends," I protested. "Are we not with Breadalbane?"

He paused to fill both goblets, balanced on his horse's saddle, before packing the flask away and handing me one of the drinks. "Not today," he said. "If Breadalbane knows we're here, so many things will get more difficult. Now – time to earn your shilling," he hissed as the three redcoats galloped to where we stood. "Hello there!" he bellowed in a warm tone towards them. There was no warmth in their expressions as I turned to watch. In truth there was little chance they were not Campbells, for this was Glen Orchy, the country of the unfortunate Captain Colin Campbell – a name which had been in my consideration since we journeyed through Glen Dochart, following our separation from Kirsty.

One soldier dismounted while the others remained in their saddles, rifles drawn upon us. "Identify yourselves!" barked he who moved towards us on foot, drawing a pistol.

"Captain Fraser and Sergeant Fraser," Simon responded smartly, waving his glass in a gesture of welcome. "Lord Murray's Regiment."

"Lieutenant McArthur, Argyll's Regiment," said the other, his naturally narrow and suspicious face poorly lit by small, dark eyes, tightened with more dubiety than I could tell they displayed normally. "What are you doing here?"

"We're taking an urgent message to Inveraray," my lord replied.

"Let me see your papers."

"Ah." Simon made an appealing gesture. "Well, we've been ordered not to come into contact with other troops, or anyone else, for that matter. You've got us into trouble by stopping us."

I would not have thought it possible for McArthur to look even more suspicious, but he achieved that feat. Just then one of his men called to him. "That's Simon the Fox — the one who was at Loch Dochart!"

Simon grinned and flashed me a sideways glance. "No, no. I just look like him. I'm his half-brother. You want Lieutenant Fraser – he's in Perth with Colonel Murray. I think. Right… papers!"

I wanted no part in what was to happen next; yet I was trapped in the moment and its consequences, and I could do no other than at least follow Simon's lead. He replaced his goblet on his saddle and opened a pocket of its pack, while the Campbells, even more tense and alert, shared their own glances for a moment. "Turn round!" McArthur cried — but he was too late, for Simon was already doing just that. The pistol in his right hand blew the lieutenant off his feet and, in the same instant, that in his left knocked one dragoon from his mount. The second fired his rifle, but in his panic aimed high and sent the ball over our heads.

"Bolla!" cried Simon as the last Campbell turned to gallop away. Yet, terrified as I was, I ascertained that there was no further immediate danger; and so I remained with my hand in my jacket, tight around my pistol, still determined that I would not kill. Instead my lord moved forward and grabbed the weapon McArthur had dropped. He took a moment – a long, leisurely moment – to settle his aim on the retreating soldier, then delivered his shot into his back.

Silence fell. I realised that almost a straight line led from my feet to the body of McArthur, that of the first Campbell, and, some distance further, that of the third. In the long grass I could not see how the last man had fallen, but if he lay facing the sky, his arms above his head, it would almost have seemed as if someone had arranged the bodies.

"Devil choke me, Bolla!" Simon said, strangely calm. McArthur's pistol still smoked as he recovered his wine, which, astonishingly, had remained balanced upon his saddle. "I could have done with a bit of help there." I said nothing. I was trapped in a moment but recently passed: a moment in which three soldiers of our own army lived, breathed and asked my lord a reasonable question, expecting a reasonable answer instead of sudden death. It seemed to me that, even as my eyes swept across the tragedy, I could still see those men as they had been: one unmounted, two on horse, three alive.

"I really do need help now," my lord said, emptying his goblet, then mine, repacking them and pressing me into action with a push of his hand. "Let's get these lads out of sight." One by one, we recovered the warm bodies and threw them into a nearly-dry burn that ran beside the road. McArthur moaned a little as we carried him; but Simon stood over him and forced his head into the shallow water, which proved deep enough to bring him to peace.

The grim task done, my lord inspected the packs of the two horses which remained with us (having previously examined the contents of the men's pockets, offering me a few coins, which I refused); and, discovering two papers, declared himself satisfied. "Orders to detain one Captain Simon Fraser, and to shoot him to death if he attempts to resist," he said, grinning, waving a sheet of paper towards me. "Signed by Ian Cam, would you believe?" I was not sure whether I believed; and I could not read the document myself to be sure; although by now I felt certain I could identify some often-seen shapes from my days of copying. "And one rather more interesting wee note," he said, adding them to his packet, before shouting by way of changing the mood: "Now! Where were we? Aye, the best man in the Highlands. Onward, Bolla! We're not finished for the day yet! Although God knows we've earned a proper drink…"

My horse followed his on the road without the need for me to offer guidance; and so, instead, I reflected on the first time I had witnessed Simon kill a man. Corpses were a common sight to all of us – I do not remember the first such thing I beheld any more than I remember who brought me forth into this world. Therefore I could not question his lack of interest in the cadavers; but I could, and must, find query in his calm reaction to having caused the demise of those who had lived within them. It is for us all to consider new experiences as we enjoy or endure them; yet Simon betrayed no evidence of fright, relief, anger, doubt or even simple curiosity: he had taken three lives the way he might take three cups of ale, and had given them as much consideration. In the same fashion as it was impossible (or near so) to conclude he was blameless in all the deaths which had befallen those around us since our travels began in Aberdeen, it was also such to conclude I had beheld the first time he had taken a life with his own hands. Even his finishing of McArthur in common human contact, his hands pushing down on the other's face, seemed not to be a virgin experience. My thoughts travelled to the shores of Loch Eil and the sorry parts of a man which lay there still. Had his last touch on earth been from my lord's hands, pushing him below water into unfathomable eternal depths?

I remained drowned in realisations I knew I had ignored and conclusions I did not wish to draw, so much so that it was a surprise to me when I realised that a vision which had been gradually rising up at great distance before us now dominated my eyesight, and, indeed, had also begun dominating my thinking, even though I had not been aware of it. I awoke to full consciousness, and looked up to behold the most severe, dark and starkly beautiful scenery I had observed in all my days. "Glen Coe, Bolla!" Simon grinned, seeing my expression. "Isn't it brilliant?" It was difficult to find argument. If the flats of Rannoch Moor, across which we had rode, could be said to be sleeping, then the mountains of Glen Coe were very much awake: awake and staring proudly towards us, demanding attention while seeming to also dismiss it as irrelevant. On our left the bens exploded up beneath our feet to a great height in one movement, seeming to confound any measurement of time or distance. To our right a solid backbone of near equal height thundered to heaven and remained there. And in between our road led down into a place I would have accepted as hell if I had been advised it was such. Yet it was all stirringly virile and fatally appealing. It took me some moments to recall we had already passed the place where MacDonald of Caolasnacon had died — also from a shot to the back.

As the glen opened up around us I beheld that it was not hell, nor anything near it. The road took us down steeply, far below the level of the moor, making the mountains loom ever steeper above us and forcing the river we followed to plummet dozens of feet beneath; but far from retaining its threatening composure I began to sense a benevolent, protective feeling, as if, once we had passed the sentinels at the east end, we had been declared friends. It also seemed so with the houses we passed, with cautious faces changing to polite welcoming nods, and Simon's bag of farthings returning to use as he told MacDonalds how the Frasers had ever been united with them against Campbell of Glenorchy – and how he had struck a blow in that fight that very afternoon.

By the moment we reached the first village, the mountains had receded far enough to allow pleasant meadows to stand between its walls, and the river flattened and widened to offer a merry accompaniment to our progress. Stopped for refreshment, Simon asked one man: "Where will we find MacIain himself?"

The other laughed. "Himself will find you," he replied. It proved to be so; for, as we once again took to the road, we saw before us a group of approaching horse, and, at the centre of the party, there was one who could only be chief of this country. Even from a distance his bearing was regal and timeless, as the hills he commanded; and on closing, I could tell his broad, long-bearded form was of a great age, and yet it seemed young. Seven men lined the way before us, side by side, and without issuing any instruction our mounts stopped about a dozen paces from them. He who commanded slid from his saddle and, as if we had been ordered, all of us followed – even Simon. The great man approached alone, his motion speaking of a power and authority I knew to be unquestionable. They stared at one another; but, unusually, it was not my lord who appeared to be the natural leader. The breadth of communication which travelled between the two, without a word shared, astounded me; until, finally, my lord said with a dry mouth:

"MacIain," and bowed.

The other did not break his gaze. "Simon," he said with a slow, quiet and yet powerful voice. "The Fox." My lord made to laugh but managed no convincing performance. Then the chief's eyes turned to me, and I found myself locked in the same deep conversation without sound. I could not look away; and I did not want to. For this was no interrogation: it was in many ways a simple inquiry, but delivered with authority: "Who are you?" And I had no choice but to answer – as did he, unbidden. Suddenly his eyebrows rose and he smiled, and clasped me on both shoulders with hands I knew could crush me if they so chose. "Your name?" he asked with his understated authority. I told him. "Bolla Fraser, you are welcome in Glen Coe!" he cried, and hugged me. He turned to his companions, placing one arm on each of our shoulders – it was the first moment he had made contact with Simon – and called: "These are friends. And they need a drink!" If my lord felt any reaction to the difference in our treatment, he did not show it.

MACIAIN WAS A MAN APART; of that there could be no doubt. As I beheld the communication he conducted with his people on our brief journey to his home, I saw him make much use of that strange ability to say much with few or no words. They clearly expected it and were comfortable with it, although I saw no one else display such a talent. The reason — or at least, a reason — was offered to me later in the evening by the chief's ghillie, one giant of a man named Cathal Hendrie, with whom I sat for dinner in the crowded MacDonald hall. "He has the sight, you understand," that one explained. "They say when the gift falls on a man it falls all the stronger. It is said of him that he was born knowing the day and time he will die."

"He does not look as old as he must be," I said.

"It is said he counts years not of men, but of mountains," Cathal told me. "It appears to me that he has looked as he does now for all the life I have known him. I cannot explain it – although he has tried to tell me often. I have not the mind to see."

I looked over to where MacIain and Simon were seated, near the fire, although the house was not cold. "I fear they should talk somewhere more private," I said, almost entirely to myself.

"There is nothing to fear about," Cathal replied. "Himself hides nothing from any of us — there's only what we hide from ourselves for want of understanding." He finished with a laugh: "And that is a lot!" as I saw Simon gesture for me to approach.

"Bolla will tell you what I said as we raised the company," my lord was explaining to the chief. "That we were to fight for King Jamie and no one else." I confirmed his words as I seated myself beside them, but MacIain did not appear interested. "I can only get the information I need for us all if I'm on the inside."

"So you are Murray's man?" asked the MacDonald.

"I speak with many and I speak for many," Simon grinned.

That did not appear to upset the chief. "So, then, you are not with Breadalbane?"

"I have a connection with him," my lord acknowledged. "But we aren't close."

"It is like choosing to fight a bear or a wolf."

"But you agree we have to fight."

"Aye," MacIain said. "And I have fought both bear and wolf, and killed both. Breadalbane was behind that talk at Achallader."

"The money he promised will come to you."

"Never say 'promise' and 'Breadalbane' together – the power of those words clashing will break your mind, just!"

"I know there's no love lost between MacDonald and Campbell —"

"That is not true," the chief replied sternly. "Stories told by folk who do not know their history. My own son is married to a Campbell. We have our run-ins, of course. They want our country – they want every country. So we have to fight. And everyone is always at the *creachadh*. We take forty of his cows, but he took fifty of ours before that; after we took a hundred, after he took two hundred. That is how it has always been. But Breadalbane himself? That is a man who will break any rule for gain. That is not the way. It is not the Campbell way either."

"You'll get what you were promised," Simon repeated.

The other laughed. "I was promised nothing. Others were. Grand Locheil, that high-minded man – he was shouting for twenty thousand pounds, and Breadalbane said he would be given twelve. He mentioned a few hundred for me — but the price was too high and we made no bargain."

My lord appeared surprised. "So little? Perhaps I can do something about that," he said.

"No — I tell you the price was too high: betraying King Jamie. And my own Abarach." As if to demonstrate he bellowed the clan's name for itself, and the assembled dozens bellowed it back. "The king will return," he stated with intense confidence. "So I will not promise anything to anyone else."

"It's said King Jamie is going to tell the clans to sign the peace treaty," Simon replied, watching the other carefully. "Because a promise made by force is no promise at all. And it gives us the time we need."

MacIain shook his head. "I do not need time. I need my honour, and I need not to have a lie put on paper in my name. The king will return, and the Abarach will be there, and all I have to do is wait."

"Listen to me," Simon said. "There's a few things you may not know, but I know, and I've brought you the letters to prove it. Breadalbane will come out for Jamie if he comes back. So will Murray. A temporary peace in the Highlands will make it all work out. If —" he waved a finger in the air — "Billy's men are satisfied the clans really mean it."

"What you tell me leads me to trust Breadalbane and Murray even less than I do now," the chief replied. "And I don't need to see any letters. If Jamie orders me to sign on pain of death I will do it. Otherwise I will not. Because the king is coming back." With a single look MacIain signalled the conversation was ended, and he fell into a distant, thoughtful silence. Simon watched him for some moments afterwards.

The following morning I found myself outside the house, staring up in awe at the mountains which shot away and above me in every direction. It was long after sunrise, but there were still many secret corners of the glen yet to see its face, such were the angles of the rock. I could not begin to estimate the distances between myself and any hillside; and I was engaged upon attempting to gather a rough measurement by means of assuming the height of a faraway tree, when I heard MacIain's voice behind me. "This country screamed its way through a birth of blood," he said with his soft yet strong tones, as he came up to me with Cathal Hendrie by his side. "But its days of anger are gone. It knows it will be here long after kings fall and papers are worn by time."

"Simon thinks it important you see the letters," I replied, with no doubt as to what he referred, and without feeling any strangeness at speaking so directly – even though I seldom did.

"Paper does not last long enough to take seriously," the chief told me. "We kill wood every day. You cannot kill stone. Or spirit."

He signalled for me to walk with them, and we wandered among the foothills while he told me the names of each summit and a little of his clan's history. After a time we approached the steep eastern end of the glen; but instead of following the road, which was a difficult climb of itself, he led us to the southern bank of the river we followed and led us through a steep and treacherous ascent. "The scenic route," he told me as we stopped, somewhat strained, at the summit. "You may find it useful to know. But show no one – not even that Fox."

"Simon is —" I began, but I had not the words to form a defence.

"I know who he is," MacIain replied. "And I know what he is. I've had cause to think about him since the death of Campbell of Glenorchy – and our Alex of Caolasnacon. Aye, I know Simon the Fox well enough. And I know you, too."

"How?" I asked bluntly, sure that it was the correct way to speak.

"Did they tell you I have the sight?" I nodded, and he looked at Cathal Hendrie before he answered, although the other made no response. "Well, they are right and they are wrong. I see things about people that others miss. But it is not because the story is not told – it is because they do not know how to listen for it. Oh, it is a grand and useful trick to be able to play," he smiled. "To silence your enemy with a look, or silence a crying child with a finger, or silence a scared cow with a hand. But if you took the time, and you watched and learned, you could do it too.

"New tricks are coming, though," he sighed. "Tricks of paper and ink. Now, those tricks are beyond me as much as mine are beyond them. But it is nothing to worry about."

"They appear to be very powerful," I said. "I've seen them change things."

"Change is for out there," he responded, waving across Rannoch Moor beyond his own country. "I can only speak for the Abarach, and it is my duty to speak well. The king will come back – I have seen it. And, yes, that is the sight." He turned to me and stared at me intently, placing his hand tightly on my upper arm. His voice changed and I felt my hold on the world around me slipping just beyond my grasp as he said: "Jamie will set foot on this land once again. He will come with just a few friends, but the clans will be waiting for him, and MacDonald will be among them. The Highlands will march south, and we will fight hard, and we will take so much of England that it will seem no hardship to let us have Scotland. God is with Jamie, and with MacDonald. And my duty is with the king and God." As he spoke I believe I saw shadows of his ideas in my mind; nothing I could swear to in certainty, and nothing I could fully describe. The images felt strangely wrong, as if dark were replaced by light and vice-versa; yet what I felt I remember still: feet on a shore, torches raised on a hillside, the knowledge of thousands of people around me, the fear and rage of fighting, the swing of a sword and reaction from a fired rifle — with an incredible sensation of belief and confidence. And the greatest shock, and also the strongest impression, came through a vision of Kirsty: but somehow different, and somehow more important, and more loved, to me.

"They say you know the time of your death," I whispered.

"No," he said. "But I have my part to play. So do we all, Bolla Fraser – you, and that fox."

"It's not our dance, but we must follow the rules," I heard myself saying.

"Very good," MacIain said, and disengaged his stare and his hand. I began to stumble as the world around me seemed the distort again, returning to that which I felt to be normal, but seemed for the moment strangely slow and dull. The reason I did not fall was Cathal Hendrie, who had positioned himself behind me and supported me by my shoulders.

"Be at peace," the ghillie said, retaining his much-needed grip as the chief moved towards the river. "Time is what you need. And so does he – that tires him out."

"What happened?" I asked, remaining dazed.

"Nothing — for he has not the sight," my companion replied, laughing quietly. "Whatever happened, you saw what he wanted you to see. Not many people can."

"Who is he?" I asked, fighting the urge to deny to myself that anything unusual had just happened; while also fighting to establish control over my own thoughts, in which it had taken place.

"He's Himself," Cathal said simply. "I have fought with him, killed with him, taken cattle with him and laughed with him, and if it is to hell he must go then I will go also. But I think it is you who knows better who he is. I think you understand."

MacIain had stooped at the edge of the river and was now returning to us. He held out his hand, wet from the waters, and showed me a small number of pebbles. "That burn, the Cona – it often worries me," he muttered. I found it difficult to believe anything could perform such a feat. "The blood of this country's birth washed away long before the Abarach came — and yet the stones in the water will burn red."

He turned himself so his body no longer blocked the sunshine from his hand, and, as he had said, there seemed something in the stones which rendered them more crimson than anything I had seen, except blood. "There is something I cannot see, and I think it is because I do not want to," he told me. "But whatever it is… If it is my duty to deal with it, then I will."

WHEN WE TOOK OUR LEAVE of MacIain the following day, I was disposed to believe him when he said we would meet again. As we rode north towards Fort William I sensed that Simon, who had seemingly spent less time in the chief's company than I, desired to know more about what we had discussed. I said little; not through any need to keep the information from him, but through the sure knowledge that he would dismiss it – and I knew the importance of what had happened to me. It was only as we approached the town of Maryburgh ahead of the fort that I realised our danger. "Should we not avoid this area?" I asked. "Since we have no passes? We're certain to be stopped." I did not say the obvious: that even Simon could not attempt to destroy an entire garrison and hope to succeed.

Yet he simply shrugged. "We'll see," he said. Soon afterwards my fears were confirmed as a patrol of six redcoats on foot appeared behind a bend in the road ahead, and we had been sighted before being able to cover ourselves. Without being asked I leaned over to make ready my pistol, but, seeing me, Simon said: "Put it away, Bolla. I think we'll be fine."

We were halted as I expected, and demands were made about our identities, which my lord dealt with as he had in Glen Orchy. Yet the similarity in situations ended there – for on establishing the redcoats were not from these parts, he produced a document which satisfied them that we were to be allowed to continue unmolested.

"You had a pass all the time?" I asked, incredulous at the thought of three men having been killed when a slip of paper might have made all well.

"Not for Campbell eyes," Simon replied.

"But surely it came from Breadalbane? You would not have got one from Murray."

He shrugged again. "I need to be careful until I know what everyone's going to do about the peace treaty. I needed to know what MacIain plans to do — but I didn't want Breadalbane knowing that I knew. Or Murray, for that matter."

"And you're not concerned that MacIain won't sign?" I asked, feeling bolder than I had in the past about examining him. "What about the time you need?"

"I keep telling you: the plan's so good that knowing it can't stop it," he replied. "Anyway, I don't care what MacIain does. I just needed to know what it was going to be."

"So does any of this make any difference?" I cried, thinking of the three men who lay in a burn in Glen Orchy.

"God knows," said my lord with a grin.

For much of the rest of the day, I wound myself in silent thought; but as our shadows lengthened, then faded as the sun fell below the mountains to the west, I began succumbing to a great tiredness which rendered me equally quiet, but less capable of thinking. I believe it was the longest day's journey I had undertaken since my injuries at the Bass, and I believe I was only moments from pleading with Simon for rest when, at last, the shape of a tall castle appeared above the trees ahead of us. Four men appeared from the woods which hid the prospect of Loch Oich from our view, and our names and intents were once again demanded of us. "Simon Fraser, the Young MacShimi!" my lord said, with as much grandeur as he could muster in his own exhaustion. "Here to greet my cousin, the Young Glengarry."

We appeared to require no further investigation, and instead we were escorted to the looming towers of Invergarry Castle, which rose to the height of six storeys, perched on a rock overlooking the loch. Our horses taken to enjoy their own relaxation, we mounted the protective stairs to the castle's first floor, where a messenger bade us wait until those within could be advised of our arrival. It was not long until a tall, ferocious man, clearly a warrior, appeared before us and marched up to clasp Simon's arm. "Simon!" he said with a voice I suspect he wanted to sound warm – yet there was no disguising the natural aggression which surrounded his very being.

"Alasdair!" my lord replied. "I see you're well! How's Isabel?"

"Aye, she's well too," that man said. "She's not here, mind – I don't want her this close to Fort William. That *amaideach* Saxon, Hill, could be here any day. They want this —" he gestured around himself to indicate the building — "out of Jamie's hands. Did you hear Maclean surrendered Duart Castle?"

"I did," Simon said. "But I think—"

"What a *gorach*! Have you seen the thing? They could have held it for years! Anyway, come away in. My father is here too."

"Good. I need to speak to you both."

We followed him into a dimly-lit room where two more men sat near the fire, rendered silhouettes by its flames. "Friends, it is," our host announced. "Simon Fraser."

"The Young MacShimi," my lord added.

They both stood in response, the traditional rules of hospitality dictating that, as new arrivals, we should be seated at the warmth. For a moment I believed my lord was about to refuse the kindness, which would have near broken my spirit; but he sat, and, grateful to end the day's movement, I settled into a chair which could not possibly be as

199

comfortable as my mind told me. From there I took the opportunity to assay our companions, estimating all three to be hardened fighters by their tall, heavy yet agile constitutions. "My sergeant, Bolla Fraser," Simon said, and I nodded as he continued: "Bolla, you remember the big man who had Jamie's standard at Killiecrankie, and who broke the line? That's him – Alasdair Dubh MacDonell, and his father Ranald, chief of Glengarry."

"I didn't see you at Killiecrankie, Fraser," Ranald growled, his old features twisting with his words.

"No? I saw you, though – spectacular sport!"

"This," Alasdair Dubh said, arm extended toward the last man in the room, "Is Father Robert Munro." I returned my gaze to that person, for I had never seen a priest before. Despite Fraser, like most clans, keeping the old faith alongside the new, the severe penalties for harbouring one of its spiritual leaders – let alone hearing Mass – meant very few of them remained in Scotland beyond prison gates.

"We've met before, Father," Simon said. "You came through our country three or four years ago – I think you'd just arrived from France?"

"That I had," Munro replied with a delivery every part as aggressive as the MacDonells. "I've not been back to you since – but I should."

"We'd be proud to welcome you," my lord said. "We all need spiritual nourishment in these hard times."

"We'll start now, then," Alasdair Dubh said, pushing cups of whisky into our hands. "Rob?"

The priest bowed his head, as did we, and he let peace settle upon us before, in a voice more rounded and toned than in the speech he had previously given, he said: "Dear Father in Heaven, we give thanks for your gift of the Holy Spirit, that gives us the power to fight against the evils that torment this land. We ask that the false king, William, is cast out of Your holy sight. And we pray for the return of the King James Stuart, placed on the throne by Your divine goodness. We humbly beseech all through Christ, our Lord. Amen."

We chorused "Amen" in response, and, holding up his cup, Munro said: "King Jamie," which we all repeated before drinking. I have had cause on many occasions to be grateful for the warming, empowering effects of whisky; but at that moment, in my exhausted state, it seemed to me the liquid had been sent directly from He to whom we had so recently spoken.

Without warning, the atmosphere changed: Ranald glared at Simon and said accusingly: "You've come from Breadalbane."

"*Ochone*, I have not!" my lord replied loudly, seemingly unaffected by the level of threat in the other's voice. "I've come from MacIain – and I had the privilege of removing three of Breadalbane's men from this earth on the way."

"Good upon you," Alasdair Dubh said as the priest made the sign of the cross upon himself, although he bore no expression of anger or regret. "So what news?"

"You know of Achallader?"

"I was there," Ranald said darkly. "That Campbell turncoat offered money for those who'd betray Jamie. I saw enough of them agree to make me sick — Jamie needs none of these *gorachs* with him!"

Simon paused for a moment. "Well... I have good word that Breadalbane's not going to pay up anyway. That – and MacIain will sign the peace treaty if Jamie tells us to. Which he's going to."

I was tired, and the second drink served by Alasdair Dubh had moved straight into my mind. Yet I was not somnolent enough to miss that Simon had spoken the opposite of which he had told MacIain, and which MacIain had told him, just one night previously. "And one more thing," he continued, preventing another outburst from the chief of Glengarry. "Breadalbane has committed that, as soon as King Jamie returns, he'll come out for him – with at least a thousand men."

"*Ochone!*" whispered Alasdair Dubh. "He would do that?"

"I have a paper to prove it."

"Traitor!" Ranald spat. "Jamie doesn't need him."

"Aye, he does," Alasdair Dubh said. "Of course he does."

"It would be dangerous for him to sign a paper, though," Munro said quietly. "I think he would have too much to lose if that got into the wrong hands." He raised his cup to his face as he stared intently at Simon. "Which it may have done."

My lord shrugged. "I can't tell you how it came about. But I can show you it." He opened the packet of letters which was never far from his hand, and, carefully selecting one while ensuring no others were seen, he opened it and held it out. Despite the dull surroundings, the tiredness I felt and the brief moment I had to look, I felt I recognised the document – some of the larger flowing patterns triggered a memory. All three read the page, as Simon said: "You can see the seal for yourself." At that Munro lifted the lowest fold to examine the wax, and a low whistle appeared to suggest his doubts were withdrawn.

"Paper, is all it is," Alasdair Dubh said after a time. "He could have another one saying the exact opposite, just."

"And why won't he pay the money then, if it's going to those on Jamie's side?" the priest asked.

My lord shrugged again. "I don't know the whole story – yet. But at a guess, he's keeping it for the king. It'll be badly needed when he comes back. And MacIain tells me the king's definitely coming back."

"He has the sight," Ranald nodded. "Even though it would seem he's set to be a traitor when it suits him. But —" he spat, remembering something which inspired him to greater anger — "What about you, Fraser? You're in Billy's army, yourself and enough of your men. MacDonell has had cause to fight you in the past…"

"Generations away," Alasdair Dubh snarled. "The big fight was near a hundred and fifty years ago. We were with the Saxons then, remember, before peace was settled. And we're family now – I'm married to his cousin, am I not?"

The chief grunted, as if he felt in some way required to start a fight, and honour had been served even in his failure. "So, Fraser… What is to be done over what you have told us?"

"Take that paper," my lord said. "Make sure it's seen by others. Let them know that Breadalbane won't be doing us good in the short term, but he's with us all the same. Let them know MacIain is ready to sign the peace treaty, and they should sign too when the word comes. It gives us the time we need."

It appeared that even these MacDonell warriors were capable of sinking into thought, for there came a lull in the conversation, until Munro said: "A thousand men? Breadalbane has maybe five or ten times that. What would the rest of them all be doing?"

"That's just caution in the letter," Simon said quickly. "He's giving himself something to argue if it's ever found out, as you said. Nothing wrong in being careful. You know that, Father — that's why you're still here! How many priests have they taken this year?"

"Four in the last two months anyway," Munro replied. "More that I haven't heard about. Most of them jailed, one or two banished to France."

"Then there's probably fewer priests in Scotland than Jesus had disciples," my lord reflected quietly.

"Is that meant to be a joke?" Ranald growled; and, being persuaded that it was not, he continued: "Still, Breadalbane…"

"I've met him, and —" Simon began.

"See?" the chief cried. "You admit it!"

"You've met him too," my lord pointed out, "at Achallader. For similar reasons. We can't ignore the man, can we? So, I've met him, and for what it's worth, everything adds up for me."

Alasdair Dubh shook his head. "Paper. Letters. Promises. It's just a big fight we need to send Billy to hell – and all his treacherous chiefs and ministers!"

"And it'll come," Simon said. "But you make a good point, MacDonell: there's always the chance Breadalbane plays both sides."

That man frowned. "Trust him, you say! Then, *don't* trust him!"

"You know it's not that simple. But if I could offer some advice, it would be to look for support from someone the Campbell doesn't like. Just to make sure there's enough power on your side."

"What do you mean?"

"Atholl?" Munro said.

Simon nodded. "Murray and Campbell will never be friends even when Jamie returns. I think it's worth having contact with Atholl, or his son, Ian Cam."

"Your commanding officer!" Ranald said.

"Exactly," Simon replied, "Although God knows there's no love lost between us."

"That I've heard," Alasdair Dubh laughed. "They say every time Murray gives you a captain he ends up dead or mad. Was there a ship?"

"There was," nodded Simon with a grin. "And a fully-supplied fort put safely into Jamie's hands. But that's not the point. I'm saying it's worth playing a careful game in these careful times. I'm sure Father Munro would agree with me." The priest offered my lord a steady stare, but it seemed to me there was much agreement in his expression.

Pleading a long day's exertion, and adding that I was still recovering from injuries received — along with the promise of an account of events on the Bass — Simon asked Alistair to send us to our couches. As I fell into welcome sleep, I still could not close the distance between what the Fox had told the MacDonells, and what he had told MacIain.

MONIACK CASTLE LAY less than a day's ride from Invergarry; indeed, the hills facing us from across Loch Oich were part of Fraser country. We were glad of the lack of distance as, at last, the long summer appeared to be failing, and it was the first cold and overcast day we had seen for some weeks. With the addition of having secured the promise of Father Munro following us shortly, Simon was pleased with what he had achieved since leaving Huntingtower, and declared, "All is done, and done well!" with delight.

Yet it seemed not entirely so; for, when we reached home, there was instruction to haste onward to Castle Dounie. After a brief stop during which I confirmed Kirsty was not there (I had not thought she would be) I was pleased to continue our journey in the hope she had returned to service with Lady Amelia, and I might see her yet. It was the lady herself who met us as we entered the castle courtyard. "Simon!" she cried with a wide smile, before adopting a more serious expression. "Where have you been? Hugh and Tom have been waiting for you."

"I was at Huntingtower," my lord replied. "Settling things with your brother, just like I was told."

"You were sent for," Amelia replied. "They know you left there last week – and they know why."

"A tragedy," Simon said after a pause. "A terrible, terrible accident. Everyone must know that?"

She ignored his unspoken request for succour. "Where's Kirsty? What have you done with my handmaid?"

"She's not here?" Simon asked. "I thought — she didn't come with us to… on the wee mission I had to do."

"No, she's not here," the lady said grimly. "I hope you haven't been up to anything."

"Just delivering a letter," he replied shortly. My lord and I continued up to the main hall, and, seeing it empty, moved into the lord's withdrawing chamber, there to behold the Lord Lovat and the MacShimi seated at a table beside the Reverend Jamie and a third man I did not know – but who nonetheless looked somewhat familiar.

"Father!" my lord cried, nodding to Hugh and the sennachie, before his expression stiffened. "And... John."

"How are you, Simon?" said the other. "I'm fine, of course."

"Bolla, my brother: John Fraser of Beaufort," the Fox said to me, waving arms with a noticeably resentful air. "John, this is Bolla."

"I've heard about you," that man smiled warmly. "A good influence on Simon, yes? Well, God knows he needs it."

"What are you doing here?" Simon asked him curtly.

John made a comical frown. "Is that the best you can do? I'm back! Isn't that grand?"

"I called John home," Hugh said weakly. "*We* called John home."

"Good, good," the Fox nodded. "So all is done in France, then? King Jamie's throne secured?"

John laughed. "The work in France goes very well," he said. "But it looks like there's a bit of work needing done here." Simon said nothing; instead he seated himself opposite his clansmen and gazed at them with an expression which displayed a demand for an explanation – but also a strange stubbornness I had not seen upon him before, and which I suspected was barely-suppressed childish rage.

Finally Lord Tom spoke. "There's been a bit of talk, son," he began slowly. "It's been said that you've — that you're... things aren't going well, just."

"Things are going very well," Simon retorted. "I'm just back from seeing MacIain and Glengarry. I've laid a position with Breadalbane. I've even got a priest coming to see us. Father Robert Munro."

"Munro?" Hugh looked delighted.

"A good man!" cried Reverend Jamie, to my surprise. "It's been too long."

"That is grand," Tom said. "We may manage to keep him all winter if it closes as it looks like it will." His attempt at lightening the conversation failed as my lord simply recovered the expression he had previously adopted. Finally his father continued: "We've had reports about the Campbell of Glen Orchy. And the Bass. And… the young Murray."

"Sad tales," Simon agreed. "But none of it my fault."

"Murray thinks otherwise," Hugh said. "The Earl of Tullibardine, on behalf of his father, Atholl, has asked us to —"

"Keep you out of trouble for a bit," John said. "That's why I'm here."

"What exactly is that to mean?" Simon asked coldly.

Lord Tom found a stronger tone of voice. "You're making too much noise, son. The Lord Lovat's Company has only been standing a few months and you've already killed a captain, lost a siege, lost a warship… and killed the son of our most-needed ally."

"That's not what happened!" Simon shouted.

"That's what everyone *thinks* happened!" his father shouted back, half-standing in anger, offering a hint of the man he must have been in his younger years. "And you, boy, of all people, should understand that when enough people say something, it's as good as truth."

"Father — I…" my lord began, shaking his head, trying a more apologetic approach.

"Just listen," Lord Thomas replied. "Of all the people we need on side, Murray comes first. That clan is big and powerful, and close. When — *if* — King Jamie returns I want to be standing here, welcoming him to Fraser country. Not Murray country. What's more important, son: the king comes back or the clan survives?"

Hugh cleared his throat at that; then Simon said: "Murray fights on paper. I fight on paper. Who else is going to do that?"

"Me," John said with a grin which carried more than one message.

His brother laughed. "You? You're just a wee *gorach*!"

It was John's turn to laugh. "I've come on a bit," he said. "And anyway, Father's right. You've drawn too much attention to yourself. Just tell me this: has anyone recognised you who shouldn't have?" My mind raced back to the moment in Glen Orchy when a Campbell trooper identified Simon, and died for his trouble; and with a momentary doubtful glance towards me, it seemed my lord recovered the same memory. That was enough for his brother, who, I assumed, knew him far better than I did. "So you've got to be silent for a bit. I'll keep things moving. That's what's been agreed."

Simon changed his approach once again. Calmly, as if he were reciting a list of army supplies, he said: "I've worked night and day to make sure Fraser's position is safe no matter how bad things get. I've dealt with the leaders of King Billy's government. I've dealt with the leaders of King Jamie's forces. And I will *not* —" here he banged both fists on the table — "be told that some wee *gorach* can come back from France and just take it over, and I'll, what? Be off to France in his place and drink wine all day?"

"No," Hugh said, apparently taking confidence from Simon's apparent defeat. "You'll captain the Lord Lovat's Company of the Lord Murray's Regiment, as detailed by Tullibardine. And that is all you'll do, for the time being. He will be sending you orders in due course."

Simon said nothing. He looked first at the Lord Lovat, who managed to return the stare without breaking it; then at his father, who seemed still to be on the verge of rage; then at his brother, who appeared to be comfortable with proceedings. "It's not as bad as it sounds, Simon," said John. "You'll see."

My lord held his silence as he stood up and moved to the door. Turning, he gave each of them another look, but again failed to achieve any kind of victory. He pulled the door open, and, just before he disappeared behind it, said: "Munro will be here by the weekend."

It appeared to me that John allowed a carefully calculated time to pass before rising and following his brother out into the courtyard. It also appeared to me that my place was to follow them, despite never before having felt, as I had just then, that Simon wanted no one near him. "Simon! What's wrong?" John called.

The Fox abruptly halted his march away, yet seemed to recommence movement back towards his brother without having altered pace at any instant. In fact, I doubted for a moment that he would stop even when he was within inches of the other's face. "What's wrong?" he cried directly into John's countenance. "Me? What in the devil's name, John?"

"Dad told me to come back," the brother cried back, hands raised in a signal of innocence. "What am I supposed to do — say no?"

"How fast did you say yes?"

"I've been holding him off for months!" John replied, and at that, an amount of Simon's anger appeared to abate. "I couldn't tell him why I wanted to stay in France, could I?"

"So you didn't tell him?"

"No – that would just tear it all up. And it's not torn up — not yet, anyway. I've brought some of the... work... with me."

Simon paused. "You still shouldn't be here. Anything could happen in France now."

"It's not my choice," John replied, his tone stronger. "I get the feeling Murray told Hugh to send for me."

"What, months ago?" Simon said. "But that would have been before —" he paused, and a new expression appeared on his face. "Devil choke me. Devil choke me! What a *gonuch*!" It was clear from the way his eyes flashed that new ideas were rushing into his mind; yet as soon as he realised we could observe those signals, he adopted another more neutral attitude. "You still shouldn't be here. Keep your distance from me, John."

"Why?" his brother said quietly, with a dangerous tone beneath his words. "Is something going to *happen* to me?"

Simon once again lost the ability to reserve his feelings, and his face flooded with resentment and fury. "Just keep your distance. Clear?" he said, and, pushing John in the chest with more suggestive than violent intent, he turned and marched away once again.

I remained where I stood, behind John, and saw that man shake his head slowly before turning back to the castle and beholding me. "The boll o'meat Fraser!" he said, smiling warmly. "I'm sorry to meet you like... this." Gesturing behind him he added: "That's a good man. But he has a lot in his bowl – and I think some of it falls out at the wrong times."

"It seems that way," I replied carefully.

John smiled again. "He has a lot of work ahead of him, and he's going to need his friends. I'm glad he has someone like you, Bolla. He might not think so just now, but he'll soon remember to be glad he has me, too." He patted my forearm as he passed me. "We should have a talk soon, you and me."

I offered no reply.

FATHER MUNRO SOON FOLLOWED US from Invergarry to Castle Dounie and was welcomed as a lost hero returning from war. After spending some days in discussion with the clan leaders – much of it in animated discussion and heavy drinking with Reverend Jamie – he spent the following weeks travelling around our towns to lead Mass, hear confession and bless the many births, deaths and unions which had taken place since his previous visit. I found myself uncalled upon by Simon, who, at least for the meantime, appeared to have accepted his change of fortune. "Ach, it's maybe no bad thing, Bolla," he told me. "Winter's coming in and we've had a good harvest. Maybe a wee break is exactly what we need." He nudged my elbow, adding: "The wine cellar is full – and I've still got the plan. It's still magnificent mischief, and it still can't fail!"

He seemed also to soften his spirit towards John; notably at a loud and drunken night in Dounie after Father Munro had led a memorial Mass for the soul of Alexander Fraser, during which my lord read an emotional lesson from the Bible which drew tears from all, and a new – or renewed – warmth for the reader from many. Soon afterwards John became my lord's guest at Moniack; although it was at the command of Lord Tom, and I was not at first convinced that either was comfortable with the situation. On a number of occasions it seemed to me that the younger brother made a task of waiting until Simon was not present before sitting down with me in an attempt to learn what I knew of the elder's motives and motions. Yet on the whole I held my peace – sensing as I did that John, while appearing to be of a warmer, lighter spirit than his sibling, presented a personality not dissimilar to that which I had met once in an Aberdeen alehouse.

Keeping my distance as I could, I was also glad to treat Simon in the same manner — for in my mind, and while my time was my own, I became more concerned with my failure to find Kirsty. If she had returned to Moniack or Dounie to collect any belongings, no one would tell me; and if she had spoken to any of her friends in either place, none would say. I already understood that so many villages, townships and even houses standing alone were there across the country of the clan that, if she did not want to be found, I had no chance of achieving a different conclusion. Yet I did what I could in the time I had; but soon an evil thought, one of the darkest I have ever imagined, began to enter my mind – a vague image I would not allow to form, of Simon having followed on her northward journey while I slept, and of what might come after. I forbade myself to think it; and yet it lurked, just at the edge of my awareness. I had seen him kill, and I had seen him involved in further deaths. Had he arranged the death of Lord George Murray — a clearly unnecessary act? And if he felt able to dole out destruction to innocents such as he...

Soon, however, there were other matters with which to be concerned: a heavy autumn frost was followed by a severe freeze, leading those women who could read the weather to warn that an evil winter lay ahead. On the orders of MacShimi all those homes which needed repair were to be attended upon, requiring the efforts of all who could help. Despite the remaining pain of my wounds (which already whispered through my scars the threats of poor weather, and would continue to do so for the rest of my days) I was pleased to help with the transport of wood for frames and rafters, the replacement of roofing thatch and the gathering in of cattle. I confess that I found the honest labours a great relief of body and mind; and, retiring at the end of each day, I found new joy and gratitude in the warming powers of meal and whisky and a warm couch in a room within the castle. When Father Munro, who had accepted his imprisonment in Fraser country until the ice might permit his onward journey, led grace before meat in the evenings during his visits to Moniack, there was no lack of whole-hearted response in my "Amen."

At last the clear skies darkened with cloud and the impotent sun gave way to unrelenting snows; and almost all movement stopped across our country, as must it have done elsewhere. On many days we were confined within the castle, which was yet a great comfort when set against the hardship of survival in small, cramped houses where clansmen slept beside their cattle for warmth, and bled them to add blood to their meal in the hope that both beasts and people could see the storms through.

I cannot explain how Simon continued to keep his lines of correspondence open. I only know that he did; for much of my confinement was spent copying new documents which appeared from that packet before winding their way to God knows where — and although I was at least suspicious of the work he had of me, I had not enough knowledge of it to conclude that I should play no part, or even object to that which I did. Simon had not said that I should keep my copying tasks secret from John, but I had the conviction he would like it to be so, and therefore I was careful to be prepared to conceal papers if the chamber door opened. It was hardly possible that John had not guessed at least the notion of my labours; yet he did not ask about it, and I suspect his silence was as much for my benefit as his own.

When the snow forbade even letters to pass we reverted to the form of drinking we had fallen into so commonly in our early days together; and at those times I found both my lord and his brother to be excellently sociable companions, with the wit and humour to continually entertain each other, which was entertainment in itself. As the winter waged on their relations appeared to thaw; and soon they began to spend a great deal of time engaged upon business with a collection of small bottles and powders, the mixing, measuring, burning and boiling of which appeared to require much consultation of old, yellowed papers John had brought from France. Their concern, on occasion, resulted in the generation of stinking clouds of evil smoke which forced the abandonment of castle more than once, the brothers at first seeming terrified and then heartily amused at what they had done.

The Fox, of course, made merry with a number of womenfolk — some who worked within the castle, some who lived nearby; some who blended so poorly amongst the rest of his company that we retired in embarrassment, and some who matched our spirits so well that, it must be admitted, we saw and shared an amount of his attraction for them. Yet there were two who lay long in my memory, for they both accompanied my lord at the same time, although, of course, on different nights. The one was named Isobel, but known by all as Issi Sona: her hair shone like sunlight, and her near-constant laughter, which could so easily have been a hardship had her tone not been so musical and her taste so clever, was a delight as she sat with us all at the hearth, then went elsewhere with Simon. The other was called Margaret and could have been no more different: she laughed constantly at nothing, and the sound was chilling to the ears, and spines, of all who heard it. She was not attractive in the way she looked or even the way she held herself; I wished her no harm, but it took many years to forget the poor quality of her company, and the sound of her mirth which, I was sure, flew up the chimney and soured the land around the castle.

Issi simply vanished one day, to the general disappointment of all. I only saw her again once, some weeks later, at the entrance to the castle. As I approached I beheld she was collapsed upon the stairway, crying pitifully. Simon appeared at the door above and a conversation took place, all of which I did not hear. Yet I did hear my lord telling her: "Why don't you get off home? You're no fun in that condition."

"I need help!" she wailed in response. "Simon, for all we had — help me!"

He laughed, and threw a few coins down at her. "Give your husband that," he said. "He's young and fit. He can ride to Inverness and back in a day with a doctor. Oh – and, good luck!" With that he turned away.

I rushed up to offer assistance as Issi, with some difficulty, raised herself from the stairway, still in floods of tears, and made to pick up the money. "Leave me alone!" she shouted furiously at me, throwing her arms in the manner of a wildcat. The force of her assault sent me reeling backward, and I stood a distance away, only for a moment catching the expression of torment on her tear-stained face. It was as she struggled away from the castle, grasping her belly, that I understood she must be in pain with child. Unable to assist I moved within, to find Simon opening a flask of wine. "I think Issi Sona is in trouble," I said simply, unsure how to open the conversation.

"I think you're right," my lord said with an attempt at a laugh. Then he shrugged. "You know how it is, Bolla," he said. "It's the way of the world. It's a man's job to hunt around and it's a woman's job to stop him. We both try to win, but on the whole, Fraser wins – with a new generation of the clan." I said nothing, clear in my mind that he was simply trying to justify his own behaviour. "They talk of sin," he went on, "but isn't it sinful to deny the honest urges God gave us?" At that moment Margaret entered the chamber, bellowing her twisted laughter even though she had not heard what Simon had said, and I left without attempting to endure a reason for it.

In the coming days I made such inquiries as I could about Issi and her husband; but I could discover nothing. I detected from the tone of some clansfolk that it would be better if I did not ask further; and, reminding myself that I was no true Fraser, I at last relegated the concern to the back of my mind, and the winter continued as if the episode at the castle entrance had never occurred. Soon, the unpleasant company of Margaret had taken itself away, to be replaced by a seeming never-ending supply of replacements; but never again did I recall such a stark and disconcerting contrast between those the Fox chose as partners.

There came one evening, just after the solemn celebration of Christ's birth, but before the revelling of the new year (and soon after another forced abandonment of the castle while dark yellow smoke poured from the windows of the lord's chamber, to much laughter from Simon and John) when my lord received two papers which he persuaded me need be copied with haste — this despite the fact we had been in our cups for some hours, and the charred skies promised a particularly severe fall of snow in the coming night. "Time to earn your shilling, Bolla," he said, seating me in the chamber beyond his drawing room. "Although if you're as drunk as I am it'll look like two shillings. Think of it as a challenge – you might find it easier to close one eye." Observing that he appeared in a better condition than I, I asked whether it might not be more fitting, since it was important, for him to copy the letters. At that he patted my back and laughed: "There's only one of you, old friend – well, there is if I close one eye!" and, taking his bottle with him, returned to the other room where John sat by the fire.

I know not why these two papers, of all those I had handled, caused such a strong response within me; yet as soon as I settled into the task a great anxiety came over me. I have felt such internal upheaval seldom in my life, and at that time I had felt it only once before: during my interview with MacIain. Perhaps it was for that reason that I found myself, despite my drunkenness, alert like a hunting animal, and aware of more than normally I would understand. I had copied many shapes over the recent months with little recognition of what they meant – but

213

on that occasion it seemed that some of the curls and lines danced out of the page and through my vision into my mind, doing nothing to calm my emotions. Realising that the voices from the next chamber were altered in tone from the light-hearted chattering I might have expected, I stepped towards the door; and I did not need to approach too closely in order to overhear.

"I don't care," John told his brother. "You have to let him know."

"Think for a minute, will you?" Simon replied. "If we pass it on the obvious question will be: how did we find out? That puts us right in the middle of it all with no way out. No one wins."

"You're talking *cac* – there's always a way out. You know that."

"Not this time. Don't you think I'd use it if it was there? But it's not. He put himself there. He just has to live with that."

"Live with that? You mean die with that."

"I know! But he wasn't going to sign it anyway. So it's just as if we didn't know. Everything will happen the way it was going to, just."

"If he knew what we knew, he might sign. I think he would."

"Have you met him? Do you know what he's like? He told me – and these were his words: 'If Jamie orders me to sign on pain of death, I'll do it. If not, I won't.' And he meant it, man."

"But it *is* on pain of death!"

"Not for certain."

"Of course it is – and you've got the proof. Jamie says sign, and Dalrymple says kill everyone who doesn't sign. And he takes time to name the MacDonalds of Glen Coe!"

"You're too new at this," I heard my lord saying after a long pause. "You need to get used to it. People are going to fall by the wayside. It's *cac*, complete *cac* – but that's the dance we're in. I like MacIain. Who doesn't? But if he has to go to keep the plan moving…"

"Go?"

"*Die*, then! *Die*! How's that?"

"It's not just MacIain and you know it. That letter says to kill the MacDonalds of Glen Coe. All of them." Another silence fell, broken eventually by Simon's repetition of points he had already attempted to make, followed by John's repeated rebuttal. I did not feel the need to hear more; instead I returned to my table and continued copying.

Yet instead of simply completing the task my lord had set for me, I did it twice, carefully concealing the additional papers within my plaid. I sat in silence for a time, almost as if I did not know what I should do next — but I knew more certainly than I could say. When Simon finally appeared to see whether I had completed my task, I suggested that it had taken so long because of my drunkenness; congratulating me, he invited me into the next chamber for more wine, but I feigned tiredness and instead went to my couch. There was no great sleeping to be had, and in the long hours before morning I found little rest. As the effects of the wine receded, I realised I was filled with a great, calm patience – and then realised it was no such thing, but instead was a cold, calm rage.

Simon was in possession of evidence that MacIain and his clan were all in mortal danger, and he intended to keep it to himself. However, I, also, was in possession of that evidence — and I most certainly was not going to follow my lord's example.

IT WAS A SLOW PROGRESS TO GLEN COE in that bitter weather, so poor that a horse would have been hindrance rather than help, made worse by the certain knowledge that I could rely on no Fraser or even MacDonell for assistance, since my journey had to remain in complete secret. The days were not long, and during those I resolved to hide as best I could in what shelter I could find. Moving by night when the world was coldest, rather than attempting to hide among my plaid during those hours, almost certainly kept me alive; and I had cause yet again to be grateful for my years as a beggar, for the knowledge of survival gained in those times served me well on that journey. I fell often (although at least twice I was thankful it was winter, since I landed upon solid ice and not deep water) and found that my leg injury rendered walking sometimes near-impossible, and yet I carried on with the aid of a staff. The biting wind off Loch Linnhe was the most difficult to endure, and on the day I reached Maryburgh I took the risk of asking for hospitality, leading to a sleep so comfortable that I did not re-awaken until nearly noon the following day; and then my anger at myself was monstrous.

At last I reached MacDonald country, and in truth I could have travelled not much further when I fell into the small home of one clansman and called on him to fetch one of his chief's household. I was in a state of near-collapse when two men lifted me up towards the face of a tall third who demanded my identity with a voice of suspicion and threat. "Cathal... Hendrie?" I whispered in reply. "I am Bolla..."

"Bolla Fraser!" the big man replied. "Himself said you would be coming! Give him a drink, someone!"

"No time," I replied. "I have to see MacIain!"

"You won't make it without a drink," said the ghillie, forcing the contents of a small flask into my mouth. Then he wrapped me in a warm plaid like a newborn child, threw me onto his back and carried me from that house, I know not how far, until the effects of the whisky finally began to work upon me; then I found myself seated near a fire next to MacIain himself, who was surrounded by over a dozen children.

"But it has been colder, my fine young heroes – colder even than this," he was telling them with the musical tones of a sennachie. "It was so cold the sun itself froze before it could rise into the sky. It froze solid, stuck to the hills before it could light up the glen. Do you know what I had to do?" They all shook their heads, their bright young eyes twinkling in the firelight. "I had to climb up the sun's rays, cold as they were, then breathe on the sun with a big warm breath —" he heaved his lungs with an elaborate throwing of his arms — "Then I had to climb down as fast as I could before they all melted again. And do you know how many days I had to do that for?" They shook their heads again.

"Well, it was a lot. It was so many that some of the wee animals came to me, and they said, 'MacIain,' they said, 'The snow is too deep for us! We cannot see above it, and what if we are eaten by foxes?'

"'Well, that is no good,' I told them. Then some of the big animals came to me and said, 'MacIain,' they said, 'The ice is too hard for us! We will break our legs walking on it, and what will we do then?'

"'That is no good at all,' I told them. So I thought, and I thought, and I came up with an answer. Have you ever seen a rainbow crow?" The young ones offered a long, doubtful negative sound. "I am not surprised," said he, "For it is a long time since a crow looked like a rainbow. But he did once – he was all the colours in the world, and he had a beautiful singing voice. What do crows look like now?"

One small voice replied: "Black," and MacIain nodded seriously.

"You are right, Eilidh MacDonald. And what do they sound like now?" The chief's hall erupted with children making crowing noises; then, with his encouragement, they ran about waving their elbows for wings. Despite my condition, and the cold rage still within me, I felt a great joy at the sight – one of the happiest things I had seen in many months. Yet with a wave of his hand they were his again, settling down intently. "That is exactly how they sound – *ochone*, I thought my house was full of crows, just! But back in the old times, the crow had a beautiful voice. They say he could make faeries cry, and make the bad ones turn good, just with his voice.

"So I spoke to the rainbow crow, and I told him, 'Rainbow crow,' I said, 'It is too cold for the wee animals and the big animals, and to tell the truth, it is too cold for me too. I am tired of climbing up to melt the sun every morning. I want you to fly to Heaven and speak to God. Tell God it is too cold, and ask Him if he will help us.

"Well, that crow did not want to go, but I told him he was the only one who could do it – for it is a long, long way to fly, and I would get nowhere myself without wings. In the end he did it: he flew up, up, up into Heaven, and he sang to God. And God is very busy, but He heard the rainbow crow's beautiful voice and He asked, 'What is wrong, little crow? Why have you left Glen Coe? Are you not happy there?'

"'Oh, aye, very happy there,' said the crow with his beautiful voice. 'But it is cold, and the wee animals are getting stuck, and the big animals are getting broken legs, and poor old MacIain is climbing into the sky every day to melt the sun.'

"'*Ochone*, that is no good at all,' said God, and He gave the crow a burning stick. 'Hold this at the cold end and take it to MacIain, and tell him to light fires in Glen Coe so everyone can keep warm.'" He made a sound with a finger in his mouth. "Well, I do not know what the crow said with the stick in his beak, but that's what God heard. What do you think he said?"

The children's consensus was "Thank you for the fire, God," which MacIain accepted with a grave nod.

"So the crow flew down, down, down, from Heaven," he continued. "But the stick was burning away all the time, and the smoke turned his rainbow colours black, and it choked his voice. But that crow brought me the fire, and told me what to do, and I lit the fires God gave us. And here is one that we are sitting in front of right now!" His audience gasped in awe, gazing into the fireplace with new delight. "But poor old crow, he has been all black ever since. And how does he sound?" As the children dissolved into more bird-like performances, the chief turned to me at last; and I took great solace in the expression of joy and satisfaction in his countenance. "I am sorry to have kept you, Bolla Fraser," he said gently. "But if you do not have time for the bairns, you do not have time for living. Will you come with me?"

Cathal walked behind, as he had when we wandered round the glen; but I felt able to move without assistance as we entered MacIain's drawing room. He turned to me expectantly, and, finding myself unsure of how to begin such a conversation, I simply presented him with the papers I had brought with me. "Simon received these a few days ago," I said. "If I understand, one is a letter from King Jamie telling all chiefs to sign into William's peace. The other is a letter from someone called Dalrymple, talking about killing you."

Behind me, Cathal let out a gasp and a series of curses, while MacIain looked closely at the papers. "These are not real," he said firmly. "There are no seals for a beginning."

"Simon has me copy all letters," I said. "He has other people doing it too, I think. But he has originals, with seals. I would guess he also has false seals hidden somewhere." I had not thought of that before. "And none of them will ever be in his hand."

"So this is fighting on paper," the chief murmured, reading the words before him over and over again. Then he looked at Cathal. "King Jamie says I've to sign, but he does not say on pain of death. But the Master of Stair — that's Dalrymple — he gives orders that MacDonald is to be destroyed before winter's end. As outlaws!"

"So what are you doing to do?" Cathal asked.

"As I said," MacIain shrugged. "It is not pain of death, and I do not fear the words of a man who thinks he can send his soldiers into my country while the snow lies heavy. He must be mad!"

"But if the two papers are placed together, as they were received, the *effect* is to be asked to sign on pain of death," I cried. "Dalrymple talks about wiping out your people!"

"Dalrymple is the secretary of state, a small man who hides behind a desk in Edinburgh," MacIain said confidently. "He has no power here. But still, Bolla Fraser, this is important news, and I thank you for bringing it." I made to protest again, but the chief laid his hand on my shoulder with a warm smile. "There is time to think on it," he said, although I felt he did so in order to calm me, rather than because he planned to do so. "And you must rest, my friend." As in most things, he was right – I suddenly realised how close to exhaustion I had come, and also that, had I laid one more night in the snow, I would not have risen again. Cathal conducted me to a couch, and I do not remember falling upon it before I was asleep.

The next vision I had was of the ghillie once again, shaking me awake. "We have a visitor," he whispered to me. "Himself wants to know if you know him. Come with me." It was daylight, so I knew I had slept, although I did not feel as if it had been long. He guided me through a small passage to an opening behind a curtain, and pulled it back just far enough so that I could see the back of MacIain sitting in his hall, opposite someone I did not recognise. "Well?" Cathal asked.

"I have never met him," I replied, shaking my head.

"Wait here until he goes, then," said the ghillie, and disappeared, only to appear moments later at his chief's side from another passage, sharing nothing but a short glance with him. Soon the visitor departed, and MacIain turned to where I stood, beckoning me forward. He held up a letter. "I have news, from that Fox of yours," he said. "Telling me that King Jamie wants me to sign the peace treaty. But he doesn't tell me that Dalrymple wants me dead."

He fell silent, and Cathal looked into the middle distance while I fought for something to offer. "I do not understand," I said finally.

"Simon the Fox wants me to know that I am to sign, but he does not want me to know what might happen if I do not."

I nodded slowly. "But why?"

MacIain shook his head, then held up the new letter. "Look at it." I took it from him, and although I could still only make out the most simple shapes, I knew it was the other copy I had made; only it also bore a seal. I admit I was not surprised.

"If I had only got this, and I had not heard from you, I would have stuck with my decision not to sign," he said slowly. "There are only two things I know. First, Dalrymple does not want me to sign, so he can outlaw me. Second, Simon the Fox does not want me to sign, so he can — what?"

"He once said it didn't matter what you did, as long as he knew what it was going to be," I offered.

The chief slammed his fists together. "He does not care who signs, as long as *somebody* does not! It could be anyone! But whoever it is, the entire Saxon army is going to come down on them. And Dalrymple does not know it will be MacDonald – he just *hopes* it will!"

"You've got to sign, then!" I cried.

Yet he was unsure – an emotion with which he was not familiar, I think. "To sign a peace treaty, with no plan to keep it… That is not right."

"You either fight on paper, or not on paper," I countered. "And you have the king's permission."

"A man's word is his alone to value, not the king's."

"Then God's fire could go out in Glen Coe," Cathal said quietly, attracting a surprised look from his chief.

There followed an exchange of glances between the two, which, I realised, was their way of communicating; a method which seemed to translate much more than words. After a time MacIain nodded. "Then I must sign," he said. "But I have less than two days to do it. And in this weather, Fort William is more than two days away."

WHILE THE PEOPLE OF THE GLEN made ready for the celebration of new year, MacIain, Cathal, two others and I made ready for the journey north; just over a dozen miles, but difficult travelling, as I could testify, especially with the chill wind from the loch to the west. Glen Coe's own loch had frozen over unto near midway, which made the early part of our movement a little easier, but only served to heighten the contrast when we attempted to traverse land. The chief's estimate was accurate – although in summer we could have easily made the passage in less than a day, the shortness of light hours and howling gale and snowstorms forced us to perform a painfully slow walk, bereft of communication for the noise in our ears and the need to hold our heads low.

For a reason I did not at first understand, MacIain led us towards the shore of Loch Linnhe where, denied the protection of bushes and trees, the wind tore at our very beings. He ordered us to stop at a distance from a stone which stood alone in a field facing out to the water, and I recognised it was one of those placed by the ancients. "Himself will talk to the *Cailleach Bheur*," Cathal shouted through the storm to me.

"The witch of winter?" I shouted back, bewildered; and the ghillie nodded, his eyes fixed on his chief. I watched as he moved carefully towards the stone, then reached both hands out to it, although not making contact. It seemed to me, then, that a strange distance grew up between the place where he was and where we stood; it appeared that in some way he was living and moving faster than were we, while a faint aura appeared to prevent the snow from falling between the two figures in the field.

The event lasted just moments before MacIain trod his way back to us, his face grim through the snow and ice on his beard. "The worst cold we have ever known," he said, shaking his head. "She says it will last for ever." Then he seemed to cheer himself. "But then, she always says that. Let us move on!" We stopped overnight in the remains of an old house, stripped of its roof as was the custom, relying instead on what remained of the partitions within to build small shelter against its north-west wall. MacIain offered me a flask of whisky and called above the gale: "A good new year to you, Bolla Fraser. We will celebrate it properly on the old day in March. Midwinter is not the start of anything good. Did I ever tell you all works of evil are begun at night? And the worst evils are begun at night in winter?"

It was after noon the next day when we approached King William's fort and were challenged by the guards, no scouting patrols having been encountered during our travels. The wind had died down, yet snow continued its assault from above as the chief of the MacDonalds of Glen Coe grandly announced himself, and the power of his expression made even trained enemy soldiers fall under his command. An English officer, cruel of face and tight of mouth, told MacIain curtly he would have to wait until the governor could be fetched, and placed us in a small room with no warmth – hardly a discomfort to such as us. After a time Cathal began cursing the Saxons for what certainly appeared to be a deliberate rudeness in keeping us waiting without hospitality; yet MacIain himself sat on a low stool, silent, his thoughts likely in a world I would never see. Finally he, Cathal and I were directed to a room in which a tall, smart officer sat, with the cruel-looking one behind him. That one snapped: "What do you want with the governor?"

The chief did not even look at him, but turned his gaze upon the seated man and said: "I am MacIain of Glen Coe. I would sign my clan into King William's peace, as the law requires, Colonel Hill."

The other stood, unbidden, taken aback by the knowledge that no authority in the room came above the natural power which surrounded MacIain. "Is that so, then?" he finally murmured with an unconvincing tone.

MacIain nodded. "I would sign now, and take no more of your time."

The cruel man leaned forward and whispered something to Hill, even though the two leaders' gazes were never unlocked. "It's not possible, I'm afraid."

The chief frowned. "Are you not King William's representative in this country?"

"Well, yes, yes – of course. But, you see…" the colonel paused again while his assistant advised him, then, with a more firm tone, continued: "The document you must sign pertains to civil law, while my authority extends only to military law. So you see, I cannot help – my apologies."

"Nevertheless, present the document and I will sign it, colonel," MacIain said. "You will witness it, and it will be recorded, and all will be well."

"I cannot!" the other cried. "It is beyond my power! This is a matter for the privy council!"

"And the Master of Stair," MacIain added quietly. "If necessary I will write my own declaration and sign it without your assistance."

"That won't do," the colonel said firmly. "No, Glencoe, I cannot accept your surrender."

"There was no talk of surrender."

"I mean you cannot sign here! You must find a magistrate."

The chief leaned over the governor's desk, leading the other to lean backward, and causing the cruel one to lose his footing behind. "I am required by law to take an oath of allegiance to King William by today," he said darkly. "I demand that the king's representative allows me to obey the king's law."

Hill shook his head, but could no longer meet MacIain's eye. "No. It is impossible. You must go to Inveraray and see the sheriff of Argyllshire. He will record your surrend — your oath."

"It will take days to get there," said the chief. "And then you will be responsible for the law being broken."

"I will write you a letter of protection," the colonel said with a tense tone, at which the cruel one frowned deeply. "Yes – a letter that explains you were here on time, but I could not help. I'll tell the sheriff to take your oath... as a lost sheep, if you will."

MacIain smiled. "In this weather that is a very good description, Colonel Hill. Very well. Write your letter, and I will go to Inveraray today." The governor sat down again and reached for paper and pen. We watched as he wrote briskly, without pause, and his assistant craned to see what was being put down. At last Hill held the letter out to the chief, who looked over it, nodded, and watched as it was sealed then returned to him. "Good day, colonel," MacIain said, placing it in his plaid and bowing slightly. That man stood up again, without being bidden, and his chair caught the cruel one's foot as it slid backward.

Nothing more was said as we left the governor's building, rejoined by our two companions, and moved across the courtyard towards the gates. Suddenly MacIain stopped, and, standing upright with his arms out and behind him and his face directed into the snowfall above, cried: "Cathal!" That man stepped immediately towards him and held him from behind, the way he had done to me in Glen Coe. The other two each took one of the chief's arms, as if trained in the movement before. They gave the impression of holding the great man down, as if he might be dragged upwards into heaven if they let him loose.

"He sees!" Cathal shouted, although the soldiers who paused in the duties to watch could not have understood. There came an expression upon the chief's face which I will never have the words to explain — as if all the feelings one is capable of expressing were exploding from his

223

soul at the same moment. He cried out with a great, long, animal roar, so loud that it even generated something of an echo in the snow-covered land. One of the MacDonalds, grappling to keep his grip on his right arm, was thrown aside as MacIain reached into his plaid and drew out Hill's letter, crushing it in his fist and holding it towards his chest.

"*Cailleach Bheur!*" he cried. "Evil!" As suddenly as it had started, the episode ended: he fell limp against Cathal and our companions (the second having caught hold of his right shoulder) and dropped his head. Nothing happened for many moments; then I witnessed the most surprising sight of all. MacIain was sobbing — great, silent sobs of deep, dark agony, a rainstorm in the snow which fell around us. Cathal, it seemed, had also never seen such a vision, for he, too, began to sob in fear, still holding his chief from the ground. At last they both collapsed down, with three of us standing helpless aside and those soldiers who watched becoming bored and returning to their business. At last MacIain stood up, holding onto his ghillie for support, yet still looking downward so we could not see his distress. He turned to Cathal, eyes red, and his face looked many years older than it had seemed at any time before. "The winter queen said this winter will last for ever," he stuttered through barely-controlled cries. "She is right."

"Let's find shelter," Cathal said quietly.

"No — we must go to Inveraray. It is late. So late."

"Just for a wee while," Cathal replied soothingly. "Just for a wee sit down." MacIain nodded, and allowed himself to be led towards the town of Maryburgh. The two clansmen and I followed behind, unsure of what to think or how to act. Yet the impression I had from what I saw was that there was no longer a chief and a ghillie; and instead there was a dutiful young man helping an old man walk in the snow. We found an alehouse and sat with flasks of whisky in a corner away from the fire, in complete silence. Eventually, whispering as if he hoped not to be heard, Cathal asked: "What did you see?"

MacIain shook his head. "I saw... almost nothing," he replied slowly. "Night and fire, and snow. And the red stones in the Cona. But I was lying in darkness for the most. I saw almost nothing. But I heard... *pain*." He covered his eyes with his hand and barely stopped himself breaking into tears once more. Then he looked at me. "I saw you, Bolla

Fraser. But you were not with me. You must not come to Inveraray – you have much to do elsewhere."

"I will come with you," I said. "I might —"

"No," he said, sounding once more like a clan chief. "Our paths separate here, my friend. The fighting on paper has ended, for me at least. I will sign that meaningless treaty, then I have to prepare for a proper fight. The kind we will be proud of, Cathal," he grinned at this last, and the ghillie did so too. "The time for sitting and talking is done. Let us go." With that he stood and marched outside, leaving the rest of us to gather and follow as quickly as we could. In the fading evening light MacIain took me by the shoulders. "I have two things to tell you," he said, looking straight into my eyes. "The first is this: if you must be the hands, then you must know what the hands are doing. And the second is this: you will find what you need near the place you found it first." I frowned, but he smiled. "It does not need to make sense now – I find it makes sense when it needs to. There are many things I have seen that did not make sense until much later. Just like then," he gestured with his head to indicate the episode I had recently witnessed. "Do not worry, Bolla Fraser. Just keep going." With that, he drew me into a hug, then set me back upon my feet, nodded, and turned away.

Cathal took my arm and nodded. "*Slàinte mhor a h-uile là a chi 's nach fhaic,*" he said, then followed his chief on the road to the south, while I turned north. I was already set upon the road to Fraser country long before I realised that was where I intended to go. Yet my thoughts continued to travel with MacIain: that strange, elemental character who simply seemed to find explanation and meaning where I only beheld doubt and confusion. As I struggled through winterbound Fraser country I could not but wonder why he had not offered me more than riddles for assistance – concepts which I vaguely understood held some message for me, but which I only found more baffling as I set my mind upon them. When my awareness returned to me it was almost as if the chief of Glen Coe had shaken it from his shoulders and thrown it over the earth towards me; it landed in my head and woke me to realisation of the breathtaking sight I beheld. The snow clouds had entirely gone, and the full moon bathed the frozen world in a silver-blue light. Descending towards Moniack from the hills to its south I could follow the lines of blazing landscape into the darkness of the waters of Beauly Firth, then on into the deep indigo of the star-crusted sky. And all was utterly silent – including, at last, the concerns in my mind.

It was only as I approached my home, realising it was likely Simon and John would be deep in their cups, that I began to worry once again. It had not struck me before the extent of the betrayal I had committed – for the decision had been made in an anger colder than the season. At that moment I understood that anger was still present within me; and instead of seeking a cautious entry to the castle I marched, tense, and with more noise than I needed to make. If they were to come at me, then I would suffer the consequences. To my amazement, no such conflict took place; instead, as I mounted the stairs which needed to take me past the hall and my lord's drawing room, I heard the usual sound of drunken laughter and chatter, with several voices in addition to those of the brothers. Even when Simon appeared in the doorway, carefully holding a handful of the small bottles which appeared to consume so much of his and John's interest, he offered nothing but welcome: "A shroud upon me, Bolla, where have you been in this weather?" he cried, grinning. "You missed new year – well, *new* new year anyway. And another smoke-out, and it really stank this time. It's good to see you!"

"I had… a matter to address," I replied doubtfully, unable to gain full control of my temper, yet not wishing to become responsible for any argument.

"Of course you did," he said. "Of course you did. But you chose some weather for it, eh?" Offering a leer I had not seen in some months, he asked: "Did you go far?"

"Far enough to be tired," I told him. "I must go to my couch."

He leered again. "Tired? Aye, I'll wager. You won't have a drink? It's not been as much fun without you, you know."

"Not tonight," I said, turning away.

"Tomorrow, then?" I sensed an almost hopeful tone in his voice, but I could not tell whether it was how he truly felt.

"Maybe," I replied.

"I'll take that," he said from beneath as I continued upon the stairs. "We've got lots to talk about — mainly *cac*, of course." I could detect no threat in his words.

SUCH NORMALITY AS ever surrounded the Fox's household settled upon us once more. The snow stopped but the cold air remained, turning all to frost and ice and rendering travel as difficult as it had been in the blizzards. On occasion Simon produced more letters for me to copy; and, with my earlier suspicions all-but confirmed, I made certain to make two copies of each. My increased proficiency and speed with the pen meant he had little reason to suspect I was doubling my labours.

Indeed, despite my preparations for angry outbursts there was almost nothing but calm and warmth in our fort, locked fast against the winter. My lord seemed to have a new enthusiasm about him – and it seemed sensible, to me, in some way, that he refused to share the reason for it with his brother.

One evening John demanded: "Out with it: what are you planning?"

Simon smiled and waved his fingers over his wine cup. "Wouldn't you like to know?"

"That's why I'm asking, you *gorach*."

"Sorry; I can't share," smiled his brother.

"Whatever it is, you'll need to be quick," John told him. "You know Ian Cam has plans for you."

"And I think I know what they are," Simon grinned.

John laughed. "And you've already worked out a way to… turn them in your favour?"

"Perhaps."

"Tell me!"

"*Non semper erit aestas* for that one," my lord said. "Or, indeed, *hiems*. If I'm right, my wee idea will take time. And if I'm right about Ian Cam, I'll have time to work on it. Then his summer will end – or his winter. I don't give a groat, but it'll end." He laughed, but I noted a darkness to it; and it was a deep darkness. I began to consider that the Fox before me was no longer the Fox who had played an idle game of letters in Aberdeen — or the one who had rescued me from my beggary.

"Anyway," he said briskly, changing his expression as if he had closed a desk drawer, "Never mind that *cac*. Bolla, when are you going to own up about your wee new year holiday?" I must have paled as both Frasers stared at me intently. "Go on," my lord encouraged. "What were you up to? Or more interestingly, *who* were you up to? As if we don't know!" Again came that leer, recently returned.

I had no clue how to respond. Then it came upon me that he referred obliquely to some kind of tryst — and in the same moment, it came upon me the person with whom he thought I had spent those days. "I would rather not talk about it," I muttered, hoping my face gave away none of the thoughts which had thundered into my head.

"The perfect gentleman, as always," Simon said, approaching and touching me on the shoulder. "You should bring her back here, Bolla. She's always welcome – you know that." His words confirmed my suspicions. Unable to gather my mind I took leave to visit the garderobe; and as I pulled Simon's chamber door closed I heard him laugh, followed by an instant's pause, followed by a laugh from John. It seemed to me there was time for just one word to be uttered between the two outbursts: Kirsty.

In the following moments I beheld the prison I had built for myself. Simon believed I had been with Kirsty, which showed that he knew where she was – and given his invitation to bring her back, she was probably close to Moniack. If I admitted I had not seen her, and asked him to say where she was, he would be forced to do so because of the words he had recently spoken. Yet if I revealed I had not been with her at new year, I would needs say where I had truly been, or at least conjure a false story; and Simon would know it for a lie even as I spoke it. My love was near to me — and I could not ask where. I decided on the only course of action which involved no direct falsehoods: I would have to act as if I had seen her, but offer no details. And then I would have to find her. I wondered if Simon had seen her, and his words meant she had spoken warmly of me, and that he expected to see us together once more; and it reduced me to a shaking fit with the notion that she was waiting for me and I had not known. Yet, if I found her and she would not accept me — What then? I already knew I had to try. I needed to find Kirsty; I simply needed to.

For once, fate appeared to step in on my account when, the following day, Simon told me: "It's time to earn your shilling, Bolla." Father

Munro, he told me, was planning to move on from Fraser country regardless of the cold; and Lord Tom had found a reason to stay his departure. "It's nearly *Là Fhèill Brìghde*," said the Fox. "Father has asked Munro to wait and celebrate with us. We're to have a big Mass at the church near Dounie – only the roof caved in. Munro says he'll do all the weddings and birthings and blessings we need for ten years, if only we get the church ready. I want you to do whatever Father says to make it happen. The clan needs this."

MacShimi was pleased to send me on a number of errands, to secure men and materials for the rebuilding of the small church. I in my turn was pleased to go, despite the cold; for travelling round our country was, I believed, the best way to find Kirsty. I understood why she might have hidden herself from the castles of Fraser: with the happenings at Huntingtower she would easily wish to pursue a quieter, more simple life. I easily wished to do the same – with her at my side.

The feast day of St Bride was an important one among those who held strong to the old faith – because the celebration held strong to an even older faith. The saint was named for Brigid, the goddess of the Highlands, of the coming spring and of all high ambitions and promises. While I was never clear upon whether some of my clansmen followed one faith or the other (and, I suspect, nor were they) it was certain that a day valued by both was doubly-blessed. On the morning itself our work had been completed to Father Munro's satisfaction; indeed, he sang with a simple joy as he blessed the church ahead of the main ceremony. "For, this kind of work, hard of hand and full of brotherly spirit, is the best way to ward off the darkness of all else that befalls this sorry Scotland," he beamed, the aggression in his voice tempered by the passion of his words. "Leave rich men to their games and live in love, good Frasers. Live in love, and King Jamie will return in love!"

Somehow – I do not know how – the womenfolk had succeeded in bringing flowers out of their winter sleep. Every home had a cradle, a bed for Brigid, fashioned from straw, and a small doll, a *dealbh*, to lay upon it, representing the return of the goddess among us for the season. If the tradition upset Munro he said nothing; and, indeed, allowed a *dealbh* in its cradle to sit in the small porch of the church.

Among Lord Hugh, Lady Amelia, Lord Tom, Simon, John and such lairds as had managed the journey, Munro led a joyful, uplifting Mass which almost seemed to raise the cold around us, if only for a short time. Afterwards the recently-wed (and, often enough, the longer-wed) came forward to have their marriage blessed in the eyes of the Church. Then came the women in child — and in that procession, finally, I beheld Kirsty for the first time since that September day in Perthshire. I was not versed in the understanding of lifegiving, so I could not guess how long she had been with child. Yet such was the pride among those who were to be blessed that they all attempted to display the girth of their bellies as best they could; and hers was by no means the smallest. Yet it was also clear from her cloaked head and averted gaze that she wanted to remain unknown. How could I fail to recognise my own Kirsty? I could not − I did not. I stood, transfixed, not twelve paces from her in the crowded church, as she received Munro's blessing on her forehead and belly; then turned away, without so much as a glance in the direction of me, Simon or even Lady Amelia.

I realised that she intended to leave immediately. Without further thought I pushed my way past my lords (I am ashamed to say it) and through the throng of pregnant women (again, to my shame) — and even then I was barely able to catch a glimpse of her dark brown cloak as she made to rush round the corner of the church wall in order, I knew, to hide from me. "Kirsty!" I shouted after her, seeing that she was barely a dozen paces from me again. Within moments I had caught up, for of course she could not run full well; and finally, after months of painful loneliness, I stood before her. Yet she would not meet my glance. "Kirsty," I said again, quietly. "My own Kirsty."

Still she would not look. "Leave me alone!" she said, the passion in her words but not in the sound. "Just leave me alone!" Since I knew I could say nothing to change the direction of conversation, I followed the only path open to me: I simply stood there, my hands on her shoulders, staring into where, if she would only look, our eyes would meet. It seemed as if forever passed; then, finally, she turned her glance upwards towards me. Sobbing in almost silence her eyes met mine at last, and she said my name almost as a whisper. Then, a little louder: "Bolla."

"*Gràdh mo chrìdh*," I said.

"No. No! I'm married now —"

"Are you, truly?" I knew the answer. She gently shook her head. "I have missed you so much," I told her. "I never want to be parted from you again."

"But —" she replied, looking down at herself. "You see I am... it has been five months since..."

"This is not the time," I said.

"There can never be the time!" she cried. "Bolla, if you still want me... if you do, you must never ask. I can't tell you! I don't want to tell you! It would —"

"Then I will not ask," I replied; and it had not taken a moment to reach my decision. "Will you come back to Moniack with me?"

She paused for a moment; I could not blame her if she was considering a return to the house of he who had set her on the course which saw her involved in the death of Lord George Murray – and involved with Mungo. Then she nodded. "I've been staying with my cousin over the hill," she nodded to the north-west, a part of Fraser country I thought was almost uninhabited, wherein I had barely searched for her. "I'll have to go back and get my things."

"We will go together," I said, as those who had been celebrating Mass burst out of the church in cries of song and laughter.

"I'd like that... *gràdh mo chrìdh*," Kirsty said, and I closed my eyes to let those words wash the pain of the last months away from my mind.

ONLY TWO WEEKS OF LIVING AS IN A DREAM were given to me. Kirsty had seemed in dread when first we approached the white walls of Moniack Castle, as had I been on my return at new year; but on seeing us together Simon embraced us both, and ordered that we should be given a new, larger chamber, over the kitchen and therefore warmer. Soon those white walls were a haven of cheer against the white frost, and then the snow when it returned with full fury. In truth, if the castle had not been such a haven, I might not have been able to endure what came next.

On a mid-morning, as I worked upon a second copy of a letter (for

I remained sure there would be need of them) a ghillie entered Simon's chamber to tell me I was called for below. I had not had time to gather the papers when a lumbering, staggering shape of a man appeared behind the ghillie, pushed him aside and called my name. Regarding the large character with his torn plaid, in dull tartan whose colours I could not make out; his red skin, telling of extreme cold; and his battered face, which spoke of violence, I felt sure I had not met him before, and made to say so. Then I saw something in his eyes which lit up a memory. "Cathal Hendrie!" I breathed. "What has happened to you?" It was as if acknowledgement of his identity marked the end of a great endeavour: Cathal slowly made to collapse to the floor, and only his leaning on the door frame gave us time to arrest his fall, then guide him to a chair by the fire. I bade the ghillie pour some whisky then leave us, then asked again: "What has happened?"

It took another two cups before I began to see meaning in his face and he felt ready to speak. "Bolla..." he said, staring me in the eye. "Bolla... Himself told me to find you."

"Where is MacIain?" At first I believed the chief might be in a similar state nearby, for I remain sure that only my youth had kept me alive on my trip to and from Glen Coe.

"He is gone!" Cathal cried. "MacIain is gone – and MacDonald is gone! He told me to find you. He told me to tell you."

"What?" I urged; but the big man had slumped in the chair, and I knew I could not press him.

Then, much more quietly, he began to speak. "A seven-night ago Campbell of Glenlyon came to us. He asked for beds for his men – around a hundred; and we offered them willingly. Three of them slept in my house." He shook his head. "Archie, Davie and Johnnie, they are. Good men. Good soldiers... until —" he broke off, having nearly reached a crescendo again. "They killed us all, Bolla! They killed us all in the dark! Johnnie, nice wee Johnnie – he made a snow-fort with my eldest son... then slit his throat in the dark! *Chan eil mi 'tuigsinn*! Murder, Bolla — Murder!"

I gave him more whisky, knowing that only the water of life had kept him from death as he had made his way to me. In truth I could say nothing, so I simply bade him drink, and waited until he continued.

232

"Archie told me to run. He said they'd had orders to kill every MacDonald of Glen Coe, but he wouldn't do it. Johnnie did. Davie did – my own wife, my own wee girl – but Archie didn't. He told me to run. I ran to Himself." He paused then stared at me once more. "He gave me his last words, with Glenlyon's knife in his back. His own son-in-law, Bolla, his own son-in-law..." he dissolved into silent tears.

"Bastards," came a voice from the doorway. "Bastards."

I know not how long Simon had stood there, but it seemed he had been able to gather the thrust of Cathal's words — until the big man shouted: "You knew, you Fox! You *knew*!"

Yet my lord seemed truly shaken by what he had heard; and he shook his head very gently. "No. No, I didn't," he said slowly.

"We saw your lettermen passing!" Cathal insisted. "Not a page is written but you know of it!" He made to stand up, as if to throw himself upon Simon; but he had not the power, and slumped into the chair once more.

"Good MacDonald, I assure you —"

"Cathal Hendrie. MacIain Himself's ghillie," I said.

"— And Himself is?"

"Gone," Cathal said bitterly. "Gone, with two hundred MacIains. But he signed the paper! He went to Argyll and he signed!"

I turned furiously to Simon, finally making the connection which must have been so clear to others. My lord looked back at me, shaking his head and holding his hands out. There passed long moments; then I realised Cathal had fallen into unconsciousness. I took a blanket and wrapped him in it, then moved towards the door. Outside, my lord seemed to understand that he owed an explanation. "MacIain didn't sign the treaty," he whispered to me. "I knew they were going to outlaw him but —"

"He *did* sign," I said firmly. "He went to Fort William, then to Inveraray, and he signed."

"He didn't, Bolla. I'm sorry, but he just didn't. He decided not to."

"He saw," I insisted. "He had a vision. He said the winter would never end if he did not sign. He would have died instead."

Simon gave me a sideways glance. "How do you know that?"

"Cathal told me," I said quickly, hoping my lord had been sent for

233

by the ghillie, and had therefore missed the first of the conversation.

He shook his head. "This is bad stuff. And to send Glenlyon to do it? That's damned personal. MacIain may have been right — this winter might never end now. I need to think..." He walked away, biting the knuckle of his thumb in thought, and I believe the Fox was genuinely upset by what he had heard.

Later, Cathal offered us a fuller account of that evil night's work. He told how government troops, under the auspices of enforcing a tax collection, had requested billets in Glen Coe, and how MacIain, despite misgivings, said it would never do to refuse hospitality to anyone who asked. The soldiers' week-long stay had been pleasant, on the whole, with not just a few couplings having strengthened relations between Campbell of Argyll and MacDonald of Glencoe. Then one Captain Drummond had arrived, it seemed, with new orders. MacIain and Cathal knew him: he had prevented them from reaching Inveraray for three more days, so that the treaty, which was to be signed by the first day of January, was not signed until the sixth. Yet the grand old chief had given him hospitality; and it had been repaid with the brutal execution of orders to wipe out MacIain's clan. Only a handful of men, women and children had escaped the gun, sword, knife and snow. Cathal again accused Simon. "You knew he had signed, and you knew they planned... *this!*"

"I can't know everything!" the other protested. "And with this weather..." he turned to me. "For God's sake, Bolla, you don't think I'd let this happen?"

I did not answer, and he left the chamber. Then Cathal brought out a small pouch from his plaid. "Himself told me to give you this," he told me. I opened it; inside was a handful of those stones from the bed of the Cona, the ones which turned red in the sun. "He said the winter would last for ever, and the river would run red for as long."

The next day I bade the ghillie accompany me to Castle Dounie, where I asked for an audience with Father Munro. At first he declined, telling me he was busy making his preparations to leave; but when I gave him the name of my companion (for word had moved quickly across the Highlands) he led us into the church, the better to speak in private. After having heard from the big man's own mouth the events

234

of that dark night, and after having spoken a prayer for the souls of the departed, I enacted what might have been the single worst act of betrayal in my life. I had brought with me the copied letters which Simon did not know about, and I asked Munro to read them.

"In the name of God!" the priest whispered on occasion as both Cathal and I continued to look round towards the door in case we were seen. "Do you know what all this means?"

I nodded. "It's part of the plan to bring King James back," I said.

Munro laughed. "If it is, it wouldn't be clear to Jamie himself. It's a book of double-dealing! If even half of it is true..."

"I think not," I told him. "I believe much of it is made up to press others into action. But I must know if there is anything that pertains to what happened in Glen Coe."

"I can't unsee what I've seen," he warned me. "Some of this will have to be told about elsewhere."

I did not wish to think about those consequences, yet I nodded in terse agreement. "I need to know about Glen Coe."

The priest told me there were some letters, sent back and forward, regarding Simon's previous attempts to persuade some that MacIain was planning to sign the treaty, and persuade others that he was not; yet without the details of who was supposed to have written the words, and to whom, only guesses could be raised. I confess that I should have paid a great deal more attention – but I was determined upon the discovery of one fact. I cannot full explain my feelings when it was discovered. "This," Munro lifted a page. "Dated the eleventh day of January, promising letters of fire and sword – but forgiveness still if those who have not taken the oath will submit." He looked at me. "That's a week after MacIain signed.

"And this – dated the sixteenth of January. 'As for MacIain of Glencoe and that tribe, if they can well be distinguished from the rest of the Highlanders, it will be proper, for the vindication of public justice, to extirpate that set of thieves.'" Cathal roared in anger, but I waved my hand to silence him. That's government language – it's from Edinburgh, I'm sure," the priest told me.

"But is there anything about MacIain having signed?"

Munro glanced again through those papers he had separated from the bundle, but shook his head. "What difference?" demanded Cathal. I did not answer; for the difference was only such to me. There was at least a hope that Simon had not lied, and that he had not known what was planned at Glen Coe. I made to gather the papers, with some protest from Munro – but I was able to persuade him that I could better keep watch on future proceedings if it was not known I had been making extra copies. Yet when I bade Cathal to return with me to Moniack, he refused angrily. "I will not meet eyes with that Fox without taking them from his head!" he shouted. "He knew! He *knew!*"

I realised his anger and loss meant there could be no discussion. "Then what will you do?" I asked.

"I will go… out there!" he waved his hand away. "I will keep going, village after village, keep telling them what happened – what was done to my people. I will bear witness to the death of a clan."

"You will come with me," Father Munro said sternly. "Aye, man, you will," he said as Cathal made to protest. "Together we will travel among the faithful and spread the word. I'll spread the word of God, you'll spread the word of how those who hate King Jamie behave. Besides," he added with a small smile, "These cold winters and months in jail have aged my bones. I think I could only fight three-quarters of a Saxon company on my own. You could probably manage the other quarter." At that moment, perhaps I saw a little of MacIain in him; and, perhaps, so did Cathal, for instead of arguing, he nodded, then bowed, then began taking instruction for the pair's journey to the next country which had not seen a priest in some years.

I HAD NOT KNOWN that Simon was at Castle Dounie while I had been there, and it certainly did me no harm that he had not been aware of my presence. Therefore I paid little heed when, as I discussed the day's events with Kirsty in our chambers, I heard a commotion in the yard. In truth there was much commotion between the two of us within. "You shouldn't have done it," my love was telling me urgently. "I just know, somehow, he'll find out. You know what happens to people who get in his way. We should get out of here."

"He needs me," I replied, as I always did.

"I'm not sure he does, any more," Kirsty replied. "Bolla, this is getting all too big. Soldiers and ships is one thing. Having a clan murdered —"

"We don't know he did."

"We don't know he didn't! Would you put it past him? After what we saw at Loch Eil? If you can kill your brother you can kill anyone. And remember he did that himself – not just by writing letters!" I had not told her about the three soldiers on Rannoch Moor, and this was not the moment.

"I think —" I began.

"You *feel*," she said. "I know how you feel. You're like his faithful old sheephound. Oh, don't take it like that. I don't mean it like that! But what happens when a sheephound starts killing the sheep?"

I fell silent. I knew she had the rights of it. It mattered not whether Simon knew I had shown his secret letters to Munro; it only mattered that I had. In doing so, I had become one who stood in the way of the Fox – and that way led to the grave. "I need to think," I told her.

"We need to act!" she cried. "Let's get moving. I don't want this child born under his roof!"

That could have commenced a completely different argument, had not the door burst open and John hurtled in. "I'm sorry," he said, smiling doubtfully. "Bolla, you're to come at once. It's bad." Kirsty looked at me, and I at her; yet at this moment there was only one course of action. I dared not say anything to her; instead I followed John out of the chamber. "It's bad," he repeated as he led me along corridors I knew well, but which seemed strangely longer, wider and darker than usually they did. "They say there was a big fight today. I hear Simon tried to attack Lord Hugh..." He opened Simon's chamber door, but left me to enter alone.

If John's words had not already piled concern upon concern, the distinct pallor and wild eyes of my lord did. He strode up and down before me, his strange face attempting to construct a look of confidence before crumbling again, until he said: "Time to earn your shilling... *cac*, I don't even know if it is! Bolla, Bolla..." He touched me on the shoulder. "We have to go our separate ways now." I was at once at full alarm, and just short of panic; he must know of my betrayal! When had he been at Dounie – was it before or after my interview with Munro? As he lifted a paper from his table I felt sure I was about to be confronted with my own copying work. Yet it was not the case. "Sign here," he told me, giving me a pen. I delayed, glancing at him in doubt, and that seemed to raise some of his usual character. "I am your chief, and you've got to obey me in anything reasonable," he said. "So sign the damned paper, there's a good lad, eh?" I applied my cross and stepped back, leaving him to stare at the document for some moments. "And that's it," he said, folding it up and finally looking me in the eye. "You're out of the army."

"What?" I asked, astonished.

"Pensioned out, Bolla — you get paid and everything," he said. "We're taking different paths, for a while." I still could not follow what was happening. Then, at last, he sat down. "I have orders from Ian Cam," he explained. "The Lord Lovat's Company is to garrison the Palace of Holyroodhouse, the better to serve King Billy – or the better to be kept under guard ourselves. Myself. In Edinburgh, out of the Highlands, out of touch, Bolla," he shouted. "Don't you see? If I'm not here, anything could happen with the plan. You can't stop letters if you're not half-way along the chain, can you? And you can't delay the damned things if they're only sent a few hundred yards down the road of that city!"

"Perhaps the time for letters is over?" I asked quietly, more in hope than with the aim of being helpful.

He glared at me for a moment; then shook his head. He picked up a bottle of ink thoughtfully, then smashed it into the fireplace. Finally he seemed to relax. "I have another plan, of course," he smiled a little. "And the main plan — it's still so good you couldn't stop it. Even if you knew the whole thing, which I hope no one does.

"Anyway, you're needed here, with Kirsty and everything," he continued. "I'll leave you in the care of John. But be careful of him. Keep an eye on him. He's not on your side the way I am. You know what I mean?" I nodded, but I could say nothing. "Of course you do."

Simon took his leave of Moniack Castle the next morning, the better, he said, to put some distance between himself and those in Dounie who appeared determined to lose the land for the king ("But don't ask me which king," he repeated with a grin). I had not had time to consider what the change of directions meant to me; yet I could not help feel somewhat elated that, for one, I was able to spend as much time as I wanted with my love and the child to come; and, for another, that the storm of intrigue which surrounded my lord was finally lightening around me.

John, Kirsty and I stood in the yard as he made ready with his horse, clad in the fine uniform of a captain of militia. "It's going to be a freezing journey, this," he said. "Still, others have done it. Garrison Holyroodhouse — it sounds truly dull, doesn't it? Just as well I saw it coming. I have a few wee tricks planned to keep things… interesting!"

"Look after yourself," John told him.

"You too – and them," my lord said gesturing towards us. To Kirsty he said: "You give him a fine son." Then, after a moment's thought, he added: "Daughter. It's always daughters." He offered me a smart salute; then turned his horse and rode off, his bag of farthings no doubt at the ready. Before distance had taken him from our sight the first billows of a rising snowstorm hid him from me.

CHAPTER SEVEN
THE CROOK OF THE CASTLE

IT SEEMED AS IF the snow swayed and swirled onto Fraser for the following four years, with flakes so harsh and heavy that there was more darkness than light in the world. It was as if the *Cailleach Bheur* lived amongst us — and as her frost fingers settled over our land and under our feet, there were to come many footsteps we would dread to hear crunching through the cold.

In the first year she danced alone, and, as the frozen world shines in full moonlight, there were moments of brightness: the first cry of baby Mairi as Kirsty held her in tears; and even the joy and relief of a good oat harvest in the late summer of 1693, despite a frost which did not rise until the end of May and began to fall again even in August. Yet of darkness there was much more. Only weeks of Mairi's life had passed before I saw in her a natural, determined expression that I knew well in only one other face; and the answer Kirsty offered to my questioning stare told me all. I did as my love had bade me, and we never discussed the matter; but as the girl fought her way through the particular challenges those years presented to a newborn — and bravely so — there could be no denying among those who saw her that she was the child of the Fox.

On the few occasions the sun shone it failed to lighten my heart; and soon its light failed as the winter returned. It seemed to me that it was not just a darkening of the sky I beheld, but an even deeper darkening of spirit; and an encounter with John, in which a mill exploded while I was within and he without, led me to doubt he planned to keep the word he had given his brother with regard to protecting me.

Soon the snow wheeled and whirled around us once more, leaving no time for even machinations of the Fox's brother. The *Cailleach Bheur* danced among us for the second year, her feet heard in the thunder, her hag laughter in the wind. In that time we lost the harvest to cold rain, and many homes to the storm; even Moniack suffered at the hands of a brutal wind, which tore off part of the roof and broke down part of a wall, destroying John's entire collection of bottles and powders – and almost all Simon's papers.

There came to me the dim light of a prospect of joy in the birth of my son, Tom, even in the depths of a blizzard that smashed windows around us. That light became brighter when, during the boy's first months, it became clear that Mairi was determined to watch over him as his very own clan chief; and the wit and charm of her real father brought smiles and laughter to his small face, then to ours also. In that year of hard labour, in which those of us who were able spent most of our time working to assist those of us who were not, my little family enjoyed our own private world of warmth against the winter's writhing rage. It was not to last. In the third year the *Cailleach* tired of dancing alone, and returned with an evil lover to enjoy her wicked ways. It was many generations since the name of the *Crom Dubh* had been uttered – but suddenly that bent devil appeared to be under every dead animal, within every broken house, and behind the froth and lash of the ever-present snow.

There was little more brightness in Tom's last months among us — the only time spent in this world by a life I had made myself. He was one of many young Frasers who stood almost no chance of survival in the face of famine and frost. And when the twisted night came for him to set down his sword and surrender, even then it was not simple: for by then the ice queen's king had made his own deep paths through every snowbound road in our land.

In many ways I could not blame those clansmen who turned to worshipping that spiteful spirit. While Christ's followers fought to the death over which of their faiths He wished them to follow, the *Crom Dubh* took his killings for himself. Long-forgotten voices awoke from the deep corners of old minds, and told how, in previous dark times, he would exchange young souls for easy living. Whispers became cries, and cries became chants; and as the winters worsened, the harvests hollowed and the mills made no meal, young children went missing from their cots in the evening and were never seen again; while, in the mornings that followed, fresh blood painted above doors told of those who had turned to such black acts in their desperation.

Tom took his last laboured breath even as John and I fought off a group of masked Frasers who demanded I give up my son to the *Crom Dubh*, on the promise of a warm summer and a strong harvest. While Kirsty, weeping silently, laid his blanket over his face, I was on the stairway of Moniack firing pistols into my clansmen's faces. To have killed one, and then identified him as not only one I knew, but had helped fend off others from the theft of his own son, was simply another dark moment in those dark years.

The winter howled on as the laughter of the devils who surrounded us. Between them they held back the power of the sun with a dark haze in the sky, even through the summer, and its influence overtook us all. Many rivers did not run even in the middle of the year, and many of those which did were poison. The only water to be had was the tears of starving Frasers; and even those tears froze, to be lost among the billow of the boiling blizzards. The harvest failed again, and with it, our hopes. We took to growing and cutting what we could, when we could, the farmers fighting the ice-like earths which even dominated the warmest months. Many of us took on the aspect of the weather ourselves: the pallor of snow on our complexions, the deep tracks of hard travelling scratched across our faces, the bent shivering gait of proud trees burst by ice from within. Some never spoke the tongues of men. Some never spoke again. The uncounted deaths of those we once knew (although came close to forgetting in our own struggle for survival) were still more real than the passing of Queen Mary, or the results of the inquiry into the massacre at Glencoe, which appeared to blame many and yet punish few.

Lord Hugh, who fared not well himself, lost his three-year-old son to followers of the *Crom Dubh*; these daring even to break into Beaufort Castle and steal the child away as Lady Amelia screamed in terror and rage. Before a single day without snow had passed since that

dark moment, the demon had taken an entire town by his own hand –
– throwing the sands of a full beach over the people of Culbin, whose
bodies and belongings were never found.

In the fourth year the *Cailleach Bheur* and the *Crom Dubh*, as bored
children, simply played with us at last — and Fraser, as servants
attending at their dance, could do nothing but wait. The demons' curling
cries in the wind blew soul after soul into otherwhere; the only respite
in the constant background noise coming when a clansfellow's cries of
animal agony were closer, and so louder. A desperate attempt to warm
our hearts on the part of Lady Amelia, by arranging a new year
celebration, became a violent battle between Christians and devil-
worshippers. The mood was so angry that, rather than intervene, we let
it burn itself out like the weak fires made of what fuel could yet be
found. Parents died to keep their children alive, with women walking
out into the night just to leave food remaining for their bairns – to no
avail as the little ones died also. One of the last victims of those days
in Hell was Lord Hugh's new son, aged no more than a twelvemonth;
whose body, like many, was buried in a hidden place rather than in a
churchyard, the better to protect it from the dark dance of the devils'
disciples. (I am not the only Fraser to have lost the place where my son
lies, because the snow distorted our world so badly that I would have
had to mark the location somehow, and dared not.)

At last the spirits tired of mocking our clan; and in the early spring
of 1696 the snows softened, then failed, the clouds melted, and the
fingers of frost finally drew off. When the *Cailleach Bheur* and the *Crom
Dubh* carried themselves from our country they took with them the
strength of many who remained behind, and left anger and sorrow
amongst those who found themselves lit by God's sunlight in the
knowledge they had followed false fleeting shadows. Those frost fingers
left many of us bent between them: Kirsty never breathed fairly again
and felt winter's chill keenly; John lost much of his light expression and
gave himself more to frowning — although in the intervening years the
force of focus on the helping of others had led to something of
warmth between us, such that I no longer feared any designed accidents;
MacShimi never retained the lightness of himself, and clearly entered
the twilight of his years; there came a hardness to Amelia's eyes; and

Lord Hugh, who had never truly enjoyed a summer of his life, moved straight to his kinsman Tom's autumn.

Yet Fraser survived. And the Fraser land itself seemed relieved to see that time pass, for a great earthquake shook the entire clan one March morning, soon after the rivers started to run at last. I cannot say I was surprised that Simon returned to us that same day.

NATURALLY IT WAS NO straightforward appearance. John and I were engaged upon the task of helping re-roof the house of an elderly woman near Moniack, and it had been a challenging afternoon's work. As we looked upon the results of our labour we heard a confident voice bark from behind: "Which of you is Bolla Fraser?" We both turned to behold a young, bright-eyed man in the uniform of the Lord Murray's Regiment, pointing a pistol and attempting to look stern, although his as-yet incomplete control of his face resulted in more of a comical appearance.

"That is me," I said flatly. The experience of recent times had, I realised at that moment, rendered to me a different attitude than I might have taken to such a situation in the past.

"You are under arrest, sir!" the other shouted, his voice slightly breaking as he did.

John and I looked at each other, sharing the thought that after so much turmoil, this was an issue we could easily handle. "On what charge?" I asked; then, louder: "Identify yourself – boy!"

"I am Sergeant Fraser of the Lord Lovat's Company," the other replied grandly. "And the charge is desertion!"

John laughed first, at which I could not remain calm myself. Sure enough, from behind the edge of another house strode Simon the Fox, also laughing, directing the bewildered other soldier's pistol to the ground as he passed. "There is no fooling you pair of *gorachs*!" he bellowed. "Magnificent mischief!"

He shook first John's hand then mine, his other hand resting briefly against my shoulder; while our companion, finding it difficult to follow what had occurred and how he should respond, returned his gun to his belt. "Do I arrest him too, sir?" he asked, nodding towards John.

245

"Shut up, Jamie — he's my brother!" Simon replied. "And this —" he touched my arm — "is a better sergeant than you'll ever be. Calm down, man. Meet Bolla and John. Give them one of those salutes you're so damned good at." Jamie Fraser seized the opportunity to throw himself into an alert position and shot off the smartest salute I had ever beheld. That led to more laughter from Simon, who seemed to have changed not one trace since last I had seen him. It was a matter of moments more before he perceived it was not the same for his brother or me. "Devil choke me," he whispered, looking first me then John in the eyes. "Have you been through the wars, lads?" There was no answer save to return his gaze, which we both did, leading to a watering of his own eyes. He looked down for a long moment, but on looking up once more he had recovered his cheery disposition; which was at once welcome and incongruous. "Well, thank God I'm back, then!" he laughed. He directed us to turn back to the roof of our recent labours. "Have you done well for Auld Maggie?"

"The best we could," John replied slowly, the first of us both to recover. "Hold on, hold on —" he interrupted himself, before growling slowly: "Where have you been all this time?"

"Duties, man, duties," Simon grinned. "It's not been easy looking after the king's affairs these last years — and don't ask me which king. But, come on: I'm back! How's that for you?"

For a moment my spirits made to rise to meet his own; then the hand of darkness of those four winters grasped me again. "There is work to be done," I said in place of anything he might prefer to have heard.

"I know," he replied quietly. "That's why I'm back." We walked with him the short distance to Moniack, while Jamie followed with their horses, trying to look as if he were part of our company, and failing. John made to summarise recent events; yet the truth of it was that no quick explanation could detail how difficult our lives had become.

"All the bottles?" he cried, interrupting John as he pointed out the repaired parts of the castle.

"And the papers. Well, most of them," his brother said.

"Damn the papers! But the *bottles*!" It ill befell him, I thought, to appear so sanguine about the dozens of deaths and the devil-worshipping of which John had spoken, only to become enraged at the loss of some glass and powders.

"Simon —" his brother said, and I realised it would have been the first time the other had heard such a tone of voice from that man.

"I'm sorry," the Fox said, holding his hands up. He shook his head. "I can see I've been away too long. But that Ian Cam... Ach, later, later." It seemed strange to feel drawn into a world I had nearly forgotten – that of Simon's intrigue – especially in that it bore no comparison to the real torments that had plagued Fraser as a clan.

If my lord was learning quickly, the pace of his education increased as we entered the great hall of the castle. Kirsty and Mairi were sitting at the fire, engaged upon some task of tapestry, as we approached. It suddenly struck me what was about to happen, and I stopped short soon after the doorway, leaving Simon to march forward, and John to pause as realisation struck him too. "Kirsty Fraser, you little —" he began, but cut off as the two looked up towards him. "My lady!" he bowed deeply to Mairi. I do not know what he expected, but the girl of just under four years froze the room with the deep stare she turned upon him; and as he looked up, even from behind I could see he struggled to meet her.

She very slowly stood up from the fireplace and stepped towards him, her glance never leaving his, Kirsty's never leaving mine, mine aimed at the back of Simon's head, and the brothers trapped as if in crossfire. Simon remained in his bow but I could see his shoulders shaking a little as the girl came within four paces of him, stopped, then moved around him almost as a cat, bringing his stare with her, moved towards me and grabbed my hand. "Dada!" she whispered, although loud enough for Simon to hear as he turned to follow her path. "Who?" The moment lasted for some time. I felt the little warm hand in mine, then her tiny body as she pressed against my leg, as all the while she refused to allow my lord to avert his gaze. He wore an expression I found difficult to read, although certainly there was doubt and fear. Yet more so (or at least I would like to believe) he displayed wonder; and I began to perceive a sensation of achievement, and perhaps even victory, in my own spirit.

"You're back then, Simon," Kirsty said flatly, and I think that only she could have broken the spell.

My lord took the opportunity she offered. "Back to help!" he grinned. "Did any of my wine survive the winters? Will somebody get me a damned drink?"

"Watch your tone!" Kirsty shouted furiously, and I am sure I heard a gurgle of approval from Mairi, who suddenly demanded that I lift her up; something which had last happened as I grieved for my son.

All eyes were on the Fox, who could do nothing but laugh. "Where's that *go* — what happened to my new sergeant?" he asked, pacing towards a window to summon that young man, who remained in the yard.

"*Gorach*," Mairi said loudly from her position with her arms wrapped round my neck. Simon made to turn towards her but stopped himself.

"No!" Kirsty shouted in order to break her own laugh. "Don't say that to Simon!"

"Simon," the girl said slowly and thoughtfully, then repeated his name in a more demanding tone, to which he finally turned towards her.

"It's nice to meet you —"

"Mairi," I finished.

"Mairi," he said, finally finding his usual demeanour and flashing one of his brightest. grins. "A real pleasure, my dear!" He stepped over towards us and held out his hand. She looked at me, and I at her, and in that moment I perceived a new understanding between us.

Suddenly she matched his grin in the manner that had caused all who had seen it to understand her lineage — but in the presence of he who had created it, hers appeared altogether more genuine. "Simon!" she said brightly. "Simon *Gorach*!" She and Kirsty laughed loudly, while I heard John splutter behind me. I managed to contain myself as my lord, realising the game was lost, looked to me for support, then seemed to accept Mairi's authority in the exchange.

"I prefer The Young MacShimi," he said with a rueful laugh.

She turned to me and shared a glance in which, at last, I saw something of myself. "No," she said, satisfied. "Simon *Gorach*."

Soon afterwards my lord took charge of our small gathering once again, despite the suggestion it was only upon Mairi's permission. He explained there was a specific purpose for his visit, something of which

John appeared to have knowledge, and asked his brother and I to accompany him to Castle Dounie without delay. Kirsty only briefly met my glance as we left, but I understood something had passed between us, and the result was a new warmth in her eyes. Mairi made much of hugging and kissing me, and telling me she loved me, as I set her down by the fire.

My sense of uplift did not last long. During our short journey I began to feel truly sorry for my lord, whose attempts at his usual light-heartedness fell on deaf ears among the precious few people we met on the road. On several occasions even his farthings fell at people's feet; and one clansman demanded to know what use a coin would be when there was no food to be had. It seemed the Fox truly did not know how to deal with the severe change in fortune he beheld among us. By the time we arrived at our destination he had long since fallen silent, and Sergeant Jamie remained on the whole a mystery – a situation I am sure would not have arisen in the past. When Simon set eyes on his father I believe he began to feel at once guilty for having been absent during our dark days, and also relief that he had not had to witness them. For in truth Lord Tom, who had appeared an aged man for some time, now seemed older than even when I had last seen him a moon ago. "Father," said Simon, almost doubtfully; and whereas a dynamic thrown hug would have been the method of greeting previously, I saw how gentle the younger man was with the older.

"It's good to see you, Simon," said Tom. "I wasn't sure…"

"My orders," his son cut in. "I couldn't. I wanted to, but —"

"Of course," the father said, attempting to imitate the commanding tone he had once displayed with ease. "You were doing it for the clan. How goes it with Ian Cam?"

"He's still *amaideach*," the other said, and both laughed at last. Yet faces fell once again when Lord Hugh and Lady Amelia entered the hall; for it was clear that the Lord Lovat was not long for this earth – and clearer still that he appeared to have accepted his lot. We offered our usual respectful greetings, but he did not want to know, and Simon's half-hearted attempt at engaging the lady in their usual jocular exchanges was quickly brushed off by that sadder, quieter woman. Hugh simply sat down at the table and gestured us all to join him. He did not even ask for refreshment, leaving Amelia, who stood stoically and dutifully behind him, to deal with such things.

"Simon," he nodded, holding his hand up to prevent any conversation. "You are to bear witness to the signing. There is to be no discussion – it needs done for the clan." He took from his robe a large paper and passed it to Tom without reading it. That man took a moment to look over it, but he had clearly seen it before; then passed it to Simon, who offered more attention. After a time he nodded, giving away no feeling, and returned it to Hugh, who, without any words, lifted a pen and signed his name at the bottom. Tom did the same, as did Simon, then Lovat stood up, with a little difficulty, and moved to the great hearth. Tom and Amelia shared a glance, then followed.

Simon slid the paper across the table to his brother. I went to look first – but John nudged me and took it towards himself. "Agreement of Settlement," he read out. "Between Hugh Fraser, Ninth Lord Lovat, and Thomas Fraser of Beaufort..." The contents made arrangement that, in the (almost certain) event of Hugh dying without male issue, the title and properties of Lovat were settled upon MacShimi and his descendants. I watched Simon as John read, wondering how much of a sense of victory he might feel that, with the swoop of a pen, he had taken a great leap towards becoming the all-powerful master he had clearly always wanted to be. Yet his face betrayed no joy; and he appeared concerned with the wellbeing of Hugh, at whom he stared grimly. I wondered if, at that very moment, the severity of Fraser's condition had finally become entirely clear to him.

Leaving the paper he joined the others at the fire, where Hugh had sat himself close to the flames. As John and I stood up from the table he nudged me. "It's best Simon doesn't know you can read and write," he told me quietly. "That's why I read it out." I nodded. Over the previous winter, the differences between us resolved, John had taken the time to complete my learning of letters. I had often given thought to what might have been revealed to me had the Fox's papers not been lost.

We followed him to the fireplace, where he was seated beside Hugh, speaking gently but firmly. "I can do more from here," he said. "It's important to —"

"You must do as Thomas says," Hugh broke in weakly. "You must always do as Thomas says."

"You need to be with Tullibardine," Lord Tom said more strongly. "Murray has not suffered the way we have. The knowledge may encourage him to act in certain ways we do not want. You need to keep close to him."

"And I have been!" Simon cried, before lowering his voice as Hugh winced. "He's engaged on matters of state. Most of Scotland is wrecked – even King Billy's men know there are fundamental problems they have to deal with. No one's got the stomach for a fight right now."

"You know that's not true," MacShimi said. "If Jamie comes back now there's not many won't support him — they're desperate for things to change. He wouldn't even need to bring money. Bags of oats would buy hearts right now."

"Jamie's not coming," Simon said.

"Do you *know* that?" asked Lord Tom sharply.

"No," his son admitted after a pause. "But they see things differently in France. I don't know how differently. I don't get as much information as I used to." Here he glanced towards John, who ignored him.

"Well, there you are," Tom replied. "You don't know enough, so you have to stay in Edinburgh until you do."

Simon shrugged. "I might need a couple of people, a couple of things. Let me stay here for a week or two?"

Tom nodded. "But no longer, son."

"Agreed," Hugh muttered, and that appeared to end the discussion. We began to move away from the fireplace, leaving the two seated there.

"How are Kirsty and Mairi?" Lady Amelia asked me.

"Good," I told her — knowing that was the best any of us could say about any other of us.

"Wee Mairi saw Simon off," John smiled. "Put him in his place. Called him a *gorach*!"

Amelia paused for a moment, considering the value of such an exchange, then laughed. "It's about time someone said that," she said. "And you, Bolla? How are you?"

"Good," I replied, and I meant it. I glanced back as we moved towards the doorway, to see Simon staring into Hugh's eyes, his hand on the chief's shoulder. I had seen such conversations before: the offering of moral support, the lending of some of the Fox's seeming endless energy to shore up an exhausted soul. Yet I also saw my lord hand over a small bottle, which he placed in Hugh's cloak, pointing towards it a number of times before rising and following us out, leaving a shadow of what had always been something of a shadow of a man, near fading among the shadows cast by the flames he sought to warm his ailing blood. There could be no doubt that Lord Hugh would not survive the winter, even if it were milder than those we had recently endured; and that by year's end Tom would be the Lord Lovat — and Simon the Master of Lovat.

THE FOX WAS NOT LONG about returning some of his old spirit to Moniack, with the help of his near-abandoned wine cellar. Kirsty yet kept her distance, but he, too, appeared to understand that need and did not force her to join us. In truth it had been some time since John or I had felt able to relax as we did that evening, and it gave me cause to recall warm, joy-filled summers in Aberdeen with Mungo Murray. At last, too, we came to know more about Sergeant Jamie Fraser; and quickly surmised why Simon enjoyed his company when my lord asked the young man what he made of the Earl of Tullibardine. "You should challenge him to a duel, sir!" he barked excitedly. "You'd have him dead in seconds!"

"Probably," grinned Simon, "but you can't call a superior officer out. It's a hanging offence."

"They'd have to catch you first, sir! I bet they couldn't. You could hold the castle against them!"

"Castle?" John asked.

"Not for Fraser the grandeur of Holyroodhouse," Simon told him. "They moved us up to Edinburgh Castle last year."

"No one else can be trusted," Jamie said confidently. "They know we'll fight anyone off. Captain MacShimi will do it himself, probably!"

"Captain MacShimi!" John spluttered.

Simon pretended to misunderstand. "Yes, this wine's awful. Who's been looking after it?"

"No one," I said quietly, then regretting it, for I wished not to disturb the pleasant feeling in the room.

My lord shook his head. "Philistines – a wee bit of cold and you can't look after the drink? If I'd known I'd have brought some claret from Edinburgh."

"You can drink anything, sir," Jamie announced. "I've seen it. You're still going when everyone else is under the table."

"An art, to be sure," Simon said agreeably. "Although – Rob Roy does not bad at keeping up with me…"

Jamie's eyes sparkled. "Tell me more about him, sir!"

"Ah, the Red MacGregor!" Simon said, staring off into the distance. "Known him for years, so I have." He ignored the looks John and I offered him. "The number Saxons we've killed together…"

"Tell me about Killicrankie, sir! How you and Rob Roy smashed the enemy line!"

"*Ochone*, that's dull," my lord replied. "We did what we did. But I remember a time it was just the two of us, cornered at Portnellan in a storm, with an entire government company coming at us…" He appeared to be reminiscing to himself, then I realised he was waiting for Jamie to plead for more information. When that one finally did, Simon instead sent him to bring more wine. Jamie, as was clearly his way, marched aggressively off into the castle; and even before he was out of earshot Simon laughed long and loud. "Stupid wee *gorach* doesn't even know where he's going! He'll find it eventually."

"When did you fight with Rob Roy MacGregor?" John asked.

"Ach, the boy likes stories – it's good for him," Simon replied dismissively. "What's wrong with having all that passion for life? I mind a time when you were like that, John. And you, Bolla."

"Things have changed. You know it," John told him. "One out of every five Frasers are gone these past four years, while you —"

"Did my duty in the name of the clan," my lord frowned. "Do you really think it would have been different if I'd been here?"

"Yes," his brother said frankly, saving me the trouble. "That devil stuff — you could have talked folk round. Nobody else had time to talk."

"Maybe," Simon said thoughtfully. "I think while I'm here I'd better take a bit of a wander round, see what people are saying for themselves."

"That would be good," I said, knowing that he could do for many in the clan what he had done for us in the short time we had sat down together.

"A progress!" he suddenly grinned. "The Young MacShimi returns — so let's celebrate! I'll get some meat and meal sorted."

"Where from?" John asked.

"Did you read the agreement? The settlement? Father gets a payment on account, and so do I."

"How much?"

"Five thousand merks," my lord grinned.

"Five thousand?"

"And you get a thousand yourself, so you can help too." John looked surprised; clearly he had not been aware of the entire agreement, nor had he read it all that day. "We're the Lovats, more or less, and that's official, so let's act like it – by getting drunk. Where's Jamie? Jamie!"

"Don't wake Mairi!" I cautioned.

"I'm sorry," Simon said almost dismissively, then looked at me with an expression of gravity. "I'm sorry," he repeated, and I believed he was contrite. "Yes, a progress round the country," he said more quietly. "Let's remind Fraser who we are. Then, Bolla —" he paused briefly, doubtfully, "Will you come back with me to Edinburgh? I need you."

His words came as a shock, although at the back of my mind I must have been expecting such a question. Did I want to return to the world of the Fox, or stay among the people I had fought so hard with – and Kirsty, and Mairi? "I do not know," I admitted at last. "Let me think about it."

My lord nodded. "Thank you," he said, and I considered that he was beginning to realise just how much had changed between us.

Finally Jamie charged back into the chamber carrying more bottles of wine than was safe for one who deported himself in such a manner. "Wine, sir!" he said proudly, nearly dropping everything as he landed his wares on the table.

"Devil choke me — how much wine?" Simon laughed.

"Some," the other replied, his round eyes betraying emotion some-

254

where between childish excitement and lapdog-like vacant enthusiasm. "Did I miss the Rob Roy story?"

"Most of it," my lord told him, enjoying, I am sure, the near panic in the young man's face. "But for you, Jamie Fraser, I'll start again." I found I could not blame him for playing with the lad, such was the joy he received from those words. "Well? Fill my cup if I'm going to dance for you!" That done, Simon began his story. "How long have you been with Lovat's Company, Jamie? Two years? It was a few months before that. After Rob married Mary – and what a party that was, I can tell you. So it's raining like in the Bible, with a wind to blow you to hell, and we're looking out the window at the burn. Rob's saying, 'It's going to burst its banks – we'll need to move the cattle.' I'm saying, 'In this weather? We'll lose the lot!' He says, 'We can always get more' — because you know what line of business he's in, don't you?

"But before we can do anything, a ghillie batters the door down and tells us there's a company on the way to take Rob. He's been calling himself MacGregor again, and that's against good King Billy's law – the name's proscribed; to use it means death. Normally there wouldn't be problem – Rob's not stupid and there's always a secret path to get away from anywhere. But in this weather, he says, the road he had in mind will likely kill him sooner than the soldiers.

"So Rob tells me, 'Stay here and stay out of it.' But I'm saying, 'We're friends, man – we're in it together.' So he says, 'Right, then,' and we get out the back door and follow a wee path he knows. But just a couple of minutes along we see a couple of soldiers coming our way. Rob's raging: 'Someone betrayed me!' and he's all for going right through the soldiers. I tell him we don't know how many there are, or how many are behind them, and we'd better just get off the path. Which is dangerous enough when you can hear the wind's bringing down trees all around us.

"But the same happens again — someone who knows all about Portnellan has opened his gub to the army, and whatever direction we try, we see the lights coming at us. Now, you know animals will always go uphill when they're being chased, and how much use it usually does them. We're the same; we end up getting forced up a wee hill with a cliff at one end, and the soldiers are coming at us from all directions.

"Eventually that's us at the end of the road. There's nowhere else to go. I tell Rob, 'Give me your gun — if they catch you with a weapon that's a double offence.' But he says, 'No! I'm taking a few of these *gorachs* to hell with me!' So we're standing there, trying not to get blown off the cliff, back to back, waiting for the soldiers. From over on the left, six of them appear, muskets loaded, and at this distance they're not all going to miss. Then on the right we see eight more, and they've all got two pistols each. Then from in front of us another twenty come up, with a captain at the front.

"'Rob Roy Campbell!' he shouts. 'It's MacGregor!' he shouts back. 'Then you admit it! Surrender or we'll shoot you right now!' Rob looks at me, and I look at him. 'Time to go to hell,' he shouts — and just as the captain orders his men to open fire, Rob pulls his trigger."

Simon fell silent, staring into the fireplace, the candlelight dancing off his face and betraying no emotion. The silence continued almost painfully as he took a long drink from his cup, and, considering the container, clapped it down on the table.

"So what... what happened?" Jamie asked at last.

"What *happened*?" Simon repeated, staring at him. "We damn well died, didn't we?"

John and I exploded with laughter, as did the Fox, all of us enjoying Jamie's refusal to accept how he'd been misled. The young man nodded seriously for a moment, at least offering the effect of thinking deeply; then he finally smiled. "I knew they'd never get you, sir!" he said with great confidence.

Soon afterwards, the rigours of heavy drinking reaching into every fibre of my body, I went to retire; leaving the young sergeant sitting by the fire waiting to be told when to pour more wine, while Simon and John began discussing how they might replenish the lost collection of bottles and powders. Had I been more aware, I would have made more of John's insistence that certain items should not be replaced, citing as a reason the lessons in life he had learned in recent years. I would also have made more of Simon's insistence that everything must be put back as it had been, because it was part of his plan. Yet I did not think of the conversation until many months later, and instead retired to my chamber, where Kirsty stirred as I settled down beside her. "Did you have a good time?" she muttered, half-awake.

"It is good to see him," I replied; then, after a pause, I added: "He wants me to go to Edinburgh."

"I thought he would," she said. "Are you going?"

"I don't know," said I. "Part of me thinks I should — if he needs me, as he says."

"He will need you. But think hard about it, because I need you too. And so does your daughter."

Mairi: my daughter. The word at last settled in my mind, and I slept soundly.

SIMON'S PROGRESS DELIVERED ALL that could have been hoped of it. His performance in every village of the country was never less than brilliant; and it surely helped that his return to Fraser coincided with a period of just the right amount of sunshine and rain that an early crop was all but guaranteed to grow well. The provision of wine and grain at his own cost, alongside his usual outpouring of good humour, energy and farthings, sowed its own crop: one of hope. If at first many kinsmen found the idea of a celebration to be at odds with their recent lives, the following morning saw all invested with a new spirit. I had cause to remember a number of occasions, such as that on the Bass, when Simon had focused such attention and intention on me. The harvested of his labours was, in a very real sense, new life.

Yet the land itself bore scars which would take longer to heal. We passed many broken houses, their inhabitants long lost to the dark times – some with the faded stains of blood over their doors as a sign to the demons who had ravaged our people. Rotting wood and cloths on well-trod circles aside the road told of places where craftsmen had toiled, but would no more. Fallen gates lay abandoned, the animals once kept behind them no longer in danger of wandering. And for those who knew where and how to look, private signals scratched upon trees told of places where small bodies lay buried.

For a time it appeared to me that Simon either did not notice those scars, or otherwise discounted them. I thought as much until, soon after our journey had been completed, I chanced upon him, drinking alone in his chamber in Moniack. He was deep in his cups and not able to speak much sense; but among the ramblings he briefly directed at me were mentions of passed Frasers he had once known and memories of times he had shared with them: a dalliance with one Mary, apparently a willing accomplice; a hunting trip with an elderly ghillie known as Charlie; a horse race with a lame man named Andrew, who had been the victor despite his ailment. Those, and many more, he mentioned by name, shaking his head and throwing still more wine into his belly. Then in moment of clarity he stared at me and said: "Your Kirsty, Bolla! She used to be so..." I did not feel anger at his words. His absence over those years meant he was not able to see that, while she had lost some of her youthful appearance, she had gained so much more genuine beauty. He stood up and staggered towards me, laying his hand on my shoulder. "Was it really that damned bad, Bolla?" he asked. I simply nodded, returning his stare. He turned away, sat down again and fell back into his drunken mutterings. Yet next morning there was nothing maudlin about him (or, indeed, hung-over) and the only reference he made to our interaction was a brief touch of the shoulder before he mounted his horse to run some errand or other.

Finally there came the words I had been expecting: "Time to earn your shilling, Bolla!" And I had decided that, despite some misgivings, I would travel with him to Edinburgh. He displayed genuine delight at my assent, and even asked whether I had discussed the matter with Kirsty. "I'd say bring her with you," he told me, "But I'm not sure how things are going to pan out. If we need to make a sharp exit..."

"She would not come anyway," I replied. "There is still much to do here."

"And no one better to do it," he grinned. "Your woman is the best Fraser there's ever been."

"I know it," I said.

We left our country a far happier place than it had been before Simon's return; except, perhaps, for John, who appeared upset when his brother told him to expect packages from France. That, in turn, cast a cloud over the Fox's own face for a time. It soon passed once we were on the road again – he, myself and Jamie.

"Edinburgh is amazing!" the young man enthused loudly. "You'll love it, Bolla!"

"I have been there," I told him. "I have stayed there."

If that disappointed him, Simon's next words did so even more. "*Ochone*, Bolla — remember that drink with Baldy Menzies? That *gorach* could drink, right enough. Can't take that away from him."

Jamie's face lit again as he thought of something new to tell me. "Captain MacShimi has served with Captain Ackermann of the —"

"Dandy Dapperman," I corrected him with a small smile.

"Now there's a real *gorach* for you!" Simon bellowed with a laugh. "Remember that swordfight on the Bass?"

Jamie finally appeared to understand that, regardless of his own desire in the matter, I had spent more time with Simon than he had, and in what the young man would regard as more interesting circumstances. "You can get a drink any time of the day or night in Edinburgh," he said, as if the previous few exchanges had never taken place. "It's grand."

The journey felt longer than usual. Nevertheless it passed uneventfully, and soon I found myself passing the highest houses of the city, and approaching a castle I had only previously beheld from a distance. It was a massive, impressive structure, towering over the city from its rocky perch — and yet, on close inspection, it was clear that it desperately required the attention of many masons. The outer walls stood thick, but broken down in countless places; and though the main defences behind appeared in better condition, mounds of rubble and distinct gaps told of a building that, if not addressed in the near future, might crumble all but to dust. Gesturing at the shattered ramparts, Simon told me: "It might not look like it, but this *cac* makes it easier to take the place than if it wasn't there at all." He responded to my doubtful gaze by offering an insight into how he might attack the castle; but I confess his words simply confused me further. I remained convinced that any defensive structure must be an advantage; but he assured me it was not so, and that the only real protection against invasion was the large portcullis gate which we climbed towards as the castle towered over our left shoulders.

The condition of buildings within was not significantly better. Our horses stabled, Simon led us past a series of outhouses that seemed to droop with shame at their appearance, up a steep path towards the main accommodation at the top of the castle rock. I was pleased to see an extensive half-circular platform from which cannon stared sternly over the approach to the outer wall and the city below; yet, seeing my appreciative look, Simon said: "The half-moon battery – completely useless!" and led us onward to four main buildings assembled round an open square. Here he pushed open a doorway at the south-east end, revealing his own chambers, wherein he appeared to have created a haven against the dilapidations of everything else I had seen. Jamie Fraser took on the aspect of a broken building when Simon gestured towards a couch and told me it was mine, and sent the young sergeant back to the guards' barracks.

"You could almost call it Castle Fraser, if you wanted to," my lord said as I looked out of the window. "The Earl of Leven only has fifty men in the garrison and there's a hundred and fifty of us. But God knows what this place could do for you, unless..." he broke off, and I wondered if he had become used to talking to himself in my absence. Then he laughed, and touched my arm. "It's grand to have you back, Bolla," he grinned. "Like old times, eh? Plenty of fun to come as well. Spectacular sport!" My thoughts returned to Kirsty and Mairi, and all we had endured; and I hoped he was wrong.

EDINBURGH CASTLE WAS AS UNIQUE a prison as it was a fortress; the which I discovered the following evening, when Simon bade me attend dinner in the constable's chambers. As I followed my lord into a warm and well-lit room with the remnants of a painted ceiling and a large table at its centre, the rumble of voices which had indicated our direction through the maze of corridors settled into the sound of agreeable, if loud, conversation. As the door behind me was closed by a servant, I was presented with two surprises: the first, to be told to sit at the table beside Simon; the second, to find myself seated beside the only other man I recognised in the room — the Earl of Tullibardine. "Sergeant Fraser!" that man said with his challenging accent, although he spoke warmly. "It is good to see you."

"Mr Fraser now," Simon grinned from his place opposite. "The right hand man of the clan in these difficult times."

"So I hear. So I hear," said the earl. "You are to be congratulated. I understand that many of the name Fraser owe their lives to you." I made a doubtful protest, yet I could not but take the hand he offered me, apparently in friendship and as an equal. "And it is good to have you back under this roof, Captain Fraser," Tullibardine said.

"Damned certain!" bellowed an elderly man from behind a large pipe. "It's been bloody boring without you!"

Simon bowed slightly. "Bolla, may I introduce Sir William Bruce to you? One of the greatest architects Scotland has ever known."

"Trapped in this dunghole without the wherewithal to fix it!" the other grumbled, before adding: "A pleasure, sir."

Another gentleman was named as David Melville, the Earl of Leven, in command of the castle, who appeared to be in every way a professional soldier, even in the manner his half-aware eyes appeared to contemplate objects in the distance rather than those immediately before him, and his grim expression did not lift even as he attempted to make a welcoming gesture to me. Of a similar age, but a completely different temperament, was William Keith, the Earl Marischal, who appeared to care little about his appearance and much about the wine in the decanter in front of him; and he shook his long unkempt hair and his large body and laughed as he speculated upon the mischief I had seen if I knew Simon well. A younger fellow laughed along too – he a fine-looking personage of classic dark looks and a glint in his cheerful eyes, who was introduced to me as Lord James Drummond, son of the Earl of Perth.

I spoke little as a grand dinner was served to us – grander than anything I had seen in several years. Yet I paid attention to the details of conversation between these six strong characters, even though it was much in the realm of small-talk, and I began to discern something of a distance of thought between two distinct parties. In time I began to conclude that, as Bruce had intimated, some of these were warders and some prisoners — and eventually concluded that Simon, Tullibardine and Leven played the former role while Marischal and Drummond joined Bruce in the latter.

Dinner eaten, the constable called on my lord to make a toast, since he had been absent in recent days, to which that man stood, held up a glass and said: "The king!"

"The king!" the others echoed; and, after a moment, realising my position, I did so too.

Then Simon added: "And the other king!"

"And the other king!" we all repeated, the doubt clear in my voice.

Simon laughed. "We find ourselves in strange times, Bolla," he told me as the others listened, seemingly intent on observing my reaction. "But we have to find a way to survive, no matter who's on the throne. It makes more sense than killing each other, doesn't it?" At that I was able to offer a confident and positive response, which appeared to relax my companions; and the conversation opened up to the discussion of current events, of which I had no understanding. Bruce appeared upset over the efforts of someone named Paterson to persuade, it seemed, everyone in Scotland who held any coin to present much of it to him, an exercise he referred to as the Bank of Scotland.

"I still don't see it," Drummond said to my gratitude. "This Paterson will take our cash — and for what?"

Simon laughed loudly. "If we could all think like him we'd all have much more money," he said. "I'll explain it to you in words an idiot can understand, if you want?" To Drummond's nod he said, "Then an idiot can explain it to you!" As the room echoed with laughter my lord drew a small chest across the table towards him. "We all have a few farthings to our names, do we not?" Drummond nodded. "You all give me a farthing and I put it in this box. So there's six farthings in there, and you've all still got a few each. But Bruce here, he needs three farthings to fix up this castle —"

"I'd sooner burn it down," Bruce glowered.

"— so I lend him the three farthings. He pays it back, plus a farthing for the loan, so now there's seven farthings in the box. Got it? Now you, Jamie Drummond, you want four farthings to get married." There was much laughter once again at the young man's expense. "Somehow you get the cash back off your wife and pay me one farthing for the loan. Now there's eight farthings in the box. You see? Everyone gets a loan according to their need, they pay for the loan, and everyone ends up better off."

"Paterson ends up better off!" Bruce cried.

Simon grinned. "That's the genius of it. He's never going to lend the original six farthings — he's going to lend the farthings he's made out of lending other farthings. It works as long as he *says* he's got money in the box. And if he hasn't, who's to know? And where do you think those six farthings go?"

"Paterson!" Bruce repeated.

"Exactly!" Simon cried back. "Well, a little goes back to the original investors, but most of it goes to him. It's genius!"

"It's theft, just!" said Marischal.

"Entirely legal, though," Tullibardine replied thoughtfully.

"Won't he end up with all the money in Scotland?" Drummond asked.

"That's the idea," Tullibardine nodded. "I think."

"And that's why he's creating his own new country," Simon added. "Darien – and, yet again, everyone else pays! Magnificent mischief!"

Tullibardine did not laugh. "Mungo wants to serve in Darien," he said, looking over at Simon.

"Mungo... hasn't spoken to me since..."

"I know," said his brother, making no other reference in face or word to the tragedy of Huntingtower. "He says he wants to get out of this civil war and do some good work somewhere else. They will have need of soldiers in that God-forsaken place. Who can tell what terrors they will face, thousands of miles from home?"

"It's completely stupid," Simon insisted. "For all we know Paterson will sail them round the islands a dozen times, take their money and send them home."

Bruce barked a laugh. "Paterson's not going himself — be clear on that!"

"*Ochone* — so it's a real expedition then," Simon smiled.

"What else can be done? This whole country's reduced to poverty," Bruce muttered angrily. "If I wasn't stuck here I'd go with them. They'll need buildings when they get there. At least I'd get some work done."

"You'd never survive the voyage, you old goat!" Drummond laughed.

"Forfeit, boy!" bellowed Bruce with glee. The others laughed as Simon opened the small box and Drummond deposited a coin within.

263

"We have some rules about what you can and can't say at the table," Simon explained to me. "For example, no one's allowed to have a go at Sir William for his age — and no one's allowed to argue over who should be on the throne. Don't worry, Bolla! A quiet chap like yourself isn't likely to need the box opened!"

"I do have a complaint, though," Drummond insisted. "And we don't have a rule about it." The others bade him continue. "Simon," he said, turning to my lord, "Can you please not bring that bloody girl Anne to my room again?"

Everyone laughed. "You are in jail, Jamie Drummond," Simon told him. "There are limits as to what – or who – can be brought for you."

"I know, but… she's so…"

"The thrill of the chase, young man!" Bruce laughed.

"My room is too small. There's no thrill in a chase that size."

"She tells me so!" Bruce replied, and cheerfully threw a coin in the box.

"Gentlemen!" Leven objected. "Decorum, please!"

"Quite right," nodded Tullibardine. "We are cultured folk in this castle."

Later, as the party separated to its various chambers (and no signal of any guards required to send the seeming prisoners to their cells) my lord gathered a large bundle of I knew not what, and told me to bring a torch and follow him down several flights of stairs. As we descended into increasing darkness and silence, it became plain to me that there were indeed jailrooms as I understood them from my youth; and that we were fast approaching the worst of them. Simon took a key from a wall and opened a heavy wooden door. Within I beheld a small chamber with a tiny window at the far end — but it was the stench that struck my senses. He took my torch and used it to light two more on the walls, at which I realised that what I had taken to be bundles of cloth on the floor were in reality two men. They sat up cautiously (and from my own experience I knew the half-stupor from which they rose, and the suspicion they felt) and remained nearly still until my lord whispered: "It's me – the Young MacShimi!"

"Simon!" answered one of them. "How long?"

"Just six hours or so," he said, "I've brought mutton and wine." It appeared, then, that even the inhabitants of the most lowly chambers in this strange place were better fed than much of the Clan Fraser.

"Any news?" asked the other.

"I'm still waiting," Simon said, and I saw both prisoners' shoulders slump, even as they made to eat what they had been given. "But we're on the move, lads – here's Sergeant Bolla Fraser, the one I told you about. Not long to wait now." I saw the shaded figures stop eating only briefly, before returning to their food. "John Stewart, Laird of Balleahan, of Atholl, and his brother Alex," he told me, gesturing at first to one and then the other; although they both ignored me.

"Too long now," one said. "You have to get us out of here."

Simon stared at them silently for a moment. "I know, lads," he replied quietly. "Four or five more days, that's all."

"You said that yesterday!" snarled one.

"You said it before you left us!" the other agreed.

"I'm working on it!" my lord cried. "Please – trust me." He went to move forward, his intention being to touch one or other of their shoulders, I am sure; but both crept back from him without standing up, to which he also stepped back, clearly in some doubt. "Not long," he repeated quietly. "Not long, lads."

"More blankets!" one said.

"Yes," Simon replied, clearly glad he could do something to help. "I'll bring them tomorrow morning."

"Now!" one shouted, spitting meat from his mouth, and scrabbling on the floor before him to recover the shreds.

"I'll have it done!" said my lord. I realised he was glad of a reason to leave the chamber; and as he closed and locked the door behind him, I was not surprised when he bade me to run the errand for blankets. "It's *cac*, of course it is," he told me. "But they won't be there for much longer."

"How long have they been there already?" I asked quietly, but he did not answer. "Who put them there?"

"I arrested them," he said, not looking at me. "It's a wee part of the plan, Bolla. Only — it wasn't meant to take this long. To bring men of Atholl to... *this*..." Suddenly he found the disposition of the Fox once more. "But it's grand, Bolla!" he said, holding me by both shoulders.

"The fun's going to kick off within a week or two!"

"Not four or five days," I replied quietly.

"Not quite," he shrugged. "But come on, my lad! What's a couple of days for a king's throne?" It occurred to me to ask which king, but I did not.

AS A ROPE HUNG FROM A TREE BY A CHILD will often cease swinging between fore and aft, and begin instead winding fitfully in all directions, so I felt myself to be wound between worlds. At first it had simply been between Moniack and Edinburgh; now, I drifted also between the prisoners above and those below in the castle. The box on the dinner table – soon labelled "The Bank Of Edinburgh Castle" – filled with coins as each diner took his turn offending another, with light-hearted jest almost always defeating any real argument. An example of the latter came when Sir William Bruce proudly displayed an old paper he said had written near forty years previously: a secret message between Cromwell's General Monck and the exiled King Charles II, which Bruce had carried at risk of execution, and successfully delivered, leading to the general's changing of sides and the restoration of King Jamie's brother to the throne. Leven objected that its presentation at the table made a mockery of their gentlemen's truce; but after the matter had been settled I saw Simon deep in conversation with Bruce, and I could imagine the contents of the exchange – as could Tullibardine, who watched with a stony expression. Meanwhile, in the bowels below, his kinsmen spoke less and growled more as their incarceration robbed them of their humanity, despite the continued supply of good meat and drink.

Several days after the Athollmen's wait should have been over (although I knew not for what they waited, except freedom) Simon told me: "Time to earn your shilling, Bolla," and led me, along with Sergeant Jamie, to a row of broken outhouses near the portcullis gate. "I want you to look for secret tunnels," he told us with a grin.

"Yes sir!" cried Jamie, and marched off in the direction in which he happened to be facing.

Simon howled with laughter. "You're a *gorach*, Jamie," he said. "You have no idea where you're going — but you're going there right now!" Bewildered, he stopped and half-turned back to his captain, as a dog who has been instructed to wait. "I haven't told you the story yet." At his words the young man scampered back. "This place has been here for centuries," said Simon, "And you don't have a place like this for long without it becoming haunted. You see?"

"Yes, sir!" Jamie cried again, and I had the strange notion that the pattern of his voice matched exactly that which he had used on the previous occasion.

"They used to call it the Castle of Maidens," the Fox continued. "It's said that in times of attack all the virgins of Edinburgh would come up to the castle for protection against —" he paused, then shrugged – – "whoever was attacking. One time they were up here, holding out against a great siege. After about four months they started running out of food, so it was time to escape. And there was an old mason, whose father's father helped build the place, and he said there were tunnels that led out under the city. Only, he didn't know where they were.

"So they sent a couple of young soldiers to look for them. And they found them too! Then the maidens gathered behind a piper, who led them through the tunnels with his pipes as a signal to follow. But suddenly the pipes stopped. No one knows where, or why — but the pipes stopped, and the piper was never seen again, and neither were any of the maidens. They say you can hear the pipes and the crying women under the city streets at night when it's quiet. And they also say that's why Edinburgh's full of whores, and men who can't hold a tune!"

My amusement was increased by Jamie's serious reaction. "So we're to find a pile of skeletons, sir? I can do that!"

Simon grinned. "Good man. Now, they tell me there's a secret entrance in that back wall there. But it's hidden to the eye — the stones are piled so as to match the wall behind, so there's a gap but you can't see it. The only way in is to march straight up to the wall, and suddenly you'll find yourself through it. Take a look, Sergeant Fraser!"

Jamie barked his affirmative again and marched away, leaving me to ask Simon: "Is any of that true?"

He shrugged again. "God knows." Then, in a more serious tone, he told me: "I'm having a bad feeling, Bolla. All this waiting is starting to anger me, and you can see what it's doing to the Stewart lads. So if things aren't going to go the way I hoped, we need another way out of here. Keep the bairn busy —" he nodded towards where Jamie had last been seen — "but I want you to see if there's any way of getting out the castle unseen, but towards the city, not onto the cliff. If not, I want you to see if the portcullis can be blocked or jammed. But don't let anyone see what you're doing. Not even Frasers. I'm not sure who we can trust in this place…"

I nodded my agreement as Jamie returned, looking somewhat shaken and sporting a bleeding nose. "No secret entrance?" Simon asked, touching his shoulder. "*Ochone*, keep looking, just!"

We spent several days exploring the lower reaches of the fortress, often finding ourselves at the mercy of treacherous wreckage; and while the task itself was not onerous, its execution alongside that young man of seeming boundless enthusiasm was altogether more taxing. He spoke of expecting wolves round every corner; of the best way to distract a bear so one could jump on his back and ride him as a horse; of an easy manner in which to tame wildcats – and in each story I heard the voice of Simon behind him, which was the reason, I assumed, that he could not hide his pride at telling such tales. He also went on at some length about skeletons of long-dead warriors who would rise up and fight on being woken from their long sleep. I could not tell whether the story had come from my lord or he had created it himself.

Tiring of his seeming never-ending speech, I fell back upon that most stable of conversations between soldiers: that of how each came to serve. Having offered my own feeble explanation (and in doing so, being forced to recall the person I had been at that time) it was, once again, Jamie's turn to speak. I was at that moment engaged upon climbing a pile of fallen masonry that rose from the floor of an outhouse to my waist, and it was no easy task, since, due to the gloom of the building's lower level, I also had to hold up my torch. The conditions did offer me the opportunity to make much noise as I threw pieces of stone to the ground behind me, and I confess the attempt at drowning my companion's voice gave me some satisfaction. Yet I soon had cause to reconsider as he described the path which had brought him to this place alongside me. "It was about five years ago," he said.

"My wife went away one night, and that was me on my own. No other family." The brash, confident voice with which he normally spoke was replaced by the delivery of a confused, doubt-laden young man, and I said nothing as he continued, his back to me as he battled his own pile of stone. "She just went away. She was getting ready to birth our bairn as well. It hadn't been easy for her but she was a real fighter. I don't know why she went away."

Despite my previous desire to keep as much of a distance between us as possible, I felt the urge to offer some kindness. "What was her name?" I asked quietly, pausing from my labours, and, although our backs were to each other, I knew he had stopped also.

"Isobel," he said after a moment. "She was always happy, always laughing. Everyone called her Issi Sona."

His words chilled me — was that not the same girl, the once-cheerful girl, Simon had sent away when she had begged for help outside Moniack in the snow? The one he had said he could make no more fun from now she was with child? I did not know for certain, yet my mind was entirely made up upon the matter. "There was no one to fight over it," Jamie said, recommencing his overbearing act. "You can't fight nothing. So I went out looking for fights. I fought for money in Inverness, but after a while no one would stand against me. I joined a ship instead, but it was boring. In the end I signed up with Captain MacShimi – he promised me a real fight. It's been spectacular sport!" Again I heard the echo of my lord's voice in his words. "Simon's the best thing that ever happened to Fraser. Without him we'd have been a sept of Murray years ago!"

I returned to my work, reaching the top of the stones and searching the back wall for any sign of an entrance; yet now Jamie's constant chatter was drowned out by the thought of the last time I ever saw Issi Sona, abandoned to a mysterious but doubtlessly agonising fate by Simon's refusal to assist, leaving her so desperately miserable that she spurned my own offer of help – and was never seen again. The question of who, between he and Jamie, was the father of the child also arose in my mind; but I could only speculate. The young man, meanwhile, boasted of adventures I either knew better than he did, for I had been present, or knew to be untrue.

Then he spoke words I found barely able to hear without exploding with rage: "Do you know Simon used to fight with MacIain of Glencoe? He even tried to save him from the massacre —" At that I felt myself lose control of my temperament. I still possessed the red stones the great MacDonald had sent to me, and in my soul I remembered every moment I had spent with him. To hear Jamie's corruption of a tragedy I knew well, and felt still, was too much. Yet, instead of turning my anger on him, for I knew there was nothing to be gained there, I instead threw my torch at the wall with as much force as I could muster. It was not the act of the throw which stopped Jamie's chatter: it was the fact that the wall, when struck, offered the unmistakable sound of a hollow behind. It was the work of moments to find a point at which a stone could be pulled away; and others soon followed, providing a space large enough to thrust Jamie's torch through, revealing that the hollow was no simple recess, but a passage that stretched away into the rock on which the castle was built. "We've found it!" breathed Jamie.

"We must report to Captain Fraser," I said.

"We should get in there!" Jamie cried. "I'm not scared!"

"I didn't say you were," I replied. "The captain needs to know."

"In case he wants to fight," the other nodded.

"Fight who?"

"The *skeletons*!" he said, drawing the word out such that I wondered if it would ever end. It occurred to me at last that this young man was not entirely in possession of his mind.

On approaching Simon's chambers we could hear raised voices from within, and it was no hardship to detect the unusual tone of the Earl of Tullibardine sparring against my lord. I motioned for Jamie to wait, despite it being a skill beyond him, and I listened for a moment while my companion acted as a dog on a rope who has smelt blood. "It cannot be agreed to," Tullibardine was saying. "Under no circumstances, Fraser. I am sorry —"

"It's essential!" my lord cried in response. "It won't start with a full-scale invasion. It'll start with one ship, and we need to be ready."

"You cannot know that for certain."

"I do. It's going to be one ship, and it's going to be soon."

270

"There is no way we can make such arrangements. Think of the miles the messengers would have to travel!"

"We don't need to send messengers," Simon replied, thumping one object against another for emphasis. "The act will be the message itself."

"We could never hold out for long enough," Tullibardine said doubtfully.

"How long did Gordon hold out? Four months? It's easy!"

At that point I could restrain Jamie no longer and he bolted into the room. As I followed I was sure our delay outside would never be imagined, far less suspected, for the sergeant's impatience would be well-known. Simon, stood near the fireplace, and Tullibardine, seated at the table, looked round in shock. "Sir!" Jamie barked, saluting smartly. "We've found the tunnel!"

"You haven't," Simon replied, taken aback.

"There is a tunnel," I confirmed, glancing briefly towards Tullibardine, wondering whether it was wise for him to hear such news. "Down at the back of an undercroft, leading towards the city. We do not know how far it might go, though."

"Devil choke me!" my lord laughed at last.

"What now, sir?" Jamie asked.

"Well, go and *guard* it, Sergeant Fraser," Simon said, as if talking to a child. "Guard it until we've assembled a proper search party. Send a lieutenant to me then go back and don't move until we get there. Go!"

Jamie ran off, and I observed a moment of silent communication between the two others, as if to end the conversation which had been interrupted. Tullibardine appeared to become fully aware of my presence and leapt to cover a paper on the table, but Simon offered him a shallow shake of the head, as if to put him at ease. "I take your point, your lordship, but I must press the urgency of the matter as soon as you have time."

"It's a waste of my time, Fraser, and yours," the earl sighed. "What you propose simply cannot take place. There's an end to it. You must apply your thoughts to a different solution." He stood and nodded briefly to Simon, then did so in a more friendly fashion towards me as he left.

"A shroud upon me..." my lord murmured, sitting down. "Never

271

try to work with a Murray, Bolla. Have I ever told you that? Bloody *amaideach* turncoats to a man." I could not fathom the subject of their conversation, so I said nothing. "Still — a useful wee discovery!"

"If it goes anywhere," I replied. "Jamie believes it is full of fighting skeletons." Simon stared at me, bewildered.

THE FOX WAS LATE FOR DINNER the following evening, leaving me to find my seat in the constable's chamber on my own – a position which would have vexed me just weeks earlier, but did no longer since even the three earls who sat with me had offered me nothing but congenial company. When Simon did arrive, I was surprised that he brought Jamie with him; but he explained it was time for the young sergeant to learn the ways of serving officers at table, the better to advance himself in his career. The conversation, at first pleasant, became heated over the subject of a new act of Parliament which was to cause every parish in Scotland to create a school, complete with schoolmaster, with the necessary funds raised from a new tax. While the argument raged back and forth, with several coins thrown into the Bank of Edinburgh Castle, the only agreement amongst all came over the suggestion that, with hearth tax, window tax and whatever more besides, King William appeared overly interested in the contents of his subjects' purses.

"We don't need more schools," the Earl Marischal said strongly. "There are plenty for those who have need of schooling."

"You miss the point!" barked William Bruce. "In your Catholic Highlands you may have the instruments to teach what must be taught. Elsewhere it is not so."

"Which, I think, is part of the point," the Earl of Leven said. "The old religion still does quite well – the new one, less so. If Protestantism is to become the only religion in the land it must earn that place."

"Which version?" Simon asked. "Presbyterian or Episcopalian?" That gained him general censure, on the basis that he had simply asked for the purposes of mischief; the which he admitted and happily threw several coins into the box. "But, my lords," he continued, "If I may quote from the paper itself: 'the erecting of English schools for rooting out of the Irish language, and other pious uses.' Is eduction to be a political tool?"

"Better, I think," said Tullibardine, "that children are taught to read and write than simply wrong from right. Otherwise how will this new Scotland fare in the future?"

"There's no need to make a fight of it," Lord Drummond said. "These things can be better managed."

"Not with Johnston as Secretary of State," Marischal told him. "That one does not have what it takes to strike a balance in Scotland. And it's important."

"Surely a temporary appointment," Bruce agreed.

"Stair was a good operator," Leven said. "But they had to blame someone for Glencoe, because they could not blame the king. Therefore we lose a good Secretary of State, and the real guilty ones go free."

"It's normal for there to be two secretaries," Simon said. "There has to be two again. And Johnston needs to be neither of them."

The room found itself in general agreement — but at that moment the chamber door was thrown open and one of Leven's men rushed in, near forcing Jamie Fraser to the ground as he pushed past in urgency. "Sir!" the arrival cried, saluting roughly to the constable. "The Stewarts have escaped!"

It took a little time for his words to make an impression; and, as if to emphasise his point, two shots of gunfire rang out from somewhere distant. "Escaped!" Leven shouted. "How?"

"I don't know, sir," said the other.

"You've called out the guard, Captain Mallon?"

"Yes sir — but we've found nothing so far."

"Escaped?" Simon said slowly. "Well, they can't have got far. They'd been in that prison so long they were nothing more than... skeletons."

"*Skeletons!*" Jamie cried. "Sir — the tunnels!"

"Tunnels?" Leven demanded.

"You know, into the rock," Simon said. "We haven't explored them yet. But they'd be easier to get to than out of the castle..."

"Then let's move!" cried the earl. All except the three prisoners, who appeared to understand their position, made for the door. With Leven summoning such dragoons as he saw to follow us, we went down to the undercroft; where, in the light of many torches, we beheld that not only was the gap much wider than when I had last seen it, but also that there lay a discharged pistol on the ground beyond.

"Get in there!" Leven shouted at his men.

"Wait!" Simon said. "We don't know where they go. There's a few different tunnels and they go in different directions."

"Split into fours," the earl told his men, and there were enough of them to create three hunting parties. At his bidding they sped into the darkness, Captain Mallon leading, and Simon told Jamie and I to follow him, while Tullibardine and Leven waited behind, shouting for more dragoons to attend.

Silence fell upon us as quickly as full darkness, seeming to push with palpable force against the torchlight. At first we could hear the sounds of the other soldiers, echoing strangely from rough-hewn walls; but it did not last, and soon even the noises we made ourselves were being consumed by the chasm, which had started wide and tall, but had tightened such that we could not move side-by-side and were forced to bend slightly. "Where do you think they go, sir?" Jamie asked. "They must go somewhere."

"Not necessarily," Simon replied slowly. "They could have been built for storage, or just hiding maidens — or anything. They might not be actual tunnels. Silence!" He stopped us in our tracks, but if he had heard something it was not repeated. We came upon several larger chambers with more than one tunnel leading away; and soon I, for one, had lost any sense of where we had come from. After a time my lord said: "*Ochone*, this is pointless. if they're down here they're dead — they just don't know it. Let's go back." We turned, so that I was now leading the party; and that was the moment we realised Jamie Fraser was nowhere to be seen. "Ah, for God's sake…" Simon sighed. "You could have put safe money on that, couldn't you? Shoosh, Bolla."

We stood stock-still in silence for several moments, hoping for a noise which might lead us to the sergeant. Yet all was still and silent, and my hearing, in desperation for something upon which to cling, magnified the sound of my own heartbeat such that I felt I should apologise for it. "Jamie Fraser!" Simon cried, shocking me out of a moment of near insensibility. His voice simply rebounded upon us after an instant; but then, a few moments later, came such a twisted, tortured rendition of his words that it chilled me. Yet there was no other response. "We'd better go back," my lord said. "Stupid wee *gorach*."

At the first larger chamber he took the lead, appearing to be confident in his direction. Soon we began to make out the sound of movements, which he told me were without doubt those of the other soldiers. Sure enough, we came upon Captain Mallon and his three companions in the next chamber.

"Found anything, Fraser?" that man asked.

"Lost something, Mallon," Simon replied. "Sergeant Jamie has disappeared."

"Doesn't surprise me," the other said. "In all my days I've never met such a waste of a uniform. Why ever did you promote him?"

My lord shrugged. "Let's go and report. The Stewarts are either well away, or they're starving to death in the dark."

We turned towards what the others appeared to believe was the exit — but just then we heard a cry altogether more unworldly than the echo of Simon's voice, approaching from the depths behind us. As we turned again I heard several pistols lifted and primed, and Mallon, nearest the tunnel from where the noise came, held up his torch in a forward direction. The ferocious noise grew and grew, filling our heads and seemingly our entire beings, as the flickering light threw shadows and shapes into our wide eyes. Then there came a screech the likes of which I had never heard, and never have again — seemingly the cry of a soul in hell, fighting for freedom from a nameless horror. And Jamie Fraser came flying out of the darkness, casting himself at full pace into Mallon.

Two soldiers fired before Simon was able to stop them, but in their fear they only struck rock. "Hold! Hold!" my lord bellowed, dropping his torch and seeking to separate Jamie and Mallon, who were tangled in a writhing heap. "Sergeant Fraser! Attention! Jamie!" At last the struggle ended, and both men rested against opposite walls of the chamber, gasping for breath. "What the hell was that all about?" Simon bellowed into his sergeant's face.

"I'll have you on a charge, you crack-brained wretch!" Mallon spat from behind.

"Sorry, sir! Sorry!" Jamie breathed, staring first at his own captain, then the other. "I... I thought you were a skeleton..."

"A *what?*" Mallon cried. "Are you mad?"

Yet Simon was already on the ground between the two, helpless with laughter. "A skeleton! What have I said you are, Jamie?"

"A stupid wee *gorach*, sir," the young man said, with shame in his face.

"You'll hang for this!" Mallon muttered angrily.

"Leave him alone," Simon told him. "I mean, he's right — you are a skeleton, partly!" Mallon, still breathing heavily, looked away; but I thought I saw a hint of amusement in his own face.

Any such emotion was shaken off when we returned to the undercroft, the last of the search parties to do so. Leven and Tullibardine remained without, and, on hearing Simon's report, set about recriminations. "So you don't know whether they're in there or not?" Leven demanded.

"No," my lord admitted. "If they are, they're either lost, or they've found a way out that we haven't found."

"Well, keep a guard on the place," sighed Tullibardine. "The main guard has been doubled, hasn't it, Leven?"

"Not quite doubled," the constable said. "We already had extra men on the half-moon battery in case the ship came in."

"What ship?"

"You were not aware? A ship of war has been seen off the coast. We think it may be French."

"It's probably just passing by," Simon suggested, drawing a strange glance from Tullibardine.

"None of this answers the question: how did the Stewarts escape?" the constable said. "They were well under lock and key, there was sufficient guard – and as you say, Fraser, they were unlikely to be in a fit state to fly fast."

"Who was last in their cell?" Tullibardine said.

"I was, sir," came the meek voice of Jamie Fraser. Simon groaned loudly.

"Well?" demanded the earl.

"I swear, sir, I left them locked up and lying on the floor, the way they've always been. They had a couple of blankets between them and

276

bread and water — there's no way they ran out." He became more distressed as the silence of his superiors became more pointed. "Even if they got the key they probably couldn't have lifted it!"

"What leads you to believe they got the key?" Leven asked, his voice calm yet threatening.

The sergeant tried to affect his usual brash expression, but his eyes showed his fear as his voice broke, lending it the tone I had heard when he spoke of his wife. "I... don't know, sir," he admitted quietly.

"He attacked me in the tunnel, sir," Mallon offered crisply; and it was clear Jamie's fate was sealed. "He could have helped the Stewarts escape then turned on me as a cover!"

"You're under arrest, Sergeant Fraser," Leven said immediately. "Pending an investigation. Mallon, take him to the cells. In fact, take him to the Stewarts' cell." He pointed at the young man. "Sit there and think seriously about what story you will tell."

MATTERS RETURNED TO NORMAL after the brief interlude of activity, although there was a slight cooling in the conversation at Leven's table for some days. Jamie remained in prison, and there seemed to be no hurry in investigating the situation surrounding the Stewarts' escape; and since there came no word of the Athollmen's progress it seemed at least possible they had perished in the dark beneath the castle. The men of the Lord Lovat's Company, as might be expected, were offered no opportunity to visit their sergeant, although Simon managed to talk to him on occasion; and reported, sadly, that he appeared to be taking on the aspect of those who had previously inhabited his room. I began to wonder whether there was the possibility of Jamie following the Stewarts' course of action – although I did not suggest it. There appeared to be no suggestion of Simon's involvement in the events, and I did not wish to make it easier for any such to be made.

The half-moon battery (built, I was told, more than a century previously following a long siege) may not have been a useful device, as my lord claimed; but it offered impressive views across the city and its surroundings, and in the pleasant weather of that summer I spent much time leaning out over its walls. I was there with Simon, as he made another failed attempt to explain to me why the construction was pointless, when Tullibardine approached and announced that a visitor was expected. "Lord Hugh will be here before day's end," said the earl, to some surprise from Simon.

"I didn't know he was on his way!"

"Well, he is, Fraser — although I hear he is not well."

"He isn't. He shouldn't be on the road."

"And yet, he has much further to travel. I am taking him to London."

"London!" Simon cried. "You'll kill him!"

"Not I," Tullibardine said. "There are important changes afoot in the government of Scotland. It would be well for Fraser to be closer to the king."

"Fraser *is* close to the king," Simon stated, with an expression upon his countenance that I could not read.

"It would do no harm to be closer still," the other said. "I have arranged for Hugh to approach the royal court. Do not tell me that is a pointless gesture!"

"No, it's not," Simon said after a pause. "But — seriously, your lordship, Hugh is a frail man. At least allow me to care for him here before you go?"

Tullibardine nodded. "I hoped you would say as much. We leave within the week, but I will hold off as long as I may. My brother-in-law may be ill but he is still the Lord Lovat, and must be treated as such."

"Of course," Simon agreed.

I barely recognised Hugh when I set eyes upon him: in fact, I confess I believed at first that I was looking upon one of the living skeletons Jamie had discussed with such animation. His complexion was even more grey than the old castle walls, and a sheen of damp illness covered him. He was almost entirely bereft of hair on his head and his watery eyes had sunk into shadows under his brow. He uttered a weak greeting from thin lips as two ghillies all but carried him from his carriage and held him between them in the courtyard. "My lord!" Simon grinned with great energy. "It's good to see you!"

"Simon," Hugh nodded in response. "You know why I'm here?"

"Ian Cam has told me everything. Are you sure you're fit for the journey?"

"I must be," he replied with as much resolve as he could muster. "If this is the last thing I do as Lovat, I must do it."

"Don't say that," my lord encouraged. "We just need to get you indoors. It's not warm on this rock, even in summer." As we approached Simon's quarters one of the ghillies, who I vaguely recognised, thrust a paper into my hand, and gestured with his eyes that I was not to acknowledge it; yet I was convinced my lord had caught sight of the transaction, no matter how brief it had been. Within, we discussed the state of the nation with Lord Hugh, he insisting that I sat alongside him and Simon. It was clear, however, that even the trip from Queen Margaret's Ferry – not even a morning's travel in normal circumstances – had exhausted him. We laid him on Simon's couch and left the ghillies on watch while we returned to the battery.

"He cannot go to London," I said.

"He must," shrugged Simon. "I'll go with him – it's the best I can do."

"It will be the end of him!" I cried. "You know that!"

"We need to make sure that doesn't happen," my lord replied quietly. "I'll send for Paddy Abercromby. Although I don't know if he's doctoring any more – he keeps going on about a book he wants to write about military history. Still, he might want to look round the castle. That'll bring him here anyway."

I did not have the opportunity of privacy until after dinner that evening; with Lord Hugh as guest the conversation at table had been of a gentle nature, and did not move towards some of the matters we often discussed – almost as if all present were aware that his state of mind was not given towards talk that could be termed by some as treasonable. Afterwards Simon made much of attending upon our chief alone, and so I took advantage of an empty guardhouse on the castle's north wall to open my letter.

It was from John; and it was written in cheerful, familiar terms, advising me of the wellbeing of Kirsty and Mairi, and indeed of himself, his plans to travel to Glasgow to continue his incomplete university studies, and the latest news from some of those we had assisted through the difficult years. In short it was a note between friends, and I realised John had composed it under the assumption that Simon might read it. My first reaction was disappointment that I could not be offered a more honest estimation of events at home; then, recalling that I was sure Simon did indeed know of its existence, I came to understand why his brother had chosen such a course of action. Returning to his chamber, and observing that Hugh slept fitfully near a fire which was all to great for the season, I presented Simon with the letter. "Will you read it for me?" I asked — and I suspect it was the greatest lie (although more by deed than word) that I had ever attempted to execute upon him.

"*Ochone*, we never finished those lessons, did we?" he said, seemingly apologetic. "Of course I will! Pour yourself a cup. Pour me one too — — news from home is always worth a drink, isn't it?" He spoke the words I had already understood, with no omission, for in truth there was nothing to be hidden. Yet when he read a line near the end I perceived it might have more meaning than I had understood at first. "Tell Simon there can be no more bottles from France," John said via the paper, "and he must consider a different course of action. I will tell him the same myself. I assure you of my faith and duty at all times. Your friend, John Fraser." Simon folded it and returned it to me. "I'm glad all's well," he grinned. "You know, Bolla, I could be jealous of you. Kirsty is a grand girl, just grand; and wee Mairi, well, you've got a real heart-breaker on your hands there. You've done well. You're probably better looked after than you realise — although not so well as you'll ever deserve."

I knew he had mustered as much honesty as he could in his words; and yet I was given to pause over John's mention of bottles, for I felt sure he referred to the substances contained within the collection he had lost. The subject had vexed me in the past and I had never managed to find a reason. "Does his message to you mean anything?" I asked.

"Maybe," he replied lightly. "I don't know if he mentioned this – he probably did – but John had unfinished business in France. Him coming home was the nearest thing to a tearing the plan ever got. But I've worked around it. It's still a brilliant plan!" His tone changed as he considered Hugh's sleeping figure. "But we have need of powders — medicine. I sent a note to Abercromby today. I know he's in Edinburgh so I hope to see him tomorrow."

I did not set eyes upon the surgeon at any time; and I would have

280

liked to do so, recalling how Simon had recruited him to save my life after the Bass Rock adventure. Yet the following day, my lord presented me with a jar of powder supplied by that man, and insisted that I learn the usage of it, so that all who attended Hugh knew best how to do so. In the evening, alone with the Lovat, I dissolved a measured amount into a cup and presented it to him. He drank slowly and with difficulty (as he did everything, it seemed) but as I made to leave him to rest he bade me sit on the couch. "You know Simon better than anyone, I think, Bolla," he said, his voice weak, his words broken with struggled breathing. "Do you think — will he stand for Fraser at the end?"

"Of course," I said without a pause.

"You know what I ask," he persisted. "The clan must survive. In the old days there would have been battles of swords, but now the battles seem to be fought on paper. I know he can fight those — but on whose side?"

"I believe Fraser is important to him," I replied after a pause. "No matter what else is important to him too."

Hugh nodded, a motion that turned into a cough. "I hope you're right, Bolla. And I pray that you bring all the influence you have to bear on him to remember what's important."

"Influence?"

"I think you have more than you know. More than me. When I am gone —"

"Do not speak of such things, my lord," I said as gently as I could, but he waved his hand in a gesture of dismissal.

"This is not a time for me," he said. "I have not been what the clan needed. But I have raised up Tom, and I have given Amelia all the strength I can. And yet, I know it will all rest upon Simon in the end. And I do not know how to make sure it's for the best. So promise me, Bolla: you will do all you can."

"I will," I said, and I could say nothing other; although I was filled with doubt that I could deliver much through any such promise. Then, inspired by the moment, I asked him: "The powders... do they all come from Simon?"

"Most of them," he nodded, closing his eyes.

"And do they make you feel better?"

"Most of them," he repeated, as he drifted into sleep.

When it came to the matter of the Fox travelling with Hugh and Tullibardine, the Earl of Leven forbade it. Despite an argument over the dinner table which became somewhat heated (causing a flurry of coins to be thrown into the Bank of Edinburgh Castle), the constable was able to successfully argue that the recent escape of the Stewarts, combined with the suspected complicity of Sergeant Jamie, and the sighting of an enemy ship off the coast, added up to an assertion that the captain of the garrison could not absent himself for any reason. Simon could see he was outplayed in the discussion and was forced to admit defeat. Later, deep in his cups, he muttered long into the night about Murray betrayal, and demanded to know how it came about that Hugh's visit had been kept from him – saying that things might have been different had he known. So it was that the Lord Lovat was entrusted to the care of the Earl of Tullibardine; and the Murray vowed to take such trust seriously; and the effective Master of Lovat in waiting was made to act as if he accepted that vow, while it was extremely doubtful that he did. As the party moved off the castle hill towards the city, and towards London, Simon stared after the horses and carriage from the half-moon battery, and remained there long after there was nothing more to be seen.

The following weeks were uneventful. While Jamie Fraser rotted in prison for far longer than the Stewart brothers (and I could only hope, while I doubted, that he was as well-provisioned as had they been), there came no more alerts regarding warships, and no more explosive exchanges across the dinner table. That changed only when a letter received by the Earl of Leven caused a great amount of excitement among us all: it declared that Tullibardine was to be raised to the position of Secretary of State, replacing the unfortunate Johnston; and that he was also elevated to High Commissioner to the Parliament, Master of the Privy Council, Commander of the Army and Viscount Glenalmond. In a twist I did not fully follow he was also named Lord Murray and the Earl of Tullibardine – titles which I understood he already held; but it seemed that he only held them within the Scots nobility, and the addition of English titles was significant. "He's the most powerful man in Scotland," Leven muttered, shaking his head as he dropped the letter.

"The most powerful man in *lowland* Scotland," Marischal said, a finger raised, drawing glances from all.

The news sent Simon into his cups once more, but on this occasion his seeming rage was tempered with bouts of extreme amusement. He was far too drunk for me to understand the explanations he offered, and I could not reach a conclusion upon which of the emotions ruled the moment – and which would rule his later actions. Later that same night I was shaken awake to find him, the stench of sour wine upon him, demanding of me whether I could help him with a rhyme. "I'm writing a song!" he slurred. "I need a rhyme for 'Tullibardine'…"

I took a great deal of time to marshall my thoughts, while he swayed above me. Finally I suggested: "'Garden'?"

"'Garden'?" he repeated, staggering backwards. "'Garden'? I've got 'garden' – everyone's got 'garden.' Got anything else?" I admitted I had not. "Maybe a bad idea, then," he muttered, staggering away. "Maybe I should do a pamphlet instead." I returned to sleep.

WHEN THE ELEVATED TULLIBARDINE RETURNED from London he did not make for the castle, preferring instead to settle himself in the Palace of Holyroodhouse at the opposite end of the city, and in doing so causing Sir William Bruce to drop many coins in the box, as the newly-completed work on that royal establishment had been in the main led by himself. The summer, such as it had been, was passed, and the days bore all the signs of bringing more harsh weather; another crop failed, although to a lesser extent than in previous years, and the danger of war receded once more as thoughts turned to the more urgent matter of remaining alive through the coming winter.

Soon afterwards a note brought from the city below send Simon into a flurry of activity. I was with him in his chambers when a soldier of the garrison brought it to him, and a previously light-hearted conversation was shattered with the words: "A shroud upon me!" He did not explain further, but bade me collect my cloak against the cold and rushed me out of the castle, whereupon we moved quickly to the Fraser lodgings near the city's south wall. We did not often visit that place, but we had appeared there often enough for Mrs McGourty, that stoic housekeeper, to be unsurprised at our arrival; yet on this occasion she seemed to have expected it. "He got here an hour ago," she told Simon, her face set in sternness as two Fraser ghillies stood behind her, matching her expression. "I set him a fire and put him to bed."

The figure of Lord Hugh lying prone upon a couch upstairs was barely recognisable. He had not reached his thirtieth summer, and yet here was a man one would not be surprised to learn was in his eightieth, completely bereft of hair upon his head and with drawn, pale skin; and in truth, were it not for the near-constant mutterings which tumbled from his twisted mouth, I might have thought him dead. When he opened is eyes upon our arrival and sat bolt-upright, my thoughts turned to Sergeant Jamie's talk of living skeletons. "Treachery!" Hugh rasped, his swollen tongue too large for his mouth. "Murray betrayed us! It was no oyster, Thomas – it was no oyster!"

"Calm, my lord, calm!" Simon said, stepping quietly but briskly to the couch, saying nothing of the lord's misidentification of him as his father. "You're safe enough here in your own home."

"They said there were oysters, but there were none," the other insisted, grabbing Simon's arm with what strength he had, his wide eyes suggesting a terror beyond the subject of his speech.

"I'll get you oysters. As many as you need."

"It's too late! They've gone, Thomas – they've all gone and they won't return."

If Simon did not know how to deal with this clear delirium, he did not display it. "I'll send to Inverness right now," he said in a soothing voice. "We'll have oysters in Castle Dounie within in the hour, if you'll just sleep."

"It can't be done!"

"It *will* be done. Lord Lovat orders and Fraser obeys."

Hugh's appearance did not change, but his tone did; and he became aware of who was truly beside him. "Murray has betrayed us, Simon, just as you warned me," he said with anger rather than fear. "He presented me to the king, right enough – but then he got me to take my leave. I didn't know!"

"Didn't know what, my lord?"

"If you take your leave you can't return unless invited. He tricked me into removing myself from court, without getting what I went for! I stayed with Lord Tarbat – Murray would have nothing to do with me. He left London without me even though he had my papers. It took me four days to get new papers and catch him up. And when I did he said nothing! Nothing!"

"May he fall and not rise," Simon said with a ferocious glower.

"He shamed Fraser!" Hugh insisted. "You have to do something, Thomas, or the oysters will never return!"

"I will act, Hugh – leave it to me," Simon told him in a voice which he tried to make sounded like his father's. "Simon and John will —"

"Simon! Yes, Simon! It is all with him now, Thomas. You must forget what we said before. It is all with Simon!"

"Sleep, now, Hugh," my lord said, pushing him down upon the couch. "When you wake all will be in hand."

"Amelia…"

"She's on her way. She'll be here when you wake."

At last the frail figure settled into a restless slumber. Simon loaded the fire, even though the room was all too warm already, then went to the window and stood with his back to me. "This will be the death of him," he whispered.

"We have to send for Lady Amelia," I urged.

"Of course we do," my lord said, moving to the table, where a pen and paper lay ready.

"And Abercromby?"

"Of course, Bolla," he told me, scribbling off two notes and sealing them. "Will you take these to the castle and despatch one of our men to Amelia? I'm not going to trust anyone else while Ian Cam's crowing round like a peacock."

"I'll go to Abercromby first," I said.

"This one's for him – he's at the Cowgate. Ask for MacIntosh, not Abercromby, in case he's not there. Tell Mrs McGourty to bring up some water, will you?"

As I left upon my errands I saw Simon draw a small bottle of powder from his pocket. After passing his message to the housekeeper I moved with haste towards the Cowgate, glad that both my errands were more or less in the same direction. Coming into that part of the city I asked and was directed to the rooms of one called MacIntosh; but I was surprised to discover it appeared to be a printer's establishment and not, as I had expected, that of a physician or barber-surgeon. Despite my hurry I paused to look at the note, and saw that Simon had indeed addressed it to MacIntosh, and not Abercromby. I entered the premises, and, on asking for the name my lord had told me, I was directed to a gentleman who showed recognition when I named he from whom I had come. "Is Abercromby, the physician, here?" I asked cautiously.

"Not now," was the reply. "But I expect him soon." Satisfied, I left the first note with him; then made my way to the castle and selected one of the Fraser men for the task of travelling home with as much speed as he could muster. Afterwards I returned to the lodgings – where I was surprised to see Simon helping Hugh make ready for the road, with the ghillies assisting. "Help me, will you?" my lord asked, telling the others: "Get the fastest horses you can find and set them on the carriage." As the two sped off on that task, he told me: "Hugh insists on going home. His mind's made up."

At that the ill man made to speak, but instead collapsed into a painful, rattling cough which would have sent him to the floor had not Simon held him. Finally he managed to whisper: "No time to lose…" and despite my misgivings I decided that following his wishes was the best course of action.

If the slow journey was agonising for Hugh, it was the same for those of us who witnessed his suffering. There was little talk as we progressed as quickly as we dared, aware that the sands of his life were running shorter with every mile. On occasion he appeared to find some of his old character, such as it had ever been; but those episodes did not last long, and led inevitably to bouts of delirium, panic and then fitful unconsciousness. It took four days to reach Perth, and on arriving at that city, it was apparent, without any discussion, that he would not travel much further. I fear Hugh spent near half of his remaining vital force when he exploded with rage at Simon's suggestion we should find lodging with Murray, upon whose land we stood. He displayed more spirit than ever I had seen in him as he insisted there would be no resting among traitors, and instead bade us find a simple inn where he could lie. We did so; and I confess to feeling envy when one of the ghillies was sent onward to intercept Lady Amelia, for that man was free of the burden and the scent of oncoming death.

Hugh did not speak again. Two days later, Simon, the ghillie and I were seated in silence in a small chamber, where Hugh's tortured frame finally stopped shivering on his couch, and he issued his last troubled breath with his face to the wall. My lord quietly stood and drew the bedcloth over his head, while the ghillie uttered an ancient prayer, with which we both joined in. So ended the life of one who, I was bound to agree, had been born into the wrong position in the wrong time. *"Forsan et haec olim meminisse iuvabit,"* Simon whispered, looking upon he who must have been the saddest of all Lords Lovat.

Lady Amelia arrived later that day, by which time we had done what we could to present her husband's remains. On her arrival I left the room without a word of greeting, to leave her with Simon in whatever reverie she found herself. After a few moments, I heard murmured exchanges between them. Their tone seemed almost conversational; but then, it had been clear since the spring that Hugh was not long for the world, and perhaps more than anything his release was a relief to his widow. I was surprised, then, to make out Simon snarling the phrase: "Damned Murrays – don't give a care about anyone but themselves." For, of course, Amelia herself was a Murray, the sister of Tullibardine. After that he left the room, and, passing me in the hallway, looked at me and repeated: "Damned Murrays!"

CHAPTER EIGHT
THE CHURL OF THE CHARGE

SIMON'S CURSE HAD BECOME a refrain. "Damned Murrays!" he spat regularly as we carried Hugh home on his final journey – despite the glances Amelia drew when he did so. "Damned Murrays!" he seethed under his breath during the funeral service led by Reverend James Fraser at the mausoleum, near the site of the dismantled Castle Lovat. "Damned Murrays!" he shouted from the ramparts of Castle Dounie, in his cups, after Lord Tom was hailed tenth Lord Lovat – anticipating official consent. "Damned Murrays!" he slurred drunkenly as he settled to sleep in Moniack, having offered himself a toast under his own new title, Master of Lovat, also to be confirmed; although, as ever, he said he preferred "The Young MacShimi." Kirsty was unsure whether he truly meant much of his apparent anger. During the proceedings she continually nudged me to point out what she said were signals between Simon and Amelia. Yet I could see nothing, and suspected that anything detected by my love was an extension of the signals displayed during the journey home. She agreed – although she did not agree with my estimation of their meaning.

"Damned Murrays!" he cried again on our return to Edinburgh, discovering that he had been put on a charge of dereliction of duty for his attention to Hugh. "Damned Murrays!" he shouted from the half-moon battery after a heated exchange with the Earl of Leven, which, although resulting in dismissal of the charge, all but destroyed the good relationship between them. "Damned Murrays!" he hissed through his teeth as we waited outside Tullibardine's office in the Palace of

Holyroodhouse; and: "Damned Murray devil!" he mouthed as we were bidden to enter by a servant.

"Fraser," said the most powerful man in Scotland – lowland at least – seeming to make his accent more difficult than usual. He ignored me.

"Your lordship, your lordship," grinned Simon, standing to attention, his attitude completely the opposite of that which it had so recently been. "Congratulations on your great improvement! Lord and earl twice!"

The other frowned. "I am glad to hear you resolved issues with Leven," he said.

"A simple misunderstanding, your lordship, your lordship. The good Earl of Leven understands the importance of going to the aid of one's family, since he's a good Scotsman – and sounds like one too."

Tullibardine frowned again. "Take care, Captain Fraser," he warned. "Much has changed in recent days. You would do well to listen to the advice of a friend." My lord looked round the room expectantly, as if seeking the friend to which the earl referred. "Sit down – and for the love of God let us speak plainly and without performance."

"Of course, your lordship…" Simon smiled, acting as if he were about to repeat the words, but not doing so.

"We have business to discuss to our mutual advantage," said the earl after a pause. "My new position allows me to make certain situations… easier for my allies." He looked for a reaction, but finding nothing more than an expectant expression, continued. "As you know, I am now commander of the king's army, and it is usual for one in my position to resign the regiment I command."

"Indeed, your lordship," Simon replied flatly.

"I would like to resign it in your favour."

I believe those words came as a genuine shock to my lord. "My favour?" he asked after several moments.

"Yours. In return for a consideration."

"You want to sell me your regiment?"

"Not so. I would resign in your favour… if you will sign to me the lands of Fraser."

Again, Simon could not hide his shock. "Be off!" he said.

"Fraser!"

"It's not even mine to give!"

"It will be. Your father is, what, sixty years old and more? And not of good health. You will be MacShimi in due course. And when you are, we can simply activate an agreement already in place. I have had papers drawn up."

My lord still appeared to be in shock. "You want me to give you our country," he said slowly, as if discovering the meaning of each word for the first time. "You want me to hand over the country of the Fraser clan – the very moment it's my turn to look after it?" He shook his head slowly at first, and then with more vigour. "I don't believe you think I would do that."

"Come now," Tullibardine said, a half-smile sitting not well on his face. "Think about it. The land has done you no good in recent years. The harvest has failed again, and will probably do so next year. I can help. There will be enough food for Fraser through Murray. And you – you will command a regiment. To do with as you wish. As you wish, Fraser. And it pays four thousand a year. And you will keep the title of MacShimi."

"I would be no MacShimi if I agreed to a deal like that," Simon said strongly, waking from his surprise. "Sell the clan for four thousand a year? You have me wrong, sir. Sadly, sadly seriously wrong." They stared at each other. In truth I could not tell whether my lord was bluffing – whether the offer appealed to him, but he could not be seen to agree readily; or even that he hoped, by objecting, to gain an even better offer. I could not image what four thousand pounds might look like, much less what one could do with such a figure; and Tullibardine was correct when he said the land had failed us. Yet the land was part of Fraser — could a clan remain a clan without claim on the ground beneath it? "But I'll think about it," Simon said at last.

That appeared to be all Tullibardine had hoped for. "Do that," he said, "But do not take too long. Things are changing quickly. It may be that the offer will be withdrawn in the near future."

"One thing, your lordship — surely, in law nowadays, the land goes with the title of Lord Lovat, as opposed to MacShimi, the chief of Clan Fraser?"

The earl held an even expression. "The details we can discuss once you have seen the sense of my offer."

"I'll think fast about it," my lord nodded, standing up and saluting. As we left the room he said in a voice loud enough to be heard within: "Damned devil Murrays!"

From that day the rate of his letter-writing increased until it seemed to eclipse that of the period following our Bass Rock adventure; yet he no longer had me, or anyone else of which I knew, assisting him with the task. All his correspondence appeared to be produced by his own hand and with his own seal. As might have been predicted, he trusted few within the castle to handle the documents, and instead sent me back and forth between the fortress and the Fraser lodgings, where the redoubtable Mrs McGourty took them from me in person. I could see only that many of them were addressed to his father; then after the passage of several weeks, more and more were directed to Breadalbane and his cousin Argyll, the Campbell chief – who, Simon reminded me, had been raised to Lord of the Treasury at the same time Tullibardine's power was confirmed. "King Billy's not entirely stupid," my lord grinned. "He's making sure those two block each other. And if one of them won't dance to your tune…" At first the only replies I carried back to the castle came from Fraser, yet soon the seals of the heads of Clan Campbell became prominent among my packets.

Tullibardine was correct on the pace of change – indeed, it was clear that he was instrumental in pushing such change forward. Work on reinforcing the castle became markedly more concentrated, and the garrison began slowly but relentlessly to be reinforced. Leven, given orders and granted funds to effect such moves, moved quickly to bring new guards onto the battlements; and as he did, the number of Frasers sent elsewhere, in the main back to Inverness, increased. Almost daily, Simon was ordered to send two, three or four men homeward. Yet one group of our own men caught my attention, for, while much of the building work was being carried out on the outer walls, they appeared to be concentrating on the row of ruined outhouses near the portcullis. I beheld them beginning their work as the shadows of night drew in, and returning to their quarters soon after dawn.

Intrigued, I waited one evening for their approach, and, recognising one I had met in the past, intercepted with a polite greeting. "'S fhada

292

bho nach fhaca mi thu, Bolla Fraser," said he.

"*Ciamar a tha thu,* Johnny?" I asked. "I cannot help but wonder what you get up to of a night."

He laughed. "Just following orders," he told me, then, turning to his companions, said, "This is the boll o'meat Fraser." They looked at me with a different expression, but I had seen such before.

"I am sure Simon would be interested," I said with a strong tone. "He may need to know in the near future."

"The Fox can do his own asking, then," Johnny said, to which they all laughed, and continued upon their way.

Those words led me directly to my lord's chambers, where, writing finished for the day, he was embarked upon a journey through flasks of wine. He laughed as Johnny had when I told him of the curious excursions. "That's soldiering, Bolla," he told me. "Probably a complete waste of time and effort, as usual. But damn it – it's Ian Cam's effort! Still, since you're so keen-eyed... remember I asked you to look at the portcullis?" I replied that I did, and that I had. "What did you think?" he said.

"It seems to be a simple mechanism, if large," I told him. "A thick rope on a pinion, assisted by counterweights. It will drop quickly and can only be raised slowly, and it is held in place with two heavy brakes."

"Is there any way to prevent it from closing?"

"I think not," I said, wondering why it could matter. "Perhaps by forcing the brakes to lock."

"And do you think it could be done without anyone noticing?"

"I cannot see how. In any case, cutting the rope would cancel out the effect – the gate would close and it would be difficult to open."

"Go and have another look tomorrow," he said, nodding. "Tell me if you can think of anything better." I did as I had been bidden; but I had to report that the situation was as I had previously seen, that the gate could be made to drop quickly, and rise only slowly, and that any attempt to prevent its operation would be obvious, and closure could be achieved quickly after an attempt had been discovered. My reward for my observations was a touch on the shoulder and a satisfied grin.

IT WAS SEVERAL MORE WEEKS before Tullibardine arrived to inspect the improvements; and, declaring himself pleased, invited Simon and myself to join Leven at dinner for the first time since my lord had clashed with the constable. Simon was pleased to accept, yet spent the intervening hours in fervent activity, both at his writing desk and among the corridors and ramparts of the fortress. I could not but detect the tension which appeared to adorn the very walls of the place: it was clear that some dramatic act was expected soon. It began to play out as soon as we entered the chamber we had previously found so strangely relaxing: Marischal, Bruce and Drummond were not present, only Tullibardine and Leven, with four large soldiers I did not recognise, and whose intent was clear with their severe, almost animal-like, expressions, each holding a pistols and a sword. The great table had been moved aside, yet the seat which had been at its head remained in place, taking on the air of a throne – and here Tullibardine sat himself, with Leven, in clearly a subordinate role, stood behind.

"Captain Fraser," said the Murray sternly. "You will surrender your weapons."

"I don't think I will," Simon replied immediately, at which the soldiers moved forward   only to be stopped by a wave of Tullibardine's hand.

"The time has come for reckoning. I told you it would not be long," the earl continued. "Have you considered my offer?"

"No, my lord, my lord."

He ignored the jibe. "No, you have not considered, or no, you will not accept?"

Simon shrugged, his right hand slowly moving towards his waist, as if to make for a pistol. "Either, my lord, my lord."

"Very well," the other sighed. "I feared it would not be possible to make you see sense. Fraser cannot survive without Murray – you must know that."

"*Ochone*, maybe it's all just too difficult for me to follow," Simon replied tensely, a response I would not have expected from him, leading me to wonder whether, at last, his confidence had deserted him.

Tullibardine ignored that too, and gestured towards Leven, who put a document into his hand. "Then I needs must have evidence of your loyalty to the king," he said. "You must sign the Oath of Abjuration."

"*What?*"

"You heard me, Fraser. You are ordered to sign into record your agreement that James Stuart has no claim upon the throne, and that William is the rightful king. It is expected of all officers."

"It's expected of no officer in Scotland!" Simon spat. "Not a single one has even been asked — never mind ordered!"

"That changes," Tullibardine said stiffly.

"Who else has signed — sir?"

"Fraser will set an example by being first," the earl replied.

"It's not legal," Simon said. "There's no law compelling me to do it. So I won't."

"You are required to obey the orders of your superior officers."

My lord laughed, regaining some of his usual spirit. "I won't so much as touch that paper of yours, the devil choke me. Nor will anyone of Fraser. Nor will anyone with any honour upon them."

"Honour!" Tullibardine laughed. "What do you know of honour? I have evidence, Captain Fraser, that you and your father have been at work on a scheme designed to take Edinburgh Castle in the name of James Stuart!"

Simon paused, clearly to regain control of his composure; then, slowly, quietly, and furiously, he said: "You Murray devil."

"And I have a witness," the earl continued, with another wave of his hand. The door opened and two soldiers entered, carrying between them a dishevelled form of a man, clothed in a mound of ancient, weathered blankets, who appeared to hold something small but of great value hidden in his hands. "Sergeant Fraser! Attention!" The shape took on the form of the shade of a soldier; and I realised with horror that it was indeed young Jamie – but such a twisted, ruined version of him that there seemed barely anything of the enthusiastic character I had found so irritating.

"You will speak, Sergeant Fraser," Leven said, failing to meet Simon's glare as he offered it. "Tell all you know."

"Captain Fraser..." whispered the young man, his left hand turning over the small item he still held, his sunken eyes seeming to look straight ahead yet see nothing. "Captain Fraser —"

"Jamie Fraser! Be silent!" Simon shouted. There appeared a small glimmer of recognition in the young man's face, yet it passed.

"No!" Tullibardine bellowed back. "Sergeant! You will continue!"

"Captain Fraser... con..."

"Conspired," Leven said.

"Conspired with prisoners in this castle to set them free as soon as James Stuart sailed from France. They were to take the castle in James Stuart's name and hold it for his arrival, to launch an invasion."

"What else did you witness?" Leven asked, while Simon appeared to be lost in thought, his mouth locked tight, his head turned towards his left shoulder and his eyes moving wildly.

"Captain Fraser... arranged for the escape of the Stewarts of Atholl in order to raise traitorous forces in the Highlands, believing that James Stuart was about to land in Scotland," Jamie whispered, and his shoulders dropped as he finished.

"Very good, Sergeant Fraser," Tullibardine said gently, with a slight emphasis on the word "sergeant" — and I realised the item he held in his hand was the cloth badge denoting his rank. "Captain Fraser, you are hereby charged with treason."

All eyes, except those of Jamie, fell upon my lord, who appeared still to be lost in thought. "No doubt you have more evidence, my lord, my lord," he replied quietly.

"I have papers that prove you and your father to have designed the entire plan."

"Of course you have." Simon raised his head slowly until he met the earl's gaze, and it seemed like neither of the two would break the moment. "You Murray devil."

In a flash he had drawn his pistol; he fired it at the first guard and that man was thrown back, instantly dead, against the chamber wall. Even as the others in the room made to react, he had drawn another pistol from within his jacket, a second guard lay dying. "Bolla! Bar the door!" he cried. Without thinking I did as I was bidden; and in the meantime he threw himself towards the dying man as the two remaining guards made after him. He recovered the fallen soldier's pistol and set it off in the same move, sending down a third enemy. Even as that one fell to the floor my lord threw himself sideways to evade the last guard's shot. He danced along the walls leading his enemy, sword at the ready, until the dance took him past first one, then another fallen blade. Now fully armed, he turned to face the guard, who stepped backward, waiting for an assault.

"Drop the sword, soldier," I shouted with more ferocity than I felt, having finally drawn my own pistol.

The chamber fell silent, save for the heavy breath of the combatants. "You took your time, Bolla," Simon said with a half-smile, his eyes never leaving the face of the other swordsman. "I have no quarrel with you," he said. "Drop it and live."

"You are a fool, Fraser!" Tullibardine cried, finally waking from his daze. "The garrison will be on their way!"

"The garrison are held back by sixty good men of Fraser — who need their sergeant back. You hear that, Jamie?" The young man gave no response, but stood where he had been abandoned by his guards.

"Treason! And murder!" Leven cried, fear in his voice. "Guard! Take him!" That man, faced with two sword and a pistol, finally dropped his own weapon.

"You are in no position to shout orders, my lord earl," Simon said, before turning to Tullibardine, blade raised, his voice turning colder than the deep winters. "Ian Cam Murray, this has been a long time coming. Draw your sword and fight to the death, you waste of life."

The most powerful man in lowland Scotland withered before us, his expression appearing to crumble like the walls of the ancient fortress which held us. As the moments passed I became aware of a sound I could not place from a direction I did not expect; until, finally, I cried: "There is a secret door!"

Simon looked towards me, incredulous. "What?" At that moment a panel behind Leven burst open; and I was already upon the task of unbarring the main door.

"Jamie!" I called; and, seeing the blankness on the sergeant's face, I repeated the name at my lord, who, pushing past the bewildered last guard, ran over, grabbed Jamie's shoulders and forced him towards the door.

"Fire! *Fire!*" Tullibardine bellowed; but the soldiers who entered from the hidden door could not make sense of the scene they beheld, still thick with powder-smoke, and with two earls stood between their position and their targets. Those few moments were all we needed to throw ourselves beyond the chamber and race along the corridor without; where, just yards beyond us, we beheld a dozen or more Frasers.

"Time to move!" Simon called as they stepped aside to let us pass. Shots rang out from behind us but our men returned fire. Soon we found ourselves in the twilit courtyard, where, it seemed, all our remaining men waited. "Alright, lads?" my lord shouted. "It's been a while, but let's show these lowland *gorachs* what Clan Fraser can do!" As the last of our garrison joined us from behind, we made towards the castle gate; but within moments it was clear that the path was blocked by many enemies, perhaps three times as many as we were. "Form up!" Simon ordered; and I began to understand that a plan had been laid in advance — and that I knew what it entailed. Since those who blocked our way were downhill from us, and even though the narrow passage forced us to arrange ourselves in six ranks rather than one, it was still to be a Highland charge.

"*A Mhòr-fhaiche!*" my lord called, pushing his way to the front, ensuring Jamie and I remained with him; and we all took up the ancient clan slogan, swords held high, forcing ourselves into a frenzy. The thought that I had only previously seen such an assault, rather than participated, crossed my mind; but then I recalled the power of what I had beheld, and realised that those we faced had likely not even observed that – and I realised we stood at least a chance of success.

Simon looked down the hill, to where nine or more ranks of soldiers stared up at us, not one of them sharing the ferocity and confidence we bellowed upon them. He rubbed Jamie Fraser's shoulders, shouting the clan slogan into his face, and that appeared to bring something of life into the young man, although he remained clearly bewildered. Then, with a start, I recollected an important point. "The portcullis!" I cried to my lord. "The gate!" For it was behind those we faced, and represented certain death to us. My lord turned to me, still shouting, and his almost senseless glance led me to believe that he had been waiting for me to advert him to the danger. Yet without changing the pace of his rhythmic chanting, he raised his voice; then his arm; and then we began to run.

There was nothing I could do but strive ahead of my near-crazed clansmen. The rhythm of our feet on the ground stamped along with our slogan, at first matching it, then setting against it; soon we were simply bellowing through our breath. Enraged by sheer terror, I no longer thought as a conscious man; but instead I knew at last what Fraser was: a single, solid force of life, determined to survive and determined to destroy everything that was not part of it. *A Mhòr-fhaiche!* This was more than a gathering of men exploding down a hill — this was a thousand years of pride, passion, love and rage; and there was no power on earth to hold it.

The engagement lasted mere moments. During the first there appeared in my vision the shape of doubt-ridden, scared dragoons some footsteps ahead of us. In the next, there was a cloud of blood-red mist and cries or mortal agony, pushed away from our ears by the noise of Fraser: *A Mhòr-fhaiche!* In the last, our charge continued beyond whatever had stood before us, and it was gone. Every fibre of my being, everything I had lived through, everything I was, existed in those moments and furiously refused to bow for anything that was not Fraser. *A Mhòr-fhaiche!* We ran on, still shouting, still feeling the euphoria of a fury that would last for ever. Then I remembered the portcullis.

The final barrier stood ahead of us, just moments in our future. I could make out the faces of men in the guardroom above, ready to drop the gate. Yet I did not care; for I believed with all my soul that Fraser was invincible, and the only course of action was to keep running, crying *A Mhòr-fhaiche!* Which is what we did — and passed through the gate unhindered.

I am not certain whether we were followed, or how many of our former enemies died in our charge. I recall the sound of some few shots fired at us from behind; but even though, as our anger faded, I had a passing sense of dread when I recalled the cannon on the ramparts, nothing came of such thoughts. Instead the men of Fraser spread out and faded through the streets of Edinburgh, as even the flames of the hottest fire will wither and fade, with the last echoing cry of *A Mhòr-fhaiche.* Finally Simon, Jamie and I were alone without the Fraser lodgings; and soon within, seated, gasping for breath.

"Devil choke me, Bolla!" my lord said after a time. "Bar the door!"

"The portcullis!" I gasped, after doing as he had asked. "It did not fall!"

"Johnny Fraser," nodded Simon. "He arranged it."

"It could not be done – release the brake, or even just cut the rope, and it comes down…"

He shook his head, trying to laugh even as he fought for breath. "Different rope," he said. "Johnny diverted the real rope to another pinion behind a wall. The pinion you could see wasn't attached to the gate!"

"You knew this was going to happen?" I asked as I understood.

"Suspected," Simon said. "Now Ian Cam has the king's ear and after he tried to get me to sell the country, it was just a matter of time." He turned to the young sergeant. "Your first Highland charge, Jamie Fraser — what do you think?"

At last I saw something I recognised in that man's face. "Magnificent mischief!" he gasped weakly, but with more character than I had seen since before his imprisonment. Then he fainted.

"Stupid wee *gorach*," Simon said, looking at him with pity. "After the Stewarts escaped there was no way to keep him out of trouble."

"What of our men?" I asked suddenly.

"I told them all to get out and go home."

"And us?"

"I was thinking of going out for a couple of drinks…" he began. "*Ochone*, Bolla – we've got to get going as well. But first, it's time to earn your shilling." His words came as no surprise. "There's a wee stack of papers in that drawer," he said, pointing. "Take them round to the place I sent you for Paddy Abercromby. Then get back here, and be ready to run like a devil."

All my instincts called for flight, and the idea of pausing for an errand did not sit well with me. "Perhaps Mrs McGourty —"

"For God's sake, do you think I'd get an old woman involved in this? I sent her away for a bit. Now get on, my lad. Every second counts."

Doubtfully, I retrieved the papers, unbarred the door and peered out into the street. The prospect without was eerily usual: night had drawn fully in, and with the exception of the sound of casual footsteps in the distance, all was quiet. I waited for my eyes to settle, such that I could make out the different shapes within the shadows; but nothing of danger appeared to be present. Quickly I moved into those shadows myself (dully aware that my old leg wound was beginning to ache after my recent exertion) and I remained shrouded in whatever cover I could find as I pressed on with haste towards the Cowgate, and the premises of MacIntosh. That man was labouring over his machinery when I arrived, but stopped upon recognising me and tore open the package of papers I presented (I had no time to examine them myself). "So the Fox is going through with it, is he?" said MacIntosh, leaving me no option but to agree. "Well, it's up to him," he went on. "I've told him my name isn't to appear. Did he have anything to do with the trouble at the castle just there?" I did not know what to say — there had barely been time to catch breath since our adventure, and I was astonished that it had already become a point of discussion. "They'll close the town gates for sure. If he's still inside by morning he'll be caught. You tell him that!" I nodded agreement and took the inference that I should leave, returning once again to the shadows.

Yet as I approached our lodgings I heard the unmistakeable steps of running soldiers from too close behind me; and my instincts took over as I bolted down the hill. Cries behind me told me I had made the wrong decision – but it was made. By the time I gained our door and battered for it to be opened, my pursuers were not far behind; and by the time Simon closed and barred it behind me, two shots had been fired upon us.

"You've made it so damned easy for them!" Simon berated me. "Grab a couple of pistols."

I beheld that he had made something of a fortress out of the premises. A number of rifles, complete with powder-horns and shot, stood arrayed against the windows, which had been partially covered by wooden panels, apparently the bases of chairs.

"Open up in the name of the king!" came a cry from without, as the door was rattled against its hinges.

"Be off!" Simon cried back. "Jamie, are you ready?"

"Yes, sir!" said the young sergeant, apparently completely rejuvenated in spirit from his time in the cell; although he remained a pathetic sight.

"Bolla, get that table down across the door. When they get in we just fire. They won't keep coming once a few of them are down. They'll have to back off. There's no other way in."

"There is no other way out," I replied, my sense of alarm beginning to increase.

"*Ochone*, details, just!" Simon grinned – he was enjoying the fact of our helplessness. "The more mischief, the better sport! Just pile up some guns and get ready to fire like your life depends on it. Because it does!"

I toppled the table beside me and cast over a number of pistols and rifles, along with powder and shot. The three of us settled behind it, the first of our arms ready to be set off towards the door. Without, the soldiers appeared to have fallen silent; but a crowd had gathered around them and hecklers were shouting advice, criticism or bawdy suggestions. I could make out one broad voice advocating that the house be set on fire — I could only hope it was not one of the garrison.

Moments passed. Even Simon began to appear doubtful, while Jamie said: "Sir, why don't we shoot our way out?" Rather than berate him for such a suggestion my lord seemed to consider it; at which point an authoritative knock came at the door.

"Captain Fraser!" a new, and somewhat strange, voice called. "Open up in the name of the king!"

"Which king?" my lord called back.

"Fraser – it's Tom Livingstone. Open up!"

"A shroud upon me!" Simon said quietly.

"Hurry up! You don't have much time!"

"Who is he?" I asked.

"He's the commander in chief of King Billy's forces in Scotland," my lord said. "I didn't know he was here."

"It's a lie," I said firmly.

"If it is, it's a damned stupid one." Another call for immediate action came from beyond the door. Looking first at me and then at Jamie, Simon stood up, a pistol pointed before him, and made cautiously to the door.

"Colonel Livingstone!" he called.

"Captain Fraser!" came the unusual voice. "Let me in."

"On your own?"

"Yes, on my own. But hurry!" That seemed to decide it: Simon unbarred the door, at which point I would have expected it to have been forced in against him, had there been a party waiting beyond to gain entry. Instead, my lord drew it towards him; and a short, stocky man of middle years stepped in. "Fraser," he said curtly, nodding at my lord.

"Colonel —"

"No time," he said, a hand held up in a dismissive gesture. "Look, I do not want to hear what has happened. All I know is there is hell to pay at the castle and your name is all over it."

"I don't —"

"Shut up, you young idiot!" Livingstone bellowed with the unmistakable tone of a lifelong soldier. "You have one chance, so do as I say." With that he drew out a tablet and wrote down a brief note. "Your orders are to march immediately north and detain as many of the deserters from the castle as you may. Those who agree to fall in may be spared. Those who attempt to run are to be shot or hung. Go quickly!"

He thrust the note into Simon's hands; but my lord seemed frozen into inactivity. "What in the name..." he said slowly.

Livingstone sighed. "They call you a fox? You're a damned slow one! No one has any love for Tullibardine. Me least of all, since he's no soldier and yet I must answer to him. I was in Holyroodhouse. I have not yet received orders from him, but I will. In the absence of those orders, I understand that some of your men have deserted. And as a good captain of His Majesty's Army I order you to go after them."

"What?"

"Fraser, much as it pains me to say this out loud, your letters have been... of use to me in the past. You have a role to play in whatever is to come, although God knows I would rather it was as far from me as possible. Is that simple enough for you?"

At last my lord grinned. "Yes, sir!" he replied brightly.

"Well — go!"

Simon saluted, then barked orders for Jamie and I to fall in. What Livingstone thought of that – one dishevelled sergeant wrapped in old bedclothes alongside one pensioned former sergeant with a limp – was not apparent. He moved out of the doorway ahead of us and ordered his men to let us pass; and they did, even forcing the onlookers aside so we could quick-march towards the nearest town gate, where our orders allowed us to pass through just as the instruction came to let no one in or out. We gave no thought to the city we had left behind until we were engulfed in the safety of darkness, looking back towards the lights that shone over a scene I had truly believed would be that of my death. Finally Simon said: "Mrs McGourty's going to kill me."

SAINT JOHN'S TOWN OF PERTH was within my sight, down a smooth slope away from the bitter wind which had left me so cold I barely felt it any longer. Grey smoke rose up from the grey houses and became one with the grey sky, with mountains covered in grey snow all around. It hurt my eyes to look, and it hurt my mind to keep thinking. Yet still I stood beneath the sad shelter of a broken, dead tree, unable to make the decision which could draw an uncrossable chasm between Simon the Fox and myself. Finally I made my choice — and tore open the letter.

The road which had led me here had taken me first, joyfully, to home. Once it was clear we had not been followed out of Edinburgh the journey had become one of laughter and merriment; for surely, after the finality of such an episode, my travels were over. Simon had cheerily mocked the government of England, the which, he said, had used the fact that one Robert Charnock owned a blunderbuss to prove it meant he aimed to shoot King William. He had poured scorn on the same thinking which had led to the arrest and imprisonment of some notable Scots in the previous months, including those with whom we had broken bread in the castle. He had railed against the suspension of the law of "*habeus corpus*," saying it amounted to the demise of law itself, and arguing that the Highland ways were much more scrupulous and difficult to pervert, being, as they were, consistent with common-sense. He had made mirth from the new window tax, accusing those who ran the nations of having brought the populace into such a dark time that no one would find fault with knocking out their glass to save money. His high spirits had more than recompensed me for the increasing irritation of young Jamie, who seemed to all but have forgotten his prison ordeal — in fact, on several occasions as we sought to avoid groups of government dragoons (not because we believed we were chased, but only to be certain) he advocated the ambush of the same, going so far as to challenge my lord's authority to stop him; the which, of course, Simon dealt with easily.

Eventually we had come to Moniack, and my Kirsty and Mairi. I had shared with my love the perplexities of recent events, admitting I had no way to calculate their meaning. She had simply told me to hope it was all over, and that without doubt Simon was taking risks with much greater and more dangerous powers than ever he had before. She also took pains to persuade me that Jamie in no way replaced me in my lord's estimations; a point I believed had never occurred to me.

Yet soon, again, it was time to earn my shilling. As the winter began to close upon us, Simon took upon the writing of more and more letters: to Campbells in Argyll, to MacDonells in Glengarry, to Camerons in Locheil; yet no longer was I expected to undertake the journey myself, but only to move beyond Fraser country before passing the task to arranged messengers. The only exception had come nigh upon the year's end, when he told me to take the letter I now held to an inn at Perth – – that place where Lord Hugh had breathed his last.

It was addressed to "J.M." and sealed with a mark I did not recognise, that seal now broken by my own hand. It was too late to change the course of my actions, and so I began to read, grateful for the loneliness of my location as the words cast image upon image into my thoughts, and I struggled to make some sense of what my lord had written. "Right Honourable, I am overjoyed to know that your Lordship is softer once more in thoughts of me. I am fully persuaded that all designs your Lordship had against me proceeded from base representations of me. All vindication I shall make is that I am mightily aggrieved your Lordship should have occasion to have bad thoughts of me. There are none more faithful and ready to obey your Lordship than I, which I hope to have proved in my recent obedience to your commands in the matter of the castle. I know since you cannot suffer me to stay in your Lordship's regiment, your Lordship will help me change to a good other regiment, where I will continue to be, Right Honourable, your Lordship's most faithful and obedient servant — Sim. Fraser."

At the first I was only certain of two things: that the letter was intended for the John Murray, Ian Cam, Earl of Tullibardine, and that there had been some collusion between them over recent events. I had already known I could not deliver the document once opened; but of a sudden I was overcome with awareness that, having ensured it would never be received, I had at the very least increased the chance of Simon's plans becoming undone — and since I knew not what they were, I should never have involved myself as I now had. Yet it was too late: and whatever damage I had done might never be measured. All I could hope was that it would never be known. Resolving to return home, I also resolved to move slowly, the better to gather my thoughts, and I was grateful of the excuse that I had to take a longer road in order to avoid Huntingtower, the home of Tullibardine and the scene of such tragedy during that bright summer long ago. The letter was quietly burned in the hearth of an inn on the way, where I was certain that it left the world entirely, and that I was not observed while it did so.

To my horror, the first eyes I met on my return to Moniack were those of he whom I had so recently betrayed — but I believe my shock was so great that it took my expression longer to tell than I realised. "Welcome back, Bolla!" cried Simon, his hand on my shoulder. "Shilling earned?" I could not reply save to nod slowly, but he appeared to misinterpret my manner. "Devil choke me, go upstairs and see her!" he laughed. "I know she'll be waiting for you." Without a reply he moved away, leaving me near to fainting with contradicting emotions.

Moments later I fell into Kirsty's arms and told her what I had done. As ever I had cause to be grateful of her wisdom, her support and her passion, as she held me, calmed me and advised me. "You had to know for sure," she said soothingly.

"I know nothing for sure!" I said, near to tears.

"Yes you do, *gràdh mo chrìdh*. You know the dance is too fast for the likes of us — and that it's not over."

I knew she was correct. "Should I go to John?" I asked, my head buried on her shoulder, my mind calmed by being lost in her long red hair (although I could not ignore the strands of grey, recalling my vision over Perth).

"That I don't know," she whispered. "We'll worry about it later."

Simon's brother himself called upon me that evening, returned temporarily from his studies in Glasgow — but in marked contrast to my near-fearful disposition, his was near-mad with pleasure. "Bolla, you've got to read this!" he cried, waving a paper towards me. "It's hilarious!" It was a pamphlet, the likes of which I had seen circulated in Edinburgh; showing a tall, slender caricature of a man towering above the buildings of a town. He had but one eye, and the and horns of a devil, and held in one hand a sceptre of state while in the other were a roll of papers. The title read "The Witch In Parliament" and it did not take me long to understand it was a satirical poem about Tullibardine himself. In truth it was so well-written that I shortly forgot my despair and joined in with John's laughter as I recited the lines I liked best.

Good Scotsmen pay heed, for you must understand
What manner of creature rules over the land;
He sits in his abbey and drinks of his fill
First toasting Jamie, and then toasting Will!
Warn all your children, he'll keep casting spells
For even the devil don't want him in Hell!
With one of his eyes he looks just at himself
The better to keep an account of his wealth…

— this last a reference to a rumour that the earl was blind in one eye;

He digs in the Forth in the hope of a fortune,
But boots filled with water is all that he's gotten…

— a clear allusion to the Murray clan motto, "Furth, Fortune, and Fill the Fetters;"

While his people fight famine he sits on a hill,
Writing poems and songs that make people feel ill

— making fun of the translation of "Tullibardine" as "hill of the bard;"

He only goes hunting within his own tower —

307

For outwith the walls it's the Fox that has power!

There could be no doubt over the author of the work; and I was preparing to tell John of my errand to the printer in Edinburgh – when, of a sudden, I realised that Simon himself was standing in the doorway, grinning, but watching me as I read out the poem. "You like it?" he said brightly.

"Truly brilliant!" John told him, not realising, at first, what had occurred. "When did you do it?"

My lord spread his palms widely, affecting an exaggerated movement as he entered the chamber. "*Ochone*, I don't know what you're talking about, brother – you don't think I'm capable of writing something so funny, do you?" He lifted the pamphlet from my grasp and looked it up and down. "Very good work," he nodded. "I've seen those arms, with three stars, somewhere before, haven't I?" He knew he had; they were the arms of Murray. "I wonder if there'll be any more published?" he asked, a glint in his eye, before returning the paper to me. He touched my shoulder before he moved away, saying: "Well read, Bolla."

John's expression dropped for just a moment, before he recovered. "Bolla was learning with me over the winter, when we were stuck inside," he said quickly. "He's doing really well."

"Brilliant!" Simon replied happily. "It's bound to come in useful. Don't give up on it!" As he departed John forced out more laughter and called upon me to give him the pamphlet — an attempt to act as if there had been no import to the exchange; but, I fear, one that fell short of its intent.

After that, I was barely surprised to find that I was no longer required to run errands for him, nor that we saw less of Jamie Fraser in the castle. I noted also that, on the occasions we gathered in Simon's chambers for drinks and conversation, no papers were left upon his table any more. Still doubting whether I could discuss the matter fully with John, I could not gather whether he too had been distanced from my lord's confidence; and Kirsty, attempting to learn what she could from Jamie, received a series of impertinent replies such that there could be no doubt he spoke Simon's words when he offered them.

Yet there were more pressing concerns as the year ended: another season of cold rain had caused another harvest to fail, and, although many among the clan had abandoned the traditional timings of planting and sowing, the better to reap at least some food from the land, it was clear that shortages were soon to become severe. Simon impressed upon all his determination to stand with Fraser through the months to follow — but if there had been a time, several years previously, when they all would have followed him without question, the turmoil of the recent winters left many in a mood of doubt and suspicion. Clearly understanding the situation, my lord worked hard to address it, and by the season of Christmas it could be seen that, through his efforts, grain arrived from the south, the east and even the hard-torn west. He would not say how he had struck these arrangements, and few pressed him to do so. It sufficed that, as the frost returned, not to loose its grip until near Easter the following year, Fraser was less likely to starve than many. Indeed, as his habit of dispensing farthings among those in need was replaced with the giving of small bags of oats, the name of the Young MacShimi was once again celebrated in the Highlands – not simply alone in our own country. Many boll o'meal men joined the clan that year, and Simon professed himself pleased, saying they would be of use come the next season.

There was even enough stock of food and drink to make merry at year's end, and it was a happy scene in Castle Dounie on that night, with Lord Tom celebrated among us all as Lord Lovat; and one with notably more spirit than the previous one, even if he was beginning to age with more speed than in the past. Yet there was cause for more serious conversation before the pleasantries took over, and I found myself in Lord Tom's withdrawing chamber, alongside Simon, Lady Amelia, Andrew Fraser of Tanacheil and several other lairds. "We have word," said Tom, "That Ian Cam intends to pursue Fraser through the courts, on a claim of high treason."

There came a moment of silence – swiftly broken by Simon's laughter. "He's a complete *gorach!*" cried my lord.

"He tells his sister —" here Tom bowed towards Amelia — "that he has letters of proof. Proof that you, Simon, and I, were involved in a plan to take Edinburgh Castle in the name of King Jamie, ahead of an invasion from France."

All eyes turn to the Fox, who shook his head dismissively. "There are no such letters," he began strongly. "And even if there were…"

"Well?" Tom demanded, and it seemed there was more to his query than I understood.

Simon paused, looking round the room. "There's no damned proof," he said quietly, staring at his father.

"But was there a plan?" Tanachiel said loudly, clearly echoing the thoughts of many.

Tom lowered his gaze. "There was talk, Andrew," he admitted quietly.

"Then he can prove what he wants!" Tanacheil cried. "Ian Cam is Secretary of State – anything he says is all but law before he has finished saying it!"

"It's not that bad," Simon said strongly. "There are… circumstances we can point out."

"In court?" Tanacheil said. "In Ian Cam's own court? He is as a king there! What was the plan with the castle? What does he know? What can he prove?"

"There was some discussion…" Tom began.

"On paper?" The chief nodded slowly. "Then we're ruined!" Tanacheil shouted.

"You fly too high, Simon – again!" another laird growled, as murmurs were raised from all in the chamber.

"*I* fly too high?" my lord bellowed in reply. "The whole damned thing was Ian Cam's idea!"

That brought sudden silence to the room, with only the crackling of the great fire, and the low echoes of merry-making elsewhere, invading upon the moment. "*Cac!*" Tanacheil spat at last.

"May I fall without rising, it damned well was," Simon said, taking to a chair. "The plan was that we filled the castle with King Jamie's men in prison, then the garrison was to overtake Billy's men and set the prisoners free. There were nearly two hundred of us and only forty or so for Billy. Ian Cam made that happen — who do you think ordered me to garrison the castle?"

"Tell them the whole thing, son," Tom said.

"There's not much more to tell," said Simon. "We were meant to take over the minute French ships appeared in the Forth. But Jamie decided not to invade this year — damned stupid, but that was his choice. I changed the plan so that if just one ship appeared, we could take the castle. If we had, the Highlands would have risen long before the government could act. A ship was coming. But something else changed: Ian Cam got himself elected to on high, and suddenly decided he was Billy's man – *this* year." His tone changed. "So, yes, there's written evidence of a plan, but his name's all over it too!"

"It will be gone by the time it gets to court," Tanacheil said angrily. "He fights well on paper."

"So do I, Andrew!" the Fox shouted. "So do I – for Fraser! As I was told to do!"

Another silence fell. I observed Lady Amelia looking at Simon with an expression I did not understand. Finally Tanacheil said: "We are undone at last."

"We're not," my lord replied. "Not by a long shot. Nothing is going to happen until the spring. There's plenty to be done before then. We all know why this is happening: Murray wants Fraser country. Always has, always will. Well, Murray can be off – can't he?" There came a slow yet focused murmur of assent. "We're the fighting Frasers. Let's fight the winter, then let's fight Murray. I'll tell you what, my lads: one way or another there'll be a war next year!"

That raised more sounds of approval. "A war on land, or on paper?" Tanacheil asked carefully.

"Both," Simon said, "And we can win both. There's still a plan. You can't stop it, even if you know what it is. But… winter, lads. Let's fight winter. Murray can't move during the winter."

"Paper can," Tanacheil said quietly. Meanwhile, Lord Tom stared into the fire, taking no further part in the conversation.

It seemed that Simon was satisfied with what had been said. Soon he was making merry among the men and women of the castle. Lady Amelia spent much time with Kirsty and I, yet for a great part of it she appeared distracted, looking beyond us to something which took place elsewhere. At first I speculated that she was still in grieving for the late Lord Hugh – although I knew that was dubious in the extreme. Finally I found a reason to look myself, and beheld the Fox talking and laughing with Amelia's daughter, of the same name; a lady who, in recent months, had come into her womanhood, and displayed younger versions of all the advantages her mother offered.

"Amy's looking nice," Kirsty said, as if it were no more than a passing comment. "What age is she now?"

"Fourteen," was the curt reply.

"You'll have a marriage in mind by now," she pressed.

"Oh, probably!" Lady Amelia replied, and I knew she did not feel as light as she tried to sound. "All in due time. You must see my new tapestries…"

Glad to be away from such a conversation, I wandered among the happy folk of Fraser, strangely aware of the contrasts I balanced between: famine and festival, winter and war, dancing and drama. I was surprised to find myself soon upon the tower, where, once, I had begun my love with Kirsty. Looking out over the battlement (a much different and limited prospect in such snow and fog) I was surprised to find myself touched on the shoulder by Simon. "Thought you'd need a drink," he told me, handing me a cup, taking my empty one and casting it away. "God knows I do."

"Where is Jamie?" I asked him, cautious of raising any topic.

He shrugged. "Away with a woman if he knows what's good for him." His tone changed; and I believe he detected something in my question that I was not aware existed. "He's no… He's a stupid wee *gorach*, Bolla. He's not you. You know that, don't you?"

"He's not me," I agreed, raising a laugh.

"Not by a long shot. I'd rather have one of you with me than a thousand of him. Damned living skeletons! Stupid wee *gorach*!" he repeated, then drank deeply. I understood I should say nothing; and, surely enough, he continued in a new tone. "Do you realise how rich I could be, Bolla?" he said. "I could take myself off to London tomorrow morning. Terrible trip in this weather, right enough. But I'd be there within a fortnight. Lord Tarbat would give me lodging. There's so much money to be made down there. Do you realise it takes twelve Scots pennies to equal an English penny? Twelve Scots shillings to make one English shilling? Twelve Scots pounds — *ochone*, you see it." He took another drink, and, emptying his cup, he absently took my own and drank more.

"But that's not what I mean," he went on. "I could get out of all the in-fighting in Edinburgh. I could stop writing letters. I could stay here. I could spent all my life making sure Auld Maggie's roof never caves in again. I could just keep the grain keeps coming from Campvere. I could get us a priest – a real, proper priest – and have a hundred men guard him wherever he goes. I could be the best MacShimi Fraser ever had. MacShimi-*mhor*, I could be." He stopped again.

"But it's not my choice, Bolla. I didn't write the rules. The world is changing. If you're not on the wheel that's rolling, you'll get crushed under it. They —" he gestured across the clan country — "don't see it. They never will. And they should never have to. But *I* see it, Bolla. Sometimes I think I'm the only one who does. I can't help Fraser if I'm not one of the voices in the room where the decisions are made.

"A shroud upon me, but I'd be a richer man with a twelfth of the money and twelve times the time to stay here with the clan." He looked down into my cup, which he had now also finished, then turned to me. "You're a damned lucky man, Bolla Fraser. I hope you know that." He touched me on the shoulder and moved off down the stairs. When I returned to the great hall soon afterwards, he was once again dancing and laughing with young Amy — although just for an instant he caught my eye.

THE WINTER WIND BROUGHT SNOW AND STORIES from far away. Some were welcome, such as a newly-written tale from France of a young girl in a red cloak and her escape from a cunning wolf, which John in Glasgow was pleased to translate into our own language, and which became such a favourite of young Mairi that she demanded a red cloak of her own. Simon told his own fairy-story: that of a man wanted for murder for several years, and found hiding in Edinburgh. On being beheaded at the mercat cross, my lord claimed, his body ran a hundred paces along the road, while a gnome lifted the head from its basket, followed the body and set it back upon the neck, upon which the unworldly pair vanished from sight for ever. Such stories brought great laughter from young Amy, with whom Simon spent an inordinate amount of time – indeed, he seemed to lose interest in most (but not all) other women; about which Kirsty had nothing to say, and nor, it seemed, did Lady Amelia.

It seemed the presence of the Fox did much to protect the clan from the threat of famine, and even though it was as cold as it had been over the past several seasons, there was not such a notable number of deaths. Simon gathered grain, and papers, from the south and east more often than the north and west. He reported upon the spread of rumours about the Earl of Tullibardine practising witchcraft, about the chance of war between England and France abating, and about a turn of fortune which seemed almost impossible to me: General Tom Livingstone securing his transfer as captain from Murray's Regiment to that of MacGill. The role took him away from Moniack as the weather improved, and, to my relief, took Jamie also. That left me, Kirsty and Mairi to ourselves for some weeks, and we were grateful for the time, even though I might admit to just a little impatience at being called upon to recite the story of Little Red Cape, and a tale about a sleeping princess, so often.

The prospect of a good harvest season at last set a warm disposition upon the clan, and some of us dared to hope that, perhaps, our world was to settle down; for there could be no question that we deserved a time of peace and comfort, even if it were a fraction of the length of our time of woe and sorrow. Yet that was not to be; and when Simon returned, with Jamie at his side, and another great packet of papers, it seemed as if the summer ended that very moment. "You're here, Bolla!" he cried as he appeared in the hall, where I sat with Mairi. "We found the messenger. Dead."

"*Gorach!*" shouted my daughter, all attempts to persuade her to refer to him otherwise having failed. "You always turn up when you're not wanted!"

He offered me a look as if to say her behaviour was another matter, but then grinned at Mairi. "My lady, it's a curse I must live with. Come on, Bolla — get your gun and your horse. We don't have any time at all!"

"It's killing time!" Jamie said from behind him, resplendent in a new sergeant's uniform, drawing his pistol and waving it dangerously around the chamber.

I asked no questions but instead stood up; yet such behaviour was not good enough for my daughter. "Where are you going with *Gorach*, Dada?" she demanded, staring at Simon all the while.

I paused, looking also at my lord. Finally he spoke – to Mairi. "Not far, my lady. Perhaps to Inverness, perhaps to Castle Dounie, but no further. Three days at most."

"You bring him back in three days," she said firmly.

"Of course, my lady!"

"Promise, *Gorach*."

He looked at me, then back to Mairi. "I… I'll try," he said; and I realised he was unable to lie to her. She held his stare a moment longer, grunted unappreciatively, then ran off, calling: "Mama!"

"Come on — this is damned serious," Simon told me, and I believed he meant it. "I'll get you a horse, and I'll send new messages out. Meet me outside." By the time Kirsty shouted my name from the courtyard, I was already beyond speaking distance with my lord and his sergeant. All I could do was wave back at my love and my daughter, who returned the gesture, somehow managing to impart their suspicion and doubt while they did so. "I had a feeling the message wouldn't get through," Simon told me. "Murray devils — they're out to get us this time, and no dancing about. They had the poor ghillie killed, or else he shot himself in the back." He stopped short. "It's grand to see you, Bolla!"

"Back in action!" Jamie enthused from behind. "Killing time!"

"Be silent," my lord told him. "It's a long story," he continued to me, "But you'd best hear it." It was indeed a tale of length, with twists and turns I confess I did not understand, and did not attempt to. The thrust of the matter, I gathered, was that the Earl of Tullibardine and his father, the Marquess of Atholl – and indeed all the leading men among clan Murray – had spent a great deal of effort on moving to claim all rights over Fraser country, using the power of law, letter and persuasion. That effort had finally resulted in physical action, the which we were riding to intercept – and, said Simon, prevent.

"Remember that time we were in Holyroodhouse?" he asked me. "Ian Cam wanted me to sign the country over to him. He didn't really give a damn whether I did or not. Because he knew, and I didn't, there was a clause in the marriage contract between Hugh and Amelia. It said

315

if he died without male issue, the lands and title of Lovat went down through the female issue." He gave me a moment to make my own calculations, but I could not follow his point. "Devil choke me, Bolla – wee Amy gets the country! I mean, it's not legal. Not even close. But when did that ever stop those Murrays?

"Ian Cam says he's going to publish papers that prove Father and I were behind the Edinburgh Castle plan. He's written a nice clean version of events that leave his name right out of it. As if it could have been done without him! But the threat of those papers – just the *threat* – has been enough to persuade Father to keep quiet. He'll never be confirmed Lord Lovat if that comes out.

"Meanwhile, wee Amy is to be married to Fraser of Saltoun's son. It's damned clever, isn't it?" He laughed. "It's the kind of thing I would have thought of." I remained unclear as to what he expected from me by way of reaction. He let out a dramatic sigh which sent birds flapping from the trees around us. "*Ochone!* If the new Lord Lovat is still a Fraser, even if it's lowland scum Fraser, the clan might just go along with it. And guess who's very best mates with Fraser of Saltoun?"

I began to understand. "Murray?"

"Murray," he agreed, forcing far more fury into the word than could I. "Saltoun is heading to Dounie to make the marriage deal. Amelia's in no position to hold it back, not with her dear brother pulling the strings. The devil thought I'd find out too late," he grimaced, his expression changing to one of angry determination as he stared at the road ahead. "Someone's been telling them where I've been and what I've been doing." He glanced sideways at me, but I was able to offer a look of blank innocence with complete honesty. "Not you, Bolla — never you, my lad!" he said after a moment, and I was not sure if he fully meant that. "But *someone*. Some Fraser not worthy of the name. Not even worthy of the lowland scum version of the name.

"So," he continued in a different tone, "We're going to make sure Saltoun never gets to Dounie. And we're going to make sure he understands there aren't going to be any damned wedding bells. If I'm right we'll meet them at Inverness. Don't worry, Bolla," he grinned, seeing my reaction. "Maybe all we need is a nice wee chat over a drink. That would be the best result." I heard Jamie complaining under his breath.

We arrived in Inverness after dark and made directly for Abertarff House, the Fraser lodgings in that town, a large building on two floors with a tower, which near matched Moniack in size, and appeared only slightly less of a fortress. Lord Tom was present, as were a number of clansmen who had answered the messengers Simon had sent from Stratherrick. There too was Fraser of Tanacheil, and there came the expected momentary pause before he and my lord exchanged greetings.

"You came, then, Andrew," said Simon.

"Of course, Simon — what else would I do?"

"Then… *Tapadh leat.*"

"*Se do bheatha.* But I also want to see how far into the mud your meddling may take us all."

Lord Tom interrupted the stilted talk. "We're too late, son," he said. "Saltoun and his men were seen crossing the river a few hours ago. They're likely at Dounie by now. I only just found out."

"Damn!" Simon spat.

"And… Mungo Murray is with them."

"Damn!" Simon repeated, although this time more slowly. "Well," he continued thoughtfully. "We can't get anything done tonight. Let's see how many we are tomorrow and we'll get going at first light. There's a lot to tell you, Father. We'll be needing some wine."

As the MacShimi moved closer to the light, I was shocked to see how much older he appeared to be than the last time we had met, no more than a few weeks earlier.

THE NEXT MORNING, I AWOKE in a corner of the attic, and made my way downstairs and into the yard, where in the half-light I beheld near forty men of Fraser, wrapped in their plaids, who had assembled during the night. A frost had settled upon them; yet a handful of oats from their pouches, followed by a mouthful of whisky from their flasks, had them ready for action, no matter the cold. "Are we getting a fight today?" One of them asked me with a knowing grin of broken teeth.

"Time will tell," I said cautiously and returned within, where Simon,

Lord Tom and Tanacheil were finishing their breakfast. My lord gestured for me to eat something myself while he made ready for the day.

"Saltoun won't want to hang around," the Fox said, "But he's a soft lowlander, no better than a Saxon. He'll still be in his cot, dreaming of his son owning lands he's got no right to even walk on. He needs to be... *persuaded*... to be off and never come back. Just how we do that remains to be seen. But I'll —" As he spoke a ghillie rushed in and presented him with a note. He took a moment to read it, and another moment to ask the messenger his name, tell him the name of his father and grandfather, offer him a farthing and direct him towards refreshment. Then he said: "It's changed. Mungo has managed to wake Saltoun early and they're going to try and avoid us on the road. So we've got to get moving while we know what road they're on."

"However can you know all that?" Tanacheil demanded with his usual suspicion.

"Andrew, come on," my lord replied in an impatient tone. "If I can keep an ear open to what's going on all over Scotland, I can do a better job at home, can't I? Actually —" he changed his manner to one which more matched the laird's — "How is it *you* only got my second message? The one I sent yesterday bringing you here?"

"It was the first message I received," Tanacheil shrugged. "And I came, did I not?"

"But when we found the ghillie dead, he'd already been past your place."

"I saw no messenger," the other insisted. "Except the one you sent yesterday."

Simon forbore to persist; yet he offered Tanacheil a number of glances in the following moments – an act I felt was surprisingly obvious for one known for his tact and cunning. Those moments passed, however, as he directed Lord Tom to remain in the house (and indeed, I might have said any journey might be the end of him), and bade the rest to prepare for departure. "Time to earn your shilling, Bolla," he said next. "Go round to the church with a spare horse and do whatever it takes to get the Reverend Munro out of his cot and on the road. Catch us up on the way to Dounie as soon as you can." He wrote a short note, gave it to me, then also grabbed a flask of wine from a shelf. "This will probably help," he said, touching me on the shoulder and nodding for me to leave.

The High Church lay not far from Abertarff House, such that I could hear the sound of our clansmen departing as I approached the place of worship. Looking round, I believed I could make out the shapes of dragoons moving on the ramparts of Inverness Castle, not very far beyond – although there was doubtless little they could do to prevent the chiefs of Clan Fraser behaving however they might in their own country. I found what I thought to be the minister's house, a small building just off the low hill on which the church stood, and knocked upon the door. After a few moments I believed I could hear the sound of snoring from within, leading me to knock again with greater volume. Achieving nothing, I moved to peer in the window of the front room, wherein I made out a figure in the black cassock of the reformed Church, collapsed against a table with a number of bottles around him. It took a great deal of rattling at the window before the figure began to wake; and, finally, with an equally great deal of unsteadiness, a blearing, greying man with a red nose and heavy paunch peered back at me through the glass.

"Reverend Munro!" I called.

"Later... later!" the other pleaded.

"I bring greetings from the Lord Lovat," I told him. "Your attendance is required as soon as possible."

"I have a lot to do today..." he stammered, then groaned as I held up my flask of wine. "No — please!"

"I have a horse. You must attend!" I said strongly, to which he appeared to wither and bow. Yet there was another delay before, finally, he emerged blinking into the daylight, and I gave him Simon's note.

"Lovat," he croaked as he read, looking at me as if disappointed I had not lied. "Dowager Lady Lovat. Murray of Atholl!" He groaned again. "Can we go later? It's too bright." I admit I considered tying him to his horse, the better to ensure his compliance and his ability to remain mounted; yet, once we set upon the road, he appeared a sufficiently experience rider, and I was pleased to go ahead of him rather than follow, the better to remain up-wind of him and the evidence of his night's work. "I don't understand," he protested after a mile or so. "Why does Lovat need me? What about James Fraser, the sennachie? Will he not do?"

"Perhaps he wishes to hear a different voice," I replied. "He will tell you himself."

"Different voice?" the minister grumbled. "I'll wager Reverend Fraser would be glad to be about more God-like business than whatever that one and his son is up to. Especially his son." I allowed myself a smile; but I had cause to reflect on the difference between this cleric called Munro and another I had known.

We had not made the half-way point between Inverness and Castle Dounie when one of Simon's men appeared ahead of us on the road and directed us off into a clearing among the trees to one side. There, my lord had some thirty of his followers lined up in a formation ready to attack, and he bade me remain on my horse, as had he. "The Reverend Munro," I said, presenting that man.

"Thank you for coming, Reverend," Simon said. "You'll be thirsty — I have some wine."

"Oh, not yet," the minister groaned, the unpleasant sheen of a hangover's sweat upon his skin, which appeared at once greyed and reddened. "I'll take water, though."

My lord feigned surprise, and had a clansman help Munro from his horse, before turning back to me. "They're minutes away," he whispered. "About a dozen of them. We're going to take them by surprise, then have a wee chat."

I did not have long to wonder at his meaning — a whistling signal came from ahead on the road, and Simon waved his arm in an order of preparation. Just then a group of figures appeared around a bend, about a dozen, as my lord had said, and all mounted. I observed an open area of some thirty paces round between us and them, and it was no feat of strategy to understand that was where we were to stage our "wee chat." Sure enough, at the moment the approaching men appeared to be the same distance from the opening as were we, the Fox waved his arm again, and the Fraser clansmen stepped forward onto the road. "Come on, Bolla!" he cried as he urged his horse into action; and myself, Jamie and Tanacheil followed him out of the clearing. The reaction from before us was instant: the figures made to turn their mounts when they saw us, and indeed several of them managed to set off back along the road from where they had come. Yet moments later they turned back as a dozen Frasers more appeared beyond to block their escape. The language of their movements displayed doubt and fear as they circled, unable to find an exit. It was clear they understood the danger of their situation, with enemies approaching from both sides, while, in the centre of the charged arena, Simon acted the one in control.

Of a sudden one rider broke out of the enemy group and dashed forward, a pistol in the air. He stopped some paces into the opening; and, seeing this, Simon raced ahead of us then stopped also. We understood we were to wait a little behind, and so we did; and by the time our men had fully enclosed the space at either end, all eyes were settled upon the two opposing horsemen.

"Fraser of Beaufort!" called the enemy.

"It's Fraser of Lovat now!" Simon called back. "But I still prefer 'The Young MacShimi!'"

"It's Fraser of Beaufort," the other cried. "And it's treason to prevent passage on the king's highway!"

"Which king, Mungo Murray, you turncoat devil?" my lord shouted; and then I recognised the good looks and fine clothes of that man, despite not having seen him in over five years.

"Damn you, Fraser!" Mungo shouted. "Be off — or face the consequences of being a traitor!"

"Traitor?" Simon cried in rage, drawing his pistol. "You'll answer for that, you Murray *gorach*! Get off that horse, now!"

The pair slid off their mounts and marched towards each other until they were only a few paces apart. Each set themselves into a side-on pose, legs slightly apart, right arms held forward, pistols held straight. "Yield, Fraser, or prepare to defend your honour!" Mungo called.

"Honour, is it?" Simon snarled. "Just count to three!"

In the moments that followed even the birdsong appeared to stop in the surrounding trees; and I cannot have been the only witness unable to breathe, and unable to decide which of the two to watch. "One!" Mungo called. "Two!" Yet before he completed his count there came the blast of a pistol-shot — Simon had given fire ahead of time. I saw the powder explode, and immediately drew my glance across the opening, almost as if I could see the shot fly, to the place where Mungo stood still, a cloud of powder also rising from his weapon. My glance raced back to my lord, but he also remained in his position. They had both fired early — and they had both missed.

"*Ochone*, honour is served then!" Simon called, lowering his gun and moving forward. At the centre of the opening the two exchanged a brief conversation, but no one could hear their words, and no one could read their expressions. Within moments Tanacheil and I had ridden up behind my lord, as one of Mungo's companions arrived behind him.

"My lord Fraser of Saltoun," Mungo said by way of introduction.

"My lord!" Simon grinned, bowing slightly. "You are welcome to the country of the proper Frasers — although you should have told us you were coming. We'd have been able to meet you sooner."

The other was a tall, slender character of some forty summers or more, and his motion and expression carried something of the late Lord Hugh about him. "Beaufort!" he spluttered.

"Lovat."

"This is… inappropriate!"

"Not as inappropriate as it's going to be," Simon muttered. "My lord Saltoun, my lord Murray, and friends — you are now the guests of the senior branch of Fraser. And we have much to discuss."

"We've discussed everything with a better part of your branch," Mungo said dismissively. "And had a better welcome."

"Do you want another duel?" my lord said. "Show a bit of wisdom for the first time in your pointless life. Now, my lords, as you can see, you're surrounded by the fine men of the Clan Fraser, who would like to spend a little time with you. If you'd hand over your weapons, that would be grand!" He stepped forward, hand open, to receive Saltoun's offering, giving that man a stare which displayed as much threat as it did welcome.

Just as the lord slowly and carefully drew his pistol, another shot rang out and a bullet burst the air between Simon and I, missing us both but surprising all. All attention turned to a young man who sat mounted a few paces behind Saltoun, a smoking carbine in his grasp; and we were all still watching as another shot came from behind me and threw him from his mount, instantly dead, with a hole in his forehead.

"Damn you, Jamie! Hold fire! Hold fire!" Simon shouted in fury, and I turned to see the sergeant's face appearing from a cloud of powder-smoke, his eyes displaying that curious and disconcerting blankness — even though he had just killed.

"My footman!" Saltoun cried after a few moments of shock.

"Throw your weapons down before anyone else gets killed," my lord said severely. "Saltoun — order them!" In the absence of a decision Mungo gave the order; and, very quickly, the enemy party disarmed themselves. Simon glanced back at Jamie, who was reloading his pistol, seemingly unconcerned over his own actions. "My apologies, my lord," he said to Saltoun, and I believed he was sincere. "The matter will be attended to."

"Murder!" the other said weakly, still astonished. "The lad was just seventeen years old!"

"He fired first!" Simon pointed out, yet insisted: "It will be attended to. Now, let's go somewhere we can discuss things properly." He glared again at Jamie, then turned to me. "Bolla, will you be my sergeant for now? Form a guard round our guests. Scouts front and back. We're going about eight miles." I did as I was bid, and our party set off in the direction Saltoun had come. No one spoke to Jamie, who was given the task of leading the horse on which lay the body of the footman he had killed. He showed no great emotion as he carried it out.

I WONDERED AT FIRST whether we were making for Castle Dounie, even though I knew it to be closer than the distance Simon had given me; but after a time we passed the road to that place, and continued on a way I do not think I had travelled before. We made good time for a party of about sixty men, most of whom were on foot, and before dusk we arrived at a sheer cliff-face, below which ran the waters of Beauly, and a narrow bridge which led to an island on the river. My lord identified it as Eilean Aigas, and directed us along a path where we found a moderately large house, another Fraser property, of which I had never previously heard. Setting guards on the bridge and around the house, our guests (for want of a better word) were told to settle themselves for a stay of some days, and locked within the rooms of the attic. It said much to me that the Reverend Munro was also detained above — as was Jamie.

Not long after Simon rested himself on a chair by the fire in the great chamber, he sent for Mungo Murray, who was released from his prison and brought to attend. "You nearly hit me, so you did!" my lord said with a mock tone of accusation, opening a flask of wine and pouring into three cups.

"I didn't even nearly," Mungo replied easily. "Although it's a fair while since we played that game."

"Too long, Mungo," Simon replied.

"New games, now," the other said. "What's going on, Simon?"

"I could ask you the same – about most of your family!"

Mungo shrugged. "What can I say? I take it you know Saltoun's son is to marry Amelia's daughter?" He expressed no surprise at my lord's positive response. "Hugh signed the deal to let the title descend through the girls. It was part of the marriage contract with Amelia. I don't think my father would have let it happen otherwise."

"And all because Murray has always wanted Fraser country."

"It's not about that – it's about protection. Murray needs a secure neighbour —"

"It's about control, and ownership, and power, and riches. And don't tell me anything else, you *gorach*! Anyway, how have you been?"

"Well enough," Mungo shrugged again.

Simon stood up and touched his shoulder. "I was sorry to hear about you and Margaret Campbell."

"Aye…" his friend stared into the fire.

"There's plenty more fish in the firth."

"There isn't."

"Ach, come on! She wasn't all that when —" he cut himself off, flashing a brief glance at me, and I recalled one of my earliest adventures with the Fox, in which I stole letters from a house in Aberdeen, believing them to have been written by one Lady Margaret Campbell, who had been Simon's guest for several nights afterwards. "I met her once," he went on, his pause seemingly undetected by his distracted friend. "She didn't seem worth fighting for, is all."

"She — we… were the only thing worth being here for," Mungo

said, as if to himself. "There's nothing else worth fighting for here. Not King Billy, not King Jamie. I'm going to Darien."

"I heard so. What for, in God's name?"

"Something to fight for! Don't you see it?"

"What about Murray?"

Something of Mungo's normal fire rose up within him. "You're going to be clan chief. That's not going to happen to me. And even if it does, there's so much politics, with Clan Murray."

"I could say the same, but it's not *quite* the same, for me," Simon nodded. "But I do have Fraser to fight for."

"Maybe," Mungo said quietly. "Nothing seems as clear as it used to. We're not bairns any more, Simon."

"I don't know if we ever were," my lord said. "What's our man Saltoun like?"

Mungo paused for a moment. "He's a *gorach* – no danger," he laughed, then looked his friend in the face. "I wish you well, Simon, I really do. But I can't see how you can win."

"That's my problem," said the Fox.

He woke me early in the morning, before first light; but he was already alert and enthused. "This is going to be grand, Bolla," he said with a grin. "Just watch how this all works out – spectacular sport!"

From the great window in the main room I could see there was already much activity in the yard below: shadows shuffled in the gloom; resolving, as the day quickly lightened, into Frasers carrying long blocks of wood, while Simon conducted two housekeepers in the preparation of a fine breakfast. As the noise from without began to increase with the addition of hammering, he ordered Mungo, Saltoun and Munro to be brought to join himself and Tanacheil – the latter offering his usual suspicious expression.

"How long do you intend to continue this nonsense, Beaufort?" Saltoun demanded, brushing aside Simon's attempt at a cheery welcome.

"How long do you intend to keep getting my name wrong?" my lord grinned, gesturing all to be seated. "Please feel free to eat your fill."

Yet Saltoun dashed his plate aside, drew a paper from his jacket and threw it across the table. "Read that!" he snapped. "Then let us be on our way."

Simon opened the document with a great show of looking bewildered. "I don't understand," he said after a moment of reading.

"Then let me explain!" cried Saltoun triumphantly. "That is a letter of welcome from the Lord Lovat, granting me safe passage and welcome – which you have not provided!"

"That can't be right," said Simon after a pause. "The seal is right. But I'd know my father's handwriting anywhere. Not that he uses it much, but that's not it."

The other murmured impatiently under his breath. "It's not from your father! It's from the late, but legally entitled Hugh, Lord of Lovat. There is no other such lord of the realm! And as he was your chief —"

Simon thrust his hand in the air, stopping Saltoun's speech, with a look of distaste as he shook his head. "You see? My point is made! You *amaideach* lowlander!" He stood up and moved to the window, looking down upon the activity below. "You needs must learn a couple of important facts, my lord," he continued. "First, in every sense but the sense of a courtroom in London, my father is the Lord Lovat."

"An illegal claim —"

"Second," Simon barked, "In any case, Hugh was not chief of Fraser. Father was, even in Hugh's lifetime, and Father remains. And knowing him like I do, I have to assume your letter was written without his permission. Because, my lord, you're damned well *not* welcome and you're damned well *not* promised safe passage."

"Simon..." Tanacheil said in a long slow voice, rising and moving toward the window.

"Third," the Fox continued, ignoring him, "And I advise you to think well on this matter – the chief is not at liberty to order the clan to do whatever he likes. Neither am I."

"Simon!" Tanacheil repeated more urgently, staring out at the yard below, his tone leading those who remained at the table to get up.

"And that's why, my lord Saltoun, you'll find I'm unable to prevent what's happening out there."

I finally turned my gaze towards that which had drawn everyone else – and beheld that the construction upon which the clansmen worked was a gallows. Even as Saltoun gasped and spluttered in shock, we saw one tall man upon a short ladder atop the nearly-complete platform, affixing a rope to the crossbar; and all our eyes followed the pendulous motion of the noose as it swung below.

"What — what is the meaning of this?" Saltoun demanded, his words less than enforced by his voice.

"It's perfectly obvious, my lord," Simon replied calmly.

"You mean to hang that fellow who killed my footman?" he asked, doubtfully.

The Fox laughed. "*Ochone!* Devil choke me, no!" he said. "I'm afraid that gallows —" he turned to face Saltoun, attempting to look menacing, but unable to disguise a twinkle of mirth as he projected a pointing finger dramatically — "is for *you!*"

"Simon!" Tanacheil protested again.

"What do you want me to do, Andrew? Stand in the way of Fraser? Do you want to go down and tell them to stop? I don't!"

The other fell silent, at which Saltoun tried again. "But I am no criminal! I responded to a request for assistance from a good-brother... and had my servant killed for it!"

"That's not how they see it," my lord said, shrugging. "They see an enemy attacker who brought armed conflict into their country. They think you're damned lucky that only one of you is dead. So far."

"Murray!" cried Saltoun.

"Yes, Mungo — you tell him. If you can remember enough about good Highland life."

"They regard you as an invader," the Murray told his companion. "The rule of war applies."

"But I have a letter!" he shouted desperately, returning to the table to collect it, and waving it around his head as if to fend off the threat of the rope. "You, reverend Minister – you can't allow this!"

Munro, whose expression matched Saltoun's, simply made a gesture to suggest helplessness. "Letters!" Simon murmured sadly. "Not everyone takes so much stock in paper, the way you lowlanders do. I'll have none of it, of course, and nor will the Clan Fraser; the proper, ancient Clan Fraser that traces its roots to Robert the Bruce. He had a way with the gallows, I seem to recall..."

"Fraser, I insist you do something!" Saltoun said, yet it was clear from his speech that he was near broken; as, in the yard without, two men

327

carried a dead grice onto the platform, clearly preparing to use the large carcass to test the rope.

"I do have a suggestion, my lord. As you are a peer of the realm I wonder if I can persuade them that it might make sense to show a little respect..."

"Yes! Yes!"

"...and have them hang you first of all. Better that than waiting around all day. Let's see what I can do!"

"Simon!" Tanacheil growled, grabbing my lord's arm as he made to move away. "Stop it now! You'll have the clan hunted out of Scotland for this!"

"Then tell me what I should do?" When the laird gave no answer, my lord made a show of having had a thought, and wandered to the fireplace. I caught Mungo giving him a glance as he passed, which appeared to suggest the matter had progressed far enough. There came a cheer from the yard as the hog's body was seen to hang comfortably from the gallows, the noose tight around its severely broken neck after a block beneath had been kicked away.

"My lord Saltoun," Simon said at last (although it took some moments for the prisoner's eyes to turn away from the grice), "I have a solution. Since you like your papers, what if we write a new one?"

"Go on," Tanacheil said from behind.

"I personally don't doubt your desire to help Fraser," Simon continued, moving up to Saltoun and touching his shoulder. "It's just a shame that you didn't know enough about Highland life to go about it the right way. If we can call it a misunderstanding..."

"Just that!" Saltoun agreed readily. "The Earl of Tullibardine told me —"

"I'm sure he did, but that won't help anyone," the Fox cut in. "Let's write a paper, signed by us both, saying the Lord Saltoun regrets his unintentional act of war against Clan Fraser."

"Of course! Absolutely!" said the other.

"And that, in future, the Lord Saltoun and his good folk will take no steps to involve themselves in Fraser matters." That noble's agreement was almost joyful, until Simon continued: "And specifically, there shall be no further talk of marriage between Lord Saltoun's son and Lady

Fraser's daughter."

Those words shocked him. "How did you —" he began.

"This is *my* country," Simon said quietly, locking his gaze. "It's my duty to know what goes on here. It's my duty to live here, and die here, if I must. And I will if I have to. So might you." He turned and feigned great interest in the gallows, casually observing: "The French have a saying. 'Save a thief from the gallows and he will cut your throat.'"

"*Thief*!" Saltoun spluttered, seeming to lose the last of his lordly manner.

"You came to steal one of our daughters," Simon said. "You came to steal our country. And you came to steal the clan itself." He nodded towards the Frasers below. "That's the way they'll see it. It'll be hard to prove otherwise — if anyone wants to try."

As might be expected, the lowland lord bowed to the obvious and inevitable: a paper was drafted (surpringly quickly, it might be thought by some) to the effect that William Fraser, twelfth Lord Saltoun and eleventh Laird of Philorth, would, unless invited in writing, play no role in the affairs of Fraser of Lovat. It was witnessed by the Reverend Munro – Simon, I think, deciding that Mungo Murray's signature would cause him difficulty from his family, and that Tanacheil's might be difficult to secure. Indeed, the Fox appeared to be the only one in the room to be satisfied with the morning's proceedings.

Yet those proceedings were not yet complete. He detailed Tanacheil to escort Saltoun and his company to Inverness, there to return their arms and part as friends. Then he bade me to fetch Jamie from his room above, and prepare him and Munro for the road. As I moved to follow his instructions he called me back, saying he wished to impart a personal message to the Earl of Tullibardine via his younger brother, and that I was to bear witness.

Once removed to an ante-room, Simon and Mungo finally let loose the laughter they had carefully concealed during the previous episode. "Magnificent mischief!" my lord bellowed, before theatrically silencing himself. "Spectacular sport!" he said more quietly. "*Ochone*, Bolla, you have to admire my work!"

"A damned gallows!" Mungo laughed. "I couldn't believe it. The poor *gorach* didn't know what to think!"

"I'm going to leave it up — I might need it again!"

Mungo gradually grew more serious. "I'm going to miss this *cac*," he said. "You know Ian was expecting me to stop you doing… whatever you were going to do." My lord nodded. "After this he won't have me involved again. And anyway, I'm going to Darien."

"You keep saying that," Simon said. "Come on, Mungo, there's much more to be doing here."

The other shook his head firmly. "I didn't think you'd see it."

"Six months on a stinking ship with God knows what for company? And God knows how little drink? For God knows what when you get there?"

"For a chance. A chance to start something new – something that's not torn up with centuries of in-fighting and factions."

"You don't really believe that, do you?"

"I've got to try," Mungo said, a steel in his expression which I do not think I had beheld before. "I've got to."

Both fell silent for a moment; then, still wordlessly, they locked arms. Mungo turned to me, made to speak, but simply embraced me also. Without looking back Simon made for the door, and, just as he opened it, the Murray said from behind: "If I see you again, I may have to kill you."

My lord paused midway through the doorway, forcing me to halt close behind him at a point which allowed him to maximise the comic effect of turning to me and announcing: "He keeps saying that." Then he moved away without speaking to Mungo again.

Our horses gathered without, Simon soon led Munro, Jamie and myself, accompanied by twelve Frasers, across the bridge from Eilean Aigas. Shortly afterwards he drew out a flask of wine and bade the minister share a drink with him; and that man, having had nothing of strength since the previous morning, eagerly accepted. "To Fraser of Saltoun, a man of honour and decency," my lord cried. "And may it one day do him more good than it did this day. *While e'er a cock craws in the north, there'll be a Fraser at Philorth*! And who are we to argue?" He then attempted to involve Munro in a discussion about matters of state, leading the other to indulge in an impressive feat of broken meanings and mixed arguments which, unless one knew better, completely obscured the fact that he was saying nothing.

Such conversation kept Simon amused for the little time it took us to travel to Castle Dounie; although he also found moments to talk to each of those he had chosen to accompany us, no doubt sharing anecdotes of their personal ancestry and passing out farthings. I, meanwhile, attempted on several occasions to engage Jamie in any conversation whatsoever, to no avail. I beheld in him too much of the humour he had shown before our escape from Edinburgh, and it began to concern me greatly. I had decided to speak to Simon about it when, just as we came to within a few hundred paces of Dounie, my lord stopped short and demanded our attention. "Well, lads, thanks for your help with that wee problem – if I ever need another gallows built I know who to ask!" That raised a small cheer. "But we've got more work to do to clear up the mess. Saltoun wasn't working on his own. He came direct from Ian Cam. What do we make of that?" The response was round of growled threats. "Exactly. He has bits of paper that say anyone who marries Lady Amelia's lassie has got more right to be MacShimi than the MacShimi himself!" The growls increased. "You can fight – I know that. I've seen it. But this calls for a wee bit more thinking. It's still a fight, but it's a fight of minds. And have I ever led you wrong in one of them?" The sounds were appreciative, but pensive.

"So this next trick… it's a wee bit unusual. I don't want to do it, but it has to be done. I have to ask you, though, you fine big Fraser heroes: are you with me?" The clarity of the question appeared to be exactly what the clansmen wanted, and they offered a firm agreement in response. "*Ochone*," said Simon, with, I ascertained, a little less certainty than his voice suggested. "Let's get this over with."

He paused for a breath, as if steeling himself — then issued the most alarming orders I had ever heard from him. His words froze me, and Munro also, yet his speech to the men had assured their support; and none raised any query, but instead set immediately about following his instructions, drawing and priming their pistols. I realised then he had chosen these Frasers simply because, of all those who had been with us since Inverness, these all bore such weaponry. My concern increased when I saw my lord signalling that I, too, should prepare my armament – then doubled once more when he gave one of his own two pistols to

Jamie, who started as if out of a stupor and gripped it with both hands.

It was bad enough that we were preparing to assault the castle of our own clan. It was worse that Simon had armed a near-madman to assist. And worst of all was Simon's reason for executing such an endeavour. "I don't think it would be right to use our battle cry," he said in a loud voice, but not shouting. "So let's just go!"

I found no opportunity to object as we launched into action, the men running at full pace towards Castle Dounie around the four of us who were mounted. The few people in the courtyard at the yet-early hour appeared confused at what they saw, as well they might, and of course offered no resistance – several offering instead a wave of recognition. We sped past them all and reached the foot of the stairway, our relative silence meaning no one from within had been alerted. Dismounting, Simon waved for the men to split into three groups, each to attend one door of the building, while Munro, Jamie and I followed him up the steps. At last the *fear-an-tigh* of the castle, a tall, broad man of nearly twice my lord's age, appeared within the doorway. He grinned a welcome, which froze on his face as Simon pointed his pistol into it. "No *cac*, Willie Mackintosh," said the Fox. "I need to see Amelia. Now. Take me to her."

The man of the house frowned. "I would have done it anyway," he said quietly, with a hurt tone, and turned inside. We followed as noises began to rise from all quarters of the castle — and my heart sank as I heard one, then two, then a third shot ring out. The Lady Amelia was in the withdrawing chamber behind the great hall, not yet finished with the first chores of the castle's day. "Simon!" she cried happily, then her expression changed, as had Mackintosh's. "What on earth is going on?"

My lord turned to Jamie. "Escort Willie out of the castle, and close the door," he said, to my horror.

"I will go," I suggested.

"No," Simon said. "I need you here. Jamie can do it."

"Remember the footman!" I hissed urgently; for I felt sure the young sergeant was not of a mind to care about who he shot any longer.

My lord rolled his eyes then shook his head — but while he deliberated Mackintosh gave him another hurt look. "I will go on my own," he said quietly. "But I will not go far, my lady," he added to

Amelia, who nodded doubtfully; and he moved off to join whatever drama was playing out below.

Simon spoke a message to me by moving his mouth without sound: "It's not loaded!" Then added in voice: "Do you think I'm as mad as… A shroud upon me, Bolla!" I offered no reply; I was not sure I believed him.

Amelia put on her most commanding voice. "Will you please tell me what's going on, immediately?"

The Fox seemed to relax a little, and gave her a grin. "Well, it's simple, just. I've kicked every single man, woman, bairn and dog out of the castle."

"Why? It's rightfully yours – well, Lord Tom's, anyway."

"That's less simple," he admitted. "My lady, in response to certain… actions… taken by your dear brother and his clan of Murray devils, I find myself forced to defend the clan."

"Oh?" she replied. "And what… form… may I ask, might that take?"

"That's simple again. You and I are to be married. Now."

"What?" she cried, horrified — to which my lord pointed his pistol at her.

"To put it frankly, you're absolutely no more use to me unless you agree," he told her.

Amelia grew angry. "Of course I won't agree! Are you mad? Or are you just as much of a *gorach* as I'd always heard?"

Simon stepped forward, grinned tightly, then slapped her face. "You don't have to live long after the ceremony… if that's your wish," he said in a dark tone. She stared at him in shock, holding her cheek; and into the silence, without turning away from her, he said: "Reverend Munro will do the honours." At that she slapped him back, but he ignored it. "Reverend, it would be so much easier if you got on with it, without me having to threaten you as well. What do you think?" When there came no reply, he shouted: "Move, Reverend!"

There came an explosion. Jamie had shot Munro at point-blank range — and yet the minister remained, stood stock still in terror, his shock only matched by Jamie's failure to understand what had happened; that Simon had told a half-truth and there had been powder, but not shot, in the pistol.

333

"Reverend?" my lord said once more, and it only took a moment of pointing his pistol at the minister to make him move. I was ordered to bring Jamie closer, and had to force him by pushing his shoulders, since he had returned to his soporific state.

So it was that he and I acted as witnesses while Munro, still drunk, married Simon and Amelia while the Fox trained his pistol on first one then the other. It did not take long; certainly not long enough for me to establish whether there was any way I could prevent it. Despite the lady's scowls, threats and growls, Munro pronounced them man and wife. "Thank you, Reverend," my lord said flatly. "Bolla will see you safely on your way. You can expect something of a thank-you from me and the wife in due course! Now, if you'll excuse me…" He made towards the stair to Amelia's private rooms, roughly pushing her ahead of him.

"If you think —" she began, but he silenced her by placing the pistol under her chin.

"I very much think, my love," he said with a twisted smile. "Get them out of here, Bolla," he added, without looking back.

I considered the pistol in my own hand for a moment. Yet the only course of action was for me to follow my instructions. I directed Munro and Jamie down and into the yard, where our companions stood with those who would normally have been within. One asked me what was going on above, but I could not find the words. Instead, after a moment, we began to detect noises coming from an open window near the top of the castle; and it was no difficulty to understand what we heard. Moments later those sounds were joined by crude comments from some of the Frasers; but they did not drown out the cries from within. I looked round in desperation and saw one man had a set of pipes beside him. "Play, man, play!" I cried at him. It took him a moment to understand; but finally he broke into a strong melody, and, at last, I no longer had to follow closely the events in that chamber.

No one appeared to know what to do next. I directed one man to lead Munro to the Inverness road, seeing that he had a flask of wine to help him on his way. Then, as those around me in the courtyard began to understand that the balance of the situation had changed, any last sense of tension dissolved, and groups of former near-enemies recalled their friendships, standing in small circles exchanging conversation, while the piper played. I stood near the bottom step of the main entrance, looking up at the great walls which told of years spent defending the name and persons of Fraser against whatever might come against them; and which were now playing the role of a prison for one who had served the clan so well. Mackintosh, the *fear-an-tigh*, came to stand beside me; but all we offered each other were silent, guarded glances, and the ground became a better place to look.

Then the playing stopped; turning, I saw the piper was staring upwards, and, following his eyes, I beheld Simon and Amelia standing side by side on tower roof. He waved down at us, but had no need to call for silence. "My friends!" he shouted. "Please welcome the bride and groom!" He turned to the lady, who also waved after a pause; yet still we stood silent below. "Well? Come away in — it's a damned wedding party!" he cried, and that brought cheers from those who had followed us from Eilean Aigas; and since they now mixed among the castle folk, those cheered also.

OFFERED THE BEST FOOD AND DRINK the stores had to offer, no one voiced anything other than goodwill for the newly-weds. The explanation of the marriage as a device to prevent Murray installing a Lord Lovat who was not of the clan's blood appeared to meet with the approval of all. Indeed, Mackintosh was soon attending to the multiple duties of the *fear-an-tigh* during such a celebration, which became increasingly demanding as the word spread and more Frasers came to join the proceedings. Shortly after noon Mackintosh announced the couple, to great merriment; and my lord introduced his wife as Dowager Lady Amelia, the Mistress of Lovat, to laughter and cheering.

I could not understand her demeanour: despite all I had seen just a short time previously, she was smiling, laughing and exchanging excited glances with her closest companions across the great hall. Both she and the Fox had dressed themselves in bright clothing, and there appeared to be as much affection between them as ever there had been before. Bewildered, I remained at the back of the crowd, hidden from view by the acts of merriment, singing and dancing; watching all, with a great sense of foreboding. The only person who remained more detached than I was Jamie, who sat at a window alone.

Silence fell when a later commotion at the door heralded the entrance of Lord Tom, Tanacheil and various other lairds who had joined them on the way from Inverness. A large space opened up between them and the high table, where Simon and Amelia sat, before they stood and moved towards the MacShimi, still smiling, but with perhaps a little more trepidation in their manner.

"Father!" Simon cried in welcome.

"*Athair!*" Amelia cried, and the couple shared a warm glance, it being the first time she had referred to the chief as her father.

Yet Lord Tom looked back at them both, doubt written across his ageing features. In fact, he looked to be in very poor health, and appeared even to have shrunk in stature since the previous day. I could not tell whether his pallor was caused by his recent journey in the cold, or a more concerning condition, as he looked at Simon through tired, sunken eyes. "What have you done, son?" he said at last.

"What had to be done," Simon said, still smiling. "Now come on and join the party!"

Tanacheil matched forward. "You have killed us all, Simon, with this charade!" he bellowed.

"Andrew, Andrew – no anger on a day like today!" the Fox said easily. "We haven't killed anyone. Not even Saltoun."

"This is the worst thing you have ever done!" Tanacheil insisted furiously.

"It's the best!" Amelia cried with force. "While you spend your years ranting and raving, this man has done more to protect the clan than anyone else! And he's done it again, and you have nothing but scorn! Bow your head, you old boar!"

"Someone has to —"

"Someone has to understand," she interrupted. "Where were you, little man, when Simon secured shipments of grain from Holland while other clans starved? How much of your own money have you spent on keeping our folk alive? What were you doing when he got the commander-in-chief of the Scots army to fight off a direct assault from my brother? How many signatures have you gathered that tell Murray how many clans they'll face if they try to take our country? Fraser still stands because of Simon — not because of people like you!"

A loud murmur of approval passed round the room. Tanacheil stared at Amelia, then at Simon. "I didn't know..."

"There's more you should know," Amelia went on loudly. "Yes, my brother will increase his efforts to take this land. But he was going to do that anyway, after Simon prevented him from taking them from us by marriage. This is nothing but a fight for survival! And all you have done is whine like a girl!"

The other stood silent, his head now bowed as the lady had instructed. "We were out of time, Andrew," Simon said more quietly, although ensuring all could hear. "I discovered just today that Saltoun had been writing to all the lairds in the east, offering them payment in return for their support in his attempt to make his son the next MacShimi." Angry muttering rolled around us. "There are people in this room who've received those letters, and never told me. Did you get one, Andrew?"

"No!" Tanacheil cried, his hands before him defensively. "I didn't know any of that!"

"Well, now you do," Amelia said. "And now you have to decide what you'll do with that knowledge."

Silence settled upon the hall again; then, slowly, Lord Tom moved forward, and opened his arms to both Simon and Amelia. "Son!" he said. Then: "Daughter!" The clan erupted in cheers as the musicians started up again in the corner; and as the celebration continued with new energy, Tanacheil approached the couple himself and offered an arm of friendship – and was embraced by husband and wife together.

Yet I remained unsure of what I had beheld since leaving Eilean Aigas that morning; I could not decipher the truth from the falsehood, although clearly both were present. It seemed to me that everyone had shared some form of grand joke, and I alone had not understood the humour. Bewildered, my mind tumbling, I made to the roof in the hope of clearing my head; but staring out across the world as the snow clouds gathered above it (preparing, I hoped, less of an onslaught than they had in recent years) I realised I was simply not in possession of the information I needed to decide how I felt. Not for the first time since leaving Moniack, I wished Kirsty was by my side.

"Bolla! Where have you been?" Simon called as I made my way down to the courtyard, intent upon making for home. "Come here!" He beckoned to me from a room along a corridor, and I followed him in, to see Lady Amelia waiting within beside him.

"Thanks for your help this morning, my lad," the Fox said with a smile, touching my shoulder. "With Jamie going mad and that *gorach* Tanacheil trailing about, I couldn't have done it without you."

"You're a better man than Simon, Bolla – I keep telling him," Amelia smiled.

I said nothing; suddenly the thought had entered my head that my lady had followed her course of action in the interests of protecting the clan, and the demeanour I saw upon her was one of brave acceptance. The idea caused me great pain, which I am sure was betrayed in my expression. "*Ochone* – would you cheer up?" Simon said. "It's a damned good day, which is more than you could have said for it this morning. Devil choke me – a gallows!" he laughed, this last directed to his wife, who laughed also.

"There was no need for that!" she cried.

"There was no need for that wee performance here this morning," my lord told her. "But you know me — the more the mischief, the better the sport!"

"I do not understand," I admitted, deciding that I had to hear his explanation, even if it might lead me into further doubt.

He shook his head. "Come on! You didn't think... did you?" He frowned at me.

At that moment the door was thrown open behind us, and young Amy strode in. "Where have you been all day?" her mother asked. "We've been looking for you!"

The girl, I could see, was upset; and by the tears and redness on her face, she had been so for some time. Nevertheless she took several moments to gather herself, before saying: "Yes, I heard. Simon, can I ask you something?"

"Of course!" he grinned.

She took another moment. "Can I ask... how exactly you plan to marry me, now that you've married my mother?"

The Fox started backwards, glancing first to the older Amelia, before returning to the younger. "What?" he said uncertainly.

"You know what I'm talking about," Amy replied strongly, although it was clear she was fighting to remain calm.

"Amelia!" her mother cautioned. "Watch what you're saying!"

"Oh, I'll watch what I'm saying, Mother," she replied. "I wish I'd watched what I was doing now."

"What is that to mean?"

Simon stepped forward, his hands open. "Amy," he said warmly to the young lady. Yet as he moved towards her she lost her loose grip on her temperament, and, bursting into tears, she ran out of the room, leaving the echoes of great sobs in her wake, easily heard even though she had slammed the door shut behind her.

"I'll go and see her," Amelia sighed. "Bairns!" She gave her husband a glance I did not fully understand, although I felt I could estimate.

"Women!" Simon said after she had gone. "I don't need to tell you, though, do I?" He gave me a cup of wine and knocked his against mine. I offered a muttered response which could have meant anything. "Just tell me what's wrong, my lad?" he urged.

"What I saw today was a forced marriage," I finally said with more weight than I intended. "I saw you strike her, and I saw you point a gun at her. Then, upstairs, I heard —"

"The piper!" Simon cut in. "Was that you? Grand, just!"

"I did not do it for you!" I cried.

"Still, though," he said, and sat down, shaking his head with a rueful laugh. "She's always been loud, that one."

Once more, I could not hide my true feelings from my face. "What do you mean?"

He stared up at me. "You really don't see it, do you? The whole thing – the marriage, the whisky priest and the pistol – it was Amelia's idea!"

"No," I said firmly.

"It damn well was!" he insisted. "Remember I got that note in Inverness? It was from her. She told me Saltoun's son was to marry Amy as soon as possible, and the only way to put an end to it was if I married her. It's grand! I wouldn't have thought of it."

"But... the pistol?" I said, unsure how I felt about his explanation.

"Theatre, Bolla, nothing but theatre. It puts Amelia in a better position with her family if those Murray devils think she was unwilling. And that's exactly what the Reverend Munro will tell them. Besides, it was magnificent mischief!"

"Upstairs," I argued. "I heard —"

"You heard a dance we've done before," Simon grinned. "And she's always been loud, like I was telling you." He tapped me on the shoulder knowingly. "Is all clear now?"

"What was Amy talking about?" I said.

"God knows," he shrugged. "She might grow into a woman every bit as brilliant as her mum, but for now she's still a stupid wee lassie." He leaned back in his chair and grinned at me. "Fraser fights on!" he said happily. "Spectacular sport!"

I spoke my mind: "I want to go home and see Kirsty," I stated, without care for how he interpreted my meaning.

"Of course!" he smiled back. "Get on your way. I wouldn't want to break a promise to wee Mairi."

As we left the room he went to rejoin the crowd below, while I moved in towards the main stair; thus he did not see Lady Amelia making her way along the corridor, clearly in tears, as her daughter had so recently been. Seeing me, she made into an ante-room; and I understood that, whichever of the many possibilities was the reason for her state, I would gain nothing by asking.

CHAPTER NINE
THE ROGUE ON THE RUN

"MY NAME IS JAMIE FRASER," I muttered, my face hidden among the rags I gathered about myself against the cold. "And I have stolen nothing, sir. The kind Reverend Munro gave me the wine."

One of the Saxon dragoons laughed at me. "Now I know you're lying! Munro hand over good wine to a beggar?"

"He did, sir!" I replied. "And he gave me a bit to eat too. Could you... Could you spare anything yourself, sir?"

He laughed again. "On my pay — when I get it? Ah, go on, try if you want. But it'll never work."

I bowed slightly and scrabbled away, the broken soles of my boots clacking against the ice on the path towards Abertarff House. It had been under guard since the news of Simon's marriage had spread, as had many of the places in Inverness where Frasers were known to gather. One of the three dragoons was still watching as I knocked the door; and, I am sure, was surprised when a ghillie opened it and did not immediately send me on my way.

"Come away in!" said he, looking out towards the street. "You're a convincing beggar, Bolla."

"I have had much practice," I replied. "You have letters?"

"Always," the ghillie replied, leading me into the kitchen, where I was grateful to warm myself at the fire. "Any from you?"

"Just the two," I said, placing the documents on the table, and taking up the small bundle he laid beside them.

"Two? That's either very good or very bad news. I think it will be bad."

"Simon tells me things have been going well," I said.

Yet the other shook his head. "There's been signs," he said with a worried expression. "They say there's more soldiers on the way. The curlews are back and they've been calling night after night." He looked doubtful as to whether he should speak his next words. "My grannie saw a *bean nighe* at the burn, washing the clothes of the dead. She wished it good-day and asked who it was coming for. It just said, 'Fraser.' And you know a *bean nighe* must speak the truth if you ask politely."

"Perhaps your grannie did not ask politely?"

"My grannie is descended from the eighty women of the Battle of the Shirts," he told me sternly; an allusion which, among the clan, suggested she was beyond reproach.

"I meant no disrespect," I said quickly.

He muttered to himself as he placed a plate on the table. "Eat," he said. "How is Himself?"

"He is well," I replied – but I did not believe it; for indeed Lord Tom's health was a concern among all of us who were closest to him.

The ghillie shrugged. "Still, he's an old man now – and there's another hard winter coming."

"You speak of the MacShimi!" I cried, astonished.

"Aye," he replied after a moment. "A MacShimi who would have had us on the wrong side at Killiecrankie. And who had us near starve in the black winters."

"Do not speak of him like that in his own house!"

"I'm only saying what the clan's saying," he replied defensively. "What's he doing for us while the Fox is standing up for us against Murray?" I said nothing, and ate instead; and soon I was on my way. Out in the darkening town the guard had been changed, so I was questioned again about my name and intent. This time, the one who spoke to me was less kind, threatening me with violence unless I removed myself from his sight – the which I was glad to do. By the time I had reached the cottage where waited my horse and proper clothing it was fully dark, and I was able to continue my journey without fear of interception.

Yet the ghillie had been correct about the letters – soon after my return to Castle Dounie I stood by the fire as the Fox, once again, cursed the name of Murray to Hell, Heaven and back again. "Utter devils!" he shouted. "It's not even vaguely legal!"

"What did you expect from my brother?" Amelia asked calmly.

"Still, five thousand merks reward, Father, eh?" Simon said in an attempt to engage Lord Tom, who sat at the hearth with a cloak wrapped tightly around him, his brow damp with sweat. "For you or me, or both of us."

"It's a king's ransom, son," the MacShimi said weakly. "I know some who might take it."

"There's not a Fraser alive who'd touch it," Simon said with confidence. "Our people won't give us up for pieces of metal. You can be certain of that." He took a long drink from his cup of wine. "*Ochone*, grand, Bolla," he grinned at me. "Months since I had a good claret. But, devil choke me – five thousand merks? Don't tell me Ian Cam's putting the money up!"

"It'll be Saxon money," Amelia said. "For the better governance of the king's wild Highlands."

"And six hundred soldiers on the way! Since when can you call in the army to deal with a personal matter?"

"When you're just short of being a king," his wife replied. "Just like Tanacheil said."

"Don't bring that *gorach* into it," he said with a sour expression. "I'll write to the actual king – that's what I'll do!"

"It won't help," she told him. "Ian's had enough time to sour him against you. And the king will back his own man. He's got to."

"For God's sake!" my lord cried with exaggerated rage, pacing round the chamber, first looking at his wife, then his father, in a manner which suggested he hoped for answers from them both. All three appeared to have become comfortable with the idyllic family life they appeared to project; yet to me, and I am sure to others, much of it bore the marks of a living untruth. "And what of all my dear companions?" the Fox continued. "The clans who promised to stand firm with Fraser against the greed of Murray? Where are they as the devil brings half of England down on my head?"

"Bought off?" Amelia suggested. "Too busy with their own affairs?"

"Aye. Aye," he sighed. "And we all have winter to fight again."

"It was always a risk," she said. "You knew that."

"If you mention Tanacheil again…" he replied, but without strong feeling. He moved to the table, where lay his pens and papers. "So it remains as it was. The best plan to stop Murray becoming any bigger is to take sides with the only clan big enough to stand up to them."

"Campbell?" Lord Tom asked, with a wince of pain as he rolled his shoulders.

"Campbell," Simon grinned, preparing his pen. "Argyll has always liked me. I'll send Jamie in the morning." He paused in thought. "And there's always the chance the wee *gorach* won't come back."

"Argyll?" his wife asked. "I thought you were with Breadalbane?"

My lord offered an expression of mock confusion. "If Slippery John is half as informed as I am – and he will be – he'll sense the change in the air. He's against Murray, of course, but he's also against Argyll, even if no one knows it. He'll be looking for the chance of his cousin tripping up; and Fraser would be the bait in the trap if I wrote to him."

"But what if he discovers you've written to Argyll instead?"

"He will," Simon grinned. "I can't stop that. So it's got to be a clever letter. Fortunately —" he waved a quill in the air as if it were a blade – – "I'm writing it." I was beginning to believe I had escaped further involvement in the concern when he added: "Time to earn your shilling, Bolla," nodding towards the second letter I had delivered. "John needs to be told about what's in that letter."

"What?" Amelia asked.

"Murray's Regiment is to be disbanded!"

There was a pause. "Then it's true?" Tom asked. "King Jamie isn't coming back, and Billy doesn't need Highland forces?"

Simon laughed. "Never believe it, Father! No, the reason's much simpler: the war with France is over."

"Over! Who won?"

My lord laughed again. "The clerks, just!" he cried. "No one won it. Everyone ran out of money to fight it. So the result is… everything stays as it was before it started nine years ago. Except, of course, France recognises Billy as king of England and Scotland."

"Of Scotland!" Tom breathed. "Then… France is no longer our ally?"

"Letters, letters, letters," Simon said confidently. "And you'll note 'of Scotland' rather than 'of Scots.' You can be sure the plan will be getting more attention in France now, if only because it's cheaper than an all-out war. But the point is this: the soldiers Billy didn't manage to kill are all being brought back, and that means there isn't room for the regiments he already has here. Therefore —" he clicked his fingers — "Dismiss them and send them home!"

"So what are you thinking, my darling Fox?" Amelia asked.

He grinned. "That Ian Cam isn't the only one with access to a private army, when there's a company of Frasers armed and ready. And it just so happens they're billeted in Glasgow right now. Within hearing distance of my dear brother's skills of persuasion! So Bolla – to Glasgow with you. And, yes, I know you'll want to stop at Moniack on the way. But wherever you go, for God's sake don't take the Perth road. Murray's not going to be taking Fraser prisoners in that part of the world – not now. He'll be making Fraser graves."

I WAS NOT CERTAIN WHY Kirsty remained upset with me, since I had explained on several occasions that I was beholden to dance to Simon's tune, regardless of my opinions of the steps he dictated. Still, she seemed at pains to emphasise how dangerous those steps were becoming; as if, in knowing such, I could act differently. "It's not just Murray you'd have to worry about on the Perth road," she said, her eyes blazing (as I struggled to ignore the pleasing effect it had upon her). "The lairds of the east country are all but Murray's men now!" She counted on her fingers. "Saltoun's been explaining how much better off they'd be by supporting him. He's got a clever lawyer to tell them how easy it would be to change sides. And even the loyal lairds are split between Simon and Tom."

"It is not so bad since Lady Amelia —" I should have known that was a mistake.

"Lady Amelia!" she cried, putting on a sarcastic tone. "That one got exactly what she wanted!"

"Uniting Fraser's interests?" I asked.

"Ha!" she shouted, pacing round the chamber as Simon had done earlier that evening. "I've told you often enough! All she wanted was Simon — and she got him. Devil damn the rest of it; she's just another scheming Murray!"

My love had indeed mentioned that belief in the past; and, as before, the words "another scheming woman" entered my head, but did not proceed into my mouth.

"And how many dragoons are between here and Glasgow?" she went on. "That Fox has no idea what he's sending you out into. It's not as if he leaves the safety of Fraser country himself – oh no!"

I decided to pounce upon the possibility of her thoughts being focused upon my own safety. "I don't want to go with you so upset," I said quietly. "Yet I do have to go."

She made to prepare another barrage of fury; then, to my relief, decided against it. "Oh, Bolla!" she said instead. "Come here!" Gladly I embraced her, and we did not speak for some moments. "But I told you, *gràdh mo chrìdh* – this dance isn't for us."

"It will soon be over," I said quietly.

"No, it won't," she replied even more quietly.

The journey, although by the longer route, was uneventful, and to my surprise, almost enjoyable – for Kirsty persuaded me to take a hound with me for protection against any attack, and I had not previously spent so much time in such an animal's company. He was a large creature by the name of Fingal, who could be transformed into a vicious warrior at the use of just a few quiet words; yet for the most part was a cheerful, friendly companion who was popular in the households where I took shelter on the journey. In one place a young girl (who reminded me of my own Mairi) insisted on sleeping beside Fingal, and the great animal wrapped himself around her little person without argument.

Presently I found myself in Glasgow, a place larger than Inverness but much lesser than Edinburgh, assembled about its four main streets and great cathedral. Having obtained directions from the university as to where I might find the lodgings of John Fraser, and the hour being late, I decided not to search for him further after finding his rooms empty; and instead Fingal and I settled outside his door on the High Street, gathered together for warmth against the snow and mercifully light wind.

346

Some time later I beheld a figure appearing from the gloom, and my sight was so adjusted that I was sure I recognised the manner of his movement. I rose to meet him as he approached – and was astonished when I found myself thrown back against the door, a knife pressed against my neck. "Who the hell are you?" rasped the other.

"John!" I whispered. "It is Bolla!"

"Bolla!" He leaned in close to make out my features; and immediately his grip loosened. "Damn! I'm so sorry!"

I took a moment to gather my thoughts. "Simon sent me," I told him at last.

"Sorry!" he repeated. "*Ochone*, come away in. And is that Fingal-dog? Much good he did you!" John leaned down to greet the animal, who was panting in delighted welcome. "Ach well, he does know me, don't you, Fingal-dog? Let's get up the stairs." Within, he made up the fire, all the time talking to the hound as he bade me pour drinks. "I have to be on my guard," he finally explained, sitting opposite me at the table. "You just don't know what Murray might get up to."

"Perhaps his power is to wane," I said, presenting the letter I had previously given to his brother, and watching his expression as he read.

"Disbanded!" he breathed. "And you can wager the troops won't get their missing pay either! Oh… there must be a way to use this!"

"Simon suggested the Earl of Tullibardine was not the only man who could command a private army," I said.

John nodded. "I see that," he said. "I'll need to have a wee think, though. They're keeping a watch on me. I mean, I can get on with my studies – but if I was seen with the lads from the company, I'd soon be in the tolbooth. So I'll have a think."

He offered me a glance which I did not fully understand, then took a drink before asking: "How are things at home?"

"All is well," I replied too quickly, adding: "As can be expected."

He shook his head. "The wedding… I can see why it made an amount of sense. But I can't see how it puts an end in sight. What else can Ian Cam do except escalate things? If it wasn't personal before, it's personal now." It was clear to me that he had not yet spoken of the matter which truly filled his thoughts, so I offered no response; until finally he asked: "How's Father?"

"I am concerned," I told him flatly.

"So am I," he replied before taking another drink, and finally divulging more. "Bolla, I've never asked you this before. But you saw Lord Hugh just before he died."

"Yes," I said.

"How did he look?"

"Very sick."

"When I was in France," he said slowly, staring into his cup, "I learned about poisons. Lots of different types. It's out of use here, but in France they say like one killing in every six is down to poison. You remember the powders we used to have in Moniack?" I nodded. "Simon wanted me to teach him everything I knew. I didn't – in the end, with those winters, I... Well, I changed, Bolla. The plan's still the plan, but those damned powders should be no part of it."

He paused once again. "There was one particular poison. Easy to disguise and it even tasted pleasant. You wouldn't know you were taking it, except for one thing – in France they call it the moonlight mist. A sheen of sweat on your skin that looks like silver. It starts out barely visible, but towards the end it's almost like you're not from this world."

"That is what I saw," I said quietly.

"And... Father?"

I sighed. "I do not think even Simon —"

"Answer me."

"I have not seen what you call 'midnight mist.' But... he sweats."

John's face tightened into a grimace. "It was no accident the poisons got lost in the storm damage. I told him I wouldn't get any more. But he has his own connections."

"He would treat his own father so?" I asked.

"What of his own brother!" John responded. "What happened to Alex, Bolla? Did he really just settle down in Wales and decide not to come back? Was Alex the type of man who walked away from his responsibilities to the clan?"

I said nothing – remembering instead Lady Amelia's understanding of what Kirsty and I had seen on the side of a loch those years past. "It is hard to believe," I whispered.

"Yes. Do you know what Simon really needs right now? He needs things to become simpler. Alex is gone – simpler! Hugh is gone – simpler! He's married to Amelia – simpler! But he's not the MacShimi, Bolla. Not quite."

"It is too difficult to accept," I forced myself to say.

"I know," he replied, laying down his cup and opening his hands before him. "But I can't pretend it's not a consideration any more." He looked at me at last. "You *have* to find out for me. When you go home, talk to Father. Ask him about the powders. Get him to stop taking them and see if he feels better. And I know, Simon will be all about you — but promise me you'll try." I wanted to agree quickly and loudly; but something within my being prevented me from so readily committing to betrayal of my lord, even after all I had seen of him, and, indeed, previously done. I began to consider a form of words which might satisfy John's concerns while not being a promise.

At that moment there came the noise of approach from without – great lumbering footsteps on the stairway. I glanced towards the hound; but, despite facing the door, alert, he again did not appear set for action. John, his back to the entrance, drew a pistol from a drawer in the table, and motioned for me to remain still and silent. The door burst open, and I recoiled in shock — for there stood a man I had known for just a brief time before he had died: Ben Ali Fraser, more than a decade in his grave. "Johnnie!" said the apparition. "They're coming for you!"

John turned round. "What?" he said.

"Now!" cried the other. "We've got to go!"

Finally John burst into motion, opening another drawer to lift some papers and throw them in the fire. "Damn it! How long?"

"Minutes," the giant figure told him, seeming to take up the entire doorway.

"Bolla, tell Callum what you told me," said John, packing another set of papers into his jacket while throwing more onto the flames.

"Callum?" I asked — aware that my behaviour was too slow and inappropriate for the moment, but unable to raise myself from the shock of what I had seen.

"You remember Ben Ali? This is his brother. Callum, Bolla Fraser."

"Speak quickly, unless you want your arse booted!" Callum told me. Something about his manner put me at more ease of a sudden; and I realised that, being dressed in the uniform of a dragoon from the Lord Lovat's Company, he was not some shade from my past. I repeated the news I had given John, while he gathered some belongings into a bag which had clearly been all but prepared for a fast departure. "Disbanded?" the big man repeated.

"Without pay," John emphasised. "Now, let's be out of here."

"Me first," Callum said, leading us out of the room and into the darkness of the stairway. I followed with Fingal, who still appeared to be unaware of any tension among us, and John came behind with his bag. "I heard them talking about you in the street," Callum went on, his voice echoing in the corridor. "The order had just come through, and they were to take you to the tolbooth without delay. They sent for six men, and it won't take them long – there's some billeted on every street."

"Some in this damned tenement!" John whispered. "I've got a boat waiting – I'll head for Dumbarton. You'll come with me, Bolla?"

"Of course," I said.

"Me too," Callum added. "It's not like they won't have seen me."

The next moment we were all seen: as we stepped into the street we beheld a group of figures approaching from down the hill, their torches lighting the bonnets of their uniforms. "John Fraser!" cried a voice. "Stop! You're under arrest!"

Callum offered a reply in the form of a pistol shot. "You want him, you come through me!" he shouted.

"*Cac!*" John said, pointing up the street, where another group of soldiers had appeared.

"There are fewer of them," I said of those above us.

"We go that way then," Callum replied as a carbine was fired from below. We broke into a run, side by side, moving towards what appeared to be no more than four dragoons, who had stopped in some doubt. "*A Mhòr-fhaiche!*" cried the big man, following the battle cry with a great roar of anger.

I remembered Fingal. "*Siuthad!*" I said, and the hound exploded into a furious rage, taking even us by surprise. "*Thusa a-nise!*" I added, pointing towards the dragoons, and he set off racing, still howling, to those ahead of us. That scattered them, allowing us to break past unhindered, and John led us into the vennels of Glasgow even as shots rang out behind us. "'*S math sin!*" was all it took to end Fingal's performance; and as we leaned against a back wall to gather ourselves, the animal appeared delighted with his sport.

"Well done, Fingal-dog!" John whispered. "It's the long way round to the boat, now." We could hear raised voices and fast feet as we made our way slowly downhill by back routes, far from torchlight or witnesses. Soon enough the dull glint of water came into view, as the moon broke through behind snow clouds; and we stepped out onto a wide road alongside the river Clyde, its great bridge a silhouette about two hundred paces beyond us.

"Which one?" Callum asked, looking over dozens of masts of boats moored along the waterfront.

"After the bridge," John told him. "Let's not panic – let's just wander." Despite his words the big man bowed himself as low as possible while we moved painfully slowly, and in truth I felt certain he could not be mistaken even in the half-light of the night. Each time the moon appeared I felt as if the snow beneath us betrayed his notable size to anyone who was watching; and if there truly were dragoons billeted in every building of the town, it could not be long before someone raised a voice against us.

"There!" John said as we passed the bridge, pointing towards a small boat with its sails open, moving shadows betraying the forms of crewmen readying for departure. But even as we increased our pace, seeing the end of our journey, we saw the shapes of more dragoons appearing out of the vennels between us and our destination. "Bolla! Just go!" John whispered, pointing across the bridge, thrusting the papers from his jacket into my hands. "Get these to Simon — and talk to Father!" Just then I saw more shadows assembling from the direction we had come.

"Keep Fingal with you," I said, realising the import of the moment. "Good luck."

"I'll see you again," Callum nodded, still crouched low, and I matched his mode of movement as I parted from them, one word from John ensuring the hound remained beside him.

Moments later the sound of animal howling, shouting and gunfire told me the inevitable had happened; and the lack of movement around me also revealed I had escaped with surprising ease. It was too dark to follow the proceedings in full; but hidden beneath the far side of the bridge I was able to make out the form of some prisoners – Callum, for one, among them – being led, guards before and after, away from the river and towards their fate in the tolbooth. I remained where I crouched, wrapped up against the night; and I resolved to stay there until morning. I did not know if dragoons would be on watch for my appearance, but I could not take the risk; and therefore my road lay west instead of north, until I could find a ferry to cross the Clyde and set me on the path back to Fraser country — although I no longer knew whether that was truly the path to safety.

THE COMPANY OF FINGAL-DOG had given me great confidence on the way south, such that I had not made use of my beggar's disguise; but leaving Glasgow, alone and vulnerable, I had cause to miss those clothes. Thus I felt it to be great providence when I discovered the frozen body of a poor wild man in the remains of a cottage that evening. The act of exchanging garments lent a strange intimacy to our presence there together; and, lighting a fire, I found it somewhat appropriate to spend the night near him, without ever knowing anything about him. The ground was frozen as solid as he, and therefore it was not possible to bury him; so instead I laid my discarded plaid over him and moved on. I was in better spirits for that singular encounter, knowing now that the worst that was likely to befall me, even if captured, was a level of casual violence from those who believed themselves to be in a better social position than I. Strangely, I was also relieved not to have to explain to one little girl why Fingal was no longer with me.

The greater portion of my journey had passed when at last my hopes of safe passage were dashed. Even Maryburgh and its dangerous fortress were behind me, and my traverse through Cameron country was almost over, when I looked ahead of me into my own land – and beheld a signal fire burning from the southernmost hill. Changing direction to gain height, I made my way through the trees of Laggan and soon saw that the chain of warnings stretched far into the distance.

Fraser country was on alert, yet none of the surrounding clans had taken up the signal.

A host of urges played across my thoughts – the first of which was to spare no time in heading towards Moniack, Kirsty and Mairi. Yet I quickly understood it would be better to discover that which I could, before moving headlong into whatever crisis awaited; and, thinking for another moment, I realised it would be best for me to remain without my own country and instead follow the far shore of Lochs Oich and Ness. Making through Grant and Chisholm lands would lead me to Fraser's westerly lordships, where, I was convinced, there would be no immediate danger.

I moved on into the night; and all too soon I had cause to regret not having considered further the advantages of caution over haste. Following a bend in the road I marched full-pace into a company of six or seven men — and before I could make sense of what was happening, I found myself held close while their leader held a torch up to my face. "You are known to me," snarled a threatening voice. "Your name?"

"Cameron!" I spluttered without thought. "Alistair Cameron!"

The other growled a dangerous laugh. "That, it is not," he said. "Fraser, it is. You have been seen with the Fox!"

"No!" I cried.

"Aye!" the other shouted back, causing the torch to flicker. "And maybe it's him you'll see sooner that you think! Archie, away and tell Himself we've a fine eighth head for him!" My pistol and knife taken from me, I was marched among my captors along a road I recognised at least partly; but the waning moon combined with the blinding torch meant I was not able to make much from my surroundings. The moon had long set before we reached our destination, a large building with lights burning from its upper windows despite the late hour. I was not led to the main entrance, but to a door down a short stairway which led into a cold, damp stone passage. At the end one of my assailants unlocked another door, and its noise left me in no doubt it opened into a prison. Without a word I was pushed within, and the entrance was slammed and locked behind me.

I stood stock-still in the complete darkness, trying to make sense of what had occurred. My mind had been churning since my capture, but I had been unable to explain any element of it – other than that it was connected with the signal fires. "Hello, Bolla," said a voice through the darkness.

"Simon!" I cried with surprise.

"Hello, Bolla," Lady Amelia and Lord Tom both repeated, although I could still see nothing.

"There's a seat here on the floor," my lord said. "It's the best welcome I can offer."

"How did you come here?" I asked, incredulous, as I felt my way towards his voice. "And how did you know it was me?"

"I heard your limp," he said. "Usually when I hear that I'm thinking, 'Oh, good, here comes Bolla, let's have a drink.' This time it was, 'Oh damn it – you too, my lad?' As to how we came here… the same as you, I reckon."

"I was taken on the road from Maryburgh —"

"Fort William," my lord corrected.

"I went to take the north road after I saw the beacons. That is where they caught me."

"*Ochone*! They came from outside Fraser country. Well, that's one thing."

"Does it help?" Amelia asked, seemingly not concerned by her current predicament, her voice as strong as ever.

I heard the smallest sound of cloth moving and realised Simon had shrugged. "Maybe," he said after a moment, realising he could not have been seen. "Bolla, what else do you remember?"

"Nothing much," I said. "I think we walked a dozen miles or more from Laggan."

"How many were there?"

I pressed my memories. "Six or seven."

"I think they were looking for you, no one else. I wonder how they knew where to look? Did they say anything?"

"Nothing, except they didn't believe me when I said I was a Cameron. One of them had seen me with you in the past."

"Anything else? I find it helps to close your eyes when you're sitting in pitch black — it focuses your other senses."

I did as he asked. "Something about telling Himself there was an eighth head."

"A shroud upon me!" Simon cried.

"There are only four of us here," Lord Tom said quietly. "Think you there are four more held somewhere else?"

"No!" the Fox said. "I think it's Glengarry!"

"Glengarry!" Amelia repeated. "How?"

"The Well of the Seven Heads," my lord told her. "A few years ago the MacDonells of Glengarry cut off the heads of seven folk who'd killed a clansman of theirs. They washed the heads in a well before putting them on display – and they've never shut up about it. If you anger a MacDonell he'll say he's going to make you into an eighth head. That's what passes for their humour."

"But – he's our friend," Lord Tom objected.

"Maybe. He's also Ian Cam's friend. *Ochone!*" Simon paused again. "About a dozen miles down the glen… we're in Achnacarry Castle, I think!"

"Very clever," Amelia said. "How does that help us?"

"I don't know — yet," he admitted.

"What happened to you?" I asked.

"A thousand Athollmen!" Simon said, a surprising amount of joy in his voice as he recounted his adventures since last we had met. The Earl of Tullibardine had secured the use of one Major Anderson, commanding at Inverness, and had given orders for a large force to enter Fraser country with the intention of apprehending the MacShimi and his son. Naturally they had been warned in advance, and were able to escape from Castle Dounie in good time. I was horrified to learn they had first made for Moniack Castle, but he reassured me that my family had been sent onward to Stratherrick House on the southerly side of Loch Ness, which remained in safety. The following days had seen them sheltering first in one township, then another, as the soldiers searched in vain, the good folk of Clan Fraser making their enemies' progress as difficult as possible. Eventually Simon had decided to leave his own country with a view to preparing more solid plans. "And I did hope to run into you," he added. "Just – not like this. Anyway, what news of John?"

"He is arrested... also," I said sadly, recounting my experience in Glasgow. That brought a long silence among us; until light snoring told that Lord Tom had fallen asleep, and Simon recommended the same course of action for us all.

The daylight was cruelly bright when, later, a guard brought in some bread and water. His blank expression changed to shock when Simon, full of his natural ebullience, ordered him to tell Alasdair Dubh of Glengarry that he was expected at his earliest convenience. Nevertheless, the greatest part of the day had passed before we were finally taken from our cell and led into what seemed to be more of a large house than a castle. "There's been a mistake," Glengarry said in his gruff manner, without any hint of welcome or apology as we entered the hall. "Have a drink."

Lord Tom, Amelia and I made straight for the fire, although Simon accepted a cup, pausing to demonstrate to us with his expression that he was pleased to have been proved correct in his estimation of our captor's identity. "Damn your mistake," he said, matching the other's tone.

"My men were told to find you and bring you in for your own protection, nothing else," the big man replied. "Anderson was coming south, Hill was coming north. And remember Hill has Invergarry Castle now. I had to find another place."

"You did that, just," Simon nodded. "Half freezing my wife, my father and my friend to death on a night like that!"

"Someone will pay," Glengarry vowed seriously. "You're under my protection now."

"And Clan Cameron's," the Fox said with a glint. "So you are friends again this week?"

"Watch your words, Fraser! There's a fine price on your head!"

"And you need a new castle, of course."

The other growled, but added nothing for a time. "I have a place deep in Glen Garry itself," he said after a pause. "They'll not be able to touch you there."

Simon made a face. "I think not," he said. "I wouldn't want to put you in that position, since you're such good friends with Murray."

"That was your idea!" the other roared furiously, and pointed at me.

"You were there when he said it!"

"I didn't expect you to do it so well," Simon replied lightly. "But, no — it's too dangerous with a garrison at Invergarry. We'll stay here a few days, though. And, Alasdair? Thank you."

All tensions apparently defused, we settled down in Achnacarry as the guest of the absent Cameron chief Lochiel, while the Fox sent and received letters at an impressive rate. After that he and Glengarry vanished for several nights, leaving me unsure how to speak to Lady Amelia, given what I had seen on the night of her marriage to Simon; so instead I attempted to follow John's bidding, and asked Lord Tom about the powders my lord gave him. "I'm not well, I know that," he told me. "And I'm not one for powders at all, but I'm still here – so they must work."

"Have you tried going a day or so without them?"

"Why would I do that?" he asked, looking at me with watery eyes, tinged with redness. "I have no need to feel worse than I do."

"John thinks… it could be worth trying."

"Why?" he repeated, strength returning to his voice; and I could not speak the words required to reply. "Do you think me a *gorach* as well as sick? Do you not think I know what's said behind my back? You may be the boll o'meat Fraser, and that may give you place to say more that most — but I am the MacShimi, man! And I lead this clan until God decides otherwise!" He strode away with more bearing than I had observed in him for some years, although it soon appeared to pain him. I did not attempt to question him again.

SIMON'S RETURN HERALDED a flurry of activity, not least from Amelia, who was distressed to see a bullet-tear in the left shoulder of his jacket, and a bandage visible underneath. He arrived with Glengarry, Tanacheil, Jamie Fraser and two ghillies carrying a chest which, if the sound were any guide, contained a great deal of money. "What happened, my love?" Amelia demanded, pulling off his jacket to inspect the wound.

He laughed. "Ask what didn't happen! We've been on a right old adventure! Dragoons, close-run chases – and we might even have discovered the truth of the Loch Ness Monster, eh, Jamie?" The young man scowled but said nothing; and that was all I could make of the expressions exchanged between those who had returned. "Anyway, the point is," Simon continued, "If they really want to collect the rest of that hearth tax, they should send me! Despite everything, we got the damned money!" He patted the chest, but did not open it.

"Money? What for?" Lord Tom asked.

"For the journey," his son said, waving away Amelia as she tried to look closely at his wound – which, in truth, seemed nothing too severe. "I didn't just learn about the monster. I learned that our own country is being used against us. And some traitor Fraser is spying on us!"

"I warned you," Tom said. "Five thousand merks…"

Simon's face turned dark. "Metal! Nothing but discs of metal — to think that means more to someone of our name than the name itself! I wish… I *hope* it isn't that." He moved towards the window, his back to us; the better, I think, to obscure the honesty of his words. "I hope it's just someone who personally hates me. That would be better than having to believe there's someone out there among Fraser who's ready to sell us all."

Amelia looked first at Glengarry and then at Tanacheil, but both returned a glance which told there was nothing to say – or, at least, there was nothing they would say. Finally, simply to break the silence, she asked: "What did you mean about a journey?"

Simon turned back to us, his expression changed to one of sheer delight. "Another adventure, my wife!" he grinned. "We're outlaws, for the moment. Hunted men. A bounty on our heads and every shadow concealing an enemy. Well, we might as well play the damned part, eh? The more mischief, the better sport!" He moved towards me and threw his arm over my shoulder. "Some of us," he said, "are going to find safe cover elsewhere. Some of us, Father, are going to ask your in-laws the MacLeods for support. And some of us, my lady, are staying here."

"I'm coming with you," Amelia said firmly.

"Not this time," Simon replied airily. "There's too much at stake."

"Don't you tell me what to do!" she cried.

"Don't you start!" he spat back. "The next step is too dangerous. I have to go first and put certain things in place. You have to stay here."

"I am coming with you," she said slowly and calmly.

"We'll talk about it later," he sighed. "Meanwhile, we've got to get moving. Alasdair Dubh – if you would?" That man stepped towards Amelia, and gestured with his giant hand that she should leave the room. She offered him a look which might have crumbled a mountain; but it seemed that such a reaction had been expected; for suddenly two MacDonell clansmen appeared through the door and expertly took the lady by her arms and waist, her feet lifted from the ground, and carried her away. Her screams, at first of surprise and then of pure rage, echoed after her, from which it was clear to understand that she was carried to the first room we had encountered in Achnacarry. "Well, that could have gone better," the Fox said once silence had fallen.

"What are you doing, son?" Lord Tom cried, his voice containing the suggestion that, at last, he had tired of his behaviour. "To your own wife?"

Simon rolled his head between a dismissive shake and a shrug. "Did you not hear me? We can't go home. Until I can be sure of safety, she has to stay here. For now!"

"She can come with me to Dunvegan – if that's where I'm going," Tom said. "She will be safe there."

"No, she won't," Simon replied. "It's complicated."

"You can all stay with MacDonell," Glengarry said. "You'll have the best of welcomes at Lochcarron – and the only government men you'll see will have their heads on pikes."

Simon laughed. "My thanks, Alasdair. But, as I say, it's complicated. I have to speak to… some people."

"Then come back when you have," Glengarry said. "You'll be safer with me than anyone else in Scotland."

"Maybe," Simon nodded. "But let's not get ahead of ourselves. You'll look after Amelia for me?"

"Like my own sister."

"Or, indeed, mine," the Fox replied; alluding, I believe, to the fact that Alisdair Dubh was married to his cousin. "Now, I have some letters to write. Let's prepare to be off in the morning."

He left the room, presenting an opportunity for those who remained to digest all that had occurred. "Andrew," Lord Tom said sternly. "What happened while you were away?"

Tanacheil's mouth moved as if he struggled to prepare his words, then he shook his head. "I am sorry, MacShimi – but I am sworn to secrecy, unless Simon speaks first. We all are." Glengarry, Jamie and the ghillies all looked away, the implications of Tanacheil's words clear to us all. Tom rose up; but faltered, and he did not ask further, instead marching out of the room, soon followed by all but Jamie. That singular character appeared to have more awareness about him than I had becomes used to, and it was apparent he wished to speak to me – the which, since he was placed closer to the door than I, could not be avoided.

"I wish I could tell you about it," he said, his voice full of enthusiasm even if his expression appeared mainly blank. "It was magnificent mischief!" I made a non-committal response to his use of Simon's phrase, but he approached me and touched my arm. "I've been... not well," he told me. "I've had a mad head. But I'm getting better now, after what just happened."

"That is good to hear," I said, before leaving the room, and I meant those words; although I moved away so that I did not have to continue speaking, for I doubted still the condition of his mind. My steps, for no reason of which I was aware, took me outwith the castle and towards the outhouses where previously we had been held. Near the small passageway I began to hear the echoed sounds of an argument – and I realised Simon was talking to Amelia.

I crept as close as I dared, unsure of my ambition; but eager, I think, to know more of the understanding between the two. "Because he's a *gorach* – you know that," my lord said in answer to a question I did not hear, although their tones betrayed some anxiety.

"Just like you!" I heard clearly from through the shutter on the cell door.

"Don't! Please!" her husband pleaded. "This is difficult enough."

"Is it?" she spat. "After everything I did – after betraying my own family and telling those lies... it really just was all about you all along!"

"No!" he cried in fury. "That's *cac* and you know it. We're here now because — ach, you know as well as I do. I don't know if this next step is going to work. If it doesn't, the daughter of Murray would be a prize prisoner. And I won't be responsible for that!" When she offered no reply he continued: "Tell me you understand!"

Yet she said nothing for several more moments; and finally I made out a short question, asked between sobs, which ended in her demanding: "And don't lie to me!" Simon said nothing. Instead I heard him slamming the shutter closed, which was my warning to retreat to a safe distance. I rounded the corner of the outhouse and stopped to consider the meaning of what I had overheard. Presently my lord himself appeared round the corner, moving slowly; and if he was surprised to see me he offered no sign.

"This is a far throw, Bolla," Simon sighed as we stood in the dusk light together. "If I throw well we could win the game. If I miss…" he trailed off, his eyes scanning the horizon as if he expected to see a company of dragoons appearing on one of the snow-covered peaks at any moment. Then he counted on his fingers as he said: "Father will be safe on Skye. The MacLeods will look after him, because he was husband to their darling Sybilla. They won't help us, but they'll keep him. Amelia will be safer with Alasdair Dubh than with me – although not much. The clan should be able to deal with Murray for now."

"And… John?" I asked.

"He knows the risks," Simon replied, almost dismissively. "He'll need to make his own luck for now. And so will we." He touched my shoulder then moved away, even more slowly than he had arrived, as if constrained by an increasing weight.

Yet even as the sun set, followed quickly by the rise of a full moon which lit the winter world for a short time until it also set, and then another snowfall began, the dramas of the day were not concluded. Simon, Tanachiel and I were in the great hall, discussing plans and direction for our departure the next day, when the sound of gunfire all too near the castle sent us out into the darkness, pistols drawn. At first nothing stirred; then we beheld a small number of Glengarry's men running towards us, their shouts expressing a need to act quickly. "What's going on?" Simon cried as they climbed the stair.

"We are attacked!" one of the MacDonells told him.

"Who's coming?" My lord asked, then, immediately, added: "Get inside!" and, ushering us all within, closed and barred the door, then led us to the rampart above. From there we could again see nothing, until, in time, a group of figures became just visible in the trees beyond the castle yard, moving slowly towards us, bent double for their own protection.

"Dragoons!" Tanacheil said, and raised his pistol.

"Wait!" Simon told him, forcing his arm down. "You won't hit anything from here." Then, raising his voice to a cry which sounded strangely depressed in the snow, he ordered: "Identify yourselves!"

A call came back through the night: "Fraser!"

That surprised us all, none more than Simon, whose expression appeared almost comical. "Fraser who?" he called.

"The Lord Lovat's Company of Murray's Regiment!"

"Devil choke me," Simon said quietly. Then, shouting once more: "Well, what do you want?"

"The MacShimi!" the voice replied. "And the Young MacShimi!"

"A trap!" I whispered to my lord.

"Who calls me the Young MacShimi without being asked a million times? Only our own," Simon said, more to himself. "Come forward and be recognised!" he cried out; and the dragoons, numbering half of a dozen, stood up from the shadows and stepped forward, the light from the castle allowing us to make out the uniform of our own company – and one figure unmistakable for any other.

"Callum! Ben Ali's brother!" I said.

By the time the door was opened and our men stood within – Callum having embraced and lifted Simon the way I had once seen his late sibling do – Glengarry had arrived. "What's going on?" he demanded; in an attempt, it seemed, to take control of the situation.

"You might well ask," Simon told him. "These lads got to within spitting distance without being stopped – and you tell me my family would be safe with you?"

Glengarry scowled. "The *gorach* responsible will be found," he growled. "And dealt with."

"Now, Ben Callum," my lord said to the giant clansman. "What brings you here at this hour of the day? And how's John?"

"You were right," he replied, nodding to me in recognition and acknowledgement. "Johnnie is locked up in Glasgow tolbooth. They say he tried to get us to mutiny!"

"*Ochone*," Simon said, shaking his head. "Come away in and tell me the story."

Stood by the fire and drinking a fifth cup of whisky while the rest of us were on our second, Callum spoke while his men nodded agreement. "After you left," he said, speaking to me, "We got caught by the militia. There was no need of the extra expense of keeping me around, so they let me go, telling me I was innocent because I'd just been following orders. *Gorachs*! I'll tell you, a couple of them went home with less teeth and more bruises than they started with!

"Then they told us the company were to march to Edinburgh. It was said Murray wanted to keep a closer eye on us. But I told the boys we should be ready to fight."

"You said we should run out right then!" a dragoon offered.

Callum nodded. "But not everyone agreed," he went on. "There's been... bad talk." He clearly did not want to speak the next words. "Some of our own men said we deserved to be disbanded." He looked Simon in the eye. "They said we were only formed to be your private army, for the betterment of your own affairs."

"You see, Simon?" Tanacheil broke in. "You have gone too far!"

"Stop, Andrew!" my lord replied, before telling Callum: "Go on."

"We got to Linthligow, and suddenly that *gorach* Captain Murray told us to hand in our weapons and disperse – and if we did it peacefully they'd send a week's pay home after us."

"Damn!" Simon said quietly. "So – what happened?"

Ben Callum grunted. "Aye, we did it peacefully," he grinned as Simon laughed, while Tanacheil made disapproving noises in the background. "They'll still be cleaning the place up just now. As if they're going to send us more money when they owe us a month already! I'm just sorry Murray got away – he started running before the first shot. Anyway, the ones who gave up their guns are probably home by now, telling their wives there's money coming next week. The rest of us..."

"Six of you? Six honest Frasers?"

"No, no – we split up to look for you. There's more of us out there."

"How many?"

Callum paused. "About fifty or so."

363

"Fifty!" Tanacheil repeated, his intention not to assist in clarity.

"A third of the company," Simon said quietly. "And everyone else believes Fraser is better off with Murray than with me."

"They do not!" the big man replied. "They just think – maybe…"

My lord touched his shoulder. "I know," he said. Then, with an effort, he returned to his more ebullient self. "Well, we're bound for pastures new tomorrow – are you lads coming with us for a bit of fun?" The newcomers all nodded assent. "I can promise you one thing," he told them. "At least you'll get paid."

"And maybe a good fight?" Ben Callum asked.

WE LEFT AT FIRST LIGHT, and the Fox, his ever-present papers tied to his horse, did not even glance in the direction of the cell in which he had imprisoned his wife. Glengarry promised once again to take care of her, and also promised to stay in close contact with any news; and the pair made arrangement for a location where they could deliver and collect letters from each other. I knew we were not headed for our own country – Callum had reported that the signal fires burned still – yet I dared to hope as the road took us towards the familiar route through Glen Lochy; and despite knowing in advance what would happen, I still felt disheartened as we turned south instead of north. Presently we came to a cross in the road, where Simon called a halt and came off his horse, bidding Tanacheil, myself and Jamie (for only one other was mounted) to do the same. He moved to Lord Tom's horse and looked his father in the eye. "It's time to go our separate ways," he said, a curious expression on his face.

"I will secure help from MacLeod," Tom told him, bearing the countenance of one who was used to acting the chief. "And we will return and reclaim our country."

"That we will," Simon said; but it was clear to all the true thoughts they shared – as did we. "Jamie will look after you, and these men of Glengarry will accompany you until you're safe on Skye." I started. I could not believe that Simon was to trust the young sergeant with the MacShimi's life – despite our brief conversation the previous day, I had no evidence to support his claim that he had recovered from the

364

ailments of his mind.

One of the three MacDonells spoke up: "Himself says we're to stay with you."

Simon turned. "Would you let a clan chief march alone through enemy country?" he demanded. "You who have slept in Fraser beds and eaten Fraser meat? Is there to be another fight?"

"I'm ready," Callum snarled. All three looked shame-faced; and, indeed, the suggestion that Highland hospitality had been scorned rendered into discomfort all the clansmen who listened.

That resolved with no more speech, he turned back to Tom. "I'll get John out, and I'll get help from elsewhere," he said. "People owe us – and a lot of them love us."

"Even if our own do not," the MacShimi said sadly.

"They worry. It's to be expected. We've kept them well through worse times."

"Have we?"

"We are the fighting sons of Simon," my lord said as the clansmen joined him in the recital, "Who died for Wallace, who died for Bruce, who died for the Stuarts, who died for freedom. Simon will die again. But Fraser will never die." Even the MacDonells bowed in respect to the abbreviated clan history, and Lord Tom's expression regained some of its authority. He looked at his son briefly, then nodded, and turned his horse to the road which led, at length, to the country of his late wife's people. The Fox whispered some short instruction to Jamie and passed him a bottle of what I sadly assumed was powder; Jamie nodded, did the same towards me, then followed the chief. A stern look from my lord sent Glengarry's ghillies marching after them; and those of us who remained waited in silence as Simon watched the small party disappear into the snow-clad distance, their tracks already beginning to be lost under the latest freezing fall from the dull grey sky.

At last we remounted and continued on our way – a way which, in order to distance ourselves from the threat of arrest, soon called upon us to abandon our horses and climb into the winter wastes. Tanacheil objected loudly when Simon instructed the ghillies with the money chest to deposit it within a small cave we had discovered, and cover it with bracken. The Fox told him that if he volunteered to carry it himself it could continue with us; and that ended the exchange.

They were harsh nights, with sparse protection from the elements, and despite my misgivings over Lord Tom's safety with Jamie, I felt sure he would not have survived the journey we took. Yet our progress was swift and our traverse untroubled – until, on the third day, we entered a small ravine and our instincts told us to throw ourselves against the rocks as three shots rang out from above. "Show yourselves – or we shoot to kill!" cried a voice.

Simon was the first to recover; he stepped forward, arms open, and called: "I have safe passage!"

"Who gave you it?"

"Archie Campbell himself!"

"Campbell?" Tanacheil muttered. "We're in Campbell country? We're dead men."

"All of you come out!" the voice called. "Drop your arms and stand away!"

"Do it," Simon told us.

"I'll break —" Ben Callum began.

"Do it!" Simon repeated, before shouting upwards: "We're doing it!"

Some moments later we heard the noise of feet scrambling down into the ravine, and found ourselves facing into the muskets of dragoons, who indeed appeared to be Campbells. "If you don't have safe passage you're dead," said the leading soldier, a narrow-faced man with a mean look.

"I have it," Simon said calmly; and, very slowly, took a document from his jacket and extended it towards the other, who took it, glowered, then gave it back.

"You'll hand over your weapons," said the Campbell. "We will escort you to Auchenbreck."

"We're going to Oban," my lord said sternly; but he received a laugh in response.

"Breadalbane wants you in Auchenbreck."

"Where in hell is that?" Simon cried in exasperation.

"You'll find out," grinned the narrow-faced one. It was not clear to me whether we were being escorted, our weapons taken from us in an measure which could be understood; or whether we were, in fact, entirely doomed. I recalled from my long-ago journey to Breadalbane's stronghold in Kilchurn how that character dispensed justice; and I recalled also that, while the Campbells aimed to be the dominant clan in Scotland, there was little love lost between Slippery John Breadalbane and his cousin, the Earl of Argyll. If, as Simon had said, we were associated with the latter, it might serve us ill in the company of the former.

Achenbreck was an older castle than Moniack, with a tall curtain wall and a tower house at one corner; and on arrival it seemed plain that we were indeed prisoners, for the Campbells sent us to the single room at the top of the building, and locked us within. Callum made several motions to overcome those who held us, but Simon waved him down each time, leaving the big man in such a temper that, on finding the door to the parapet locked against him, near tore it off its hinges before stamping out into the cold air and staring angrily out across a country which, on first glance, might seem similar to our own; but was in fact completely alien and threatening to us. Tanacheil, as might have been expected, launched a new assault upon Simon, telling him he had been the architect of our destruction, and hinting darkly that those of the Lord Lovat's Company who had expressed doubts over his intentions had some justification. That brought a furious Callum in from the parapet, threatening Tanacheil with a fate worse than death if he did not begin treating the Young MacShimi with the respect his position demanded. As silent tension filled the room, Simon sighed, sat down upon a window seat, and said: "Lads, let's tie our coats together." That drew the attention of Tanacheil, Callum, the five dragoons, the the two ghillies and myself.

"More madness!" the laird muttered.

"Not madness, Andrew – sport!" the Fox told him. "These Campbells have a dark secret, and I warrant they don't know I know it." He shared a twinkling glance with each of his listeners (and it was always a wonder to see how his face could light up when he wished it to do so) before sitting back with a happy sigh.

"Long, long ago," he grinned, "Not far from here, actually, this fine clan made prisoners of eleven men of better blood. Just like us, you might say." That brought a laugh. "And they put them in a tower just like this. Well, being of better blood, and better brain, they tied their coats together and made a rope more or less to the ground. But how to cause a distraction? The better men called for a drink, and the Campbells, because even they can more or less be trusted to do things well —" that brought another laugh — "gave them a drink. They started to sing, all eleven of them, but, one by one, they climbed down the rope and took themselves off. The Campbells down below thought they were falling asleep one by one, not escaping, so they didn't do anything about it. In the end there was one voice left, then that stopped too, and the guards went to sleep themselves, thinking they still had a room full of prisoners above. But of course, they didn't — and it wasn't until the next morning that they knew it!" It was a pleasant story, pleasantly told; and it had the desired effect of calming us all and promoting a sensation that, instead of being a number of factions, we were eleven men together. Yet Simon persisted: "So we need to tie our coats together."

"It'll never really work — will it?" Callum asked.

The Fox laughed. "No, we're not going to escape. However bad it looks, lads, I need to speak to Slippery John, so here's where we're staying. It'll be funny to look as if we're escaping, just. Let's see if the Campbells have learned anything from their own stories!"

There was no denying that the sport appealed to us all; and so, under my lord's instruction, we gathered what linen there was amongst us (the ghillies bearing none save their plaid) and tied it all roughly together. Securing the make-shift rope onto the parapet door, we threw it over the side, where it appeared to fall to a level close enough to the ground that a genuine effort to use it was discussed briefly. Deciding against it for the reasons Simon had offered, we began to sing, with the Fox pointing at one of us on occasion to signal that we should stop. Presently there were but he and Tanacheil giving voice; at which point we heard a series of shouts from outside the castle, followed by the clatter of feet on the tower stair — and the door was thrown open to reveal four Campbells with expressions of concern verging on terror.

"*Ochone*, lads!" cried Simon. "Any chance of a drink?" Our laughter was louder than had been our song.

IF SLIPPERY JOHN BREADALBANE aimed to shake the Fox's confidence by conducting their interview in the tower room before all of us, it was an error of judgement; for, within moments of that man's arrival, the same four Campbells behind him, my lord was offering a good account of himself. "You had better have a good reason for dragging me from Kilchurn in this weather," said Breadalbane furiously, shaking snow from a wig which was by no means as dramatic as the one I had seen him wear in the past.

"You didn't have to come at all, my lord!" Simon replied. "I was on my way to see the Earl of Argyll, not you."

"Archie Campbell may be a fool," muttered the other, "But he knows better than to dance across a table with you, Fraser!"

"You flatter me, my lord. I wish I could offer you some hospitality... but you find me in a less than able position."

Breadalbane grunted. "Food! For all of these!" he told one of the guards. "Songs and a rope of coats – you know your history, I'll give you that."

Simon bowed. "Am I to speak to you rather than Argyll, then?"

"You'd find it better for you. These are my men and this is my country, whatever Archie has to say about it."

"A pleasure, my lord! Then, since I'm sure you don't know the contents of my letter to him —" Breadalbane raised an eyebrow — "let me explain. Murray presses Fraser hard, and Fraser has long been friends of Campbell. It's in your interest, and ours, to join forces against Murray. For the betterment of our clans, and for Scotland."

"Is this your force?" said Slippery John, waving an arm.

"Indeed not, my lord! These are my friends, who volunteered to keep me company on the journey to see Archie — or you. They've kept me in fine voice!"

The Campbell gave a narrow smile, then paused for thought. "You understand you and your father are to be attaindered for an attempt on Edinburgh Castle?"

"A sly move by Ian Cam," my lord said dismissively. "There were plans afoot, but they were his idea. When he was made Secretary of State he changed sides overnight."

"Aye, that would be right. But... forcibly marrying his sister? And

369

raping her? That's —"

"Not true!" Simon shouted with feeling. "My lord, you know of me and something of my affairs. I am guilty of many things in the pursuit of my clan's interest – and so are others in this room. But of that disgraceful accusation I am not guilty, and I demand that you accept so!"

Breadalbane stared at him for a moment; the dynamic had changed utterly and there was no doubt who now controlled proceedings. Then he nodded slowly towards my lord, whose fists were tight with fury. I believe the signal of understanding from one who could be said to bear similarities of character meant a great deal, for, in the acceptance, my lord seemed to relax to a greater degree than he had for some months. "Thank you," he said quietly; then, more strongly: "Thank you, my lord."

"What do you want of Campbell, then?"

"For now, two things," Simon said, the glint returning to his eye.

"If it's whores you want, you can ask Archie," Breadalbane told him with a frown. "That's his concern."

"No, my lord – not that. The first is: good wine. Claret, if you can."

"I hear you," nodded the Campbell with a light smile.

"The second is papers, pens, ink and sealing wax. Lots of it. And the time to use it to my best advantage."

The other nodded again, then sighed. "You're either a gift from heaven, or a curse from hell, you damned Fox," he said, with little aggression in his tone. "And I think many of us will have need of your abilities before this game is over. You have the protection of Campbell – Archie will not interfere. But!" he raised a warning hand, while looking round at us all. "You are to call yourselves Campbell from this day on. You are to be clear about your movements, and you are not to travel more than one mile from here without as many of my men as there are of you. Be honest, you Frasers, and all will be well." We all bowed; surprised, I think, at the apparent warmth we were being shown. "Now I must get back to work," he said.

"Thank you, my lord," Simon replied. "I would have enjoyed your company at Edinburgh Castle, had we been there at the same time." Breadalbane paused for a moment, laughed and shook his head. As he disappeared a ghillie appeared with a large tray of food and drink, and was waved in to deliver it. When he departed, the door was left open to us.

IT APPEARED TO ME THAT Stratherrick House was empty and locked tight against visitors; it stood cold and uninviting, an easy exercise on such a dull midwinter day, as an unhappy biting wind tore at my extremities, whistling in my ears if I turned in the wrong direction. All that was not already grey in my vision was darkening rapidly, and I realised I had no desire to knock upon the door before me. Yet so I did; and again, and again, as the night closed in quickly around me. After a time I perceived my labours to be useless, and I scanned around the large, two-floored lodging for an outhouse I might force open for shelter. Just as I moved away from the door I thought I heard a low sound from above; looking in its direction I beheld a vague shadow within a window, which, on realising it had been seen, first went to step away – then stopped, and threw the glass open. "Bolla!" cried Kirsty.

Within moments the door had been opened and I had been ushered in by a ghillie, whom I believe I recognised from some time in the past. The hallway was as cold and uninviting as was the exterior, and I still felt imposed upon by this great building. That changed in an instant when my love appeared at the head of the stairway before me. "Bolla!" she cried again, near tumbling downward in her haste to reach me. We met half-way upon the stairs, where a warm, tight embrace said more than any words — until she drew herself back, cleared my wet hair away from my face, and told me: "You stink!"

"A beggar's disguise," I told her lightly, running my hands down my Campbell clansman's clothing, unable to keep my happiness from my expression. "It will soon be off."

"If you mean what I think you mean, you'll be having a wash first," she scolded, before rewarding my return with one of her most beautiful smiles. "Of course, after that…"

"Dada!" came a voice from above, and, turning, I beheld someone I must confess I did not recognise immediately.

"Mairi!" I cried, half in question — for she had grown in no little way than when last I had seen her. "You are a big girl now!"

"I can't wait for you to be here before I grow up," my daughter said, matching Kirsty's scowl so accurately that I near exploded with delight. "I hope you've brought stories to tell me."

"I have, lass — I have," I grinned as we moved up the stairs. Within the chambers my family used as their own, the spirit of the house was much more to my liking; and as I warmed myself in front of a welcoming hearth, and supped upon a bowl of equally welcome broth, I found myself unwilling to speak, preferring instead to see my daughter at play upon the floor, and imagine my love at play upon the bed in the near future.

"Did you run into any soldiers?" Kirsty asked, pouring a cup of whisky for me.

"A fair few times," I replied. "They appeared to be around every corner. And it seems my disguise was less effective than in the past, because there were no other beggars to be seen anywhere."

She sighed. "It's not as bad as it was, *gràdh mo chrìdh*. After Simon and Tom ran away —"

"Ran away?"

"That's what everyone's saying."

"They were hunted out by Murray's men. The beacons were lit and no one came to help!"

"Let's not fight. After Simon and Tom… went away, the country was stuffed with soldiers. They really were around every corner, stopping everyone, checking everything. There was talk of a curfew and passports to leave your village of birth!"

"This from the government?" I asked, amazed.

She shook her head. "They're not government soldiers. They're Murray's private army, made up of people he kept from his regiment after it shut. Commanded by a Captain Menzies – everyone calls him 'Baldy.'" I could think no other than it was the same man who had resigned his commission in Simon's favour following the Bass Rock endeavour; but I said nothing, gesturing for her to continue. "We were told it would be instant execution for anyone found harbouring or helping Simon, any of his family – or his retinue." She said this last in a tone which suggested she was quoting from a paper.

"Execution?" I repeated. "It cannot be legal!"

372

She shrugged. "Who cares! Murray's in charge here. They can do what they like. They've got two arguments in their favour – one, Ian Cam is near enough king of Scotland; and two, Amelia speaks for Simon in his absence."

"But she is absent too," I said, failing to understand.

Kirsty shook her head. "About a week after Simon ran — went off, they caught her somewhere down the glen. She's a prisoner at the far end of Murray country."

"A prisoner!"

"I heard she was a prisoner anyway," my love said, displaying no concern and a suggestion of doubt. "They say she's refusing to testify against Simon on the charge of rape – and until she does, she's kept in a tower somewhere. It just goes to show you what happens if you get too clever."

My mind raced, but could find no purchase on an idea that made sense of the news. After a few moments I was able to offer some little entertainment in the tale of our departure from Glengarry (and the condition in which we had left Lady Amelia, which, again, drew no sympathy); and of stories Simon had told us from his letters at Auchenbreck, including Tullibardine's horror as he witnessed the Palace of Whitehall in London burning down, of a Russian emperor's decision to impose a tax on beards, and the adventures of a Scottish privateer known as Captain Kidd. Those last episodes served as stories which Mairi professed to find to her satisfaction, and she set off for her couch happily – warning me that she expected more of the same quality the following night, and, as she kissed me, warning me also that her mother was correct and I did "stink."

At last I was alone with Kirsty; and, vowing to wash before the evening became much older, I stood to go in search of new clothes. "I'm so glad you're back, Bolla," she said warmly, her expression soft. In looking upon her beauty again, I had cause to reflect that some of the lack of appreciation I had bestowed to her the last time we had been together had been entirely due to my own disposition. I could no longer comprehend how I, who loved her so much, had so recently been convinced she was a creature similar to Lady Amelia, and had acted towards her accordingly. Now, in that chamber, alone and at peace, I was once again in no doubt that she was everything I needed in my life. The thought alone rendered it close to impossible for me to ignore the urges I felt — until she said: "Let's never be apart again."

She must have seen my face fall, for her own changed, and yet she said nothing. "I must go back to him," I admitted at last, the words bitter in my dry mouth.

"No," she replied – and I was not certain whether it was a question or a statement.

"I must," I said again. "The dance is not over. But it will be soon."

"I told you last time you left me: it'll never be over," she whispered as she turned away from me to stare into the fire.

At once I realised I had attempted to lie to her, and although my intention had been honest, I knew it was wrong. "I will go back," I said slowly, "but only when I am forced. I do not think it will be before spring. In fact, I will make sure it is not before spring."

She said nothing for a moment. I watched the back of her head, admiring still the strong red hair (despite the strands of grey) dropping onto her smooth back and curving waist, and I was suddenly struck with the desperate need to put my arms round her; the which I did. "You're mine until spring, then?" she asked quietly, still facing the fire, as I laid my head on her shoulder.

"All yours, *gràdh mo chridh*. And afterwards too."

"After what?" she asked. I did not answer, for I did not want the conversation to continue in that vein. It seemed she agreed; because, after a time, she turned to me, kissed me, and said: "If you want any more you'd better go and wash."

Stratherrick, it became clear, was no bad place to live. Although not far from the road along the south-east bank of Loch Ness, it was a quiet area, surrounded by a row of townships of which none were large and all were inhabited by close relations. The result was an entirely enjoyable new year celebration which seemed to continue for nearly a seven-night, and very little engagement from Murray's dragoons, although they were sometimes observed marching up and down on errands we could only guess at, but chose not to. By the time the weather began turning warmer, with the promise of a bright season and a healthy harvest, I confess I felt myself retired from the troubles of the world and the intrigues of the Fox.

Of course, it was not to last. I was engaged one afternoon upon a fishing expedition with Mairi in a burn near the road (which I had prepared with previously-caught fish, so that she did not go home disappointed with her day's work) when a ghillie dressed in the colours of Campbell hailed me by name. Seeing no advantage in denying it — an example of how detached I felt from the world — he presented me with a small paper, sealed with quarterly strawberry flowers and crowns, the arms of Lovat. He moved on without any further comment, although I would have offered him refreshment, leaving me to consider the paper I held. I realised it was heavier than I might have expected, and by the time I tore it open I found a shilling sealed within. The paper simply read "5 – S," which bewildered me: the second character I could explain; the first I could not.

Kirsty's welcoming expression collapsed as I showed her on my return home, and all delight over Mairi's haul of fish was extinguished. We sent her to the kitchen to instruct the cook on how to prepare them for supper, while my love sadly took me upstairs and revealed, from a wardrobe, four similar notes which had not been opened. "I didn't want you to go," she said simply and quietly. I said nothing, but instead tore the letters apart, to reveal four more shillings. The first note read just "S" while the second added question-point to the initial; and the third and fourth were numbered.

"How long?" I asked quietly.

"A couple of weeks," she replied dismissively, and I knew she was not being fully truthful.

I sat down. "I have to go," I said. "I do not want to. But I have to."

"Why?" she cried, an incredible amount of passion – yet not anger – in that one word.

"He is… Simon," I said, shrugging. "From the very beginning the understanding was that I had to obey his order as long as it was reasonable."

"And what of the unreasonable ones?"

"We have said all this, *gràdh mo chrìdh*," I told her quietly. "And it makes no difference." She sat down beside me and I put my arm round her. "I do really believe it will be over soon," I told her in an attempt to offer soothing.

"What if it is?" she said in a tone which suggested she did not want to speak. "What if it's over soon — and you don't come back?"

I turned and took her face in my hands, looking into her tearful eyes; and she attempted to avoid my gaze as she had when I found her in the churchyard after having believed I would never see her again. Yet I could offer no words of comfort, and she stood and ran out of the chamber.

My preparations to depart the next morning were filled with sadness. I made a point of rising long before the rest of the house, that I would not have to perform any pretence of happiness or even calmness; for in truth I wanted to rage at the world for the unfairness of it all. I also could not bring myself to say goodbye to my daughter, for I feared her ability to know truth and say it. I did lie awake beside Kirsty for longer than I had planned, watching her life continuing as she slept, wondering how much more of it I was going to miss, and wishing dearly that somehow things could be otherwise. It was only as I drew open the great door of the house, clad once again in the clothes of a Campbell beggar, and drew in a breath of the cold air without, that I felt a touch on my shoulder, and turned to find myself held tight by my love. She would not let me speak, but simply kissed me, then pushed me backwards through the door, looking into my eyes all the time. Finally she closed it between us, her fingers taking an eternity to vanish behind into the distance, as if even one last touch would be worth everything. And it was.

BY THE TIME I APPROACHED AUCHENBRECK I believed I had managed to make some form of peace with myself. Thinking deeply during my progress across the land, I had, it seemed, come to understand some balance between the world of my family and that of the Fox; and, I think, I had imagined that if I could keep the two separate I could deal with the rigours of both. I suspect that I did not want to admit to myself that there was also a division of man and boy; the one, desirous of being a good man to Kirsty and a good father to Mairi; the other excited for the risk and adventure of dancing with the Fox. Yet if I did understand, it followed that my attempt to divide those parts of myself was partly because I wished to avoid coming to a decision over which should take command of my life; and as I felt a tugging pain in my forever-wounded leg, I knew that if I were fully honest with myself, there was only one decision I could make.

On entering the castle yard I beheld the pleasant scene of a warm evening's relaxation: a group of Frasers and Campbells sat easily around a small fire, cooking fowl upon it and sharing jokes. With some waving of arms passing between us I made immediately for the tower house, wherein I found Simon. It appeared he was concentrating heavily upon a letter; ink was spotted on his face and shirt, where he had waved the quill while considering the words to inscribe, and abandoned papers lay scattered all around his table. It was several moments before he looked up and realised he was not alone. "Bolla?" he said quietly, almost as if he was unsure of what or whom he saw. Then, after a moment: "Bolla! Devil choke me! Welcome back, my lad!" He stood, his labours forgotten, and all but stumbled in his hurry to lock arms with me. "It's grand to see you," he said, grinning in a manner I could not believe was anything but fully honest. "Let's get a drink!" He dashed to another table and poured two cups of wine. "Welcome back," he breathed again after a hearty mouthful, nodding contentedly. "Welcome back."

"I could not come before…" I said, unsure of how to state my position (and realising that I had not thought I might have to until this very moment).

"*Ochone*, you're here now," he beamed. "And I can't blame you! How are the best two girls in Clan Fraser?"

"They are well," I smiled. "They are safe."

"That's no poor story in this day and age," he told me, his eyebrows raised for emphasis. "Things are difficult." he touched my shoulder. "I wasn't sure you'd come back. I wasn't sure anyone would. Tanachiel… he's had seven, eight letters since I let him go home. Not a word."

I did not know what to say. "Perhaps he is hard-driven?" I suggested after a moment. "Murray all but owns Fraser country – I had to play the beggar's role to get in and out."

"Is it that bad?" he asked, great concern on his face, and I had cause to recall the time he had asked the same question following the black winters.

I nodded. "Tullibardine has his own dragoons patrolling all over the land. One Captain Menzies commands – they call him 'Baldy.'"

"Damned Menzies!" he said. "The same one?"

"I do not know, but I think so."

"Who else? Lap-dog toy soldier."

"It seems they have law on their side, since they have Lady Amelia," I observed — and I was not prepared for the consequence of my words.

"They *what?*" he bellowed in a voice which echoed round the chamber.

"You did not know?" I said, astonished. "They caught her soon after we left. She —"

"In the name of the devil!" Simon cried, dropping his cup and racing to a shelf where a stack of papers lay, seeming ordered in some fashion. He took a moment to select a bundle and looked through them, his eyes wide, his face pale. It took him several attempts to focus on what he was trying to read, I suspect, such was the emotion of his response to my news. Finally he discarded the notes, in a less organised fashion than he had lifted them. "Why didn't I know that?" he said quietly, staring directly at me – and although I am sure he was not truly looking for an answer, I offered that I could venture no suggestion. He returned to his table and sat once more, his hand over his mouth, unwittingly rubbing more ink onto his face. Unbidden, I took him his cup and the flask of wine; for I knew what had to happen next. As I moved to leave he said quietly: "Sorry, my lad — I've got to think. I've got to think. But... thank you for coming back. It means a lot."

It seemed that the sun was in no hurry to stop warming the evening, although the castle's curtain wall made an early dusk within, and the ghillies were in the act of building up their fire when I stepped out at the bottom of the tower house. I realised I was not in the spirit to join them; also, as I was also not aware of what was known and what was not known about Simon's current position, I could not become involved in any open conversation, which would be bound to happen as Fraser clansmen longed for news about the homes they had not seen in several moons. Instead I took myself through the open gate, planning to sit in the sun and consider my situation; but I was distracted by the sound of singing further along the outer wall; and, looking over, it was impossible

378

not to identify the giant frame of Ben Callum Fraser, seated beside a tall but much more slender character. The big man saw me at the same moment and waved me over. "Bolla!" he cried as I approached, and I could tell by his tone of voice he was something the worst for wear through drink. "How are you?"

"I am well," I smiled.

"Bolla," he repeated, pointing at me, although he could barely focus upon me with his eyes, "This is Bolla." I realised he was speaking to his companion. "And this is Sir James Campbell, master of the castle."

I nodded towards the other; yet I could not match the description with the man, for he who I beheld was barely as old as had I been when I first met Simon. "Jamie Campbell," that one bowed, equally in his cups as was Ben Callum. "Not quite a 'sir' yet, but not long. And not quite the master yet, but not long either." He was a fair-looking person with unkempt dark blond hair and a face which looked serious and withdrawn, until he grinned, the which he did. "You're the bowl of meat man, aren't you?" I nodded. "Magnificent mischief!" he replied; and I understood him to be yet another one who had come under the influence of the Fox.

"It's not magnificent," slurred Ben Callum. "It's not magnificent — it's *cac*. It's all *cac*. And I was telling you about your death!" With gratitude I understood he was talking to the Campbell, and that there was little malice in his tone.

"Callum has been introduced to a drink we have here," said James by way of explanation. "It's a heavy thing, not for everyone. We call it *sealgaire-mhor*. Here." He offered me a flask, warning me to simply sip at its contents; and, doing so, I quickly understood the danger I was in. "Heavy, is it not?" he asked, and I had to admit he was correct.

"Grand," Ben Callum said with difficulty. "Fuel for fighting. Argument juice. Singing water!" At that he broke into an out-of-tune song, the which, I slowly understood, was the tale of a battle long ago where the Clan Campbell were roundly defeated:

When it came to the fighting, everyone knows
The Campbells got flattened heads from sword blows...

"Shut up," James said, with the air of one who had being saying so for some time.

There was manure aplenty on that old field
But it wasn't dung, it was Campbell blood congealed...

"Shut up."

They shat themselves silly, they ran for their lives
They threw up their breakfast and cried for their wives...

"Shut up."

I left them to their reverie, wondering if, at last, I had chosen wrongly in answering Simon's call.

SOME DAYS AFTER MY RETURN I felt much less disconnected from proceedings; yet also I felt in some way different from how I had as I approached Achenbreck. I was now sure that, somehow or other, I had to change my life – for if I did not it would constantly be changed for me, in the interests of others; and the truth was that I had more important interests of my own. But if I believed I had surmised the young Campbell correctly I was proved wrong very quickly, and much more became apparent about his character the first time he, Simon, Ben Callum and I sat together to drink in the Fox's chamber. "We owe a lot to Sir Jamie," my lord told me, waving his cup towards that man in salute. "Not only has he extended hospitality far beyond whatever Slippery John Breadalbane had in mind —" they exchanged glances, which I could only surmise referred to womenfolk — "he played a big role in getting John out of Glasgow."

"John is escaped?" I cried, delighted to hear something uplifting regarding Fraser's endeavours.

Simon nodded. "That he is, and we have these two to thank for it."

"I just broke some heads," Ben Callum grinned happily. "Sir Jamie did the thinking."

"Nothing that hasn't been done before," said the Campbell. "Just a case of applying the right ideas."

"Aye, but very few people can think like that," Simon said with a pointed finger. "Don't do yourself down. It was seriously clever."

"And we'd never have got away from the blue men without him," the big man told me with a strange expression.

"The blue men?" I had to ask.

The others in the room shared doubtful looks. "The less said the better," Simon muttered. "Let's just say, keep out of Kilmartin Glen. Everyone else does — and now we know why." It seemed they were in agreement, for there came a pause before my lord changed the subject. "I'm glad you're back, Bolla," he said yet again. "When I first sent for you I thought we were going to go into action then. It turned out I was wrong. But if what you tell me about Amelia is true, I think we're not long for this castle."

"I would not lie," I said, surprised.

"I didn't mean that, my lad," he grinned. "It's just… it's difficult to believe that something that big would happen, and no one would tell me. I have contacts checking on the details. I wonder how they caught her? There's no way Alisdair Dubh would have left her at Achnacarry. It's too close to Invergarry. Unless…" he broke off in thought, something he had been doing with great frequency in recent days.

"What of Glengarry himself?" I had to ask.

"Nothing's been heard of him for some time," he mused. "He's not sending letters. I don't even think he's been getting letters. Perhaps he's – what did you say about Tanacheil, 'hard-driven'? It must be that. Evil times, Bolla." His tone changed. "Murray must be stopped."

"I'll drink to that," Sir Jamie said loudly.

"You'll do more than that," my lord replied. "You'll help — I hope?"

"I will," said the young man. "And I'm sure more of Campbell will too. We have some experience in this kind of thing. These lands are only back in my family's hands a few years, after certain legal action following the Monmouth business."

"Aye," Simon said shortly, deliberately leaving his meaning open for interpretation.

"Nothing is irreversible, is my point," Sir Jamie continued. "Clan Campbell has always known this is a long game. Longer even than the dispute between Argyll and Breadalbane. One of those two will win, one will lose – but the clan will win no matter what."

"Simon will die again, but Fraser will live," my lord said.

"Exactly," said the other after a pause. "It doesn't matter where, and it doesn't matter when."

"Here and now," the Fox stated strongly.

Yet Campbell shook his head. "That's not always for us to decide. I have this castle back, but I don't call that a victory. It could be taken off me again."

"You'll build it up?" my lord said.

"I'll sell it," Sir Jamie replied. "Just as soon as my father is gone and the title is mine."

"That's cold!" I forbore even to look the Fox in the eye.

"Is it? The money is more use than a broken castle. With the cash free to use wherever I want… well, I can use it wherever I want."

"I thought Campbell wanted the whole of Scotland."

The other shrugged. "How big is Scotland?"

"Big enough."

"For some. My family have titles and lands in Nova Scotia. Do you know that place is bigger than Scotland, England and France all together? Now there's a place to dance."

"But it's not Scotland," Simon objected. "It's not…"

"Not Campbell country? It could be. When we dance here we dance among old masters who rule the floor and won't leave it without a fight. We dance in the corners, in the dark. How much more fun would it be to dance on a bigger floor than they've ever dreamed of — and own it at the same time?"

"I dance for Fraser," my lord said after a pause; but there was uncertainly in his voice.

"Fraser, the clan nearly overtaken by Murray? Or Fraser the clan who could own as much of Nova Scotia as Campbell – maybe more? You're a good man, Simon. You've been dressing like Campbell for a few months now… perhaps you should start thinking like Campbell."

"*Cac!*" cried Ben Callum. "What was that old paper? 'We fight not for glory or wealth or honour, but only and alone we fight for freedom!'"

"You just like to fight," Sir Jamie said, pointing at the big man with his cup.

We all fell silent for some time, until Simon muttered: "*Fas est et ab hoste doceri*," then opened a new flask of wine.

IF IT WAS NOT THE HAPPIEST TIME OF MY LIFE, due to my distance from my family, it was certainly the easiest; yet it all came to a stark and bitter end when Jamie Fraser arrived at Auchenbreck from the north, alone save for a Campbell guide. For the most part we were seated without the castle, silently enjoying the sunshine of an early summer afternoon, the only sound that of Simon's pen scraping upon papers on his portable desk. The young sergeant moved with the unseemly haste he had shown in the days I had first known him, that strange blank expression betraying more about him than the complete absence of thought which sometimes played across his face. We all watched his progress towards my lord; fearing we knew what was to be said to him.

"Jamie Fraser!" Simon cried, looking up at last – and, immediately, his face fell.

"Greetings, MacShimi," Jamie replied starkly; and all was told.

My lord dropped his pen. As he stood up the desk collapsed before him, papers and ink spewed across the grass. "Father," he said quietly.

"He died," Jamie said in a flat tone. "Five days ago. He was old and not well. He told me to give you these." I had not noticed the second sword he carried until he took it from his side and it caught the sunlight in a dull flash of ancient metal; yet when he offered Simon a faded white wooden wand, I recognised it as the staff of authority his father had carried. Simon stared at the wand. I had never seen so much emotion in his countenance; and although I could guess the breadth of thoughts which ran through his mind, I could not estimate what the moment truly meant to him. He had achieved that position for which he had strived since the day I met him. He had overcome seemingly unsurmountable foes in the form of enemies and events. He had also, there could be no doubt, acted darkly in the pursuit of his interests – and I could not help but wonder about those powders. Watching the

Fox tremble, seeing him fighting for control of himself, was fascinating; and yet terrifying. I was minded of the two sides of young Jamie — and I could not know which side of Simon might win.

Callum stepped forward, his arm held out. "MacShimi," he said loudly, but my lord offered no response. "MacShimi!" he cried, with an almost military tone. At last Simon met the other's gaze; and, through watered eyes, held up the wand, held out his own arm and grasped Callum's. "MacShimi!" the big man bellowed with the full force of his huge frame. "MacShimi!"

"MacShimi!" we all cried – even the Campbells. "MacShimi!"

Simon looked around at us all, the inner conflict seemingly resolved. I beheld upon him that bearing of command he had always so easily held; and yet, already, something about it was new – reinforced. He cast off his own sword and replaced it with Lord Tom's.

"It is time to act," he said.

Despite Simon's words we did not depart with any haste. Instead there appeared to be something of deliberate leisure surrounding his movements, as if he were forcing upon us a mood of stately measure. Within his chamber I beheld him draw out a number of letters, seeming by the colouring of the papers and the roughness of the seal to have been written some time previously. Perhaps he had prepared them for the instance which had now taken place, yet now that it had, he felt differently about it; for all but two of those documents were discarded into the fire. I know nothing about those which survived save that one was sent east, and one, west. "Not a moment too soon, Bolla," he grinned as he lifted a small bag of coin from the far-carried money chest, showing me that it was the last of its contents. Despite my suspicions I could see no reason for the which being anything other than coincidence.

Strangely it was the other Jamie, the Campbell, who sought to persuade my lord against action. "Whatever kept you here until now," said he, "Must count for double now you're chief. You need to remain in safety."

"No," was the reply. "You know what's being going on – Fraser country under harassment day in, day out. Homes burned! Weapons confiscated! Our people arrested on suspicion of aiding and abetting us! No, Sir Jamie – what's kept us here was that Murray would find it difficult to move against Campbell and MacLeod together. Now Father is gone, he knows which enemy to work on. And when Slippery John realises that, he'll soon be seeing what can be made of it."

"Campbell won't deal with Murray!" the young man insisted.

Yet Simon insisted: "Breadalbane and Argyll both need one good move to take the entire clan from the other. I'll be damned if Fraser is the bait in that trap, sitting like an idiot in a Campbell castle — however welcoming our host has been."

"You haven't been confirmed as MacShimi," said Sir Jamie.

Simon laughed. "Aye, there's the meeting and the naming and the presenting. But who else could be chief? Fraser of Saltoun? Bolla? Tanachiel?" He laughed more loudly at this last. "He's thought about it — don't tell me he hasn't!" The Campbell considered the meaning of those words as my lord continued: "Ben Callum, will the clan follow anyone else?"

"Not if they want to keep their teeth," the big man growled, to laughter.

"So we're going back," Simon said, in a tone which suggested there was to be no more discussion. "And we're not slipping back either."

Yet still there appeared to be no rush, for he refused the offer of boats as Sir Jamie escorted us through his country. That one left us on the second night out – after a private conversation with the new MacShimi, and an emotional one with Ben Callum – whereupon we settled on the shore of Loch Leven in Glen Coe, within sight of the remains of MacIain's home; although we did not trouble the new MacDonald chief and their clan, whose efforts to heal the wounds of the evil that had befallen them would require years of labour.

As we sat around a fire the Fox told us a story of the great Fingal, who had a cave named after him nearby, and reminded us of that noteworthy saying: "Attempt and Did-not were the worst of Fingal's hounds." As we reflected upon that, sure that the task which was soon to befall us would match that of the MacIain, he told Jamie to recount the last days of Lord Tom's life. The young man's strange expression seemed sometimes to show some feeling as he spoke, telling of how the old man had become increasingly sick, losing his hair, his jowls hanging from his skull, empty skin hanging from his arms; yet had never let up upon Ruairidh Og, chief of MacLeod, in the pursuit of active support for Fraser. Tiring of his words, Ruairidh had at last removed Tom from Dunvegan castle and sent him to the smaller isle of Raasay. In that location he was no longer completely protected by MacLeod, for there was country belonging to both MacDonald and MacKinnon (and, of course, sea) separating them. Indeed, the three clans were often at war, and although they appeared not to be so at that time, all knew the situation could change at any moment. Into such concern came news from Inverness that a shipload of dragoons were thought to be approaching Skye, leading Lord Tom to decided upon a return to Dunvegan, there to renew his argument with Ruairidh, and with renewed evidence for his words. In case his plan did not succeed the old chief had written to Alastair Dubh of Glengarry, believing he might be safer with MacDonell if MacLeod continued to offer so little support. Yet the plan came to nothing – for, in storm-driven wind and rain, Lord Tom fell ill for the final time; and, on reaching the castle of his wife's clan, took to his couch, and never rose again. The flames flickered as Jamie fell silent, and we sat with the sounds of the darkling world around us, until one of the ghillies began playing a lament on his hornpipe. Simon did not speak for the rest of the night, but simply drank whisky in silence, and made certain that his face was hidden from the fire, so that none could tell what he felt.

Our progress around Fort William was by needs cautious, but passed without note; and finally, within sight of our own country, we took to the water and sailed up Loch Lochy in two boats. We entered Loch Ness on the three hundred and seventieth anniversary, said Simon, of the Bruce's death; and landed near Stratherrick, sending a ghillie ahead to tell of our arrival. By the time we approached the village my lord was master of all, hailing old friends, reminding them of their family histories, asking after their current affairs and dispensing farthings. The sun warmed our heads as the Fox warmed our hearts – and although he started out with a following of just more than double the number with which he had arrived, he was soon surrounded by dozens of clansmen, hailing him as the MacShimi; regardless of whether the traditional process of confirming him had been completed.

We stopped in the township, whereupon Simon, as had in the past, leapt up on to a barrel to act as a platform, and began to speak. "Fraser!" he cried. "It's been a dark couple of years, but you see I brought the sunshine with me – MacShimi is here!" If there was any uncertainty among those who heard his words, it was well hidden. "And MacShimi has one thing on his mind: the putting down of Murray!" That gathered more vocal support. "I know it's been difficult, especially for those of you on the border of our country with that bedevilled clan. But it's all going to change. Are you ready to fight?" None bellowed louder than Ben Callum, although many tried. "Then a fight is what we'll have! Not only that, but I've spoken to Archie Campbell of Argyll himself, and he's off to London to tell the king about Murray's lies. Once that's settled, any dragoons you see in our country will be trespassing. Not only will it be legal to kill them – there'll be a reward!" The noise continued to bring people from all directions, and in the background I noticed some I recognised: lairds, who had been named in the past as those who sided against Simon. Yet they, too, were cheering, despite their late arrival; and I was assured of a sudden that, in their eyes, all previous doubts had expired, and he was truly MacShimi, the eighteenth to hold the title. As he made his way through the crowd, grasping arms and sharing words of mischief, he paused not a moment to embrace those who had previously spoken against him, but bade them welcome – and bade them drink. Yet when some made to light a fire, trim an oak branch and prepare a goat for death, Simon told them to forbear. "We're not raising the clan this very moment," he said, to some disappointment. "I have to see everyone first... and we have a few friends to bring back to us. Just a few days, that's all, then we'll be shouting 'A Mhòr-fhaiche' into the face of Murray!"

One young clansman approached, holding up a sword, blade down, which was in desperately need of repair. "I'll fight any moment you say, MacShimi!" the slender character said, his clear blue eyes flashing under a tousle of long blonde hair. "Just give the word!"

Simon looked at him. "Roabie Fraser, eh? Son of Roabie who died at Killiecrankie? He was a good man. So was your grandad, Old Archie, who was out fighting with my dad and Montrose."

The young man beamed; although I saw Jamie offer a glance which suggested less pleasure. "Let me come with you now," Roabie pleaded. "I'll carry the flame back here when you raise the clan."

Simon grinned. "I like that idea. Aye, come along with me – we'll be in Castle Dounie by tomorrow night."

My thoughts had all day been turning towards Kirsty and Mairi, so near to me; yet my lord did not have to tell me that I had to be present for the current action, for there was no other who had traversed so many of the previous steps with him. We did not stop at Stratherrick, but moved north, although slowly, as he repeated his performance upon barrel after barrel, and our company began to expand as a number of men asked the same of their new chief as had Roabie. We rested for the night by a ford of the River Ness, where a great fire was lit and the spirit among us was of a celebration. He who was the subject of such revelry found his time filled with playing the role of chief — yet he found a moment to move towards my place under a tree, and offer me a cup of wine. "Well..." he said, trailing off.

"Indeed," I replied. In truth I wished I had more words, and I knew that was what he desired from me; yet my head was reeling with the knowledge that, so suddenly, he had achieved much of what he had always wanted, while my heart reminded me what he had done (and what I suspected he had done) to get it. "You did it," I finally added, offering the best smile I could.

He laughed loudly but stopped suddenly, a flash of a different emotion on his face. Then he laughed again, more quietly. "Devil choke me me, Bolla. We did it. All of us. But especially you. I couldn't have – – it's been... I mean, there's so much more to do. More shillings to earn!" he touched my shoulder. "But when I think back to that night in Aberdeen when you came running in, a wee stick with terrified eyes... And what you've become since..."

To hear so many years of turmoil summarised in so few words appeared to emphasise the fantastical nature of those times. I smiled more honestly and said: "Magnificent mischief, Simon." Then I added: "MacShimi!" holding up the cup and taking a drink.

He took it and drank also, his eyes never leaving my face, then returned it to me. "I prefer that," he said, grinning.

We were disturbed by the approach of a handful of men, raising their voices in apparent disagreement with others who had attempted to hold them back. We both turned to behold four figures, who halted suddenly as they set eyes on Simon. Only one continued his advance, slowly and with doubt in every move. Suddenly the Fox grinned. "Andrew!"

"MacShimi," said Tanachiel quietly, offering a salute. "I am sorry! I have been —"

"Hard-driven!" my lord said loudly, offering me a glance. "I understand. You're here now, eh?"

"I am," the laird replied, his head bowed.

"Old times, eh?" the Fox laughed, putting his arms around us both.

I HAD TAKEN IT INTO MY MIND that Kirsty would hear of our proximity and meet us on the way to Dounie; Yet it was not to be; for, soon after we had left the second township on our route the following morning, with our company, I was told, numbering a little over fifty, Tanachiel, who had recovered most of his usual poise and marched close to Simon, pointed ahead of us on the road, where we beheld a figure the size of Ben Callum moving quickly towards us. "Glengarry!" he said. "It must be!"

Simon offered nothing in response, but signalled for us to stop; and presently Glengarry – for it was indeed he – ran up to us, and, without hesitation, held out his arm. "MacShimi!" that man said through heavy breaths, to which my lord grasped his salute.

"Alisdair Dubh!" he grinned slowly. "It's good to see you!"

"I heard about Tom. I am sorry. A good man, and a grand fighter."

"That he was," Simon replied. "You're alone?"

Glengarry looked around him. "I came quickly, once I heard you were back. I hoped to meet you on the road at Invergarry."

"I'd be mad to go there," said my lord. "We came by boat."

"A good move," nodded the MacDonell. "That *gorach* Hill has patrols out everywhere. All the time. God be praised you've kept out of their way. I was lucky to get out of Glen Garry myself."

"A minor miracle," the Fox agreed. "You'll join us? It's going to be a big day!" We began moving forward again — but, some time later, on arriving at a crossroad, where one route headed south towards Castle

Dounie, I believe we were all surprised when Simon led us not that way, but to the west instead.

"What's this?" Tanacheil demanded. "You're not going on through the country, are you? The clan will come to us now."

"Just one more quick visit," said the Fox. "It won't take long. Don't start, Andrew," he continued with a warning tone, staring at the other, who, after a moment, decided to say no more; although his expression continued to say much. Yet so soon as it became clear that we were not heading south, a cry from one of our company alerted us to a movement from the woodland we would have entered in that direction — from which a number of dragoons were now emerging. "The hunt is on!" cried Simon, apparently having expected such an event. "Run, boys – run like the devil!" Even as an explosion of near-hopeless long shots rang out from behind us, we set off along the road at not far off the full pace of a Highland charge. Several men bellowed the clan slogan as we went, which served to focus those who had not yet surmised the danger of our situation.

"MacShimi!" called Ben Callum, less challenged than the rest of us. "The hidden ford!"

"Aye!" Simon retorted. The big man took the lead, finding time to shout that we must follow him carefully and match his footing. I dared to look back and observed that, while the soldiers kept after us, they were not as ready for running as were we; but who could tell what chance there was of more troops waiting ahead? It became clear that Ben Callum had considered just that possibility, and after a deal of distance he began leading us through the flats at the southern end of the firth of the River Beauly, which opened up to the size of the sea to our right. On either side of us deep bogs lay waiting to trap the unwary — but there was obviously a way through, known only to certain members of the clan: hence, the hidden ford. Soon enough we reached an easy crossing of the river, and splashed to the other side; where we stopped to gather ourselves, looking back to where we had come from.

"They're coming through!" Ben Callum cried – and it was true: the figures of dragoons began appearing through the brushland, moving slowly yet confidently towards the ford; and it appeared there were perhaps five or six of them for every one of us. "Only a Fraser would know how," he spat.

Simon surveyed his company. With the exception of himself, Tanacheil, Callum, Glengarry, Jamie and me, they were all young men with no experience of a real fight; for, I now realised, they had been selected for their keenness to run. That had held us in good stead, of course; yet if events transpired in the manner which appeared obvious, it would offer the enemy nothing more than faster than usual targets; and with six shots at each, such a game would not last long. "Roabie!" my lord said, touching his arm. "I need you to run. South, to Balblair. Tell them —"

"No, MacShimi! Let me fight!" the boy said, his face locked with stern determination.

Simon looked again at him, and then round, and his glance settled on a younger boy who carried no weapon and looked fit to burst into tears. "Colin," said the Fox gently. "Can you run?"

The other tried not to let his sobs stop his response. "Very fast, MacShimi," he nodded.

Simon grinned at him. "Then you can be my best friend now. Get on the road over there, run to Balblair — you know where it is? That's right, over there — and tell everyone that Fraser is under attack. Tell them to come quickly, and send for more help. Can you do that? Good lad!" He found time to hand a farthing over, touching the boy's shoulder. "Friend of MacShimi. Off you go!" He did not follow his progress as he leapt away, but pointed north, and looked around at us all. "Another wee run, lads, but not far. Then we'll see what we see!" We took off again, just as the first dragoons entered the river behind us, and moved as quickly as we could across land which slipped smoothly downward to the firth upon our right. We kept a strong pace, the cries of "*A Mhòr-fhaiche!*" keeping us angry. Then Simon stumbled, but waved for no one to stop, although I did; and even though we were delayed for just a moment, it left us near the back of our company.

"Stop!" he called almost without sound a little time afterwards. "Stop!" I repeated the call and so did those around us as they became aware of it. Yet the confused message served only to separate those who kept moving from those who did not. Eventually Ben Callum, still at the fore, realised we were no longer with him and called a halt at the bottom of a low hill they had traversed, paces away from the waterfront of the firth. We remained at the summit, between a number of stones the ancients had left standing, from where Simon waved for them to come back up; but at that moment gunfire began to emanate from behind us, the sound of shot landing uncomfortably close. That forced him to tell us to move downhill.

Moments later we were regrouped; yet we were stood on a midly sloping ground, the water before us, and the hill behind us, the last place demanding our attention as it began to fill with dragoons taking firing positions against us. "Too far!" Simon said, to no one in particular.

"I didn't know!" Ben Callum replied. "I didn't know you'd stopped!"

My lord dismissed his words with a wave. "Not your fault. Haven't been here in years. Forgot." No one needed to state the obvious: that in having overshot the hill, we had lost the only position to offer an advantage against a greater number of better-armed enemies.

"Simon Fraser!" cried a voice from above. "Surrender in the name of the king!" The Fox threw his finger in the air by way of response, causing unexpected laughter among us. "I'm coming down!" the soldier shouted, and, accompanied by two others, began to approach.

"Bolla! Jamie!" Simon said urgently, pushing us forward before there was time for anyone to argue. He had us run up the hill so that we were closer to the dragoons than they were to us — and as their commander came into full view I beheld that he was known to me. "Captain Menzies!" Simon grinned. "Well, devil choke me!"

"Captain Fraser," said Menzies, his expression showing doubt.

"I prefer MacShimi," my lord said easily. "Has it been a hard time being in a private army? I ask because you appear to have lost what remained of your hair."

The other bristled. "I am a soldier of the king — and a better one than you ever were," he said angrily.

"You," Simon replied casually, "are in the pay of the Earl of Atholl since his regiment was disbanded. How did it feel to sell your honour the way you sold me your commission?"

"Honour!" spat the other. "I was right about you, Fraser."

"Maybe."

"You must surrender!"

"I'll surrender to the king's men, but not you."

"You... *must* surrender!"

Simon sighed. "What if I don't?"

Menzies unhappily replied: "Then you will die."

"Not today, captain. I've made other plans. Have you met Sergeant Jamie Fraser?" Confused, the other's natural sense of order led him to nod politely towards him as Simon presented him. "He's still learning, you understand. Jamie, who has command of the field?"

"Them," said that one flatly, his hand moving towards his pistol, even though hundreds of guns were ranged upon us.

"And if we can't outgun them, and we can't outrun them, what do we do?"

Jamie paused. "Outthink them?"

"Good lad — not such a stupid wee *gorach* any more, eh?" Simon raised his voice. "This land," he shouted, so that the dragoons could hear him, "Is cursed by the ancients. Anyone who fights the proper owners is doomed to die in such a damned mess that three generations of crows will feed upon your blood – while you still live to endure it!"

"That will do!" Menzies cried; but it appeared to have had some success, judging by the number of musket barrels which dropped, and the heads which turned to one another.

"I am the rightful owner – and so is the king!" Simon went on. "But Murray is not!"

"Fraser!" barked Menzies. "Enough! I thought I'd dealt with the last of your games — well, I will today. You have ten minutes to surrender." He turned and marched away.

At the foot of the hill, Ben Callum had managed to arrange our men into something akin to battle order, although the scarcity of weapons and poor position rendered his efforts almost useless. Simon touched his shoulder by way of thanks, only to have his arm pulled by Tanacheil. "Well? How do we get out of this?"

"That is not the question," my lord replied with a strange tone. "How did we get *into* this?"

"What do you mean?" the laird demanded.

"For the last two years and more, someone has been betraying Fraser to Murray. Almost every step of the way, some *gorach* has been reporting

393

my every move to Ian Cam and his nest of chancing animals. And *that's* how we got into this. Someone's been spying on me — and I've worked out who it is."

"Name him, and I'll finish him," Ben Callum snarled.

Without warning a gun went off at close quarters and Tanacheil fell to the ground. We all looked round to where Jamie stood, the smoke clearing from around him, just as it had in the woodlands on the day he had killed Saltoun's footman. Yet his expression was different; not blank and distant. "He drew first!" he told Simon. Yet even as he spoke a second shot rang out, throwing the young sergeant down just paces from Tanacheil, who had fired from where he lay.

"A shroud upon me – no!" Simon cried, looking at both men, of which, it was clear, Jamie was worse wounded. The Fox crouched down over him. "You stupid wee *gorach*! Tanacheil's not the spy!"

The other looked astonished through his evident pain, then fixed my lord with the only honest grin I ever saw on his face. "Magnificent… mischief!" he spluttered as his life ebbed away.

By that point I was trying to attend to Tanacheil, who was also not long for the world. "Andrew," Simon said quietly as he joined me, "I'm so sorry… I never doubted your loyalty…"

"Glengarry…" the laird whispered for his last word.

We all turned to Alasdair Dubh, and it was simple to follow what he had meant; for he was the only other to have drawn a pistol, only now his hands were grasped behind his back in Ben Callum's own. Jamie may have aimed for Tanacheil — but Tanacheil had been aiming for Glengarry.

"He was going to kill you," Ben Callum told Simon. "Just before you named the spy."

"Which means I don't really need to now," the Fox said. "Alasdair Dubh, you have brought shame on the name of MacDonell."

"Lies!" the other growled.

"My wife was surrendered to Murray days after I left her in your care," Simon said in a calm yet threatening tone. "And even though you betrayed Fraser, she would not — and she's still being kept God knows where because she won't testify against me. Do you know why, Alasdair? It's because I never brought dishonour on anyone. Shame on the name of MacDonell!"

"No!" said Glengarry; but there was panic in his voice.

"You never surrendered Invergarry Castle, though. It's still yours, providing you share it with Colonel Hill and his men. The ancestral home of MacDonell, built with stones passed hand-to-hand by your clan, down from Ben Tee — sold to the friends of Clan Murray! For shame, Alasdair Dubh!" I do not think any of us had heard such poison words. For even though they were spoken relatively softly, their meaning slashed at the very heart of a clan's way of life. Glengarry was rendered speechless, half through anger, half through fear; and yet, the expression which began to take his face was exactly that which Simon had called down upon him. "Every letter I sent you went straight to Murray. And I know, because I've seen Murray's letters after them. And when my dad asked you for help, you betrayed him too. He warned me you had discovered where I was – although you tried to stop that letter too. Shame on MacDonell!" The other simply shook his head. "And at the last... at the last, Alisdair Dubh, you didn't even have the decency to shoot me dead, in case the end of me meant the end of Murray's money!"

"You devil-damned fox!" Glengarry cried, struggling against Ben Callum's grasp. "You told me to befriend Murray! And you were right! MacDonell's future is with Murray. Fraser's future is with Murray!"

"No," my lord said quietly, but with great strength. "Fraser's future is with me."

"Surrender or be killed!" cried Menzies from above.

"Ben Callum," Simon said with a nod.

The big man leaned into Glengarry's ear from behind, still clasping the other's hands in his. "My brother once had a saying," he growled. "He didn't like people fighting on paper. He said they should have their hands broken." With that there came a sickening sound as the great Fraser crushed MacDonell's knuckles, resulting in an agonising cry of pain from the shamed one. Then Callum knocked him on the side of the head with one giant fist, and he fell to the ground in a deep sleep.

"My lads, take your places," said Simon.

"What's the plan, MacShimi?" the giant asked as we lined up in the form of a Highland charge, watching as the dragoons followed Menzies down the hill towards us.

"What else?" Simon asked. "*A Mhòr-fhaiche!*" He did not give anyone time to question him, which was for the best, since the notion of charging uphill seemed to be madness itself. We broke into our slogan at the top of our voices, the anger of generations rising in us, those who had pistols ready to fire them and drop them, those who had blades ready to swing them, and all of us ready to die for our clan.

Just then the noise of hell itself came from above us — and three great cannonballs threw themselves over our heads and smashed the dragoons to pieces. "What the hell kept you, Dandy Dapperman?" Simon cried with a scream of delight, turning and waving to where the *Janet* sailed into view across the firth. The reply was more cannonshot, which forced us to the ground for our own safety. One more round came from the ship, before Captain Ackermann, waving from the deck, acknowledged Simon's signal to cease fire.

Above us, Menzies' company lay in ruins. Dozens had been killed or injured, the remainder cowered behind the ancient stones for cover, even though each would become a weapon if struck by a ball and broken to shards; and in the midst of it all, Menzies stood as if he were still in command of the situation, his bearing seeming to suggest the last few moments had simply not taken place.

"Withdraw!" Simon bellowed — but not to us, to them; and we all repeated it. They began to do just that, while Menzies, completely bewildered, stood to attention amid a cloud of dust and blood-soaked stone and grass. It took for MacShimi to offer a neat military salute before the other returned the gesture and marched away as if he had been dismissed from parade. "Baldy *gorach*," my lord laughed, waving us with his arms towards the shore, where a cutter was preparing to land, Dapperman himself at the bow. "What kept you, you sad excuse for a sailor?" my lord demanded once again. "I had to talk *cac* for ages, waiting for you take your time up the firth."

"All hail to the MacShimi, eighteenth of the Clan Fraser," said the Dutchman. "And, I think, the first to order an uphill charge."

Simon gave him a look which was something between a grin and a grimace, then turned to the south to observe Menzies' troops heading directly towards the hills over Loch Ness, the better to escape Fraser country as fast as possible. Beckoning Ben Callum to join us – although that one looked as if he would prefer to wait over the unmoving body of Glengarry, the better to knock him down again if he should try to stand up – my lord said: "Time to earn your shilling, Bolla."

"I am not coming with you," I told him.

He looked at me in surprise, his head turned slightly sideways but both eyes fully focused on me. "I wasn't going to ask you to. That's why I need you to do this one last thing."

"Very well," I nodded.

"After you told me what had happened to Amelia, it took me a while to work out how it had happened. In the end I realised he was the problem." he threw his head dismissively towards Glengarry. "Some people thought it was Tanacheil. Some thought it was wee Jamie. Some even thought you had betrayed me, Bolla — you!" I could say nothing, as it suddenly became clear to me how complex was the web of politics and intrigue upon which he perched; and that there were indeed instances in which I had risked the fate of the clan through my action or inaction, regardless of the quality of my intent. At that moment, I decided the dance was over for me.

"You'll soon receive a stack of letters at Stratherrick — I take it that's where you're going? Good," my lord continued, seeming not to have observed the thoughts which had just drawn themselves across my face. "I hope you'll never have to use them, but I want you to make copies and prepare for them to be sent to the people on the list that comes with them." He drew a document from his jacket. "I don't think they'll be needed, because I'm going to make him sign this. Read it – go on, I know you can." If I had been surprised by the harsh way he had spoken to the MacDonell, I was equally surprised by the wording of the oath, for such it was. Indeed, it was entitled "A Horrible Oath," and the description was accurate, for the signatory recounted all claims in Jesus Christ and any hope of Heaven, and devoted himself instead to the devil and all the torments of Hell, if he ever returned to the territories of Fraser, or, by action or lack of action, allowed Clan Fraser to befall the smallest mischief; all this evil to be visited upon his descendants in perpetuity were the clauses to be invoked.

"*Ochone,*" I breathed, considering that even I could not dare sign it.

"Strong words," Simon grinned, misunderstanding my outburst. "Once he signs it — once his hands are healed — I'm going to let him go. You never know, I may need him one day." He continued: "I have another copy. I want you and Ben Callum to get a squad together and go after Menzies, and make him sign it too. He won't be on safe ground for a couple of days, so you should catch him easily. In fact, get the whole lot of his dragoons to sign it."

I was doubtful that I could achieve such a result, and I was sure I did not want to try; yet I told Simon I would do all I could. "Good lad, as ever," he said, touching my shoulder. "I'm going to — actually, it's probably better if you don't know where I'm going. But I'll be back. Fraser's future is with me, and there's work to be done to secure it. Remember, I've still got the plan – and it's still grand. You can't stop it even if you know it. It's time I persuaded certain people of that; and I will. God knows how long it'll take… but you'll hear from me.

"One more thing," he said. "Stay away from Murray. Any of them. All of them."

"What of Lady Amelia?" I asked carefully.

"Stay away from Murray," he repeated, watching me equally carefully. "Until I come back." He put his hands on my shoulders and looked me up and down. "Until then," he said, "Go and enjoy your happy wee life with your wife and daughter. *Domus et placens uxor. Et filiola* – no matter what she thinks of me!" He reached into his jacket and brought out the last bag of coin from the chest we had carried to Auchenbreck. "It's a lot more than a shilling, God knows," he sighed, staring at it. "But you've earned it." He pushed it into my own jacket, then turned me towards where Dapperman stood, studying the bodies of Jamie and Tanacheil. "What do you make of that?" he asked the sailor.

That one sighed. "It's obvious what happened," he said as if he were bored. "A duel over cowardice. He —" he pointed towards the sergeant — "wanted to run away, while he —" directed to the laird — "was the type who never raised a word against you, and became angry at the suggestion of refusal."

"*Ochone*," Simon said slowly, shaking his head. "How do you do it?"

"I study the science of the brain. If you focus through your right eye you consider the facts; whereas, if you focus through your left, you consider the matter of people's feelings."

"Time to be off, you *gorach*," Simon said, as Dapperman bowed to me. "You know this firth is tidal?"

"But of course — I was charting it while I waited for you…"

I detailed some of the men to take up our two dead, while Callum lifted Glengarry as a backpack, and began suggesting where and how he might keep him prisoner until he was capable of signing the oath. As we moved towards the hidden ford I heard the sounds of the cutter pulling away, and the laughter of the Fox over one utterance or another from Dapperman; but I did not look back.